Siege Works

Jim McDermott

Acronyms and terms used in the text

DVdI – Deutsche Verwaltung des Innern: German Administration of the Interior, the Soviet-zone puppet internal security administration prior to the establishment (1949) of the German Democratic Republic. The *VolksPolizei* was administered by the department

EATS – European Air Transport Service: USAAF transport division, established shortly after the end of WW2

HO – HandelsOrganization: **SVAG**-administered official food and goods outlets, located in larger department stores in eastern Berlin, and from 1949, towns and cities across the **SBZ**

Intendani – rank of quartermaster, Red Army

K-5 – The Fifth Kommissariat of the **Volkspolizei**: police criminal unit specializing in political subversion and domestic security, precursor to the Stasi. Though staffed exclusively by German natives and ostensibly reporting directly to **DVdI**, the department worked under **MGB** supervision from its inception. During 1948, however, **DVdI** petitioned Stalin directly for a significant expansion of **K-5** resources and manpower, and this was granted despite resistance from **MGB**.

SBZ - Sowjetische Besatzungszone: Soviet Occupation Zone of Germany

SED - Sozialistische Einheitspartei Deutschlands: German Socialist Unity Party – A forced marriage of the German Communist (KDP) and Social Democratic (SDP) Parties in the Soviet Zone of occupied Germany. By 1948 it was wholly a communist entity, absolutely loyal to the Soviet Administration

SPD – Sozialdemokratische Partei Deutschlands: German Social Democrat Party

SVAG - Sovyetskaya Voyennaya Administratsya v Germanii: Soviet Military Administration in Germany, based at Karlshorst, Berlin; known also (to the German population) as **SMAD** (Sowjetische Militäradministration in Deutschland)

USFET – United States Forces European Theater; US Military administration in Germany. **USFET (G2)** was the Army counter-intelligence department to which the Gehlen Organization reported directly until, in late 1947, it was transferred to the purview of the newly-created **CIA**.

WVHA - Wirtschafts-Verwaltungshauptamt: Bureau for Economic Administration - the SS's commercial arm, charged with the exploitation of conquered peoples and assets

Berlin, September 1948

Since the turn of the year, American and British efforts to establish a distinct western German economic order have accelerated, fuelled partly by the Soviets' persistent refusal to contemplate currency reform and by their demands for further war reparations (to be extracted from Germany's Ruhr assets). It is no secret that Stalin wishes for a unified Germany with a government loyal to Moscow, and the western Allies' conviction that he is working to achieve this is strengthened in February, when, following a bloodless coup, communists seize power in Czechoslovakia. If Germany is allowed to go the same way, Soviet divisions will stand on the Rhine.

As the Prague coup takes place, representatives of the US, British, French and Benelux governments meet in London to discuss the formation of a West German state and its participation in the Marshall Plan. Moscow rightly sees this as an attempt to build an anti-Soviet axis. At an Allied Control Council meeting in March, the Soviet commander in Germany, Marshal Sokolovsky, uses US General Lucius Clay's refusal to discuss details of the London Conference's agenda as an excuse to walk out, effectively ending the Council's function.

On Berlin's western boundaries, the Soviet authorities begin to impede the movement of road traffic to and from the west, and close one of only two access road from the British Zone. They also demand to inspect all train cargoes (military and civilian) coming into the city from the west. When, on 1 April, they are refused permission to board four military trains, they block the tracks. General Clay orders a limited airlift to supply Berlin's western sectors for up to forty-five days.

Meanwhile, the political struggle between factions of Berlin's city council intensify. The Soviet authorities prevent the newly elected mayor, Ernst Reuter – a social democrat - from taking office, and 'night and fog' abductions of western-leaning politicians by plain-clothed communist agents increase. Some are beaten up and released; some disappear forever.

On 7 June, the London conference makes its final recommendations, and the Allied administration in Western Germany instructs the presidents of the western *Länder* to convene an assembly to draw up a constitution for a federal German state. Eleven days later, a new currency – the Deutsche Mark - is introduced in the western zones, replacing the highly-devalued, Soviet-printed 'Occupation Reichsmark'.

The Soviet Administration reacts immediately. From midnight on 18 June, access into the city from the west via all rail, road and river/canal routes is heavily restricted; four days later, another new currency – the Ost Mark – is announced for the SBZ, and use of the Deutsche Mark is prohibited in Berlin. Twenty-four hours later, the city assembly defies this order when it votes, despite physical intimidation from communist agents (the *VolksPolizei* look on, refusing to intervene), to permit the use of the Deutsche Mark in western Berlin and the Ost Mark in the Soviet Sector.

The following morning, at 6am, all land and water routes into the city are definitively blocked both to civilian and military traffic, and power to the western zones' offices and factories from the city's eastern electricity stations is shut off. The blockade of Berlin has begun. The US has some 6,000 military personnel in Berlin, the British 5,500 and the French 3,000. There are 1.5 million Soviet troops in the SBZ, and thirteen Soviet divisions within fifty kilometres of the city. Food stocks in the western sectors are sufficient for approximately one month, coal for forty-five days.

General Clay wants to use armoured columns to re-open the road routes forcibly, but he is persuaded by the British that an airlift to supply the city may be feasible. This seems doubtful; western Berlin, with a population of almost two-and-a-half millions, needs at least 2,500 tons of foodstuffs and 4000 tons of coal daily. American air forces in Europe are a tiny fraction of their wartime strength, and both British and French resources are heavily committed to operations in their colonies. Nevertheless, on Clay's authority the airlift begins. At first, fewer than one hundred USAF C47s make daily turnaround flights from Wiesbaden and Rheine-Main, while the British utilize a wide variety of military and civilian aircraft (including Freddie Laker's passenger-converted Halifax bombers) from Fuhlesbüttel and Finkenwerder airfields. By mid-July, these limited resources are supplying Berlin with about 1000 tons of food and fuel per day, and in the following weeks the total rises steadily. It is not yet nearly enough, but the city has a little time before General Winter returns.

What Berliners do not have is a glimpse of the future. They are the ground upon which a stand-off is being played out, an opening gambit in a vast, new contest between Powers holding irreconcilable views on what Germany's eventual fate should be. If that contest turns for the worse, they will be the front line in a new war.

The Artists' Café, Dircksenstrasse, Berlin, a late-summer morning. The establishment has history, having catered for the city's leisured classes since the fat, hopeful days of the Second Empire, but its décor is very much of the moment, being distressed and likely to remain so. Shrewdly, the management has legitimized shabbiness by the simple device of a name-change, substituting the café's former evocation of lazy Italian climes for a hint of garret *chic* and its implied contempt for bourgeois comforts. At some point this strategy will be reinforced when the old sign (damaged, it advertises *C-fé -- alfi*) is replaced. For the moment, the dislocation only adds to its enigmatic charm.

Business has been bad for several weeks now, and the café is grateful for any it can attract; but one of its only two customers this morning wears the uniform of Paul Markgraf's *VolksPolizei* and has taken the window seat, an excellent position from which to deter further custom. Worse, in moving to occupy the table he has demonstrated that he is the owner of a savage limp, an unwelcome reminder to all Berliners who would wish not to recall why, presently, things are as they are. His companion, a thick-set, hard-faced civilian, has removed his hat and dropped it on to the table. He rubs his face, trying to massage away the weariness that most underfed Germans know intimately these days.

'What's happening, Freddie?'

The Uniform pulls a face. 'What it looks like, Gerd. Rivers of ripe shit are flowing gracefully together and pointing themselves at us. Is it bad for you?'

'As bad as it could be. We'd just got the machinery set up and the first orders placed with our Berlin paper supplier when it started. Now, we can't get any of what we've paid for. Our workers – who have yet to *do* any work, by the way - want to know what's happening next, and no one who isn't a General can tell them.'

'Forget Generals. They have as much idea as the rest of us. It's become one of those messes like Barbarossa – once they kick off they take on a life of their own. Actually, more like a dysentery outbreak.'

'Don't the Ivans tell you anything?'

'They tell us lots of things, and all of it comes straight from the wrist. Firstly, they said that the business was going to last a week at most and then the Amis would drop the whole idea and go back to the old system. When that didn't happen it was a month, for sure. Now, we're told to look on the bright side – the Allies will never manage to keep it up and the city's going to turn against them as soon as it gets colder.'

'They're wrong.'

'Of course they're wrong. Statistics are posted every three days, and even a half-wit can see that they're being understated. All you have to do is look up and count. That's the thing about communism – the system relies on everyone being blind *and* stupid all of the time.'

'Like democracy, you mean?'

'Just like it, yeah. Do you want a coffee?'

'Is that what it is?'

'Of course not.'

'No, then.' Hard-Face looks around. 'I never liked this place when it was the *Amalfi*. The other bulls used it because it was only a minute from the Alex and they could poison themselves more conveniently.'

'Happy days.'

'Happier than these, just.'

A septuagenarian waitress, her grey complexion artlessly revived by dabs of rouge, shuffles to the table but executes a smart about-face when the Uniform shakes his head. He waits a moment as she retreats, in case her ears are more limber than the rest.

'So the book-binding business may or may not be a good idea?'

'I'll let you know. How's policing?'

'As wondrous as ever. Too many murders, assaults, kidnappings, thefts large and petty. Rapes are becoming slightly less fashionable, suicides more so. Not that we do much about any of it, anymore. On a single day in July we lost almost three quarters of our trained men, deserters to the new Allied force. What's it like in the West? I mean, way out West?'

'Better than it was. The Allies cut off payments to farmers, so the bastards had to sell their produce instead of hoarding it. The currency reform's helped, too. People lost some of their savings, but it could have been worse - forty new Deutsche Marks for sixty old Reichsmarks was a generous rate. Apart from that, everyone wants to know when we can start pissing again without asking permission.'

'We don't have that problem in the SBZ. Pissing times are posted prominently.'

Hard-Face smiles, says nothing. He looks at his old friend and recognizes the same doubtful, pained mood as he feels himself. They have been talking for comfort's sake, dodging the moment at which they will come to a certain point. They both know that they shouldn't be in the café together - they haven't met in almost a year, and have taken particular care not to communicate during that time. They are alive and grateful to be so, and as intelligent men know how not to attract unwanted attention. This meeting is not a good idea, even if it is a most necessary one.

'Thanks for coming, Gerd.'

'Don't be a cock, Freddie. Of course I came.'

'Should I write to him?'

Hard-Face sighs, softening the prospect slightly. 'I don't know. I've tried, several times, and got nowhere beyond platitudes. I think of all the things I could say and tell myself that none of it's worth minnow spit. But …'

'Poor Otto.'

'As you say.'

'The man deserves a bit of good fortune.'

'He got it. And then he had it stolen away.'

'I hope he's alright.'

'Someone who gets hit so many times either goes under or grows armour. Otto isn't the sort to put a gun in his mouth.'

'No, but he won't be looking after himself either. When I met him on the rail line near Stettin two years ago he looked like a work-camp original, about as far through as a heavy-smoking halibut. Marie-Therese filled him out, put life back into him. Without her he'll need to be nagged.'

'His friend Earl will do that.'

'Not with the necessary violence, he won't. The boy's too soft. Anyway, he has a family of his own now, and new husbands get distracted. If only it had happened some other time ...'

'Better not at all, if we're wishing for things.'

'Yeah.'

Distracted, both men sigh once more, each hardly hearing the other. For a few moments the Uniform taps the table, and the frown that lives as resolutely on his face as the nose beneath it deepens slightly. 'I'm going to write to him, today. I'm going to tell him to come to Berlin.'

Astonished, Hard-Face stares at his friend.' Berlin? Why would you even think it?'

'Because we're living a mild form of nightmare, and Otto's good at nightmares. If everything's falling to fuck like it seems to be, at least his mind's going to be occupied by more than his own business. He can stay with us, in the East.'

'Kristin won't mind? I'd take him of course, but Frankfurt's still a bit risky after last year ...'

The Uniform picks up his cap, which bears the insignia of a full Inspector, the fourth highest rank in the *VolksPolizei*. 'Kristin would murder me if we didn't. You know what women are like with this sort of thing - it's a blood-sport, only with hugs. Come on. If we aren't having a drink I've got to get back to Keibelstrasse and draft some more drivel to put in the bulletins.'

The Uniform leaves a couple of Ost Marks on the table and barely acknowledges the floor manager's effusive farewell as they depart the café and emerge into Dircksenstrasse. Like many other Berlin streets it is a mixture of ruin and clearance, a monumental confection of *then* and *now*, the occasional intact structure poking up amid the half-ruins and mere shells of its former neighbours. The most impressive skeleton is the long, rear facade of Alexanderplatz's Police Praesidium, where both men once worked - Hard-Face as a *kriminalkommissar*, the now-senior Uniform as a lowly *rottmeister*, a street-pounder. They glance instinctively at the building now as they always do when passing by, as if a distillation of suffering, an echo of the thousands of souls who passed through its doors as suspects and emerged as something else, lingers to entreat the innocent, the guilty and the cravenly culpable alike.

But modern Berlin has too many attractions to allow minds to dwell upon past glories. The two men turn from memories of crimes to which they had borne silent, uncomplaining witness and glance up into the crowded sky, admiring yet fearing the implications of the unending stream of machines that approach the city from the north- and south-west, deliver their bounty and then return immediately to another world, one that does not live under enduring siege and the threat of annihilation.

Technical Sergeant Ethan Potesky of the European Air Transport Service, Wiesbaden was a hero, and his unwillingness to talk about it only added to his reputation. It might have been that he had collected his six Distinguished Flying Crosses merely for completing tours of duty (it was USAF's policy to mark time-served in the North African and Europe theatres), but the last one – the rumour was it had been earned at Bastogne - had silver oak-leaf clusters attached, and those weren't handed out for managing to crawl from a fuselage to salute the flag. It was even more notable that Potesky had never flown fighters or bombers - that he had gathered his fertile crop of honours in the workaday task of delivering and collecting men and materiel. But then, there had been plenty of places where either or both had saved the day for Liberty.

Men liked to fly with Potesky. They liked heroism, liked to think that the potential for it might rub off a little in his presence. Some tried to find in his clear, young face a hint of the qualities that made him what he was, but it was time wasted. Someone who wouldn't wear his ribbons even on his dress uniform, who changed the subject whenever his past service came up, wasn't going to make more obvious claims upon their respect. *Stars and Stripes* had tried a little harder, used the chain of command to prise out some details that would gratify their readership; yet not even Andy Rooney had managed to get more than a referral to the Department of the Air Force for the official story. For once the Department had demurred, telling Rooney that if Potesky didn't want to talk about it then the man's reticence should be respected.

His crews took care not to mention just who or what he was in front of the German women they tried to impress, because if they'd done so it would have been game over, prize lost. Not that he ever seemed to want to test his attraction with local girls beyond requisitioning the occasional arm-warmer for visits to Frankfurt's picture houses. When pressed about it he admitted to Donna, a girl back home who had worn the ring too long not to deserve a second one. And that was all that anyone ever heard about Donna.

The only thing that Potesky ever opened up about was flying. He'd piloted just about every C in the sky and was presently rekindling his on-off affair with the Douglas Skytrain, an aircraft he insisted was just about incapable of being crashed. Other guys in EATS agreed, and boasted of the number of holes they'd peered out of as they landed their gooney birds on strips that would have tripped a goat. But Potesky didn't do tall tales any more than he did autobiography. It was the art, science and spirit of flying that held all of his attention - which was just as well, because he'd had plenty of flying to do recently.

What none of Technical Sergeant Potesky's colleagues knew was that his military career had been plotted more carefully than a navigator's bomb-run. It wasn't that a man could choose to live or die walking down a quiet street in a peaceful town, much less during battle situations; but Potesky had thrown himself into tight spots and wide-open crises with the deliberate intention of coming out of them very, very well or not at all. He wasn't brave, and he certainly wasn't fearless; he'd just calculated very finely the utility either of dying in combat, time-serving his shift and going home to a commercial pilot's life and Donna (if there was such a girl, he neither knew nor cared) or emerging from the twentieth-century's greatest fuck-maul with metal to his name and a reputation that would buy far more than whatever came in a services pay-packet. The choice hadn't been difficult.

A couple of his squadron leaders had thought him dangerously reckless, but sensible, circumspect voices were hardly heard in war. His nation, like most others, worshipped empty courage - courage for its own sake and to no better purpose than to mark out a man. In any case, he usually demonstrated the quality while helping to salvage desperate campaign setbacks, when heroism became the good news which drowned out quieter, wiser judgements on stupid command decisions. It was why Generals loved a hero - his shine drew attention from their shit.

He'd managed to get wounded only the one time, in flak above the Hürtgen Forest, a nice neat slice from a tricep that hadn't slowed him for more than three days. The Purple Heart it brought meant nothing – he'd always thought it ridiculous, that misfortune or plain dumbness deserved a medal – but it had silenced the last of his critics, the ones who'd said he was just strangely, undeservedly lucky. After that, he'd let the myths work for him.

One man – a flight lieutenant with the 39th Airlift – had come close to guessing something of what moved Potesky. The guy gave him sideways looks, talked too much about him to other guys; but then a remarkable piece of luck – so remarkable that Potesky almost began to believe his own legend – had nudged the flight lieutenant's jeep off the road and directly into the path of a retreating Waffen SS unit.

With this one inconvenience safely underground, anyone's chance of understanding what moved Potesky went away. The end of the war brought the greatest stand-down in history that wasn't an actual defeat, when most of the US Army and Air Force went home as quickly as God and Harry Truman permitted. Seeing where this was going, Potesky had refused his demob papers, immediately volunteered for EATS and joined a bunch of men for whom peace had descended as an equally unpleasant surprise. In his case, however, it wasn't a lack of (or too much) family Stateside that kept him with other flyers, but the certainty that a smashed continent held out more opportunities than the most highly-polished chrome corners of the American Dream. EATS pilots transported men and material supporting the western occupation forces, flying almost daily from Wiesbaden to Berlin, Bremen, Munich, Vienna, London - and, occasionally, as far as Athens and Rome. A guy couldn't choose where he was sent, obviously; but Potesky's war record had somehow stood behind him when he expressed a preference for the Berlin run, and soon he was flying that route at least once each week. The city, undoubtedly a dump of the first order, nevertheless contained lots of something that he appreciated very much, and that was Red Army personnel.

Ethan Potesky was no communist. As far as he could tell, Stalin had his hands full most days just managing to feed his people – or would have, if he'd given a flying fuck about them. By the same token, the fact that there had been nothing obviously wrong with his all-American childhood inclined the man to think that, despite its many and obvious faults, a liberal'ish democracy trumped a totalitarian state any time. But Potesky was no ideologue either. He didn't give a scoop of rats' droppings for whatever qualities defined his great society except those that had shown him how to get ahead. He had never voted in any State or Federal election, never put himself forward for any service that didn't further his own ends and regarded hardly anyone as other than a potential competitor, customer or hindrance. He had no friends, no close acquaintances and no interest in making either - in fact, the only human being for whom Potesky could claim the slightest ties of affection also happened to be the closest thing he had to a bank manager.

This man wasn't someone to be trusted with an innocent observation, much less money - but then, trust wasn't an issue.

If either party decided not to play straight with the other it would take only a 'phone call to the right department to put him before a Court Martial. In Potesky's case that would earn a couple of decades in a shit-hole prison in the mid-west; in the banker's case, a neat execution in a small room. Neither of them planned for that kind of retirement.

Potesky's war record had put him exactly where he wanted to be. A hero got noticed by men at the top, men who wanted the best of the best when just any guy wouldn't do. Standing orders for pilots flying transportation into Berlin were to get cargoes unloaded onto the concrete, to have a quick smoke and coffee and take off again. They applied to everyone except Potesky. He might be pulling food, medical supplies or fuel like anyone else, but almost always he brought or took away confidential paperwork also, dispatches to and from anyone up to and including Generals Clay and Keyes. These, he didn't hand over on the concrete. He was charged with putting them personally into the recipients' hands, which meant that he had to see more of Berlin than his fellow mule-handlers. And if on these missions he carried two attaché cases rather than one, who would think anything other than that a lot of important business was being done?

Potesky liked to have all the angles covered. He hated upsets, surprises, changes of plan or routine and weather forecasts that didn't pan out precisely; he thought ahead, gauged known odds and tried to keep the unexpected as at far a remove as humanly possible. So when, one morning in September 1948, as he took charge of dispatches from Camp Grohn, Bremen that were to be placed by him into the hands of Lucius Clay's adjutant, he was told that he had a passenger for Berlin, he didn't think *oh great, company*. Nor did he argue the point, because the news came from a lieutenant with whom he did a lot of business, a serious man who wouldn't have arranged this if it wasn't some other sort of business. He just shrugged, deployed a few silent *fucks* and asked a name.

'He's a Kraut. Does he need one?'

As much as he disliked the news, Potesky's mood improved slightly. The lieutenant was a careful guy, and this was him playing safe.

'I guess not. Do I deliver him to anyone?'

'Just to the concrete. Park, open the door and say goodbye. Or say nothing.'

'You'll owe me.'

'We're both owed. You'll get yours.'

Ten minutes later, Potesky was checking his instruments with his co-pilot when the Kraut boarded through *Donna*'s rear hatch. He turned to give him the standard list of *don'ts* but nothing made it out. The fellow was a civilian in a worn suit, probably in his late-forties, carrying a small, soft leather bag. He nodded at his pilot, who returned it as he took in the view. Potesky wasn't someone who trusted first impressions, but he decided, there and then, that he really didn't like the face. It wasn't the damage, the way half of it seemed to have been run through a meat grinder and then slapped; it was the other side, the normal part, the bit that could still express something, that gave him the heebies. Potesky was very familiar with pain. He had pulled men out of battle, airlifted them to where they could be patched up or given enough morphine to get dead comfortably; he'd seen the worst that bullets, shells and grenades could do to flesh, the way they could make something that had been human into something else, something that other folk would sooner not see at all. But he'd never seen anything close to the pure distillation of misery, of hopeless, raw loss, that was painted upon the left side of this very wrong face.

Had he not carefully wrapped and stowed his soul some years earlier, Potesky might have felt more for the guy. Still, he made an effort - told him where to sit, got him strapped in, even passed a flask that he'd filled with coffee for himself. That was pretty Christian by his standards, and an hour later, when he realised that his passenger badly needed to be dead or missing (and very soon), he regretted all of it.

3

As *pater familias* of Gartenweg 16, Kurt Beckendorp (known formerly, and to very few still-living souls, as Freddie Holleman) occupied the chair closest to the kitchen range, letting the warmth do its fine work. His stump rested upon the socket of his artificial leg, and his *Inspecteur der VolksPolizei*'s tunic was carefully hung upon the chair's back. Other than when he lay his weary corpse upon the marital bed each night, this was as much comfort as he ever experienced.

He glanced around the kitchen, letting the view work on the permanent knot in his neck. His wife, the truly fair Anneliese (née Kristin Holleman) was performing a magical ritual which would somehow transform mundane ingredients into a fine cake. Falling over her pretty eyes, her still-blond hair (never dyed, though she was now almost fifty years old) had been whitened slightly by a stray explosion of flour and looked none the worse for it. An uncharacteristic frown tried but failed to spoil the rest, its cause not any unfamiliarity with the process but a grim determination that nothing should go wrong between cupboard and table (flour, sugar, margarine and - a true wonder - essence of vanilla being extremely elusive commodities these days, secured only by reason of her husband's exalted position).

At the other side of the kitchen, well away from where its bowels could interfere with the domestic schedule, a dismembered bicycle lay at the mercy of its surgeons, Dierck and Adelmo (formerly Franz and Ulrich), the twin seventeen-year-old heirs to the modest but improving Beckendorp estate. Their frowns – unconsciously synchronised as always – stood purely upon a point of what to do next, there being (in their equally synchronised opinion) several parts too many laid out in front of them. But at least they *had* a bike, even if it was shared and forlornly in need of renovation, and expectations of cake in the very near future, and not many German children could say the same.

The false Kurt Beckendorp knew that he had much cause for satisfaction with his lot, but he struggled with it. This was partly the fault of their delicate situation, the constant effort that a family was put to when needing to be another family. For the boys it wasn't so bad (they hardly recalled life as Franz and Ulrich anymore), but their parents lived with the fear of discovery, of at best falling back into the great seething struggle that marked most of their compatriots' lives, or, worse, paying the full price of having for long deceived both the Russians and Berlin's *VolksPolizei*.

It was also difficult for them to be good communists - Kurt for want of the ability to believe in anything beyond self, family and friends, Anneliese because her profound Catholic faith - one that required attendance at Mass, not a pious longing for it – refused to surrender to realities. Deception was not a new burden, obviously; they had borne it under the previous regime, when a soldier and a good, fertile housewife had been required to eat, breathe and defecate loyalty to the Party and Führer. Perhaps it was the persistence of the effort that had worn them down, making each day a game-board to be negotiated with great attention and care; but neither husband nor wife could recall a time when they could speak to strangers without the words first being plotted, the little lies carefully shaped to reinforce the greater one of who they weren't.

There was another matter, one which Kurt did not care to share with his family, and this further depressed his mood. Being one of Berlin's most senior policemen and a leading SED councillor he had responsibilities as well as perquisites, and though murder, rape, assault and a startlingly robust black market were expected (and not at all resented) hurdles to negotiate each day, he had gradually lost any affection for his evening job. He had no problem with deceit, self-serving hypocrisy and the blatant untruths he was expected to spout constantly; in fact, his seat on the City Council (earned the honest way, via the voting booth) had provided a good deal of entertainment over the previous two years, not to be regretted or foregone upon any point of principle. What bit his arse, badly, was the cheating - the new orders to wreck what couldn't be seized legitimately by lying convincingly to the electorate, as decent politicians did. On a recent evening he had been obliged to wear both hats simultaneously, attending the City's Council as a member while plotting to break it up with a group of plain-clothed thugs from K-5, the Fifth Kommissariat. He had been following orders of course, but he was convinced that it was a bad strategy. The SDP and their allies weren't just going to roll over and do what they were told - they had somewhere to go in an extremity, and that *somewhere* was the Allies. With the way things were generally in Berlin, wasn't it just the excuse they needed?

'Father, what's this?'

Kurt dragged his mind back from politics and focussed upon the item that had been thrust under his large, unlovely nose.

'It's a washer. For one of the brake-pad screws, I think.'

It was a wild guess, but Adelmo accepted it much as his mother did God's promise of salvation. He nodded and returned to the patient. The Christian herself paused in her kneading and turned to her husband. 'I've made too much, Freddie.'

Freddie. She wouldn't call him Kurt indoors, no matter how neatly he lined up the very good reasons why. He had a dread of her forgetting to slip back into her Beckendorp skin once out of doors, out in a society that already was blessed with as many informers as the Reich had ever employed. It hadn't happened yet, but then every man tied to a firing post and still on his feet could say the same thing.

'We'll invite Engi to help with it.'

'You don't mind?'

'He's family almost. Why would I mind?

She nodded, pleased. She treated young Engelbrecht as a third son, and the boy's guardian, Rolf Hoelscher, didn't seem to mind. Kurt had no problem with it either, other than that it made his relationship with Hoelscher – a *VolksPolizei* subordinate – more intimate than it should have been. When you couldn't trust anyone, even decent people were the enemy.

'He likes vanilla, doesn't he?'

Kurt scratched the unlovely nose. 'How on earth would I know? I doubt that he doesn't. It isn't like any German kid to refuse cake, not when the alternative's no cake. If there's any left, you might even tempt Otto with a slice.'

His wife turned to him, her face a mask of anguish. 'Poor Otto!'

'I know, darling.' He sighed, wishing he hadn't said it. He wasn't even sure that his invitation would be accepted – the closest of friends couldn't be read when something like this happened. The letter had gone almost two weeks earlier, courtesy of a willing American pilot's sleight of hand at Tempelhof, but no reply had yet arrived. It was too dangerous to telephone, of course, even if a connection could be had (there were functioning lines between the Western Zones and the SBZ still, but where and when they could be found was a mystery even to senior *VolksPolizei* personnel). He had done all that he could, and it felt more or less like nothing.

He shifted in his chair and began to strap on his leg. As always, the hint of a dolour had to be dealt with, snuffed out. His preferred method was to arrest someone, but this was his Sunday off and he had to be satisfied with a short but painful walk, a matter of only five streets, to the Hoelscher residence.

'I'll go and invite Engi to the feast. What time should I say?'

The fair Anneliese-once-Kristin wiped her sticky hands on her apron. 'Oh, bring him back with you. He can help the twins with their bike.'

In the hallway, Kurt recovered his walking stick (a long-avoided but necessary item he had finally been nagged into acquiring) and stepped out into a dull but pleasant Marzahn afternoon. Their street was a Berlin phenomenon, one in which not a single property showed either war damage or evidence of recent repair. Several of his neighbours were SED men also, faithful Party lapdogs who'd been rewarded with fled or dead Berliners' homes, and though he was a beneficiary of the same largesse he kept as far from his political colleagues as he would someone else's groin infection. A little girl waved at him from the garden opposite (her father was something in DVdI); he returned the compliment, hoped for her successful early orphaning and turned right towards Hohenwalderstrasse.

His stump had only just begun to feel the exercise when Rolf Hoelscher ceased to be the subject of idle thoughts and occupied the view to the front instead. Surprised, Kurt stopped and waited for his *unterkommissar* to close the gap between them. Against orders (intended to give the *VolksPolizei* a more prominent profile than their now much-depleted ranks deserved), Hoelscher was wearing civilian clothes on his day off, but the frown on his face had nothing off-duty about it.

Notwithstanding his attire, he came to attention in front of his boss. 'Comrade Inspector, I …'

'It's Sunday, Rolf', said Kurt, mildly. 'I'm human for the day.'

'Kurt, it's ….'

'It's what? Get it out, man.'

Hoelscher left-and-righted Gartenweg like a pimp caught out in daylight. 'Otto Fischer. He's here, in Berlin.'

Kurt sighed. 'Good. I was beginning to worry that he wouldn't come.'

'He shouldn't have. Müller called me from Keibelstrasse half-an-hour ago. K-5 were waiting for him, picked him up the moment he crossed into East Berlin. They handed him straight to the Ivans.'

4

Major Sergei Zarubin glanced around Wünsdorf's elegant theatre at the ranking officers of the Soviet Union's occupation forces, Germany. Their faces wore a remarkably homogenous expression - a concoction of faint anxiety and pronounced boredom, leavened by no anticipation whatsoever. These affairs were coming to be known as The Boss Isn't Happy Meetings, because recently the same revelation had opened each of them. The phrase incited unease in any sensible audience, but there was no doubt that its repetition was beginning to blunt the edges. Even Colonel Shpak, Zarubin's immediate superior and one of nature's more exuberant lip-chewers, could hardly be bothered to pale anymore when the bad news was delivered.

Marshal Sokolovsky, their supreme commander in Germany, had brought it personally to the previous meeting. His audience had been most attentive, no spine less than rigidly to-seated-attention; yet even he hadn't been able to imbue the message with more than a perfunctory *or else*. It was as if everyone involved in this drama had read the script, shook his head and was trying to reach the curtain drop without being the first to laugh. When Sokolovsky had finished he hadn't even allow questions – no doubt to avoid the embarrassment of there not being any.

Obviously, what the Boss wasn't *happy* about was that every one of his assumptions (or those of the latest lickspittle to seize and nibble his ear) had proved to be – for want of three better words – moist cow dung. Bad judgements conceived in Red Square weren't a novelty, God knew; but lately the old gangster's cunning seemed to have signed off for a rest-cure. Even an unworldly dolt – Shpak, for instance – was aware that the moment to have stepped back from this business was the one immediately following that in which the Americans and British hadn't blinked. It was worrying that the General Secretary didn't, or couldn't, see it.

Today, their old friend Major General Kotikov, the Berlin Garrison commander, had come to deliver the bulletin. He was a decent sort, not too full of himself but definitely not the man to light a fire under his audience's arse – and, in fact, he didn't try. He gave them the latest statistics instead: of sorties to inconvenience incoming western aircraft, troop deployments to protect power stations, allotments and urban farms, and 'readiness' exercises that would prevent the American's Berlin hordes (six men and a regimental dog at the last count) from overwhelming the thirteen divisions the Red Army currently had surrounding the city. At least he stayed on afterwards to speak informally to his men, though nothing he said gave the impression he knew more than they.

Shpak pulled Zarubin to one side as the non-briefing concluded. His cadaverous frame made his uniform seem as if were an unclaimed item at the cleaners, hanging forlornly, waiting for its owner to recall where he had misplaced it. He swallowed nervously, the Adam's apple moving beneath the skin like a python's undigested feast.

'Sergei Aleksandrovich, did you not think that Comrade General Kotikov looked *meaningfully* our way?'

'No more than anywhere else. It isn't as if anyone's shining at the moment.'

'But whose fault is that?' Shpak, aware of the indiscretion, glanced around, twitched and stifled it. 'What do we have on at the moment?'

He was perfectly aware of his workload, but Zarubin assumed that its iteration would make the point he didn't dare spell out.

'The internal security review, liaison with the Fifth Kommissariat, surveillance of SDP councillors in the western sectors and the camps business.'

Shpak sighed. 'It isn't like we have the opportunity to …'

'Shine? No. But then, who else does?'

'Still, it's a shame that diligence isn't recognized.'

Zarubin tried to recall when either of them had demonstrated *diligence* lately. Six months earlier he had arranged his transfer out of the smoking end of the espionage business because he was beginning to gain a reputation for being clever - as in too clever for his own good (in the Soviet Intelligence system, any degree of cleverness was not likely to be to one's advantage). The bureaucratic backwater into which he had punted was undoubtedly safer, and, until 18 June, it had seemed a shrewd manoeuvre. Now, of course, he was on the side-lines, watching history turn but with precious little chance of putting his mark upon it. Worse, he had managed to shackle himself to Maxim Shpak, a man whose anima could enter a guilty plea before the charge was read out.

In any normal milieu, Colonel Shpak wouldn't have been dangerous company, but he had a quaint fondness for probity – for what the British would call *playing a straight bat*. This was a severe defect of character in any employee of the Ministry for State Security. His intelligence reports bore a fatal tinge of relativism, assessing the enemy's motives and actions from a broader perspective than the purely gladiatorial. Zarubin knew this because Shpak had a habit of pushing them his way before submission to Moscow, to double-check that he hadn't allowed personal prejudice or what he called *blinkered thinking* to taint the product. Obviously, no sensible person would add anything that could be adduced in evidence against himself, so Zarubin invariably gave his enthusiastic approval (verbally, never in writing) to what he'd read and then braced himself for the return fire.

To date, Moscow had shown remarkable patience. Shpak had been overburdened with the sort of administrative crap that wiser men managed to avoid and overlooked for promotion several times; but given that it was his job and duty to demonstrate a high degree of *blinkered thinking* his sins should have earned him far worse. Perhaps, Zarubin speculated, he had old friends at the Ministry. Perhaps his transfer to a listening station on the Chukchi Peninsula had simply gone missing in the post. Perhaps everyone who might have cared was otherwise occupied by the biggest strategic arse'ing they'd suffered since Second Kharkov, or possibly Borodino.

They were locked - had locked themselves - into a game that couldn't be won, short of an all-out military offensive. The Boss would have seen this once, but these days strategy seemed to serve the heart's longing. He had slapped the Allies' faces, dared them to step over the line and then done nothing – in fact, worse than nothing. With overwhelming military superiority in Germany the Soviet Administration was now firmly committed to counter-punching, to reacting clumsily to a series of unwelcome novelties. Its fearless riposte to the new western currency had been an even newer eastern currency, the Ost Mark, worth about as much as it could absorb in toilet duties. Then, faced by a growing likelihood that western Berlin could be supplied exclusively from the air, SVAG had dangled before its besieged inhabitants the irresistible lure of SBZ ration books, their coupons to be redeemed at official HO stores. So far, about three thousands of these had been claimed (presumably by the sort of *wessie* who faced fate's whims with belt, braces and a parachute harness), of which fewer than two hundred had actually been used. Most painfully, the economy of eastern Berlin had shown itself to be horribly reliant upon its western neighbour (170,000 eastern Berliners went west each day to their workplaces, three times the number who came the other way), so the siege was murdering living standards in the Soviet Zone and making its population even less likely to prefer the command economy model.

Zarubin assumed that this was all perfectly clear to anyone who had a say, but of course no one dare say it (there hadn't been a contrary opinion expressed in the Central Committee since 1937, not without condolences being sent to the widow afterwards), nor reflect openly upon the irony: that Stalin, the man who had deflected Roosevelt at Yalta as a card-sharp would a three-year-old, who had dunned the Allies for three years now at the *Kommandantura*, who had printed currency like he was the Weimar Republic while stripping the SBZ of everything that could be unscrewed, was now paralysed with outrage because the Americans, British and French had finally removed the targets from their backs and gone their own way. There was going to be a self-governing western German state with its own currency, and the Boss couldn't see that it was his doing, his particular creation, his child.

So, their meetings at Wünsdorf were no longer the happy, fraternal events of pre-blockade days (Zarubin allowed his memory a little latitude on this point). They sat and listened to complaints regarding what they had failed to do, exhortations to do more if it (but better this time), and implications of what would happen if *it* didn't, and not even Shpak listened too closely anymore because it was breath wasted. The fundamental problem was that they lacked even a rudimentary understanding of what the Americans thought, feared and planned to do, and particularly how they might react to further provocation. This data was, of course, the primary responsibility of MGB to collect, as it was they who ran an army of German informers and the occasional American traitor; who directed K-5, the Fifth Kommissariat, in its excellent work of intimidating or suborning the western leaning elements in Berlin's civic government. But, since the beginning of the blockade, Moscow had drawn the chain around MGB's collective neck tighter than a widow's purse-string. As during all crises, the Centre had decided that only it had all the facts and reserved to itself every last atom of initiative. The conceiver of this disaster was its only repairer, apparently.

Zarubin was inclined to sit back and enjoy the debacle, but they were all living through one of those moments when careers were made or ended, and he had no way of excluding himself from the process. His rank was sufficiently high to make him visible (even if it brought precious little power anymore) and his nature made him unwittingly vulnerable. He had never been able to commit the latest prescribed drivel to memory and then spout it convincingly (a talent the Party's more adept coasters had imbibed at their mothers' teats), and if there was no place for him in that chorus he would be stood out in front, a convenient objective for pointed fingers. And fingers always were, after a debacle had run its course.

A wise man would conceive a means of shining dimly, of encouraging enough faint praise to carry him, whole, through and out of it. But, tied to an unlucky commander, Zarubin saw little reason to hope for opportunity in the current crisis. On his quieter days he daydreamed of leading an elite, plain-clothed squad to snatch Lucius Clay and drag him over the demarcation line; or of intercepting a secret communique from Truman, ordering the General to give it another month and then attempt a break-out. He held onto a forlorn hope that his unusually high academic achievements would earn a recall to Moscow, to some boring but slightly more advantageous post at the Centre. He even – very briefly - considered making a direct approach to the State Committee for Material-Technical Supply, to the dreaded Kaganovich himself, reminding him of a certain young man's instrumental part, two years earlier, in removing the Boss's oldest and most embarrassing problem. Like everyone else with a brain, however, he knew full well that to place an obligation upon one of the five most powerful men in the USSR was to put oneself over a sluice hole.

When his head had exhausted the impossibilities it advised him to tread water and wait until something showed itself, but in the hapless Shpak's company that strategy might carry him out to sea. It occurred, eventually, that short of planting treasonable material on his superior and betraying him to MVD, the only realistic course was to somehow drag the man and his tiny department to a minor success. Yet if Zarubin found little enough scope for his own heroic endeavours, Shpak's virtues pushed him as far towards greatness as would a reasonable mark in an accountancy exam. Give him a desk full of paper and he was as content as a pig in its own muck, careless of the hours it took to clear the pile; give him a pistol and orders to clear the streets and he'd put himself where his panic attack wouldn't be noticed. If only …

The man had just spoken, and Zarubin had missed it. The theatre was empty now except for the two of them, it being noon and a luncheon provided for the day's attendees.

'I'm sorry, Comrade Colonel?'

An empty room, and still Shpak's eyes did the dance-around, trying to find the fatal ear. 'I asked your opinion, Sergei Aleksandrovich. On the situation.'

The *situation* was what a certain member of Berlin's *VolksPolizei*, an industrious subordinate of Zarubin's, would call a piece of prime cack, incapable of being polished into something less turd-like.

'The situation is hardly to be understood, Comrade Colonel, as we don't have good intelligence on the Americans. If you're asking whether they and the British can feed their Berliners, I believe we already know the answer.'

Shpak sighed. 'You're right, of course. If only we hadn't needed to regroup for so long on the Vistula, back in '44.'

Or after Berlin, even. In Zarubin's opinion (never stated, for obvious reasons) it was possible – perhaps likely – that even now the Americans wouldn't use their atomic bombs if the Red Army decided to go for the Rhine and managed to do it quickly. There would be no point to it, as a deterrent couldn't deter what had happened already. It would bring US forces flooding back to Europe after the event, probably; but the French would make sullen hosts, and a prompt offer of free and fair elections in Germany – carefully manipulated, naturally – followed by a promised Soviet withdrawal to the Vistula, might deflect even that. The Americans wanted, *yearned* for peace, and what the British wanted hardly mattered.

Yet Zarubin's bones told him that it wasn't going to happen. Even in the middle of this first great stand-off with the Americans, any shrewd intelligence officer could see that Red Army deployments in the SBZ weren't remotely configured or equipped for an early campaign. The Boss clung to his dream of a unified, socialist Germany despite all the evidence, so nothing that he, or Shpak, or anyone else …

A whimsical thought, something that Zarubin had played with, laughed about and then discarded some weeks earlier, politely reapplied for consideration. At any other time he might have sent it on its way once more, but in an otherwise bare cupboard it loomed more substantially than it should have. He examined it once more, momentarily, and saw no risk.

'We can't see into Lucius Clay's head, or blow it off. But we might be able to put a case for doing something more than waiting, something that would help us to *shine*. At least we wouldn't be in the middle of the road still, staring at the headlights'

'And what won't Comrade Stalin consider too provocative? Militarizing Berlin's cats?'

Zarubin enjoyed Shpak's wit. It was resigned, droll, the kind employed by a man who, facing his executioners, wanted to be recalled for more than falling down neatly.

'I was thinking that we might use the tools of capitalism against its disciples. We need to seize the initiative, and that takes time, patience and a mature network, or …'

'Or what?'

'Money, plenty of money. The real stuff, not the crap we're printing.'

'We're going to rob a bank?'

'Of course not. Just widen the Deutsche Mark's distribution a shade further than the Americans intended.'

5

Joachim Dein banged his gavel to call the meeting to order.
He did this very softly, as there were several notably fragile
constitutions in the council chamber (or Hut 46, as it was
known in its off-duty hours) and it wasn't as if aneurisms were
unusual events in their community. After a further few
moments he cleared his throat to dampen a residual argument
in the back row, and turned to the minutes.

'Latrines …'

'Point of order, Chairman.'

Dein sighed. 'Yes, Udo?'

It wasn't necessary to glance up to confirm the source of the
interruption, or to wonder whether this would indeed be a
point of order (it wouldn't). Udo Grosser regarded their
meetings as the means by which his current crop of grievances
might be advertised most efficiently and at greatest length. He
was always on the front row, always dead centre, always out
of the blocks before the rest of the field had wandered on to
the track.

'The rations have been reduced again.'

'I know, Udo. We all know. We're coming to that in a
moment, as *you* know.'

Leaning heavily on *know* wasn't going to deter Grosser for
more than a moment, but Dein ploughed on doggedly. 'After
the last outbreak of typhus the commandant assured us that

necessary measures would be implemented. The main latrine was dug out …'

'We did the digging.'

'Thank you, Dieter. My memories of that are equally clear. Since then, however, no further steps have been authorised or provided for, and early symptoms of a new outbreak have been reported by Doctor Anschel.'

'He isn't a doctor.'

This from Grosser, who bore an abiding grudge because his vertical hernia had been pronounced by Anschel – correctly - to be untreatable.

'He's had four years of medical study, Udo. And he diagnosed the last outbreak, so we must trust him on this.'

'He's not even a real Jew.'

Dein sighed once more. The other tragedy of open-ended imprisonment was that every bad habit had the chance to mature like precious wine. The camp was full of formerly enthusiastic National Socialists (Grosser included) who had faded, decayed and devolved to genteel Second Empire snobbery, offended that a near-doctor's ostensibly Jewish name wasn't attached to an equally venerable bloodline.

'I've asked for detergents, but when they'll arrive we don't know, obviously. In the meantime, we should press the Commandant to allow us to dig a new latrine and fill in the old.'

No one said anything to this. It was necessary, and nothing to anticipate with pleasure. Dein cleared his throat. 'Item two. Rations.'

He waited until everyone – even Grosser – had exhausted their invaluable personal anecdotes, and continued.

'Technically speaking, this isn't a reduction but a return to the pre-winter allowance. You'll recall that Commandant Shurakov permitted a 200 calorie per diem increase a few weeks before he was replaced. We've been expecting this concession to be removed for more than five months now, so in a way we've been lucky.'

'It's just as well. My arse is getting too wide.'

Irwin Schuldhoff, one of the camp's few remaining wits (the majority having died or abandoned their previously sunny dispositions), glanced around and garnered a thin crop of smiles.

'Thank you, Irwin. Seven hundred calories isn't a lot but we endured it for several years, and those who couldn't are dead. The weather's good right now, and we have the allotments. It won't be as bad as before.'

Dozens of frankly disbelieving stares met this bold claim, as Dein had expected. It made him wonder why he bothered to be their one-man morale committee. He hadn't applied for any part of the composite role of chairman, judge and jury, but his former career as a mayor had rather led him to it, abetted by the fact that he was incarcerated for a reason as opposed to just filthy luck or the wrong political opinions; that, in a blind, venal moment, he had embezzled his village's quarterly agricultural payment and almost reached the British Zone before a Red Army patrol caught up with him. A genuine criminal mastermind (even a failed one) enjoyed a degree of natural respect from civilians and MVD alike. He was, after all, a fixture - someone who was going to be here as long as the camp itself, whatever the Ivans eventually decided to do with the others.

He waited until it was obvious that no one was going to second his optimism, and then moved on to the day's least pleasant business.

'Disciplinary matters, then. Theft, food. Bring the accused forward.'

Two of the larger, least emaciated inmates pushed their prisoner to the small table that served as the judge's bench. He kept his head down.

'Accuser?'

A man sitting immediately behind Udo Grosser got to his feet and waved his cap at the defendant. 'He took my …'

'State your name.'

'Sorry, Joachim. Franz Webern.'

'Alright, Franz.'

'He took my bread, yesterday morning.'

'You saw him do it?'

'No. But he was sitting next to me, and no one else could reach it. I only turned away for a moment and it was gone.'

'Was he searched immediately?'

'He ran out into the yard. When we caught him, half of it was in his pocket still.'

Dein looked at the accused, Amon Friel. He was a former Berlin *zeelenleiter*, one of the professional snitches the Reich had employed to spy on its faithful populace. His imprisonment had saved his life, probably. There weren't too many of his sort enjoying a comfortable retirement, basking in the gratitude of their fallen nation.

'Did you do it?'

There was a pause while Friel examined his feet carefully. Eventually, he nodded slightly without looking up.

'Hang him.'

'Christ, Udo! Will you shut up?'

The murmur that Grosser's comment raised didn't sound disapproving. A hanging would be fair enough - when you stole a man's food in Sachsenhausen you were trying to preserve your life at the very likely expense of his. For the first two years that NKVD Special camp no 7 had been in operation, such crimes had invariably been punished by death, the 'hanging' carried out by two comrades kneeling on the condemned man's back while strangling him with a cord. Eventually, the camp's disciplinary committee had discussed the punishment's deterrence value (it hadn't any, for men who were already starving or rotting away) and agreed to commute it to a two-month tithe of the guilty man's rations - to be shared equally around his hut - and ostracism for the same period. As a punishment this was hardly less brutal than what it replaced, but many inmates (particularly the Christians) considered it unconscionably weak.

For a moment, Dein was tempted to sentence Friel to a stiff talking-to, but that would have been as wilful as the theft itself. He banged his gavel - a polished stone – once more. 'Two months' surrender of rations at the usual proportion, no one to fraternize during that time. Any other matters, or do we all want to get back to our huts?'

Half of those present were standing already when Jansen Schott (a former munitions worker who had squandered his reserved occupation status by picking up a rock and resisting the Soviet advance up his mother's street) raised his hand. Schott wasn't a time-waster; in fact, Dein couldn't recall him ever having contributed to one of their meetings. He halted the exodus with another rap of his stone.

'What is it, Jansen?

'Something very unusual, Joachim.'

6

It had been the nudge at Tempelhof, one of the unloaders brushing against him. He had hardly felt the transaction and only recalled it now, but the men who had snatched him had gone straight to the correct pocket. He should be worried, he told himself, and failed once more to take the advice.

He had been processed from police to military custody like a banker's draft - smoothly, professionally, without let or hindrance other than to the process of law (if such a thing mattered in modern Germany). Only few hours ago he had departed his home – his *domicile*, he corrected himself – and now he was lost, buried without a marker.

Some residual sense of engagement had made him pay attention following his arrest. They had driven northwards, obviously - even the Soviets couldn't disguise the sun's passage – and for about an hour. He was no longer in Berlin but very near it, and he didn't have to guess too hard. Every German knew about this place, what it was - a well-spring for everything that had followed, four hundred hectares of abomination, too valuable to let go, to erase for the sake of decency.

He had been driven through the main gate and inner perimeter fence without seeing either, bundled out of the truck and into the administrative offices, forced to sit and wait for whatever came next. No one had spoken a word to him since his interception a few metres beyond a temporary checkpoint on Wildenbruchstrasse, but he'd noticed the looks, both from the guards in the truck and the ones who'd taken delivery of him. They were puzzled; this was not normal.

The pause was just what he didn't need, more time in which to think. These days, thinking took him in one direction, to where it hurt. It was a place he had already explored intimately, decked out with his favourite recollections, painted with anguish - a place in which he intended to spend some considerable time (at least, most of that remaining to him). He should be worried, but only if they wanted to keep him in the world.

He felt it again in his chest, trying to rip out the organ that sheltered there, all the more painful because there was no one to blame. The girls at her laundry had swarmed around him, all of them crying, trying to find words that might be a comfort. They had told him that the driver, a GI, had been upset – distraught, even, mumbling tearfully that it was his fault, over and over. But that wasn't correct: he hadn't meant for his brake cable to be sheared, hadn't wanted to hurtle down Ostertorswallstrasse, had tried desperately to avoid …

Her face was unmarked, unknowing, almost serene. He had taken her home to Queerenstrasse 23, wrapped carefully in one of the clean sheets that had been waiting for their owners to claim them. Technically, it was against the law to disturb a body at the scene of an accident, but that was in normal times, and only when it didn't involve one of Germany's Occupiers, an untouchable species. He didn't think that anyone would care.

Yet someone had, in a different sense. Her funeral was attended by dozens of people he didn't know – her customers, new friends she'd made, her employees and their families, a small multitude that inhabited a parallel life to his. Only Earl Kuhn and his new wife had been familiar faces, and their anguish had been little comfort. They'd helped afterwards, poured drinks for the strangers, headed off some of the more incontinent well-wishers and then tidied the apartment while he sat in his chair, conducting a careful examination of the opposite wall.

He felt for Earl. The boy was already inconsolable, convinced that a real friend would have been able to do more. In a few days, word of this would get back to Bremen, and then he'd blame himself for having arranged the flight to Berlin, easing a favour from one of his American suppliers. He wouldn't recall that he'd argued against it (why the hell would a sane man want to fly into a siege?), or beat himself for not having argued strongly enough. A good, kind friend, Earl, better than he knew - would ever know, now.

He glanced around the office, a small, smoke-filled shed occupied by three of the sort of far-to-the-rear echelon soldiers that every army conscripted and then wondered why it had. In different circumstances he would have been shocked to be here, condemned in absentia for the crime of having done nothing, nothing at all. He didn't care to think too hard about how the mistake had come about. Perhaps, somewhere, there was another poor bastard who looked something like him; perhaps an indifferent investigator, distracted by more important business, had put too much trust in a poor description; perhaps – most likely, perhaps - *VolksPolizei* had been burdened by a spare crime they needed to fit to someone. It didn't matter, to him any more than to his captors.

An MVD sergeant, seated at the desk opposite, was glancing up occasionally, a slight frown creasing his Asiatic features. Either he didn't find the view amenable or he objected to the afternoon's calm being rippled by new business that …

It came to him, suddenly, that no-one had expected this. It was why he'd been sat here for almost half an hour now, waiting for *next*. If the prelude to an interrogation, the pause would have been deliberate, a means of working on his composure;

but he was *here* already, where a man could reassure himself that any investigation was concluded, the file closed firmly and the ribbon tied. Yet no one had bothered to send word of it, apparently.

The office door opened and a full colonel stepped in, wearing the same, standard-issue frown as the sergeant. He said something in Russian and the three clerks jumped to their feet, grabbed their caps and bundled themselves out of the room without offering the salute. The colonel waited until the last of them had slammed the door behind him and turned to his problem.

'Who are you?' A northern accent, probably Leningrad, but his German pronunciation was perfect.

The prisoner stood up. 'Otto Henry Fischer.'

'I know. At least, your papers tell me so. *Who* are you?'

Fischer thought about that. 'I'm sorry, but my offence hasn't been stated.'

'Nor to me.'

It occurred to Fischer that the frown wasn't directed at him, precisely. It had more to do with protocol, and someone taking care to swerve widely around it.

'You were apprehended by a *VolksPolizei* patrol, in the Soviet sector of Berlin.'

'I'm not sure. They weren't wearing uniforms.'

'You were found to be in possession of Deutsche Marks, an offence on our side of the demarcation line.'

'I didn't know that it was. An offence, that is.'

'Typically, they would have given you a fine or a kicking. But you're not a Berliner.'

'I live in Bremen.'

'As your papers also state. Which poses a question: a citizen of Berlin might well cross the line to go to his workplace, but a man travelling hundreds of kilometres to penetrate a blockade – and with American-minted currency – must fall under severe suspicion.'

'I see that, yes.'

'Then why did you do it?'

'The money was planted on me - at Tempelhof, I think. I came to Berlin to visit friends, nothing more.'

The Colonel removed a notebook from his breast pocket. 'Give me their names.'

'I'm sorry, no.'

The Russian looked surprised. 'Really? Because my believing your story offers the only possibility of your being released from our custody before you become too old to care.'

'I know. I appreciate that you've taken the trouble to ask.'

The Colonel replaced his notebook. 'Someone seems to want you to be regarded as an infiltrator. It isn't my job or inclination to consider that assessment, though it would have been a courtesy to have informed me of it. This, as you've probably guessed, is Sachsenhausen camp, known to us as MVD Special Camp no. 1, formerly NKVD Camp no. 7. We house the largest group of political and military prisoners on German soil - in fact, anywhere outside the Soviet Union. Please don't worry about rules. Everything that is not compulsory is forbidden, as you will also have guessed. You'll have no access to any form of communication with persons outside the perimeter, now or ever. Conditions here are challenging, though some of the older inmates may tell you that things are improving slightly. I would suggest that you make friends rather than enemies, as we allow the population to police itself – within strict bounds, obviously. That is all. I'll have you allocated to a hut.'

The Colonel turned to leave. Fischer cleared his throat. 'May I ask something?'

'What is it?'

'You've taken time to speak to me, to someone who can't possibly have the slightest right to an interview. Why is that?'

The Russian pursed his lips, looked the prisoner up and down. He found the face remarkable, but he'd been in too many battles to think it shocking, or singular. It was what ordnance or fire did to those unlucky enough to be in the way.

'Your situation isn't usual.'

'In what way, sir?'

'We have almost fifty thousand prisoners here. It *was* sixty thousand, perhaps slightly more, but disease and malnutrition have done their bit over the past three years. It's still a great number of souls, but even among them you're a little special.'

'Why?'

'We haven't had a delivery of fresh meat – not a single piece - for more than a year now.'

7

Inspector Beckendorp didn't hold meetings, usually. He attended those he couldn't avoid, made his excuses when he could, and if he needed to give his men the latest news, proscriptions or orders he had them assemble in the main investigations room at Keibelstrasse Police Praesidium and shouted at them for as long as it took to get it across. A meeting, in his opinion, was what police did when work had become too unpalatable.

But this morning he was hosting a meeting in his own office, one that he had called as a matter of great urgency and which had very little to do with normal business (if any business in these strange days could be considered normal). It was attended by just three men, men who could be trusted to say nothing of matters discussed.

The first to arrive was *UnterKommissar* Rolf Hoelscher, a man rescued from the depraved world of espionage by a Russian with a sense of humour. The two who followed him in – *UnterKommissar* Albrecht Müller and *OberWachtmeister* Sepp Kalbfleisch - were police raised up by Beckendorp personally, on the strength of their notable facility for dogged, unimaginative graft. In Berlin, in 1948, such a talent was not common, and their commander was deeply grateful (though naturally he didn't say so) that so far they had resisted the siren call of western Berlin's new police force, which the Americans were making attractive with a treacherous promise of almost liveable wages.

As Kalbfleisch - an ageing former night-watchmen - entered the office he turned, scanned the corridor with vaudevillian subtlety and closed the door firmly.

'Right.' Beckendorp waved vaguely in the direction of three chairs he had commandeered from the Bulls' pen a few minutes earlier. His guests sat down and glanced at each other, imagining they knew already what this was about. 'I'm going to tell you a story. It's not a short one, but you'll understand a lot more when I'm done. If you ever breathe a word of it, my ghostly, only foot will find your arses from the Hereafter. And if I go the wrong way it'll be on fire. Alright?'

They nodded. It seemed the only adequate response to that sort of threat, or promise.

'It begins with a noble officer-pilot of our glorious, former Luftwaffe, a late spring morning in 1940, the advance through Belgium, about a thousand metres above the river Vecht …'

Almost half an hour later, Beckendorp stopped talking and sat back. His audience glanced at each other, weighing what it all meant – most pointedly, to them. Kalbfleisch – who, as the most junior-ranked man, had the least right to speak – coughed and raised a finger.

'So, you're not …?'

'A ruthless former *kozi* street-fighter from Hamburg? No.'

'Can we ask your real name?'

'Also no, because I wouldn't want it to be beaten out of you. But you needed to know the facts, because I'm about to do things that could end a career quicker than buggering a rent-boy. I don't want you taken by surprise, and if I ask your help you should at least know why.'

Hoelscher stood up. 'Of course I'll help. Fischer's family.'

Müller and Kalbfleisch seemed as stunned by this revelation as those preceding it (or perhaps their capacity to absorb novelty had found its natural rim). Hoelscher turned and looked down at them. 'He was *Fallschirmjäger* 1 Regiment, like me.'

'You were a paratrooper?'

'Until Adolph took away my parachute.'

Müller (who had spent his war as a defence lawyer in the People's Court and was therefore intimately familiar with the Führer's whims) blew out his cheeks. 'Small world.'

Kalbfleisch coughed again. 'Comrade Inspector, you said *help*. How could we help with K-5 business? They'd cut us off at the ankles if we even glance their way.'

'Otto Fischer has been disappeared, and too neatly for this not to be something big. K-5 had him for about ten minutes and then passed him to the Russians. I need to know who ordered it, and where he's been taken.'

'We question the *Russians*?'

'Obviously not. We start at this end, at Keibelstrasse. We need to find out what happened without seeming to ask – at least, not with a question they'd recognize.'

Hoelscher was frowning at his boots. 'Could we not approach our mutual friend at Karlshorst?'

'No. You and I have had as much kindness from him as we could ever expect. And we don't know that he isn't involved, do we?'

Müller, who knew nothing (and didn't want to know more) of 'friends' or anything else at SVAG headquarters, scratched his cheek. 'I read the original report, from the *anwärter* who saw it happen. Your man Fischer was taken on Wildenbruchstrasse, just after midday on the 28th. It's a start. We might be able to identify the squad members.'

Beckendorp considered this. 'I'll get Beyer to ask questions at K-5. He's the one who liaises with their plain-clothes to break up the Council meetings.'

'Can he be trusted?'

'As much as any scorpion. But I'll make up a good reason why I'm asking.'

UnterKommissar Kurt Beyer was an important man pretending to be otherwise: no more than a middle-ranking *VolksPolizei* but one of the SED's place-men at Keibelstrasse, as was Beckendorp himself. Unlike his boss, however, Beyer believed sincerely what he preached. Since the blockade began he had commanded the police presences at City Council meetings that had ostentatiously failed to intervene when undercover K-5 personnel laid into non-SED councillors – had actually given the nod as to which of them should receive special attention. The Fifth Kommissariat were bastards but there weren't many of them, and Beyer - also a bastard - knew everyone in the Berlin branch by name.

The four men in the room regarded each other. With the exception of Kalbfleisch they had family - wives, sons or daughters who would follow them down the sewer if any plan failed. But all three of them owed Beckendorp their jobs, and one of them, probably, his life. It wasn't a matter of saying yes or no, more of trying to understand how far it might take them. Müller - whose courage, soundly whipped through the

National Socialist justice system, had never since fully emerged from its box - tried to frown in a purposeful way before he asked the one sensible, craven question.

'Will it be dangerous?'

Beckendorp sighed. 'Yes.' He opened his desk and removed three sheets of paper. 'I don't know what these are going to be worth, but they're signed affidavits, stating that everything you do from this moment on is at the express order of your *Inspecteur der VolksPolizei*, no questions to be asked. We're Germans, so paper has to mean something still.'

Hoelscher read his copy. It was succinct but carried several impressive franks. He looked up. 'And if we find Fischer? Are we going to try to free him?'

'I don't know. I don't know what it's about, why he was picked up. Decisions come later.'

Kalbfleisch folded his paper with care and put it in his pocket. 'He's a good friend, then? This Fischer?'

'He's family, as Rolf said. If that's not enough, think of him as Germany – smashed to pieces inside and out, with just enough left to make helping him more than a waste of time.'

'Who is he?'

Colonel Shpak regarded Major Zarubin's visitor with distaste. He had nothing against Germans particularly (those not in uniform, that is); in fact, his three years' pre-war studies at Leipzig University had given him a fondness for the race that made him a poor conqueror. But this specimen wasn't so much occupying as defiling space in the otherwise pristine office. He was slovenly, quite filthy, a natural sloucher and sufficiently oblivious to authority not to have thought to removed and extinguished the cigarette that leaked ash on to the polished wood floor.

'A loyal and valuable associate, Comrade Colonel.' Zarubin didn't seem offended by the soiled article. He opened a silver case and offered it; the man nodded, acquired three more cigarettes and placed them in his jacket pocket.

Zarubin continued in German. 'Please sit, Herr Gerste. You work with the Americans, yes? At Tempelhof?'

Gerste looked a little uncomfortable. 'I do, comrade. On the orders of the Soviet …'

'Yes, of course. This isn't an interrogation. We just need a little information.'

'About what, comrade?'

'Deutsche Marks.'

The German's shoulders, which had loosened a little, re-tensed.

'Deutsche Marks, comrade? What about them?'

'Where can I get some?'

Helplessly, Gerste looked from one Russian officer to the other and back again. Shpak gave him the sort of encouraging smile that a teacher would a dolt who was doing his very poor best.

'They're in free circulation in the Western Zones …'

'I don't mean a sample. I need a quantity, for reasons that needn't concern you.'

'How many?'

'A million, I should think.' Zarubin glanced at his commanding officer, who had blanched considerably. 'Definitely no more than that.'

Finally, Gerste got the point. He shook his head. 'About two hundred and fifty millions came in before 24 June, by train or road convoy. I can't say whether further amounts have been brought in by air since.'

'How have they been placed into circulation?'

The German shrugged. 'The Allies issue them directly to the Länder Bank, I assume.'

'Yes. I meant, on what basis? Were they distributed fully before the blockade was established, or are there still some to be released?'

Gerste's mouth twisted. 'I don't know, comrade.'

'Then you must find out.'

The helpless look returned. 'How?'

'With guile, and bonhomie. I assume you know some of the American pilots who land at Tempelhof by name?'

'A few. I'm always there to help unload the 'planes. They think I'm just another half-starved civilian working for free food, but I speak to them occasionally about my dream of going to America.'

'Good. Talk to the friendliest one about what comes in – the food, fuel, anything to get him preening himself about what a wonderful job his countrymen are doing, how they're saving Berliners. Don't forget to emphasise how difficult it is for citizens in the present crisis. And then, perhaps, make a joke about how you and he could snatch the next shipment of currency and spend the rest of your days by Lake Geneva. Or Lake Superior.'

'He'd report me!'

'No, he won't. He'll assume that someone who was intending such a theft wouldn't actually put the US Air Force on notice of it. Bored men like to talk, if only in generalities, and a pilot on perpetual turnaround will be very, very bored. If he says, 'Ah, if only it were that easy' he'll have hinted that further transfers will occur. If he tells you to fuck off you'll have lost only a glancing acquaintance. If he says that you should have thought of it three months ago we'll know that all the cash that's due to run the blockade has done so already. And thus we may learn something from a simple conversation.'

'You're intending to steal Deutsche Marks? I beg your pardon, comrade, I …'

'No, that's a reasonable question. We intend a reallocation, though it will either remain in, or return quickly to, western Berlin's economy. The money itself is irrelevant; what it can *do* interests us greatly. Of course, you needn't be party to any further detail.'

'No, comrade.'

'Well then, we're done. Do you need anything? Money, food?'

Gerste swallowed visibly. 'I … have a wife and two children. We live in a cellar at present, in Schöneberg. It isn't really safe, or warm.'

Zarubin made a note in his desk diary. 'A man should be able to rely upon his friends. If you do this thing I'll make sure that when it's time to bring you east there'll be a two-bedroom apartment waiting here for your family. It may not be palatial, but it *will* have a roof. And heating, if only from a stove.'

Quelling the German's effusive thanks with a hand, Zarubin nodded at the door. Gerste was out of the office in a moment.

Shpak closed the door behind him. 'Can you promise that?'

'Of course. Now that most billets in the city have been given up and officers relocated to Wünsdorf there'll be a stock of spare accommodation. I don't doubt that someone here at Karlshorst is busily taking bribes to allocate it a certain way. We find out who that is and hint at denouncement. I'm sure Herr Gerste will be placed near the top of the list.'

Shpak smile ruefully. 'You have a cynic's soul, Sergei Aleksandrovich.'

At the main reception area Rudolph Gerste surrendered his pass and departed the main building. His excellent mood stayed with him for most of an otherwise tedious trek, but as he approached a checkpoint on Dammweg and the American Zone it struck him that he had a new problem. His two MGB masters – the man who had recruited him and this one – were presumably speaking to each other, coordinating their efforts for the State and cause. His third employer occupied a different trench, however. It might be that he could serve everyone without hindrance or a bullet in the head, but doing and saying nothing seemed to him to be the most dangerous option. The third man was particularly unforgiving of deceit, however tacit. Two months earlier, another of his German employees, working alongside Gerste on the runway unloading shifts, had disappeared. He was a very garrulous fellow who enjoyed chatting to the Americans, and had got into the habit of disappearing for an hour or so into the main Tempelhof arrivals hall, usually towards the end of a shift when no one from the departing or arriving work gangs would notice his return. Then, one day, he wasn't there. He turned up again eventually, in a number of boroughs in eastern Berlin, the body parts placed where they couldn't be missed. The *VolksPolizei* had only glanced at that one before burying the mess.

Gerste could only guess how his new friend the MGB Major might take a similar disappointment, but this was a case of facing a dark cave's mouth or the bear itself. By the time he reached the airfield he was determined – if very nervously – to do the least imprudent thing. It wasn't ideal, and it was certainly going to be hazardous; but a man who had already stumbled perilously close to the edge had to take the best grip he could, even if it was upon a rifle's barrel.

9

In his first eight minutes as a resident of Hut 37, Otto Fischer lost his bedroll and a tooth, and was placed on notice that a proportion of his rations was to be surrendered each day. The beneficiary of these undocumented transactions was a gaunt but still-muscular fellow who wore a tattered *Feldgendarmerie* trench coat, an item not usually affected by anyone who hadn't served in that prestigious organization of sadists. Fischer decided not to speak to the legality of the matter. Clearly, the man was something of an expert in rules and making them up.

When his assailant had wandered off he was helped to his feet by a short, amiable rag-warehouse with thinning hair and bad skin who introduced himself as Siegfried Stolz.

'Don't worry about Adelbert. He'll only take your food for a day or two. He just wants you to know who the boss is.'

Tenderly, Fischer rubbed his jaw. 'Is he?'

'Oh, no. A little bullying isn't frowned upon here, but if he goes too far he'll lose his own rations. The inmates keep their own order quite well.'

'The Ivans don't mind that?'

'They only mind when we try to cross the perimeter. Actually, they don't mind that either. It gives them a chance to practise their marksmanship.'

'Has anyone escaped from here?'

'A few. More have died trying. For a while now, no-one's had the strength or enthusiasm to make the attempt. Could you tell me if the *Oberliga*'s been restarted?'

'You don't know? In the South since late 1945, and the rest of Germany last year. Football's the only form of combat permitted to us these days'

'Ah.' Siegfried nodded happily. 'Otto will be happy.'

'Otto?'

'Nerz.'

'Otto Nerz is in *here*?'

'Since the battle for Berlin, yes. As for many of us, it was his NSDAP membership card that did for him.'

'Poor bastard.'

Siegfried shrugged. 'As are we all. But what about you? You're the first new face we've had since I don't know when. What did you do?'

'I'm not sure. I travelled from Bremen to Berlin and then crossed the demarcation line. *VolksPolizei* arrested me immediately and handed me straight to their bosses.'

'No trial? The Russians like a legal process, even if it's a comedy.'

'No questions, even. This morning I was in my own bed; now …'

The inmate's eyebrows went up. He glanced around and whispered. 'You're the first *nacht und nebel* we've had for years. We've been assuming they off'd them straight to Siberia.'

Fischer tried to smile, but it died on the way out. 'I must be important, though Christ knows why.'

'*Were* you someone?' Doubtfully, Siegfried regarded a face that obviously had fought very much from the front.

'Not at all. My greatest achievement was …' the thought of her quelled any desire to talk about it. '… to survive. I was in *Luftwaffe*'s War Reporters' Unit, then Counter-Intelligence, East.'

'So you told lies about the Ivans. It doesn't seem much.'

'It hardly matters. I'm here now, and definitely no-one.'

Siegfried took his arm and gently led him to a bunk. 'No, no. It's too late for modesty, you've interested me. Here, this is your home.'

The pallet was just wide enough for a slim man to turn without entering free space. Two of its base-slats were missing from where Fischer's lower legs would spend much of their remaining years. He didn't mind that; he preferred to sleep on his stomach.

'I can get you another bed roll. Do you have cigarettes?'

'I gave up the habit some years ago.'

'Alright. I'll speak to the supplies committee.'

'There's a committee?'

'There are dozens of them. We have recreational committees, disciplinary committees, agricultural and husbandry committees – the last one's for rat-breeding – and even an auditions committee for the choral society. The supplies committee is *very* necessary, as you'll imagine. They have a hut in which they hold back a little from the rare occasions when MVD become sentimental and decide to supply us with necessities – and, of course, they try to requisition the possessions of dead inmates before their neighbours can snatch them. They'll probably want something from you in return. Don't worry, it won't be a major organ.'

Fischer turned to examine the rest of his new world. Other than himself and Siegfried (Adelbert the one-man welcoming-and-redistribution committee had disappeared), the hut held only three other inmates at that moment, all of them laid on their bunks in various stages of waking drowse. At a glance, there seemed to be sleeping accommodation for about eighty men in two tiers. A single stove sat in the middle of the room, unneeded on a mild, late August day, and two large tables flanking it provided the only communal arrangement. It took a singular act of will not to speculate about the toilet facilities.

Siegfried followed Fischer's gaze. 'You wouldn't think it, but this is quite lavish compared to the early days. The Ivans weren't too kindly disposed to us back then.'

'They had a lot to be not too kindly about.'

'I suppose not. It didn't help that the SS guards here lined up and head-shot hundreds of Soviet POWs in the main yard before they fled the advance. I assume the new landlords wanted to make our treatment appropriate.'

'I was told …' Fischer thought about a conversation he'd had only the previous year but seemed a dead, dusty age ago; '…

that NKVD – I mean, MVD – think that these camps aren't worth it; that their impact on inmates' families and other Germans in the SBZ is counter-productive. Stalin doesn't agree, apparently.'

Siegfried considered this. 'Really? We don't get to see their tender side, but it's nice to know they have one. Ah, this is someone you'll want to meet.'

The hut door had opened, and a thin but very upright man in his 'fifties passed through it. He was wearing what, in a different setting and condition, might have been a garment indicating rank or function. Fischer's deduction in this regard was founded entirely upon the fact that it covered the man's upper body but didn't appear to have sleeves.

Siegfried raised a hand to catch the man's attention and turned to Fischer. 'I'm sorry, I didn't ask …'

'No, that was my poor manners.' He held out his hand as the older man approached. 'Otto Fischer.'

'Joachim Dein.' Fischer got the usual, careful appraisal of his visible mementoes from the Eastern Front. 'Forgive my grand appearance, but I came straight from the hearing. We don't get many new faces.'

'Hearing?'

'The inmates' court. We try to keep our society from eating its own bowels. What did you do?'

'I asked that already, Joachim.' Siegfried took Fischer's shoulder with a discoverer's pride. 'I think we've got a rare Innocent.'

Dein seemed to doubt this. 'You're not SDP?'

'I'm not political in any way.'

'NSDAP?'

'Unavoidably. But I misplaced my card years ago, well before the surrender. Prior to *Barbarossa* I was a paratrooper. After that, I served in an artillery unit until the Ivans gave me my new face. Since 1942 I haven't done anything to offend the most fragile temperament.'

'Mm.' Dein looked at Siegfried, the two men sharing a mild expression of professional interest. Fischer understood nothing of camp protocol, didn't know if it would be polite to ask in turn of their real or inferred crimes. He didn't suppose that the sure majesty of justice need have been applied too assiduously in either case. It would have been enough to be a German in the wrong place with the wrong papers.

'He's met Adelbert.'

'Dear me. Was he rude?'

Fischer shrugged. 'He didn't hit me too hard. But I lost my bed roll.'

Dein frowned. 'My patience with that boy is thinning. If he wasn't a war hero …'

'Was he?'

'He extracted three men from a burning tank, in the fighting to break out of Breslau. The Führer had him brought back to Berlin and presented him personally with the Iron Cross.'

'In that case, I make no complaint.'

'It's your choice.' Dein turned to Siegfried. 'Adelbert isn't to touch our new comrade's rations. It's a final warning, tell him.'

'I will, Joachim.'

'Now, what can you do?'

Fischer didn't understand the question. 'Do?'

'Skills, military or civilian.'

'I have no skills.'

'What were you, before the war?'

'I was police, in Stettin. Criminal investigations.'

Dein laughed. 'You won't be bored here, at least. We have an impressive collection of criminals who desperately don't want their pasts to be investigated further, myself included.'

Siegfried grinned. 'Me also.'

Bored. Fischer couldn't conceive such a state, even under a regime designed to obliterate the final spark of human spirit. Hopeless, perhaps (though he'd smuggled in enough of the product to make its further supply pointless), and he had a full ration of regret that he would tend as carefully as winter asparagus. Boredom, though, would require that his life here be in abeyance, wanting in lieu of something better, more inviting. And that, equally, he couldn't conceive.

'Do you have a gramophone?'

Dumbfounded, Dein glanced at Siegfried. 'What?'

'Are you allowed a gramophone?'

'Yes. I mean, we *were*. And a stock of NKVD-approved martial music. But it hasn't worked since 1946.'

'I can mend it, probably. That's a skill, isn't it? All you'll need to do then is petition the Commandant for a selection of Wagner.'

Siegfried shook his head firmly. 'We've had more than enough of that shit. We can ask for some Buxtehude, or Hummel, or even Schubert. But I'm sure the answer will be the same for each.'

10

'This is a fucking mess.'

Inspector Kurt Beckendorp stood on Pariser Platz, a few metres to the east of the Brandenburg Gate. Beside him, ranked closely and armed with *schlagstocks*, dozens of his subordinates kept their hungry gaze upon a great and growing mass of protesters, gathered in contravention of the new ordinances against demonstrations. They were safe, just, on the Allied side of the line, tormenting the enemy with what might have been, but Beckendorp bore them no ill-will. His ire was directed rather at the circumstances that had brought them here, that had made a confrontation inevitable. The officer by his side, *UnterKommissar* Beyer, wasn't frowning. He seemed pleased, as though a carefully-wrought plan was coming to its expected conclusion.

'Yes, Comrade. But it's *their* mess, a very public one. If the Council elections don't happen we can blame western intimidation.'

Beckendorp removed his cap and rubbed his head. '*They'll* say that we made things impossible, that they had no other choice. It doesn't matter either way. We've given the Americans and the Brits just what they wanted, an excuse for the *de facto* separation of Berlin's administration. They say *de facto*, don't they?'

'Yes. Even so, it'll last only until we re-take the city's western zones.'

'Really, Beyer? How will we do that? Are we preparing for a coup.'

'Don't worry, Comrade. Premier Stalin's got something planned, he must have. He isn't going to let a couple of Allied battalions hold on to half of Berlin, is he?'

Common sense couldn't dent that amount of serene conviction, so Beckendorp didn't offer any. Besides, Beyer wasn't the sort with whom to share doubts about the ultimate triumph of the world revolution, or Stalin's present state of mental health. He sighed, and tried to gauge the size of the crowd. They were well-behaved so far, letting their presence do the talking. It was impressive - by far the city's largest gathering of non-herded humanity since the Weimar days.

'I'd say a quarter of a million, perhaps more.'

Beyer scanned the vista. 'It's a pity we can't …'

'Not in daylight, and not while they stay on that side of the line. I can't see any cameras, but someone's sure to be hoping we'll go in heavily.'

'A small incident might stampede them. A crowd this size, it could be terrible.'

The wistfulness in Beyer's voice would have tugged at a mother's heart. 'Not even an *incident*, lad. The Ivans didn't allow K-5 to deploy for a reason. We're here only to protect eastern Berlin from capitalist aggression, remember?'

'Yes, Comrade Inspector. May I ask why you're not at the Rathaus?'

'Why should I be? If no-one's attending but SED councillors they don't need another one to swing the vote. Anyway, *this* is my day job. Politics should be conducted in the dark, where it belongs.'

Curious, Beyer glanced at his commander. A man never knew with Beckendorp whether he was hearing cynicism or the old street-agitator, railing against all suits in plush seats. Sometimes, the things he said teetered on the brink of heresy (if a good communist could put it that way), but the men in Karlshorst seemed not to care. They had their ears (Beyer's among them) at Keibelstrasse and must have heard every word the Inspector uttered, and yet they continued to ignore what would buy a trip east if it spilled from any other mouth. Perhaps his history really was as gloriously true-red as the rumours painted it.

As if trespassing upon Beyer's thoughts, Beckendorp turned and dropped his voice.

'MGB have a little problem, Beyer. And you can help with it.'

The *unterkommissar*'s bowels flexed instinctively. 'Me? How, Comrade? And what …?'

'Like Bo Peep, they've lost a sheep and don't know where to find it. Actually, an agent, their only man in Bremen.'

'But we have nothing to do with Bremen …'

'He came to Berlin to make his report to Karlshorst, and for Christ knows what reason K-5 picked him up and passed him on immediately to some other Russians. He's gone into a hole, and MGB would like him back - or at least get an explanation as to why. They could of course go straight to K-5 and cause trouble, but it would be better if this was settled sensibly, without fingers being pointed or broken. You're very good friends with Jamin's boys; please have a word, today. He was picked up on the twenty-first.'

Beyer chewed his lip. If some interdepartmental shit was being flung around Karlshorst no sane German wanted to be caught holding a bucket. Beckendorp noticed – smelled - his subordinate's anxiety.

'It's alright, you're not in anyone's sights. MGB have asked the question – you can tell them that.'

'But …' as certain as he was of his standing with the Party and the Fifth Directorate, Beyer hesitated to risk a transfer to the Prostitution Detail; '… wouldn't your speaking directly to Direktor Jamin do the business more quickly?'

Beckendorp shook his head. 'Think about how things work. If I involve Jamin directly and if this disappearance becomes an embarrassment, he isn't going to thank me, is he? What it needs is a few quiet words being bandied between people whose names never see the light of day. That way, whatever the reason for MGB's boy being snatched, it can be put right, no ripples, no punishment beatings. On the other hand, if I took your excellent advice, blundered into K-5's offices and caused a fuss, where would the blame stop?'

Beyer nodded and scanned the crowd once more. Discretion was a quality most Germans of rank were relearning. Under National Socialism, one's position was enhanced or undermined much as it had been under the Romans – by the blade, deployed savagely and not always in the metaphorical sense. The Soviet system had more time and even greater consequences to draw upon, and its surviving players had become adept at the necessary art of negotiating darkened rooms without leaving the scent of their passing.

'Do we have a name?'

'Otto Fischer. Don't ask more than you need to, and come straight to me with what you get.'

'So he's important? Not just another disposable *Schwab* to them?'

'You really want to know? Put it this way – Bremen is the Americans' only German seaport, and Fischer's are the only eyes on what they can't bring into the country by air.'

'Oh. Right.'

The crowd was trying coalesce around a single point, from which someone had started to harangue them. He seemed to be getting a lot of agreement, and Beyer's wistful expression returned.

Beckendorp snorted. 'Forget it, lad. It's one thing to set on a few dozen fat politicians as they try to vote, but you'd need artillery to dent this lot. It would be just what the Allies want - proof that fear's the only thing keeping us married to the Russians.'

'That's a lie.'

'It doesn't matter. Truth is what people see it to be - Lenin said that, I think. If we try to interfere today the newsreels will be rolling in London and Washington before it gets dark, showing their folk what they believe already. If anyone knocks off your cap or gives you a mouthful, just smile at them. In fact ...'

Briefly, Beckendorp glanced around and counted those of his men that were close to hand; '... you can fuck off back to Keibelstrasse now. K-5's boys are there at the moment, safely indoors. It's the perfect time for you to ask the question. And with subtlety.'

As Beyer departed, Hoeschler, who was one of the police forming the left flank of the line of *VolksPolizei*, detached himself and approached Beckendorp.

'Will he do it?'

'He will, but keep your eye on him. He's as much Party as police, so if he starts to twitch, let me know. Are you working on anything together?'

'The Kaulsdorf executions.'

Two weeks earlier, a warden had discovered a shallow trench near Kaulsdorf's *Jesuskirche* in which three men had been planted, each with a bullet in the head. As the wounds were temple-shots, Soviet participation hadn't automatically been assumed and a case file was opened, and that was where things came to a frozen halt. Eastern Berlin's *VolksPolizei* no longer had the manpower to investigate actual crimes (its remaining complement was too busy beating up Social Democrats and importuning *wessies* who crossed the line to their jobs each day), but Beckendorp had insisted that his own department's caseload be properly documented and assigned on the small chance that a day might come when police were permitted to do police work once more.

'Good. At least you'll have a reason to talk to him.'

'What if he squeaks to K-5?'

'Say something nice at my funeral, get the family west. Then shoot the bastard.'

Hoelscher couldn't tell if he was joking, but then he never could - almost everything that Beckendorp said could be mistaken for something else, and sometimes nothing at all. His own instinct was to stay as far as possible from anything that K-5 touched, including Beyer. The man was too happy for a Berliner in 1948, too ready to think of too many other Germans as the enemy. Other than friendship with Otto Fischer, Hoelscher and Beckendorp shared only a sincere desire to move on from the Age of Carnage. Beyer, by contrast, was yet another eager volunteer for its next phase.

'I'm better with a knife.'

Beckendorp shrugged. 'I was being droll. You know that this is it, don't you?'

His eyes were on the crowd. Hoelscher tried to gauge their limit, and couldn't. 'I've never seen so many civilians in the same place.'

'We've lost. You can't intimidate people into loyalty unless they have nowhere to run, and this lot have. The Americans and British wanted a split Berlin and Stalin's just given it to them. Fucking idiot.'

'Stalin?'

'No, his dog. Come on, let's get closer and watch. If history's happening I don't want to miss it.'

11

It struck Fischer that MVD Special Camp no. 1 was a piece of amber, preserving a part of National Socialism in its pristine moment of defeat. Out in the world its philosophies had been expunged or chased into dark, warm corners; here, it functioned still at a bacterial level, retaining a capacity to re-infect. He wondered if the Russians knew what they were doing.

Every shade of Party fossil crossed his path between hut and latrine, a nostalgic honour guard for his imminent bowel movement. Without exception, they resembled the former Regime's administrative disappearances – emaciated, greyed out, rendered nondescript by an act of policy. Some held on to the tattered dignity of once-well-tailored suits or dress-coats, starved ankles disappearing into shoes that had been made far too stout for mere shuffling; a full colonel, leaning against a hut wall, his bony nose poked deeply into a book that held on to the barest memory of its spine, could have frightened birds from crops had a breath of wind caught him; most notably, the former deputy Gauleiter of Pomerania (Fischer recalled him from a brief, carefully-staged morale visit to Stettin's Police Praesidium in 1937) scratched his arse ostentatiously while playing dice with two other men against the wall of a shower block - at least, it resembled one, but then such facilities were often found to be something else entirely. Clearly, the man hadn't followed the excellent example of his boss, the pig Schwede, who had exhorted Pomerania's population to fight the advancing Red Army to the last man, woman and child and then motored swiftly westward to surrender to the British.

He suspected that most of them were the middle-rankers of National Socialism, their achievements too modest to deserve a tribunal, too questionable to pass over. A vast comic lottery determined who was caught and who evaded the ridiculously inefficient mechanism of retribution to reap the whirlwind of comfortable obscurity, protected by a growing web of complicity. Here, he was among his own kind in one fundamental sense – these were the unfortunates, the men whose feet had found the only remaining mine in a cleared field.

He attracted attention on his way to shit. A slim man, he was nevertheless too well-padded to pass as anything other than a new arrival, even among a population that might have filled a medium-sized town. A few stares were hostile, but the majority held only mild curiosity, an interest in rare novelty. Ridiculously, he couldn't help nodding at those who caught his eye, as if he had encountered casual acquaintances at a street market.

He noticed no guards on the ground. Between the administrative sections and the perimeter was a near-autonomous slice of Germany, able to get on with the important business of dying slowly without interference. Siegfried had told him that the kitchens staff were the only people who came into contact with inmates on a daily basis (to pass on the inedible to the irredeemable). Very occasionally, one of the inmates would attempt to take weekend leave, after which his corpse would be dragged by its ankles to the one of the burial pits that surrounded the camp. Otherwise, the sole function of the authorities here appeared to be to provide an impassable barrier between past and present Germanies.

At the latrine door, another scarecrow was selling small paper squares cut from old copies of *Red Star*. Fischer had no recognizable currency and didn't think to enquire as to the possibility of credit. Inside, the odours were familiar and overwhelming, a miasma that made anything other than a short visit fatal to most forms of life. Two men held on to the suspension post, their grips bloodlessly tight, straining to lose their last meal. Fischer regarded this as a good sign. When the camps' virus of choice paid one of its periodic visits, no-one had to strain to lose organs, much less waste-matter.

He took a place at the post and managed to do what was necessary without thinking too much. This required three intakes of air (two more than he'd hoped), but the stench stayed with him for only a few minutes once he emerged from the block. He reminded himself that this and other aspects of camp life were no worse than his first few months in post-surrender Stettin, where a prospect of living like animals would have had people queuing to sign up for it. In fact, a regular seven hundred calories a day (and Siegfried had assured him that the ration had never fallen below this) struck him as requiring only a certain economy of effort, and as far as he could see the authorities didn't demand physical labour from their charges. It was bad, but not entirely unbearable.

It was *her*, he realised, making tolerable what should have been something else. The halving of his diet, the contraction of his world to a few hundred hectares, mattered far less than it would to anyone who had a stake in life still. Really, he should have been grateful. It wasn't often that one loss gave a man the will to bear another.

Joachim Dein had invited him to Hut 22 (his official residence), to discuss how he might be useful. The ailing gramophone aside, Fischer couldn't imagine what contribution he could make other than to offer recent news of the world. The inmates were allowed no visitors or literature (other than the Red Army's official newspaper, not translated), so there was at Sachsenhausen a deep ignorance of anything that wasn't Sachsenhausen. Siegfried had told him that a few weeks before his arrival one of the more garrulous kitchen staff had made a vague reference to the Berlin blockade, which for want of further detail had blossomed into several wild theories about a new war. He could at least enlighten them on that matter, and – if anyone cared - the market for recorded jazz music in Bremen.

Disappointingly, Hut 22 was no more luxuriously appointed than his own. Having knocked rather than entered (camp etiquette being as yet a mystery to him), he was admitted by a large, bony specimen whose fixed scowl and door-blocking stance marked him as the security detail.

'That's alright Dieter, he has an appointment.'

Dein sat on a bunk, wearing a woollen cap that covered his ears, but was stripped to his shirt and trousers. He had been reading - the book, obviously contraband, was a slim volume, easily hidden. He noticed Fischer's interest.

'Rilke's *Sonnets to Orpheus*. He reminds me of a world that's neither here nor rubble.'

Fischer searched his deep memory for a dusty, long-interred school text.

'Trees I have admired, Distances which are tangible

Meadows that can be touched, And every astonishment at myself.'

Dein beamed. 'There, you've earned your place already! We *must* have a vacancy for Camp Laureate!'

'I've given you thirty percent of my entire store of poetry. The rest is filth.'

'But at least now there's someone I can inflict verse upon with a clear conscience. The gramophone's gone, by the way.'

'Stolen?'

'Burned as fuel, last winter. I'd forgotten.'

'Then I'm truly redundant.'

'You won't be that, for sure. We're a very mixed group here, but many were politicians – National Socialist, Social Democrat, and, of course, the wrong sort of Communist. Believe me, there aren't many of them who can throw together a water pump or build a wireless set, so our definition of *useful* is necessarily wide. I myself can project an air of authority and temporarily hush a roomful of complaints. That's it, the Dein talent in full. What we did *outside* rarely stands us in good stead here. Don't worry, we'll find something for you to do.'

'I would prefer to be occupied.'

'Well, we have allotments now, so if nothing else occurs we can send you out to help gather the harvest. But a former policemen – a detective, even; I can't help but think you can be useful.'

'Do you have much crime?'

'Theft, yes. Violence is endemic, and usually upon some extremely minor matter that our way of life magnifies. All but a tiny number of offences are witnessed, as you would imagine.'

'Detection isn't a problem, then.'

'No, but retribution sometimes is. There are … groups, men of a like-minded *weltanshauung*, who associate to protect their own.'

'Gangs?'

'More like lodges, defending a way of life that exists only in memory but matters still to them, at least.'

'The good old days.'

Dein smiled thinly. 'Some would say so.'

'I'm surprised that particular enthusiasm has survived the regime in here.'

'They have the advantage of a cause. Most of us haven't. At first we mourned Germany, but that passed. Our hope for our families lingered longer, but without news or any form of contact it's hard to keep hold, even in one's heart. This is a world offering no promise of better, or other, and so we gradually weaken, become ghosts like the Regime we served. Faith in something, even a thing that no longer exists, gives its possessor a certain energy that the rest of us have lost. Your good friend Adelbert is occasionally useful to their blessed circle. Perhaps it rubs off on him.'

'You're sure it isn't the extra, extorted calories that keeps him stronger?'

'Possibly. As you'd imagine, we don't try too hard to investigate their activities. A corpse that's become so other than by starvation or disease would be a matter for concern, usually. But a cut throat or a beating that fails to stop in time sends a message - that the business is not to be pursued. And it isn't.'

'The Russians don't care?'

'They don't even pretend to. Siegfried told me what you said, that MVD have come to regard the existence of this and other camps as counter-productive. It confirms my suspicion. They would be much happier if we all went away in a convenient manner, so the higher the inmate murder rate the more content they'll be. To them we're a degenerate species, overdue for extinction.'

'Yet they continue to feed us and provide other basic necessities.'

Dein shrugged. 'Moscow doesn't know what to do with us. They need to work out first what Germany's going to be. Is it true about Berlin? About the blockade?'

Fischer told him everything he knew – the events since the turn of the year, the determination of the Americans, British and French not to continue to allow Stalin to dictate terms, currency reform in the west, the close-down of road, rail and water navigation into the city, the air-lift. The old man listened intently, scratching the side of his nose with a fingernail, his eyes on the hut floor.

'It seems to me', he said at last, 'that there are two possibilities. First, that there'll be war, in which case the Russians won't need to justify their treatment of us to anyone. If so, the best we can expect is Siberia; the worst, what Sachsenhausen's SS did to Red Army POWs. Second, there is no war, and Germany becomes two Germanies, East and West. Again, the Russians will no longer need to pay lip service to the Occupying Powers' joint agreements. And yet … the border between the new states will be a front line, yes?'

Fischer nodded slowly. 'It isn't likely that the division will settle anything.'

'So, Stalin will need *his* Germans to be friends, even allies. That might mean our treatment improves. It *might* mean a decision on our future is made eventually by other Germans, which could be very good or very bad.

'You mean, whatever happens might mean anything.'

Dein looked up and laughed. 'Just about. To parse the world from in here is to read palms through gloves. Fortunately, most of us have learned the patience of the truly helpless.'

Roughly fifty thousand men, unfinished business from the previous regime and the square pegs of the new, waited upon a decision that might never be made. Fischer didn't possess the judgement gene, didn't think himself pure enough to pick up a stone and cast it; but nor did he doubt that while some men here deserved better than they had, others had missed the firing post. The trick - and he hoped to learn it, very soon – was to be able to tell them apart. He glanced at Dein. The man had the sunken, grey complexion of a man too used to bad food and not enough of it, yet he had made a footprint here, in a place intended to allow no mark of a man's passing. However far he had fallen, it was something that deserved respect.

'Are there many soldiers among the inmates?'

The question seemed to surprise Dein. 'Some. There are officers whose homes are in the east, caught and then released by the Americans or British. The Reds don't trust them not to have been indoctrinated. Of the lower ranks, we have a few men who were caught between the mass surrenders, or who didn't observe the rules but weren't important enough to go to

Nuremburg. And there are some who only did their job but took an extra portion of shit for no good reason. Why?'

'You wanted to know what use I might be. I could help to arrange something.'

'Something?'

'That might take the worst edges off limbo.'

12

The truck had been parked at the corner of Immelmannstrasse and Burgherrenstrasse for almost an hour before it was investigated by an *anwärter*. He had noticed it a few minutes earlier but hesitated for two reasons: first, this was only his third week on street duty as a member of the new western Berlin police force and he was extremely averse to coming to anyone's attention for good or bad; second, because it was an US Army vehicle and he feared that he had no business noticing it at all. The peculiar detail that made him overcome his reluctance was that the driver's door was open – that is, there was a tiny gap between chassis and door, indicating that the catch had not been engaged. As there were no US military personnel in sight, this was something (he told himself, very reluctantly) that any assiduous policemen must investigate.

The cab was empty, but the ignition key was in the transmission. Stood on the footplate, the *anwärter* had a better view than from the ground. He peered around, hoping to see a GI close by, having a smoke or urinating; but on a stretch of road with no obvious places to hide or shelter there was no sign of a uniform other than his own.

Being until recently a member of *VolksPolizei*, the *anwärter* had a keen sense of just how far a German's authority stretched in matters concerning the Occupiers. Had he access to a radio he would have called in the business and waited for someone to come and take it off his hands, but Berlin's police, east or west, had no such sophisticated equipment as yet. His only option, as he saw it, was to accost a passing civilian, demand that he or she hurry to the nearest station and report the incident while he stood guard. This, he decided, was an excellent idea as it neither allowed nor demanded any more discretion than was expected of him. He stepped down from the plate, made his choice of unwitting volunteer from a number of early morning commuters passing on the south side of Immelmannstrasse and removed his whistle.

The muffled groan destroyed his composure. It came from beneath the tarpaulin covering the truck's platform, an area he had avoided as being none of his concern, but which now demanded it. Slowly, he edged his way towards the back of the vehicle and drew aside the flap.

The cargo appeared to be foodstuffs. Crates were piled three high, with a narrow loaders' aisle between that should have been empty but wasn't. In that confined space, the *anwärter* counted four feet, all booted, one pair facing the other, and though he had little prior experience of this sort of thing (having directed traffic for much of his short career in eastern Berlin) he realised that the time and need for discretion had passed. He put the whistle into his mouth and blew hard.

He directed a woman to bring more police and conscripted a muscular fellow in manual-worker's clothes. Together, they unloaded crates quickly, exposing more of the two prone soldiers. They were bound tightly together at the knees by a leather strap. The worker took hold of it in both hands and heaved them towards the dropped tail gate.

The *anwärter* tried to control the lurch in his stomach. One of the GI's was obviously dead, his eyes wide, blood from the mouth covering most of the front of his tunic (and that of his comrade). The other – the one doing the groaning – was unconscious but twitching, and a large, purpling area was raising the veins on the side of his almost-shaved head.

The muscular fellow stared at what he had manhandled and glanced around nervously. 'Can I go now?'

Who would want to be near *this* when explanations had to be made? The *anwärter* nodded. 'Yes. Thank you.'

The man shuffled off westward along Immelmannstrasse, his collar pulled up, head down, inviting the least suspicious temperament to wonder what he'd done wrong. A siren wailed briefly, too distantly, and faded to the north. Carefully, the *anwärter* unfastened the belt and made a careful start on the knotted rope binding the surviving GI's wrists. Before he had worked out the puzzle, two jeeps roared around the corner of Burgherrenstrasse, their axles almost grounding on the left-hand side, and came to a screeching halt to the front and rear of the truck. Six American soldiers in MPs' white helmets converged upon the *anwärter*. He jumped back smartly and come to attention.

To his great surprise, they ignored both him and their comrades, and began to closely examine the crates that he and his unwilling helper had placed on the ground beneath the tail gate. Then, they moved inside to check the still-stacked cargo, prising off lids and passing the open crates out to the road to get at the lower tier. The *anwärter* knew only too well the tight, miserable feeling of an empty stomach, but even so found their single-minded obsession with the truck's load – tinned meats, flour, sugar, dried milk and eggs - disconcerting. Eventually, when every crate had been opened, one of the Americans – a sergeant – went back to his jeep and used its radio. Belatedly, two GIs inspected the dead man and then gave some attention to the survivor, and even now the policeman might have been a lamp post for all that he intruded upon their day. Had he not been the one to report the incident he might have continued on his beat, almost certain that his departure would not be noticed. But questions would be asked at the station, and he needed at least to be able to tell them that he had been dismissed.

Some minutes later another jeep arrived with an officer in its back seat. This man ignored everything that had so occupied the other Americans and walked straight across to the *anwärter*.

'Tell me what happened here.'

The man's German was perfect, with a slight Westphalian accent (probably his grandmother's). The *anwärter* clicked his heels and came to attention.

'I saw that the truck door had not been locked, sir. I sent a civilian to alert the duty officer at Kleineweg station and then noticed the ... gentlemen in the rear of the vehicle. One was already deceased. Your men arrived a few minutes after that.'

'You saw nothing prior to this?'

'No, sir. I first noticed the vehicle some minutes before I examined it. I assumed then that the driver had merely parked it here. It was only when I saw the door ...'

'Yes, the door.' The officer turned to stare at the crates scattered on the road behind the truck's tail gate. One of the White Helmets came to speak to him; their English conversation was entirely lost upon the *anwärter*, but the tension in both men's voices was plain. Again, he wondered why a cargo of foodstuffs – even one that must be vitally necessary to Berlin's besieged population – should be such a matter for concern, particularly as it seemed to him that nothing was missing.

The thought jarred a memory. When he and his reluctant assistant had clambered into the back of the vehicle to assist the bound GIs there had been a gap in the otherwise full load, a precisely crate-sized gap. It hadn't concerned him then –

why should it? There was no rule he knew of that said all trucks had to be loaded to exactly their full capacity. In any case, the space had been at the rear of the loaded area, where, logically, it would be. But what, he thought now, if *something* had been there?

Pineapples. He couldn't think of anything to eat that was more precious (but then, he was biased, this being by far his favourite fruit, sampled only once in his life so far), and even they seemed a poor return for murder. No, it couldn't be that. For a moment he wondered if he should volunteer his observation to the officer, but that surely would be pointless – they *knew* that something was missing. Why else were they here, and in such numbers?

Naturally, no low-ranking German policeman know anything of the American Military's investigative procedures, and he was reassuring himself that seven men might not be considered an excessive number (their nation had vast manpower reserves to draw upon, after all), when a column of some twenty armoured vehicles roared eastwards down Immelmannstrasse and came to a deafening pause surrounding the hijacked truck. As the *anwärter* stared at the 75mm barrel of an M24 light tank that pointed only a little to the left of his ear, thoughts of pineapples and protocols went somewhere else entirely.

13

UnterKommissar Rolf Hoelscher placed his service revolver in the bottom drawer of his desk. The Nagant was a concession, like every other gun in the hands of a member of Berlin's (now just eastern Berlin's) *VolksPolizei*. The Soviet authorities had issued them reluctantly, and only in response to repeated pleas from a force massively outnumbered and outfought by the criminal gangs that had crawled from the ruins of the war that ended Germany.

At the moment, Hoelscher didn't feel too grateful for his gift of firepower. As he closed the drawer he noticed that his hands were still shaking, badly. They brought back a memory from a bright, hot day, the sound of the Mediterranean easy upon his ears until the moment that he and his comrades had emptied their magazines at a wall and what stood in front on it. When the firing stopped the sea had gone; only the wails of women and children remained, begging God to undo time and circumstance, to restore their husbands and fathers to them. He had watched their tears mix with the copiously spilled blood, and his hands had shaken like they'd never intended to stop.

A man had stood in that same firing party, perhaps only two or three metres away, and Hoelscher had since wanted to ask him how he'd felt about it, how his hands had been afterwards. But only their eyes had mentioned the business and then momentarily, the shock of shared guilt recalled. *We don't do such things*, men of their regiment always told themselves. They had that day, though. The order had been handed down, and orders were something they definitely did, always.

Otto Fischer. You saw war in his face of course, but the hurt of it, nor the hurting. At least he could feel that he'd been punished, had had his account partly settled. Not so

Hoelscher; he had fought everywhere that Fischer had fought and further still, marching backward the entire distance from Moscow almost to Berlin through a dozen hells, avoiding the slightest harm while his former comrade had writhed in a lazarett, flayed by aviation fuel. The account with his own name upon it awaited payment in full still, no deposit to be deducted.

He looked at his hands again, the way they took upon themselves the entirety of his physical reaction to murder. Perhaps they were his soul's last, precarious bridgehead, the rest lost somewhere on that long retreat. His mind managed to agonize still, dissecting motive, but that was a form of cowardice, not remorse. If it had been more he would have thought longer, long enough to weigh the possibility of other options; but he had committed himself instantly, experiencing no more drag of conscience than would a released guillotine.

Then shoot the bastard.

Beckendorp hadn't meant it, but to have said it was enough. It had opened a door, shown a way out of a place that had grown spikes. Hoelscher hadn't been offered the *choice* – he repeated it to himself, often, trying to calm his hands.

He wouldn't be caught. Seven-point-six-two millimetre was a very common calibre for a very common gun - untraceable, safe. The act had not been witnessed, there was no known motive and the righteous anger of the dead man's colleagues would blur vision, make the likely suspects seem likelier. It wasn't fear of discovery that keeping the shake in place.

He rehearsed a dozen ways to tell Beckendorp what had happened, and each of them disgusted him. How did an assassin paint a sympathetic canvas, a not–quite *mea culpa*? He thought of saying nothing at all, of letting a vast coincidence speak for itself, however implausibly. They probably wouldn't find the body until it had floated eastwards out of the city, so one could say that it had been an execution, not definitely. Except that Beckendorp would know, even if he never mentioned it again other than as a disappearance, an unsolved crime against the *VolksPolizei*. There was a knack to meeting someone's eye (even that of someone who wasn't owed a great debt of gratitude), and Hoelscher knew that he didn't possess it.

He looked at the clock on the wall of the Bull's Pen. It was a few minutes past six am. He had come in early to avoid company, to get right what he needed to say. The night shift was supposed to end at six, but very few of those who hadn't already defected to the new western police force had bothered to hang around to do their paperwork, much less care to be seen at their desks. Morale had dropped deeper and more quickly than the *Hood*, and now he he'd done something to push it down further.

'What did they say?'

Hoelscher almost left his chair. Beckendorp, a one-legged lump of a man, had somehow managed to cross the Pen like a sylph with its carpet slippers on. He was scowling, but then he always was, at least in uniform. It meant nothing, yet Hoelscher almost lost the last fragment of his composure.

'Nothing, apparently.'

'Nothing?'

'Actually, worse than nothing. All they were interested in was who wanted to know.'

'Beyer told them that Fischer was MGB's man?'

'He said that he did. But none of his friends at K-5 seemed to believe it, or cared.'

'They'd fucking *care* all right, if they believed it. Shit!'
Beckendorp stared pensively at the wall. 'What did Beyer tell
them? When they asked who was asking?'

'He told them he couldn't say, only that it came from up high.'

'Really? I didn't think he had the balls.'

Hoelscher realised that this was as close to the right moment
as he was ever going to trip into. 'I don't know that he has. He
told me afterwards that he was worried you're playing games,
or covering your own arse at the expense of his. He said he
didn't see why K-5 shouldn't know, seeing as how they're
MGB's pet Germans anyway. He said …'

'He said what?'

'That he was going back to the fourth floor, to give them your
name and tell them to look more closely.'

'Christ. When did he say this?'

'Last evening. He asked to meet me away from the station, so
I suggested Werderscher Markt – it's all clearance or
construction there, so I knew we wouldn't be seen.'

Beckendorp sat on the edge of Hoelscher's desk and rubbed
his face. Someone at K-5 might have spoken to Karlshorst
already, asking what it was all about. If they attached his name
to it he'd probably find Otto Fischer in a matter of hours, but
not the way he'd intended. He should have thought of
something else, something that hadn't involved a man he
couldn't trust.

'Alright. Tell Muller and Kalbfleisch to keep their heads under
the table for the next few days. You too. There's nothing to
put any of you on the same shit-heap as me, so don't make
them think that there is. And when Beyer comes in, tell him I
want to see him.'

When Hoelscher said nothing to this Beckendorp took his face out of his hand. 'Rolf?'

'Beyer won't be in.'

'Why? It's not his day off …'

They looked at each other. Hoelscher could feel heat in his face, an involuntary confession. It may have been enough to keep the next, obvious question in its sealed box.

Beckendorp raised a fist as if to strike something that wasn't there, and left it hanging.

'Sweet God.'

'No one saw, or heard.'

'You're certain?'

'It was dark by then, and we were beside the Spree.'

'Someone must have heard the struggle.'

'There wasn't one.'

Beckendorp had nothing more to say that was useful. In war he had been a fighter pilot, trained to kill at a remove, at the press of a button. As a policeman, *OrPo* or *VoPo*, he had never been obliged to take a life, much less that of one of his own. He had no right, no urge, to blame Hoelscher for the great favour he had done them both.

The assassin himself was still seeing the act, walking around it like the investigating officer he was supposed to be. There hadn't been a struggle because he had shot the man in the back and let gravity pull him into the river. There had been no noise because the Ivans had supplied Berlin's *VolksPolizei* with one of the few revolvers ever made that could take a suppressor, and he had carefully attached his own when Beyer paused to re-fasten his bootlace. To the stock of his sins he could add something that smelled like premeditation.

At the other end of the Bulls' Pen, men were shuffling in to start the day's shift and clear the previous day's paperwork. One of them looked up, saw the Inspector and coughed to alert his colleagues, who began to move to their desks as if they gave a damn about what awaited them.

Beckendorp cursed his rotten heart, but the opportunity was too good to let slip. He gave them a few moments more, to let the audience build to something respectable, one that would be able to dredge its collective memory and recall the question.

He coughed, to get their attention. 'Anyone seen Beyer?'

14

'Sergei Aleksandrovich, what have you done?'

For a moment, Zarubin, lulled by the familiarly forlorn lilt of Shpak's voice, didn't give 'you' the attention it deserved. He was busy, trying to glean useful information from a small pile of reports on the movements, comments and moral imperfections of some of the host of western Berliners who commuted to work in the SBZ each day. As fiction - discounting finesse, grammar, plausibility and any feel for a storyline - they ranked with anything by Dostoevsky, and reinforced Zarubin's principal objection to the use of paid informers: that they always felt obliged to offer value for money. He was reading what they thought he wanted to read, not what he needed to read; and, being Germans, they assumed that the quickest way to an official's heart was to denounce treacherous talk and opinions.

In fact, Zarubin couldn't give a bad kopek for whether one Hans Miller, carpenter of Moabit, believed that Stalin wore frocks and took it up the arse during depraved weekends at Sochi. It did not move him that Frau Ingrid Baumgartner, bakers' assistant and widow of Wilmersdorf, had allegedly claimed that all Soviet soldiers had monkey-parts between their legs with which they intended to breed a generation of degenerate half-Germans. And he was nothing but amused that Johan Frost, electrical engineer of Kreuzberg, had confidently stated to an apparent friend that the blockade of Berlin was merely the opening gambit in a Soviet ploy to seize all of Europe east of the Rhineland (amused, because any implication of Soviet strategic planning was invariably entertaining). It was all drivel, as pointless as it was expected, a waste of his valuable …

'Me?' Zarubin paused, sat back and briefly audited his day so far. It seemed remarkably innocent of doings. 'I don't think I've done *anything*, Comrade Colonel. Who's been talking?'

'Reinhold.'

Zarubin sat up. *Reinhold* was their only effective asset at USFET HQ, Frankfurt, an agent insinuated by NKGB two years earlier. The man's real name was known to a handful of senior MGB men at most, and his intelligence, if often sparse and incomplete, was considered gospel even by his godless handlers.

'What did he say?'

'That a consignment of Deutsche Marks was flown into Berlin two days ago. It departed Tempelhof under guard, on its way to the Länder Bank. It didn't get there.'

'How much?'

'Three point five millions.'

At current exchange rates, just over one million US Dollars. Zarubin gave Shpak his guileless face. 'It wasn't me.'

'Yet this was precisely what you had in mind.'

'But I haven't submitted a proposal, much less a requisition for men or vehicles, have I?'

Reluctantly, Shpak shook his head. 'Not through me.'

'Was it done cleanly?'

'Anything but. One dead, the driver, and a guard severely wounded.'

'Shot?'

'Clubbed, I believe.'

'Strange.' Zarubin scratched his chin. 'It sounds like it was done professionally, but with no attempt to avoid damage. Is it possible the perpetrators were trying to make it look like a gang was responsible?'

'Or they *were* a gang.'

'Would a gang risk bringing upon themselves the wrath of the Americans? To take their money is one thing, but such violence …'

Shpak was looking pointedly at him. 'Perhaps someone who's too fond of his own cleverness decided to play a game and this is what came of it.'

'Comrade Colonel, the last thing my plan needed – my extremely provisional scheme, I should say - was for the Americans to know that their money was missing.'

'Really? And how could you prevent that?'

'By not stealing it.'

'For God's sake, what are you talking about?'

It wasn't like Shpak to lose his temper, and Zarubin realised that he had been goading him.

'As I said when we first spoke of it, my idea was to re-circulate the money. For that, a sleight of accounting would have been necessary, not coshes in broad daylight.'

'And we would send someone into the bank to do this? With a letter of introduction from his excellency Marshal Sokolovsky, perhaps?'

'I've been compiling a list of Länder Bank employees in the city. With that information, I had intended to determine which of them might be susceptible to persuasion.'

'Persuaded with what?'

'The usual – sex of whatever type moved them, or money; blackmail, if the opportunity presented.'

'What would you ask them to do?'

'To transfer the monies as we directed.'

'And the bank wouldn't notice this?'

'Of course. But not, perhaps, for several days. Which is all we would have required.'

'To do *what*?'

'To advertise the event, as loudly and as broadly as possible. And having done this, the inevitable recapture of the funds would have made the matter even more prominent, almost a confession. It would have been damaging.'

'Fuck your mother! *To whom*?'

Zarubin's eyebrows rose innocently. 'To the recipient, of course.'

Shpak, having finally got something of the point, calmed himself. 'Sergei Aleksandrovich, do you think you might say who that would have been?'

'Ah!' Zarubin rummaged through papers at his left side. 'It had to be someone worth importuning, obviously, who also happens to maintain a personal account at a commercial bank to which the Länder would, with a nudge from me, immediately transfer the new monies.'

Shpak thought about this for several moments. 'Define *worth*.'

'Someone whose embarrassment would also hurt the Allies, bolster our case regarding the inherent corruption of the capitalist model, and, most importantly, reflect unfavourably upon just about every non-SED politician in the city: the principal thorn in our collective arse – the man who, two days ago, rallied almost a third of a million Berliners and asked them to bare theirs in our direction.'

'Ernst Reuter?'

'The city's Mayor-in-waiting – though not waiting too much longer, the way things are going.'

'That would have been ... considerable.'

Zarubin sighed. 'It would have been. But now ...'

'Why can we not proceed? Why does it have to be *this* money in particular?'

'Because a simple switching of nondescript funds between accounts could be dismissed as a stupid clerical error – slightly awkward perhaps, but nothing more. Timed correctly, what we had – what we could have created - was a paper trail that passed physically from USFET Frankfurt to their favourite pet German, proof that the Americans rule by bribery and corruption. At the least, Berliners would have paused in their headlong rush to see them as – what do they call themselves - the *good guys*? It would have cost us nothing, risked nothing, and earned you at least a modest degree of praise from Moscow.'

Wistfully, Shpak stared at his subordinate. 'Do you really think so?'

'Is anyone else doing anything praiseworthy right now?'

'Not really. It astonishes me that with a hundred-fold superiority in military resources we've somehow handed the initiative to the Allies.'

'I know, it's curious. Perhaps the Americans have a man in the Politburo, I can't explain it otherwise. But now we have a problem.'

Unlike Zarubin, Shpak picked up on the offending pronoun instantly. 'Do we?'

'Our imagined employee, Herr Gerste. Clearly, he spoke to someone else after we discussed what we required from him. Unless this robbery is an astonishing coincidence.'

'Then we'll arrest him.'

'I doubt that.'

Shpak frowned. 'He's playing games with MGB. Of course we'll arrest him.'

'He's already dead, or sufficiently recompensed to be somewhere we can't reach him. Would whoever took the money risk having MGB looking for them?'

'Then you're saying we do nothing?'

Zarubin stared at the wall immediately behind his boss. He had wormed his way into a relatively calm corner of MGB and almost immediately regretted it. Now, somehow, he had contrived a brilliant coup that had dragged his back-office to a front line. If the Red Army gave out Complete Cock awards (for other than spectacular battlefield reverses) he would have heartily pleaded his eligibility.

'No, we need to know that our fingerprints haven't been put on the business, so to speak. It's tiresome, but I must now investigate my own clever scheme. Please volunteer us for it, quickly.'

The struggle showed on Shpak's face. He was an intelligent man, and could see how they might be exposed by the episode, but in any crisis his burrowing gene swelled prominently.

'Why would Karlshorst care about the Americans being robbed?'

'Because it was a gang from eastern Berlin, obviously.'

'It's obvious?'

'I'll make sure that it is.'

15

After three days' careful sifting of memory and discreet consultation, Joachim Dein brought nine names to Fischer.

'I didn't know how many you needed.'

Fischer looked at the list. Brief biographical details were appended to each name – background, service records and the reasons for their being here rather than somewhere either in civilian life or the Russian tundra. Two of them he dismissed immediately, former camp guards who had put their faith in the *only obeying orders* defence and thrown down their rifles when the Reds arrived. He paused at another name: Adelbert Kranich.

'This isn't …?'

Dein glanced at the paper. 'Yes, your affectionate hut-mate.'

'I thought he works for the old guard.'

'He does, but not from any conviction. He just enjoys the extra rations.' Dien tapped the paper. 'He's also a close comrade of this one. In fact, he rather idolizes him. He'll do whatever Georg decides.'

Fischer looked at Georg Schiel's *curriculum vitae*. His grand tour had taken in France, Greece, the Eastern Front and some hospital time to repair a punctured stomach; then, east again before making a last stand in the fighting for Budapest. A busy man, but not one obviously culpable of more than his military service.

'Why is he here?'

'He didn't surrender when Buda fell. He and a few others from his unit made it into the woods to the north of the city. They stayed there for weeks, during which most of them died in Soviet ambushes. Georg was wounded and captured a few days after the general surrender. He should have been sent east, but he'd managed to lose his uniform by then and told them that he'd been on Veesenmayer's staff. They believed him, classed him as a political.'

'Why does big Adelbert think he's a *mensch*?'

'You'll know when you see him. Adelbert isn't what you'd call a ladies' man – though Georg is, strangely.'

Fischer looked at the list again. 'Are there any other odd ones?'

Dein laughed. 'After three years at Sachsenhausen, who could be anything else? As far as it goes, they're fine. None of them are hiding from the tribunals, if that's what you mean.'

'All I care about is reliability. When can I meet them?'

'Do you want to see them together?

'These seven, yes.'

An hour later, a small meeting convened in Hut 5 (once part of the dormitory complex, now a blanket store). Fischer, Dein and seven other inmates eyed each other warily. Dein had passed out half of a small bar of Swiss chocolate to each of the attendees (their principal reason for attending, Fischer assumed), which disappeared swiftly into pockets. Despite this largesse, the glare on Adelbert Kranich's face might have been set by casein glue. Fischer didn't need introductions to identify Georg, his friend. Even after several years' careful indulgence in malnutrition and camp ailments, the man might have been a casting agency's main source of income: blond hair, light blue eyes and features more regular than a monk's daily routine all explained Adelbert's fondness for the man. The others were as motley a group as any, though they all shared the peculiar characteristic of not being quite the usual sort of politicals or eastern refugees whom the Russians had marked for Sachsenhausen.

Adelbert apart, they wore mildly curious expressions, tinged by a hint of anxiety at being somewhere they shouldn't. To take the edge off it, perhaps, Dein went to the hut's only window and stood watch. Fischer glanced down at his feet for a few moments, trying to put what he had to say in an order that would neither scare nor bore them out of the door.

'I want to suggest something, but let me first ask a question. Do any of you know men who've died in here?'

A laugh, short and not pleasant, swept around the group. A one-eyed inmate wearing a knitted hood tossed his head at Fischer. 'Who doesn't?'

'Disease, hunger?'

'And executions - hundreds of them, in the first year. And giving up.'

'Giving up?'

'It's easy. You'll probably do it too one day, when you're tired of things and decided it's time to go. It can be quite comfortable. A fellow just stays in bed until ...'

'What about fellows who *haven't* decided it's time?'

The seven men glanced at each other. One-eye spoke for all once more. 'Yeah, sometimes. Tempers can get going on a point of rations. No one likes a thief.'

'And the other deaths? The ones that aren't about theft?'

No one answered that one. Adelbert's face had darkened, but he kept his lips together. He stood behind his friend Georg and another man, so getting past them would give Fischer at least a moment's warning of any assault. Whether he could use that moment to good effect was another matter. He decided to push a little, to draw any inconvenient loyalties out into the light.

'I'm told there are people in here who are old fashioned, who don't like the way things are these days. I don't blame them. Me, I've never liked the taste of boots I've had to kiss. But if anyone's waiting for the restoration - for the Allies to go home, or to fall out and somehow kick the hell out of each other while we watch - well, they're pricks. I've been outside since the surrender and I've seen what's happening. In the west, Germans are writing a new constitution for themselves, and it looks a lot more like Weimar than Munich. Here in the east, we'll get exactly what the Reds want us to have, and you can all guess what that'll be.'

He paused to check the audience. No one – not even Adelbert – looked like they were about to rush him. He realised that he had caught their attention with *outside*; that they were being held by what might have been a transmission from the moon. The history of Germany, 1945 – 1948, was as forbidden to them as a weekend stroll down Ku'damm, and for want of it they had built a dozen mythologies, the most dangerous of which held out hope for the sort of miracle that had kept up spirits in the *Führerbunker*. He took a deep breath and went after it.

'It's not going to be like it was before. National Socialism's a list of dead, missing or rotting, like in here. There's no underground, no partisan movement, no nostalgia for anything after 1938. Forget it, it's gone. Anyone who says differently is helping those who think that Germany's only going to be made safe if our clock's rewound a century. Fuck them.'

This goaded a slight nod from one of the seven listening heads. To Fischer's intense relief, it belonged to Georg. He pressed on, pointing to the ravaged side of his face.

'I was with 1 Regiment, *Fallschirmjäger*. No one can say that we weren't at the sharp end. I went where I was sent, and didn't worry about what's right or not. But a man should know when he's kissing the canvas. Those who don't, need to be enlightened for everyone's sake. Herr Dein tells me that the authority of the Inmates' Court isn't recognized by some people?'

A few more nods. Adelbert's colour hadn't deepened further, but he was staring at Fischer as if will alone might reduce his problem to a puddle of tissue.

'I don't blame them for not being able to take that they've lost, it's only natural. But that sort always believe that anyone who doesn't think their way's a traitor, that there's one correct punishment for treason. They only have power in here, and the Ivans allow them to get away with it because they really don't care. Outside, how long do you imagine they'd last before someone put a blade into them?'

Adelbert shook his head. 'There are people outside who take care of their old friends. We know that.'

Fischer nodded. 'The important ones get looked after, that's for sure. They hide and feed them, and then get them out to spend the rest of their lives up to their waists in Patagonian sheep shit. There's no place for them in Germany because no one wants them here, not even other Germans. We've had time to think about things, and we don't blame Neville Chamberlain or Edouard Daladier for the war. Now …'

It was obvious that he was carrying at least five of them with him. Adelbert was the only obviously hostile party, and his friend Georg was wearing a carefully blank expression.

'… at some point, if we're lucky, the Ivans are going to get tired of keeping the camps going. That means at least some of us will get out. So ask yourselves, when that time comes, who wants a finger pointed at him as one of the sort who'd be best dealt with over a shallow trench?'

Not even Adelbert volunteered himself for that detail.

'If you think about it, that's the choice. The day the gate opens, the best connected men in here are going to be the most vulnerable. They'll be owed a deal of grief from the friends of those they've buried. Where would you prefer to be standing?'

Georg cleared his throat. 'What's being offered?'

'Not much. Two hundred calories extra each day from the pooled supplies, and for that you swear not to take anyone else's rations.'

They glanced at each other. Outside it wouldn't have been worth a polite reply, but at Sachsenhausen it would mean the difference between walking out unaided or warming a stretcher.

'Why us?'

'Because you're all ex-military, you can handle yourselves. Which is why you've been working for the bastards whose fault it is we're in here. It has to stop.'

'How? If we agree, they'll just …'

'I haven't finished. You don't get the rations just for not hurting people or not taking their food. You'll be acting as officers of the Inmates' Court.'

'Officers? To do what? Be police?'

'Police investigate things. The crimes in here are done openly, to intimidate and send a message. You'll blunt the message.'

'How?'

'Punitively. You're going to be a *stosstruppen* unit.'

A couple of them laughed incredulously; the others stared at Fischer as if he had offered to light their farts with a blowtorch. Courteously, Georg raised a finger. 'How would that work?'

Fischer shrugged. 'Let's say that someone gets killed. You'll know who wanted it done and probably *why* too, because you've worked for these people. So, Herr Dein summons you and issues a warrant, formally. Then, you come to this hut.'

He turned to a small stack of axe handles stacked against the wall. 'You each pick up a stave and assemble outside. Then, together, we find whoever's guilty – not the fellow who did it, but the one who gave the order and doesn't care who knows. When we find him we beat him - arms, legs, torso, nothing fatal - and if possible we do it in front of other inmates. In case they don't get the point, we pin a court notice to the guilty party. When it happens again, we do the same thing again. Eventually, *everyone* gets the point.'

'We'll be picked off one by one.'

'No, you won't. Herr Dein will arrange for you to change bunks, to occupy the same hut – if you're getting extra food it's necessary anyway, to prevent trouble. And you have an advantage.'

'Which is?'

'You're soldiers. Not many of them ever were.'

'Why should we agree? We can get extra calories without the grief.'

'If you're happy here, then carry on. But like I said, these camps are going to close eventually. The Ivans can see that they're becoming counter-productive – that it isn't worth the cost or ill-will they breed among Germans in the SBZ. When they do, some inmates are going to be released and the others sent east to where they can never harm anyone. Where do you want to be standing when they make their choice? On the Inmates' Court's good or bad side?'

Georg glanced around at his fellow Muscle and then back to Fischer. 'Why are you doing this? Adelbert says you've only just arrived - why aren't you hiding in a corner, weeping? If I had your face I probably would be.'

'Because this will be jolly.'

'No, really. Why?'

Fischer thought about *why*. Because his life could be defined now only by what it lacked. Because facing down the only dangerous men in Sachsenhausen who weren't manning the perimeter seemed a clever way to cut short the misery. Because he had been asked what he could *do*, and it had occurred to him that all he had ever been able to do was to inconvenience the wrong people at precisely the wrong time. Because what else could a man do, when ...

'Because I can't remember when I wasn't jumping for the amusement of scum. The war cost me my face, shoulder, most of an arm and any quiet I might have thought I had a right to. Then I starved, got used as a football, lost a wife and found myself here for Christ knows what offence, or to whom. And I find that the scum are here waiting for me, ready to issue new orders. It will be the last pleasure of my life to disappoint them.'

He made a point of staring directly at Adelbert as he spoke, and the others noticed it. Georg turned to his friend and said something quietly. It was enough to bring the colour flooding back into the bigger man's face. Whatever he heard, he didn't reply to it.

Dein had wandered back from the window. All seven men, though belonging to other men who didn't recognize the authority of the Inmates' Court or its presiding Chairman, straightened slightly as if wondering whether they were on parade. He stood considerably closer to them than Fischer had dared.

'You all came out of the war without any history that you'd prefer to lose. So, if you take on this thing, I promise that you'll get favourable reports on your conduct from the Court Committee. The Commandant trusts us, you know that. Now, you should go and discuss it, but not with anyone else.'

16

Inspector Kurt Beckendorp's stern gaze passed slowly over
the several hundred anxious policemen who had gathered in
the main courtyard at Keibelstrasse Praesidium. They
represented almost forty percent of manpower based here - his
personal command, or at least that part of it that wasn't
currently directing traffic or failing to solve serious crimes
that weren't even being investigated because of parlous
manpower shortages caused by …

By gatherings like this, among other things. He coughed, and
the low burble subsided.

'As you'll know by now, one of our own has been murdered
by parties unknown. That isn't unusual in itself, God knows;
but Kurt Beyer was an *unterkommissar*, and President
Markgraf himself has told me that he wants the killers'
testicles in a box, on his desk, as soon as it's convenient. He's
not a patient man, and I'm not either. Most of you have been
on civil order detail since the (he wanted to say *stupid fucking
stand-off*) city's administrative close-down began in June, but
I want at least ten percent of all criminal investigations
personnel to get on to this thing immediately, whatever your
other commitments. Talk to your weasels, ask about rumours
and street gossip – you can read their palms, if it gets results.
This killing's a slap in the face for *VolksPolizei*, and if it goes
unpunished we might as well give up. Should we give up?'

'*No, Comrade Inspector!*'

The response was gratifyingly robust, but it meant as much as
any pulled string. He commanded a band of variously good,
bad and utterly incompetent policemen, in reverse order of

prevalence. The new force (that part which hadn't defected westwards) had two near-fatal flaws: it comprised far too many old fellows, retired non-police recruited in the darkest days of Berlin's struggle to emerge from chaos, and its Soviet-drenched culture made it extremely difficult to retire those who didn't want to go and who weren't actual criminals. This made a career in the *VolksPolizei* unattractive to competent, younger men (not that Germany was burdened by a surfeit of that sort) and very attractive to those whose passage through life was a gentle, moist tread. Beckendorp, having been one of the latter for much of his own pre-war police career, couldn't in good conscience condemn them - but he did anyway, and often, to those of his superiors who would pretend to listen. It achieved nothing, naturally. He had what he had, he was told; make the best of it.

He dismissed the men. A few of the more useful ones remained in the courtyard, wanting to hear more that wasn't office tattle. Hoelscher was among them, looking serious, keen to get about the task of bringing someone to justice. Beckendorp only hoped that his own face shone with similar innocence. He waved this residue over to him.

'This isn't the best time to be finding a murderer, so be sharp. Keep me informed of what you're doing - I want proper reports, witness statements, the lot. If the President asks to know what's happening – and he will - I need to be able to show him the paperwork.'

One of the Bulls, a decent old hand dragged out of retirement with the promise of a pension, shook his head. 'This is shit.'

Beckendorp nodded. 'It is, Gregor. But it has a small bright side. I asked Markgraf if we could look at the gangs as possible culprits. We've been told to lay off the organized stuff while the present emergency lasts, but he admits it's possible that Beyer turned the wrong corner and saw something he shouldn't have. So, as long as he stays outraged about this we should use it. Leave the cigarette people alone – they're dying for want of business anyway. But coupon forgers, medical supplies barons and goldfiners have had it too easy in the past three months. Make things unpleasant for them. If they know anything about Beyer it's a bonus.'

Hoelscher stayed where he was as the other officers dispersed to rearrange their schedules. He had been watching faces carefully, trying to gauge what wasn't being said. For someone who was about to be chased by some of eastern Berlin's more competent police he was remarkably composed; but then, Beckendorp had seen men go to the wall with every appearance of tranquillity. It didn't mean much.

Hoeschler waited until the last of his colleagues had disappeared. 'I've lost the pistol.'

'Very lost?'

'Stripped, cleaned and sent to where turds go.'

'Good. It wasn't likely to have been matched, but …'

'I know. They're looking for a motive they can't find. Even if K-5 stay interested, there's nowhere they can start looking. Beyer asked about Otto Fischer, but no one can put him with you or me.'

'One man can.'

'Major Zarubin?'

'I don't know if he ever talks to K-5 beyond the usual operational business. If he does, I don't know how he'll react if he hears the name Fischer – whether he'll be amused, interested or sick of the sound of it and happy to drop us all into the crap. In any case, we'll probably head his list of suspects within a minute of him getting the word.'

Hoelscher hadn't considered Zarubin. Both he and Beckendorp owed their present lives to the Russian's curious refusal to be what his job title inferred. He knew their real names and histories yet had almost colluded in keeping consequence from falling upon them like a wall. In turn, they had done their best to give him their loyalty, efficiency and, above all, invisibility. If Zarubin heard anything about Beyer's final conversation with K-5 and immediate death thereafter their unspoken agreement would be ripped apart.

'Look at it this way: if Beyer hadn't died, Zarubin would probably know already that we're looking for Otto.'

Beckendorp sighed. 'He probably would. I'm not saying you did the wrong thing.'

'I *did* do the wrong thing. It just seemed very necessary.'

'Well, it's done. So, what's next? Most likely, K-5 will assume that Beyer got unlucky the same way other *VolksPolizei* have over the past three years. We'll investigate, stir up a lot of muck, get nowhere but be seen to have done all that can be done. Or, K-5 will get angry about losing their pet policeman and make a noise that Zarubin hears. In which case we'll get dragged to Karlshorst and convince him that it's a terrible coincidence. Or we won't, and get the nine-millimetre treatment. *Or …*'

'Or what?'

Beckendorp sighed again. He enjoyed the way it said how he felt. 'That's it. That's all I've got.'

The two men studied the courtyard's pitted surface, looking for clues to all possible futures in its broken RK-AG tiles. Hoelscher half removed a pack of cigarettes from his tunic, changed his mind and cleared his throat.

'What if we go to Zarubin before K-5 think to do the same?'

'And confess?'

'Everything except the last bit. You invited your close, bereaved friend Otto Fischer to Berlin, he got himself disappeared, you wondered how and why. All of that's perfectly reasonable. Then, you heard about K-5's involvement in the business and sent one of ours – a man who liaises with them regularly – to try to clear up the business on the quiet. But that's the last time poor Beyer's seen until he's found impeding river traffic. This appears to be something big, so you decide that the only sensible thing to do is go straight to Karlshorst and give Zarubin the story.'

Beckendorp thought about it. 'The man's clever. He might decide that it *is* a story.'

'But it isn't, is it? He only has to verify the facts that you give him. And when he does, he – perhaps we – will be closer to knowing where Otto's been put.'

'What if he looks more deeply?'

'What if he does? He sees the biggest manhunt *Volkspolizei*'s ever undertaken, with you leading it. He notices that K-5 – the ones who disappeared Otto - were the last people to see Beyer alive, just after he asked about the embarrassing object in question. He recalls that *you* came to *him* with this, with a tender, worried expression on your face. Who looks more likely, us or them?'

'Yeah.' Another sigh. Parked around the courtyard, the few GAZ vehicles donated to Keibelstrasse by kind Uncle Karlshorst were being claimed by the day shift. Above that clench, peering down from fifth-floor windows, their colleagues in K-5 were weighing the possibilities, wanting to know why they had been asked a question, and why it was that Otto Henry Fischer's quick, easy disappearance had become a more complicated matter.

Hoelscher followed Beckendorp's gaze, apparently unconcerned by the enemy's proximity. 'I assume you don't want *me* to look too hard for Beyer's killer?'

'If you mean do I want you to avoid mirrors, yes. That thing you were working on with Beyer.'

'The Kaulsdorf executions.'

'I'll assign Müller and Kalbfleisch to help you with it. I don't want them on the manhunt, and I certainly don't want to tell them the truth.'

'Right.'

A *wachtmeister* emerged from one of the courtyard's corner doors and hurried across to the two men, holding out a piece of paper. Beckendorp took it, read briefly and nodded the man away. Hoelscher noticed that some colour had drained from the usually florid complexion.

'A message from Major Zarubin of MGB, Karlshorst. He tells me he needs some help with a missing person. Quite urgently.'

'Now that,' said Hoelscher, scratching his head, 'is fucking unsettling.'

17

Zarubin placed the photograph on the table in front of
Beckendorp. It was a head and shoulders, an eminently
forgettable face adorning grey, dusty work clothes. Had it
been entitled 'German: male' the image could not have been
made more nondescript.

'Name: Rudolph Gerste. Age: I don't know. Address:
somewhere in Schöneberg, where you can't ask questions.
Occupation: anything that pays, though most recently an
unloader of supplies from American 'planes at Tempelhof and
part-time MGB agent.'

Beckendorp peered at the subject, willing something
distinctive to suggest itself. 'Is he likely to be alive?'

'I have no idea.'

'If not, there won't be identification on the body.'

'No.'

'Can I have this copied and distributed?'

'Only to men that you can trust absolutely.'

'Trust? To do what?'

'To not mention this to K-5.'

Surprised, Beckendorp glanced up. 'Aren't they your very
favourite Germans?'

'They might have something to do with the business, I can't say as yet. More particularly, I don't want it getting back to Karlshorst that I'm looking.'

'You don't trust your own people?'

'Not in this. Which is why I'm asking you, rather than sending a heavily armed battalion out on to the streets.'

Though he hadn't yet begun to think it through, the revelation eased Beckendorp's nagging worries regarding another matter. Deception was much happier in its own company.

'I assume this is to be done as quickly as possible?'

'It is.'

'Fine, I'll assign someone today. May I ask something in return?'

'Certainly.'

'Otto Fischer.'

Zarubin closed his eyes. 'Oh God, no.'

'He lost his wife in a road accident. I invited him to Berlin to stay with the family. He never got to me. He was picked up at a checkpoint – by K-5, according to a passing *anwärter* who saw it happen – and handed to your boys. I'd like to find him, to find out why. I assume it wasn't you?'

'Believe me, I would hide in a latrine to avoid old times' sakes with dear Otto. When did this happen?'

'A week ago.'

'He could by in Irkutsk by now.'

'I don't think so. The further he travels the more people get involved in the business, and someone obviously wanted this done discreetly. There are places in Germany he could be lost into, very quickly - if he isn't dead, that is. I'm hoping the fact that he was passed on means that he isn't.'

Reluctantly, Zarubin nodded. 'Enquiries could attract a great deal of the wrong attention.'

'Not to a subtle man. But there's something else. I tried to ask questions of K-5, using one of my men who works with them a lot. He turned up in the Spree. Or rather, down.'

'Surely you don't think the Fifth would be so bold, not without authority?'

'Probably not. But that brings me to the other half of the *something else*. I needed a credible reason to be looking for Fischer, so I told my man to tell K-5 that he was one of yours, an occasional MGB agent working at Bremen.'

'The fuck you did.' Despite himself, Zarubin was interested. He removed a silver cigarette case from his tunic and offered it. 'So, knowing this, someone still had the nerve to kill the policemen who asked the question.'

'Unless his death was entirely coincidental to the matter.'

'That hardly seems likely.'

'No.'

The Russian stared at his office wall. He could have ordered Beckendorp to devote as many men to his Gerste problem as necessary, and damn him for asking something in return. But in the past he had used Otto Fischer for reasons that couldn't have borne daylight, and rather than tie off loose ends in the sensible, brutal way he had stretched a point at some inconvenience to himself. Beckendorp fervently hoped that it had been more than a symptom of his whimsical nature.

Zarubin turned, caught the glance. 'I won't confirm or deny your story about Fischer, because if I do I'll be asked eventually why MGB is running an operation in Bremen that the Ministry hasn't heard about. There may be another way.'

'To find Otto?'

'At the least, to find out where he isn't. In April, SVAG convened a committee, to which representatives of MGB and MVD were invited. Its purpose was to discuss the condition, status and future of political prisoners held in MVD special camps in Germany. A list of 49,000 inmates was circulated, with details of offences. After an extremely brief discussion a recommendation was made and a show of hands requested. As you might imagine, agreement was unanimous.'

'Agreement to what?'

'Agreement regarding the immediate release of some 27,000 souls from the list, on the basis that they were not, nor ever had been, the slightest risk to security in the SBZ.'

'Really? They were released?'

'They were. Names and addresses were provided to K-5 to allow their monitoring – obviously, we released no-one whose home lies outside the SBZ - but no other restrictions were imposed. Which leaves only some 95,000 prisoners within the system still.'

'How does this help?'

'Further releases will be considered in due course - which could mean sooner, later or never. To permit the accurate consideration of cases, it might be suggested that up-to-date information should be provided periodically.'

After considering this for a few moments, Beckendorp grasped the point. 'Which will highlight any new inmates. But if the committee never reconvenes …?'

'It can be encouraged to. My immediate superior, Colonel Shpak, will put the case to Moscow that we have a problem. With their food deliveries to Berliners the Americans and British are winning German hearts. What better, cheaper way to redress the balance than to release a few thousand more innocents from an incarceration that achieves nothing and costs much to maintain?'

'What if your camp commandants don't care to draw up new lists?'

'That wouldn't be necessary – only a brief note from each, giving details of new arrivals since April. There certainly won't be many. Once the suggestion is made - as it will be by Shpak, who happens to be MGB's representative on the committee - no one would dare refuse.'

'He has that much influence?'

'He has none whatsoever, but assiduity can hardly be shouted down or ignored. The rest of the committee will assume that he's trying to ingratiate himself with Moscow, so they'll bend over backwards to outdo him.'

'If Otto is one of those named …'

'I can't do anything for him, obviously. I may not be able even to determine the reason for his incarceration, unless someone decides to volunteer it. But at least you'll know he's alive.'

It wasn't all that he had hoped for, but Beckendorp wanted very much to know that Fischer was alive.

'Thank you. May I ask …' he lifted the photograph from Zarubin's desk, '… why I'm looking for this Gerste fellow?'

'No, but you needn't regard him as a criminal. I just want to speak to him. If you find him alive bring him here, without telling anyone else about it.'

'Of course.' Beckendorp wanted to be gone, to set in motion the thing that Zarubin wanted, to earn credit that might lift the fog around Fischer's disappearance; but this was the first time he'd stood in front of a Russian officer for some months, and the question demanded to be asked.

'The siege …'

'You mean the administrative measures?'

'Yes. What … how do you think they're going?'

Zarubin shrugged. 'It depends what you mean by *going*. Clearly, the Allies' air-supply system is proving capable of averting starvation. Perhaps it will be able to fully provide all that western Berlin needs in the short term. It can't be maintained forever, but that's not the point of it.'

'No.'

'The principal issue is what the situation achieves for us.'

'Which is?'

'Nothing, it's a disaster. The Americans and British – and the French too, now – want some part of Germany that falls permanently outside of future Soviet influence. Premier Stalin recognized this long ago, naturally; but his sealing of Berlin has virtually guaranteed that it will happen *and* raised Berliners' opinion of the Allies beyond anything they might have achieved in the absence of a crisis.'

Beckendorp nodded slowly. 'It's what I'm hearing, too. Everyone's worrying about another war.'

'They should. No one wants it, but this sort of confrontation tends to have a life of its own. A few more air collisions, or a malfunction that brings a Skymaster down on an eastern neighbourhood, and hot heads will heat further. It may not need that, even. Stalin may bear only a little more of this humiliation and then allow himself to be convinced that the only way out is to double the bet.'

'And then ...'

'Then either Soviet troops will paddle in the North Sea or American atomic bombers will reduce our cities to rubble. In either case, Germany becomes a memory. We take it in with our mothers' milk that a reckoning with capitalism is inevitable. I just never thought it would come about by accident, a foot shot off in a stumble.'

Beckendorp tried to smile. 'Well, your brilliant idea to empty the Special Camps may ease the safety catch back into place, for a while at least.'

Zarubin opened a file, his way of ending a painful conversation. 'Soviet firearms tend not to have safety catches. It spoils the fun of never knowing.'

18

Fischer rested on his heels and waited for the man to catch his breath. This was taking some time, as most of the kicks he'd received had found his diaphragm. When the gasps receded he patted a shoulder, which cringed in anticipation of a new round of damage.

'From now on, you bring disputes before the Court. No one gets knifed, strangled, beaten to death or anything else. If you and your friends don't like it, get used to this.'

He stood up and nodded at Georg, who stood back, paused as if about to take an eighty-ninth minute penalty and then drove his foot into the man's balls. The scream was stifled, choked off by too much bloodied saliva backed up in the oesophagus.

Fischer regarded his first client without pity. A man – even someone in this place - had the right to express an opinion on the late Regime without getting his belly sliced, but this fellow didn't seem to agree. Unusually, the victim had lived and managed to make a complaint to the Inmates' Court, which had authorized redress - or rather, a correction of attitude. Correction having been applied, Fischer was happy to have his *stosstruppen* repeat the dosage, if necessary. They were here to provide a diligent service, no corners cut.

They stood around the sentenced man, whose name was Enno Blaeser. Until the surrender he had been a middle-ranking *SiPo* officer whose subordinates had once delivered much the same sort of treatment to anti-social elements (a large constituency in National Socialist Germany) seized under preventive action raids. Naturally, those beatings hadn't concluded with a warning, because censure hadn't been the point; they had been object lessons, intended to educate the public on the perils of non-conformity. At least this one would get up and limp away, eventually.

Fischer nodded at his troops and they slipped away in both directions, emptying out of the narrow passage between two huts. He reached down and pinned a note to the sleeve of Blaeser's coat.

'This is the court order that names you and your offence. You'll wear it until you're told otherwise. Failure to wear it … well, you can guess what will happen.'

At the end of the passage he paused and glanced around. A few inmates had paused, curious to know what was going on, but no guards were in sight other than those manning the watchtowers, and their attention – such as they could raise - was on the death strip between the electrified fence and perimeter wall. He stepped out and walked at a casual pace to hut 22, to report to Dein.

'We can expect them to retaliate.'

'Them?'

'Blaeser is close to five others, all former *SiPo* – though the Russians don't know that particular detail, otherwise they'd already be in a pit on the other side of the wire. Being former police, they have the idea that their once-authority should still count for something.'

Fischer grimaced. 'I was obliged to work with their sort. I never mistook them for police.'

'Well, they won't just accept what's happened. About a year ago, when we first established the Court, they tried to assert control over its procedures. I had to ask the Commandant to intervene, which of course allowed them to portray me as a collaborator. For a while they intensified their persecutions, presumably to emphasise their own legitimacy and the Court's powerlessness.'

'Clearly, it didn't work.'

Dein pulled a face. 'It didn't fail, either. Men still die for little reason, and those who don't can't hope for much better. The Court exists as much to give an illusion of human dignity as it does to keep order.'

'How will Blaeser's friends react?'

'To this? They'll try to hurt you, obviously. If you keep the company of your men they won't do anything too overt, but I should check whatever you eat for broken glass.'

'You?'

'It's hard to say. I suspect they'll weigh the odds of a gesture rebounding. If I'm harmed, someone will take my place with good reason to settle things. The Court has the tacit approval of the Russians, and not even ex-*SiPo* want to stand on those toes.'

Fischer looked out of the hut's window. He had been taking the Sachsenhausen rest cure for less than a week and already had found his way onto at least one death-list. Dein had been right: he wasn't going to be bored here.

Otto, you can't do anything about anything. Just let it pass.

She had been right, too. Neither nature nor fate rewarded a righteous cause. The best he could hope for is that they would tire of losing ribs before he ate powdered chandelier or had his grip prised from the latrine post. It was a shame - a few months more and he might have been looking forward to his lavish fiftieth birthday celebrations, warmed by the thanks of a grateful once-nation.

He looked at Dein. 'Do you ever wonder where you'd be if Frau Hitler had miscarried?'

The older man shrugged. 'Of course - a place like this encourages what-might-have-beens. To be entirely honest I can't blame the Führer for my predicament. I suspect my better nature would have been stifled in that other life, too. You?'

'I don't know. An unhappy *KriPo* possibly, made prematurely unpleasant by the work. With luck, I might have thrown it all in for a horse-stud, a nice farm somewhere outside Asunción.'

Dein's eyes creased. 'Not an unpopular choice for Germans in *this* life, too. I couldn't say it would be a worse fate than MVD Special Camp no. 1.'

'That's because you're not giving this place a chance.'

Briefly, Hut 22 echoed to the uncommon sound of two men laughing. An inmate who had been busily contemplating the ceiling from his pallet turned and gave them his back. Shunned, they went out on to the stoop.

From an elevation of forty centimetres they regarded Dein's principality. A few men were setting themselves to work of some sort: whittling, sewing (needles issued upon request, to be returned to the guards each day) or digging in one of the many allotments that had been laid out on the flanks of the outer huts. Most of the others visible from that point stood or sat in small groups, passing all the time they would ever need or want in fond memory, abiding rancour, frustration or half-starved blankness.

To Fischer, it seemed like a vast, open-air waiting area, for some rally that had been cancelled without notice. 'Why aren't escapes organized anymore?'

Dein laughed again, without humour. 'The most difficult part would be getting over, or under, the fence and wall. After that, and unlike those who make the attempt in wartime, one would be among a friendly population, unlikely to be betrayed or refused help.'

'So, why not?'

'Because the incentive isn't there. Again, unlike other escaped men, our homes lie in enemy territory, so those who managed not to die trying could never return to them. They'd be wanderers, sleeping in barns and hedges, never seeing an end to it. Family is all that a man would risk the wire for.'

'Of course. It was a stupid question.'

'No, you're new. Your spirit hasn't been fitted for its lead coat yet. A prisoner of war knows that his ordeal will be finite, so morale falls only so far. We're prisoners of a half-peace, one that's marked out our territory as a future battleground, so we don't have that certainty.'

Fischer wondered if he had been fortunate, an unusual feeling. Until Marie-Therese fell under the wheels of a Ford truck his life had been making a start on escaping the past, rearranging the rubble into a something ready to be metalled by love, time and the thousand mundane rituals that carried folk through days in which armies didn't move, shells didn't drop and bombs didn't fall. It was rumoured that any man was only ever two pieces of bad luck from ruin, but gradually he'd allowed himself not to believe it. He probably deserved this.

'Perhaps escaping wouldn't be the point.'

'Ah. You mean the discipline of preparing for it?'

'Of planning one. You never know, if we could manage to enthuse the National Socialists – tell them the rat-lines are primed to whisk them away to Spain - they might decide to steal the plan, get out and spare us the feud.'

'Or at least get shot trying. It's a sweet thought. If not, perhaps *I'll* risk the wire and try to get back to my village. Memories of my embezzlements may have faded.'

Dein had a face that was hard to read when he wasn't making it obvious. He had a slight tick to one eye that became more pronounced as he concentrated upon a thought, and it was busy now. Fischer's suggestion had been half-serious at most. This close to Berlin, the Ivans had the option – at next to no notice – of putting a couple of divisions into a chase for fugitives, making any actual escape attempt a suicide mission. He wouldn't think of attempting it himself, but then he hadn't been rotting gently here for the past three years.

The tick subsided. 'Not an escape. But perhaps the means to be more than ghosts. Siegfried told you about our many committees here?'

'Yes, he did.'

'You come to us bringing hopes for release, if what you say about MVD isn't wishful thinking.'

'It's what I heard from an MGB officer last year. He had no reason to tease me.'

'Well, then. Among our population are some of the real unfortunates, refugees from the Polish expulsions who weren't yet too old or infirm to be considered harmless. Most of them were civilians, so they had skills that had kept them out of the Wehrmacht – miners, dockers, railwaymen and similar. Ironically, hadn't they fled Silesia and Pomerania the Ivans would have employed them, put them to where they could be useful. Here, they're just surplus stock, forgotten men with a grudge.'

'I was one of them. Except for the skills.'

Dein seemed surprised. 'You were?'

'I'm from Usedom, originally - a Stettiner by adoption. I managed to get out in '46, via Lübeck.'

'Then you'll understand something of their pain. To date, we haven't even thought about benefitting from their skills but …'

'Knowledge could be shared. And it's as worthwhile to teach as to be taught.'

'There are electricians, at least half a dozen plumbers, several general mechanics, all of them quite unnecessary to life in here.'

'But not to men going out into the world.'

Dein studied the surface of the stoop beneath his feet, frowning. 'I don't want to give them hope, if …'

'When I was dragged in here I had an interview with the Commandant. For MVD he seemed almost … reasonable. Why don't you go to him and put a case, ask for permission to organize classes? Ask also, perhaps, if it's a waste of time or something else?'

Dein thought about this. 'It's a good thought. His predecessor, Rudenko, considered any living German to be an affront, but Colonel Vaisman is a cultured man. I doubt that he'd intentionally deceive me.'

'And even if the releases don't happen for several years yet, it's hardly a waste of time to occupy idle minds with practical matters.'

The older man smiled. 'The University College of Sachsenhausen - our diplomas to be certified by the Humboldt, presumably?'

'Why not? It's only forty kilometres away. The Chancellor could come out every year to award our degrees. With luck, he'll bring his wife. In a hat.'

Joachim Dein was a respected man in MVD Special Camp no. 1, so when inmates saw him on the stoop of his hut, convulsed with laughter, most assumed it to be the fault of a fine joke. A few wondered how anything could be sufficiently amusing to raise spirits in this place, and one or two of the more anxious temperaments wished that he had shown more sense than to give the Ivans an excuse to meddle with the rations once more. All were incredulous that the source of whatever wit had so taken Herr Dein appeared to be the recently arrived, half-faced veteran whose terrible luck obviously surpassed even their own.

19

Oberwachtmeister Kalbfleisch peered deeply into the incident report, as if attempting to see beneath the bald, sparse statement of facts.

'Why are we bothering with this?'

UnterKommissar Müller looked up from his own copy and frowned. 'To do justice to poor Beyer, by continuing his work.'

'But it isn't work. It's a waste of time. The Ivans did it.'

'Probably. But it isn't typical, is it?'

The report – drafted by the late Beyer with Hoeschler's counter-signature appended - was a masterwork of circumspection. Three bodies had been discovered on the evening of 12 May 1947 in a shallow trench in Kaulsdorf, by an old church warden whose sense of duty had overcome the common variety sufficiently for him to report it. The bodies – all male, aged between twenty-five and forty, were dressed in outdoor clothes, but carried no identification or personal items that might have allowed the same. All had been shot in the head from the side, a neat temple shot in each case. Therefore, none of the three had attempted to avoid their fate, meaning either that escape had been impossible (or pointless), or that the three men had been executed simultaneously, by three executioners. It hardly needed Kalbfleisch to suggest that the Russians appeared to be all over this, which is why the investigation had proceeded at a lame snail's pace until the siege necessitated that all officers be reassigned to the important business of intimidating the general population and allowed a relieved Beckendorp to place the incident file in the ever-pending drawer.

But Müller was also correct: this was not a typical case of Red Army personnel saving the cost of legal proceedings. The standard Soviet execution was a precise affair which invariably delivered a bullet to the back of the condemned man's head. To do it from the side, three times, suggested either a deliberate attempt to mislead (and why would Russian personnel bother to do that?) or that this was not what everyone assumed it to be. This one circumstance had been enough to keep the file on the very top of the not-now pile.

The victims were Germans. Before casework was suspended a perfunctory medical examination had found sufficient dental work remaining in all three mouths to remove any doubt. The brief door-to-door that Beyer and Hoeschler conducted the morning after the discovery had confirmed the inevitable – that, quite definitely, no one had heard or seen anything.

This was the full extent of evidence over which Müller and Kalbfleich now pored, an exercise that had consumed about five minutes of their morning before a familiar weight of blankness descended. On past experience, they could expect to be sent to kick over the site (now long polluted and filled in), re-interview the deaf and blind and then attach a note which would allow the file to be re-interred, to everyone's satisfaction.

'Isn't Rolf Hoeschler supposed to be helping us with this?'

There was a whining tone to Kalbfleisch's voice that managed to highlight both his pain and frustration at not being able to share it more widely. He was good, dogged police, but he preferred a thrown bone to retain scraps of meat still. No doubt a Sexton Blake or Sam Spade might have glanced at the facts and instantly identified some anomaly that would beat a clue-strewn path to the perpetrators, but all that occurred to him at this moment was that Müller had dandruff.

As the senior man, Müller tried to put a thicker lid upon his own frustration. With most of the rest of the station devoted to chasing down Beyer's killer, he couldn't understand why he, Kalbfleisch and Hoeschler had been sentenced to chasing this nonsense. *Of course* it had been an extra-judicial execution - probably of black-marketeers, to send a subtle message to their competitors about the cost of doing business in the SBZ. *VolksPolizei* had buried a hundred similar cases in the past three years without the slightest regret or uneasiness, comforted by the fact that, really, there was nothing useful to be done. Why not this one, also? They could hardly be doing justice to poor Beyer by persisting at something he had almost certainly wanted to drop like the moist turd it was.

And where the hell was Hoeschler? As Beyer's partner on the original call-out he could at least confirm that nothing was missing from their thin file, and perhaps even offer some observation he might have thought too slight to set down (Müller's collection of *krimi* novels had given him a sound conviction that a vague feeling or hunch was evidence by any other name). He turned to look at the neighbouring desk. It was cleared, obviously untouched since the previous day's shift.

'Where is he?'

Kalbfleisch looked up. 'He arrived when I did. Then Beckendorp limped in, they had a quiet word and went out. That was an hour ago.'

'They're very ...'

'They're very what?'

Müller cleared his throat. Since the previous year, when a momentary but deep concern for his own job had made him consider denouncing Beckendorp (he preferred to think of it as *expressing concern regarding*), he had come to realise that his commander was one of the few truly competent policemen in Berlin - unconventional, disrespectful to his own superiors and horribly unconcerned with the political proprieties that should have carried him to where he was, certainly; but when it came to crime – actually criminality, as opposed to whatever bit the arse of the Party – there was no one that Müller trusted more to lead them. He was also flattered that Beckendorp had trusted him enough to confide this business about his friend Fischer, even though it had something to do with K-5 and the Ivans. But …

The *but* was a big one. Beckendorp had too many secrets. He had admitted that he wasn't who he pretended to be, but not who he *was*. He was taking risks (and inviting Müller, Kalbfleisch and Hoeschler to do the same) for his friend, someone whom Müller had met just once and knew nothing about. And now poor Beyer, whom Beckendorp had sent to K-5 to test the dangerous waters, was drying out at the Beelitz-Heilstätten mortuary. Had he died because of Fischer, or some other matter? A man with a wife and children had to consider such things, however disloyal it felt.

And then there was Rolf Hoeschler, someone else with more cover than front. He had joined the force in the previous year, immediately after the mysterious Otto Fischer helped them with the Friedrichshain child killings. Hoeschler was good police and easy company, but how did a man with no previous experience enter *VolksPolizei* with the rank of *unterkommissar* unless he had the sort of friends one didn't ever ask about?

'Do you not think that they are *close* sometimes?'

Kalbfleisch considered this. 'Beckendorp and Hoeschler? What, as it brotherly?'

'No, as in keeping stuff to themselves.'

'Do you *want* to know more?'

'I want to know if I *need* to know more. Don't you?'

'I don't know.'

'I think they both have a past.'

Kalbfleisch laughed. 'They're German. Of course they do.'

'I meant, one that should concern us. Something shared.'

'Well, we share it too. The Inspector told us he isn't really Kurt Beckendorp. That would hurt him, if it came out.'

'What if there's something else?'

'They served together in an *einzatsgruppe*?'

'It may not have been anything terrible. But only four of us know about this Fischer business. What if their loyalties are to each other, more than to us?'

'You mean if this thing all goes to shit they might slip the blade between two sets of expendable shoulders?'

Müller fingered his collar nervously. 'I'm not saying that they would. I'm saying that we don't know.'

Kalbfleisch rubbed his chin. He was a phlegmatic sort, slow to be pushed in any direction without good and urgent cause. During his years as a night watchman (spared the Front by reason of a club-foot) he had faced boredom by ignoring it, and the occasional break-in by deploying to the nearest cupboard until he was certain the excitement was over. He had passed through unsettling times as part of the great, blurred background, always somewhere other than where heavy ordnance had been falling. Having survived all that, the suggestion that he might now have wandered into someone's cross-hairs was as welcome as a night-shift in haar.

'Here he is.'

Rolf Hoeschler had sat down at his desk. Hunched over, he was frowning at its battered metal surface, examining something that wasn't in front of him.

Müller dragged his chair across the two-metre divide between them.

'What did Beckendorp want?'

'Oh, just work.'

'What?'

'A missing person.'

'Another one?'

'It's a favour. For someone at Karlshorst.'

'A Russian's gone missing? Why don't they …?

'No, a German. The man who's asked the favour, I know him. Beckendorp does, too.'

'Why doesn't he use troops?'

Hoeschler looked up and around. 'Beckendorp says he doesn't want his own people to know that he's looking.'

'That's not good.'

'Probably not. It's just me who's been put on to it. You and Kalbfleisch are to keep on with the Kaulsdorf killings.'

It was wretched, but Müller felt a great surge of relief. It was bad enough being privy to the Fischer matter, to chasing something that other *VolksPolizei* couldn't know about; but chasing something about which the Ivans were to be kept equally ignorant was suicide by any other means. The fact that Hoeschler had been put on the case eased another fear - Beckendorp would hardly have handed it to a confidant, a co-conspirator. It was remarkable how one man's shitty luck could blow away the clouds in another's day.

'You say you know this Russian. How?'

For a moment Hoeschler didn't answer. He was weighing something, dealing the cards and assessing his chances.

'He got me this job.'

Astonished, Müller forgot to whisper. 'As police? Why would he do that?'

'I'm not sure. He's a strange one, can't be read. It might have been a whim. It *might* have had something to do with Otto Fischer. He knows him, too - very well, in fact. They came out of Stettin together.'

The brief, hopeful hint of sunshine faded, and a new weather front darkened Müller's day considerably. It took an effort to drag his mind back to the day's principal business, but he managed it while he had Hoeschler in front of him.

'Before you forget them, was there anything about the Kaulsdorf killings that didn't find its way into the report?'

'No, it was straightforward. No one in the neighbourhood heard anything, saw anything, had an opinion about anything. Beyer and me hadn't made a start on trying to identify the bodies before we were told to file all ongoing cases. They probably died sometime before midnight, and almost certainly because a quantity of metal passed through their heads. If I had to bet my pay packet, I'd put it on the square that said Red Army business.'

Müller sighed. 'I don't know why anyone wants this chased.'

'It was reported, and reported crimes must be investigated, eventually. When it gets to the point where the road goes nowhere except to a Russian you'll have to hand it back to Beckendorp and let him decide.'

Kalbfleisch had wandered over from his desk. 'We'd sooner be chasing the bastard who did for Beyer, wouldn't we?

Müller nodded. 'It isn't right, *VolksPolizei* being dropped like gangsters. Whoever did it should get a bullet.'

Hoeschler was weary of feigning outrage, but he made the effort and growled something meaningless. Müller and Kalbfleisch knew what business Beyer had been on before he died, which put Hoeschler in proximity, if not what the Amis called the *frame*. They could be trusted in most things, but not to understand what had made a death necessary. He opened his drawer, dropped his pistol and warrant card into it and stood up.

'I'll be gone for a while. Not too long, hopefully.'

Muller frowned. 'Gone? Why?'

'This fellow I'm supposed to find. Beckendorp says that if he's alive he's probably in western Berlin.'

20

Even when they were not informers' statements, Major Zarubin really did not enjoy reading reports. It was a grave failing in an officer of the Ministry for State Security, whose lifeblood was denouncement, betrayal, insinuation, information and misinformation - all of which, to become more than spent air, had to find its way on to a page at some point. Zarubin had ample opportunity to find his work onerous.

He eased pain's edges by telling himself that one needed to be methodical. A half-effective proposal, an operation run with less than obsessive attention to detail, usually ran into a wall and took its driver with it. He had no intention of anticipating his retirement in a region where engines had to be run all night to keep their oil liquid.

So, if a relevant event, an allegation, a crime had paper to corroborate the fact, he chased it down and then spent time absorbing the detail, even if it was a tiresome business. His conversation with Beckendorp hadn't been as one-sided as anticipated; he had asked something of the man but been asked something else in return, and that *else* required that he understood where the mines had been laid before he hopped into the field.

Fortunately, even in these wretched times the primal human need for order almost always produced paper of some value. The incident itself had been regarded as too trivial for a report to have been made, but its consequence was one of the three fundamental events that any society, however broken, made the effort to record. The paper was in his hand, testifying to what Beckendorp had told him.

To his surprise, Zarubin very much regretted what he was reading. It was a bare two lines of text, confirming that one Marie-Therese Fischer, nee Kuefer, aged approximately 40 years and originally a native of Pomerania, had died on the previous 16 July, in Bremen, the cause provisionally stated as trauma resulting from a traffic collision. He regretted it partly because all decent life wasted was unfortunate (his Mother's closely-held but sincere religious beliefs had left their small, tainting mark), but more so because the deceased had been the object of one of the few, unequivocally selfless acts of Zarubin's entire adult life. Then, she had been a wretched, battered prostitute, whom he might have allowed to die at an evil man's whim and risked nothing; yet he had hidden, dressed and then smuggled her out of Stettin during one of the city's many *Deutschevolk* expulsions. It had felt good, this novel act - so good that he did something similar for her boyfriend, just weeks later.

Back then he had used Otto Fischer, knowing that the likely consequence of his scheming would be just another German corpse, unshriven and unmissed. Zarubin delighted in playing men, in bending their weaknesses and needs to further whatever purpose they might serve; but playing Fischer had made him feel complicit. The man wore his mutilations like penances, inviting more of the same to absolve him of God knew what, and there had been no utility, no satisfaction, in adding to the sum of those wounds. To the contrary, extending a small degree of mercy had seemed the defiant, wilful course – and, to a degree, a selfish one. He had to admit to a slight but remarkable respect for a man whose mind he couldn't read, whose motives he couldn't sense, whose ambitions didn't seem to encompass the usual ends.

But now Fischer was a widower – that much of Beckendorp's account could be trusted, at least. As for his seizure in Berlin by K-5 and transfer to some element of the Soviet Occupation forces, this was the part that Zarubin needed to treat with the same care as an anti-personnel device (which it might be, if he blundered into it). Even a Major of MGB could not, without very good reason, wander the corridors at Karlshorst, demanding loudly to know who, and why.

It was the *why*, above all, that intrigued him. If Fischer really had been a resident of Bremen for the past eighteen months (and the port's business register listed his wife as joint owner of a laundry there with another old acquaintance from Stettin, Adolph 'Earl' Kuhn), what conceivable reason had someone in eastern Berlin to organize his abduction? Had he been misidentified as someone of interest? It hardly seemed likely, unless a doppelganger with a half-melted face had been busily getting up the wrong nostrils.

It looked – smelled – like a counter-intelligence operation, the sort of street-snatch at which both K-5 and MGB were adept; but Zarubin would have heard whispers at least if it had been that. MVD wouldn't be involved unless Fischer had been dealing directly with Red Army miscreants – black markets, probably – and that wasn't remotely likely. He could see only a single further option, and that was someone dealing on his own, unofficially - someone so well-connected or senior that K-5 either wouldn't or couldn't refuse to jump when he clapped his hands. How the hell was he to follow *that* trail?

It was easy to blame Kurt Beckendorp for this, so Zarubin did, volubly. If the man hadn't mentioned Otto Fischer and his little predicament he wouldn't be feeling a slight but insistent pull upon that most inert faculty, his sense of obligation. A wiser man might have attacked the problem sensibly, by staring at his office wall for a day or two and then calling it a brave but unsuccessful effort; but Fischer had been the unwitting means by which Zarubin had ascended from Stettin to Berlin, and he was not immune to his compatriots' superstition that the fates detested an unsettled bill.

At the least, he could put into motion the thing he had mentioned to Beckendorp. MVD were eager to close their Special Camps, or at least to cull them to accommodate the hard core of men who couldn't ever be released. He would draft the memorandum and have Shpak sign it, send it back to Moscow and risk his colleagues' *arse-kisser* jibes, and if Fischer was in one of the camps rather than dead somewhere in the woods they would know of it. What might then be done about it was a different matter.

It was a distraction, all the same. He had three-and-a-half million problems, all of them Deutsche Marks, gone missing with his name potentially smeared on each note. That was bad enough, but not knowing who or where to chase gave him an unwelcome sense of victimhood. Herr Gerste might have offered some enlightenment, but he doubted that even the assiduous Beckendorp would find the man alive still. Without him, there was simply no trail to follow.

He had an order in front of him. It had come from the Ministry that morning, flown in as a matter of urgency. Apparently, Moscow didn't like games being played with the Americans, not without express, iron-bound rules being laid out beforehand. Zarubin had inferred that the perpetrators had crossed the line from and back into eastern Berlin, in order to keep MGB's – his - hands on the investigation. The more he considered the matter the likelier it seemed that, however inadvertently, he was correct. Eastern Berlin had no monopoly on organized criminal behaviour, but it was hard to believe that anyone would dare to mount such a robbery in a place from which they couldn't swiftly escape the wrath of the Americans. And now that the city's outer perimeter was sealed by several Red Army divisions, that escape could be effected in only one direction - across the internal boundary. The robbery had occurred about a kilometre west of Tempelhof, which meant that the perpetrators could have been back in the Soviet Zone within four minutes, given a good engine and …

That was the thing, the worrying part. They would have needed the collusion of Soviet personnel to ensure that their vehicle wasn't searched at one of the extemporary checkpoints that were thrown up in different locations each day. Who could buy such blindness?

Gerste had spoken to someone, a man or men who considered Zarubin's idea an excellent one, who could draw upon resources to put together an operation in short order and not care about inflicting casualties, even American ones. More ominously still, the implicit threat of reprisals from the Soviet side didn't seem to be a factor either. So, again he asked himself, who had that quantity of juice?

That was the potential hammer. The anvil he had created, and upon which he now rested his head, was the approach to Moscow. He had the Ministry's order, demanding a swift resolution. In its top left-hand corner was a Central Committee stamp, which meant that someone at the Kremlin had considered the matter. He was being watched, expected to do impressive things, against someone whose own power he could only guess at.

'Christ.'

He should have strangled the idea in its crib. He should have sat on his arse, pushed paper, done nothing, waiting out the present storm like everyone else in Berlin. He had fired a shell and it had come right back at him, a man with no influential friends, a boss who wouldn't go out on a limb to shake loose a Fabergé egg and no assets other than the personal debt owed to him by a fairly competent senior officer of the city's *VolksPolizei*. He no longer needed to wonder how a Belgian front line felt.

Since Stettin he had been treading water, and now he was in danger of drowning. He couldn't see how his name might be attached to the missing Deutsche Marks, but only because his vision was blurred by a hundred possibilities, none of them amenable. Nothing had been set down on paper, but damning paper could be manufactured. No witness – the hapless Shpak apart - could come forward to lay the scheme at his door, but perhaps his opponent had the power and connections to shape the truth into whatever he wanted it to be. Nor was there physical evidence to tie him to the money, but it had never been difficult to salt suspicions with a well-padded envelope, a device he would not see coming nor have the ability to deflect. He feared that the real culprit was feeling deep gratitude for Major Sergei Aleksandrovich Zarubin's hapless connivance at that moment.

To distract himself, he re-read his orders. At least he was allowed to call upon resources to chase down the gangsters, though a platoon of MVD police wasn't the most he might have hoped for (he much preferred to keep both eyes on a problem, rather than constantly be watching his own back). They could, he supposed, be put on to the patrols' daily reports to determine where the checkpoints were located that day. They could examine the same reports for an anomaly, perhaps a half-awake *soldat* noticing a truck moving as if it were on the Nürburgring, burning rubber to get the loot to where it could be counted. Most usefully, they could do what MVD did best, which was to question men with that half-hint of menace, the unspoken suggestion that something not said was as damning as a confession. Most of it would yield irrelevant shit, but someone might let slip something. Men tended to unburden themselves to MVD, even the entirely innocent ones.

He had never been allowed such authority or resources, and he had never been so helpless, dependent upon others to douse the flames that lapped at his knees. He told himself that if he came out of this he would place his cleverness in a box, bury it the woods and devote himself to a rigorous regime of bare competence. With cautious vigour, eager reticence and a chair in the third row of every meeting at which someone was asked to take on onerous responsibilities he might look forward to retiring with colonel's pension, comfortably certain that no one would ever quite put a face to the name, if asked.

He was still warming to the prospect of oblivion when his adjutant Yelena poked her head around the door. She was a beautiful, dour creature, widely admired at Karlshorst and about as sexually aware as a sea urchin. This evening, however, her face glowed as if God, Karl Marx or an adept pair of hands had ignited all her glands simultaneously. She had forgotten to knock; now, she dispensed with the salute and regulation bellow.

'Comrade Major', she breathed, awe-struck; 'It's a great honour.'

'Is it, Yelena?' First-name terms between ranks was strictly forbidden, but the moment seemed one for oddities. 'What, exactly?'

'Marshal Sokolovsky wants to see *you* immediately. He's here in the building.'

Somehow, Zarubin managed to keep his slightly patronizing smile from crumbling.

Plan B, then.

21

Fischer waited until he and Siegfried were alone in their hut and then asked for help in removing his shirt.

It was damp, clinging to his body, and he was certain that this wasn't entirely due to perspiration. At least one of the kicks he'd received had raked his flank as he tried to turn away, and its scrape was definitely his most painful trophy. The superficial stuff hurt far more than deep-down damage, a curiosity he'd observed several years earlier, during his time on a burns-ward.

Siegfried didn't want to see what was beneath the shirt but he complied, lifting its edge with all the reluctance of a magician whose new trick had yet to work. That suited Fischer - the slower the better (with a quick tug to prise it off the scrape) was exactly how he'd have done it himself.

The damage wasn't too bad. He had managed to stay on his feet for longer than his assailants had expected, taking several punches to the ruined side of his face, where fewer nerve-endings chose to reside. When he went down they'd been too eager, each of them trying too hard to land a kick. In the scramble he'd taken about half the intended blows, and afterwards at least one of his assailants had limped away, the victim of a comrade's boot.

They weren't used to doing it for themselves. He didn't doubt that some of them had been eager participants in the old days, but back then they'd been younger and better fed, and the objects of their attention would have been strapped to a chair, or on a cell floor where a connoisseur could take his time.

Really, he should feel insulted. It had been at best a half-arsed attempt at a serious beating.

His body told him otherwise, naturally. He, too, was older, and this was his first time on the wrong end of a beating for more than two years. His bones pretended they were broken when they weren't, his head was pealing like the *Maria Gloriosa* and his right shoulder felt less like undertaking normal duties than it ever had on a frosty Stettin morning. He watched Siegfried's face, trying to take comfort from the reflected pain as his hut-mate gently dabbed something greasy on the various purpling patches. It smelled like fuel.

He gasped when the fingers arrived at the scrape, and Siegfried winced. 'Bastards.'

'No, it was fair enough. They just aren't getting the message yet.'

'How many beatings can you take, for God's sake?'

Very few, probably. 'It was over quickly, which is good.'

'Of course. Personally I'm not an expert, but a slow one must be worse.'

'No, I mean they were anxious, worried that they'd be interrupted. Which means they're already thinking about consequences. And I recognized two of them. We'll go after them, return the favour.'

Siegfried chewed an already battered lip. 'This is getting out of hand. We don't want a war, do we?'

'This is the Court establishing its authority. Sooner rather than later, they'll realise that it isn't going away - that they'll pay a price for continuing to impose their punishments. They aren't unreasonable men, merely swine. We have two great advantages.'

'I can't think what they are.'

'There are more of us than them, and they can't get away. If it came to a war, they'd be in a worse place than Poland.'

'I heard the Poles were good fighters.'

'They were, little good that it did them.'

Siegfried took a step back, regarded his handiwork for a moment and then replaced the cap on his bottle. 'There's nothing bad. But you're going to ache.'

'I ache already,'

'Really, Fischer, is this the best plan? You're relying on them being sane, but even if they were when they arrived here – and that's by no means certain – three years of Sachsenhausen isn't the best treatment for heads.'

'I suppose not.'

Siegfried sighed wistfully. 'It's a shame you couldn't enlist the Ghost.'

'The who?'

'You don't know? No, how would you? Last year there were three murders here - very bad ones, with … mutilations. The victims were all ardent Nazis, so people assumed it was someone with Jewish friends or family. But then it stopped, even though there were plenty more of their sort breathing still. The killer left no physical clues, no signs of struggle, only the butchered corpses. So we called him the Ghost.'

'Could it not have been the Russians?'

'If it was, I see no reason why it had to stop. In any case, the official executions were still happening at the time, dozens of them. Why not just add three names to the list?'

'I assume no one tried too hard to solve the mystery?'

'It was a piece of gossip for about three weeks. We wondered who might be next. When no one was, everyone lost interest. Still, you could have used skills like that.'

'We need to deter the old guard, not disembowel them.'

'I suppose so.' Siegfried sighed and scratched his head. It was occupied by a single clump of hair, front and centre, standing out like a juniper bush in a desert. Whenever he thought about things he gave it some attention, as if to reassure himself that it hadn't fled with the rest. 'One of the victims was quite famous in a way, though I'm surprised he survived the Führer.'

'Who was he?'

'He was once the Gauleiter of Berlin-Brandenburg.'

'I assume you don't mean Goebbels.'

'Before his time, before they split out the constituencies. I'm talking about Ernst Schlange.'

'I've heard the name. I don't know much about him.'

'He was a strange one. An eager anti-semite, but not the usual sort.'

'In what way?'

'For him it was a sincere thing. He wanted the Jews gone from Germany, but expelled, not killed. And he detested the strong-arm tactics of the early years - he believed the Party should have taken power respectably, and said so. Clearly, this didn't make him popular. He was sacked, then came back as Gauleiter of Brandenburg only, but was quickly sacked again, at Goebbels' urging.'

'Why is it a surprise he survived the Regime?'

'He was a good friend of the Strasser brothers.'

'Ah.' It was one thing to be squeamish about official policy; to be associated with the only two men the Führer ever regarded as rivals was definitely not something to advertise with pride.

'Perhaps someone here regarded it as unfinished Party business.'

Siegfried looked pleased. 'That was my belief also. The mutilations seemed to be a statement.'

It might have interested Fischer in another world, but his head and ribs were singing to him of his present business. Curiously, his several pains had an edge to them that he couldn't place for a moment, a sharpness that wasn't entirely the cause of physical trauma. Hurt was supposed to enervate yet he felt almost detached from it, as if he were strapped to a chair and required to assess impartially the sensations inflicted by several strengths of electricity.

Christ. Am I enjoying this?

Siegfried was looking at his bruises once more. 'It's strange that they didn't do more.'

'Try to kill me, you mean? That's the other good thing – I think they may be wary of what Joachim Dein can or might do, now that their thugs are working for the Inmates' Court. As I say, they're not unreasonable men. They're keeping faith with the old Regime, in a way; but if they'd been happy to die for it they would have picked up a *panzerfaust* and put themselves in front of the Soviet advance. No, these are the survivors, the ones who thought surrender was the better of two options.'

'You mean cowards, like me?'

Fischer laughed. 'You're in good company. I don't recall that I had any great urge to go down in glory. It's what we had teenagers for, at the end. Siegfried …?'

'Yes, Otto?'

'I never thought to ask. Why are *you* here?'

'At Sachsenhausen? For forgetting to be human.'

'If you'd rather not speak of it …'

'No, I don't mind. I was the proprietor of Stolz Munitions, a small factory in Breslau making parts for the model 24 grenade. When the city's civilians were evacuated in January 1945 we stayed put, switched to small arms repair work and kept at it as the Red Army began their siege. After two months things were pretty desperate, as you'd imagine. The local communists – the ones who'd kept their heads down through all the Hitler years - began to get bolder. They passed out hundreds of leaflets, telling us to accept the Soviets as liberators, not the enemy. One of them was a worker of mine. He agitated on the shop floor, tried to get his mates to down tools and slip out of the city. When I heard of it I told the army. He and sixteen of his comrades were shot on the orders of Gauleiter Hanke.'

'You did your duty.'

'He was my employee, like family almost. And he had three children, all of them young. No one at the factory said a word to me afterwards, about what I'd done or anything else. At the end of April I told them all to leave, to try to get out of Breslau, and it was only afterwards that I realised I'd done precisely what poor Johann had done, for which I betrayed him. Eight days later, Russian soldiers took the factory. I was waiting for them, to confess my sin. I think I was hoping they'd shoot me, but I was brought here instead.'

Fischer might have told him that Sachsenhausen was penance enough, but it would have been breath wasted. Siegfried Stolz was his own, bespoke punishment for having been German in a certain age; for having colluded with that which could not be resisted without extraordinary courage or detachment. Bonhoeffer, Rösch, van Galen, Niemoller - men like that had enjoyed the benefit of a firmament to their backs, a God to tell them plainly what was wrong and what needed to be done to face it down. The rest of them, the unrighteous, hadn't stood a chance against a philosophy that knew how to flip right and wrong like lard cakes on a hotplate. They had all been complicit, innocent of everything except knowing their part and playing it.

Siegfried seemed slightly eased for having spoken of his guilt, as Fischer was for the pain of his latest wounds. They sat on the bunk, side by side, each wondering about what came next – for one of them at least, a novel experience in a place where *next* had been suspended indefinitely by order of the Occupier. Siegfried snuffled occasionally (he had a permanent cold, gifted by a chest that had all but surrendered during his first winter here), and his fingers moved slightly constantly, flicking in some secret dance of frayed nerve-ends. Fischer, as always when movement didn't provide a distraction, thought of Marie-Therese and what she would think of him, doing this. He could see her pretty eyes rolling up, the noise her mouth made when it didn't quite form a word but still managed to convey frustration, affection and a strong urge to thump him, only reluctantly resisted. It made him smile almost, and hurt more than the wounds.

He stood up. 'Well, I'm breathing still. I suppose I should find Joachim and give him the good news.'

Siegfried squinted through the one unbroken lens in his glasses. 'Are you going to retaliate?'

'Those are the rules.'

'When?'

'Immediately. We'll do it while they're still slapping each other's back. The pain's sharper that way.'

22

Eleusis airfield, 19 May 1940.

It was the only place and time that Rolf Hoeschler could recall seeing so many aircraft assembled together, and that had been a forward base at a time of war. But then, he told himself, so is this.

He knew Tempelhof, of course. Before the war he had flown to Italian holidays from here, admired its futuristic terminal, its ingenious design that allowed a major international airport to operate from almost the very centre of Berlin. Now, it was shabby, crowded, a triumph of function over art, and he was no less impressed.

He saw himself reflected in one of the few tall, narrow concourse windows that wasn't boarded up. He looked ragged yet hopeful, one German civilian among many, waiting for the next 'plane to taxi off the field and be unloaded swiftly. It might be fuel, food, medical supplies or any other of the very basics that allowed life to continue in a besieged city, but whatever the cargo, it was becoming a boast among western Berliners that they could empty it in five minutes or less. In weeks past there had been children here too, working as frantically as their parents; now, they were outside, under the approach flightpath, waiting for the crazy American pilot who dropped 'candy' on hundreds of little parachutes. It was useless as nourishment of course, and another vast propaganda coup that the Soviets could only watch dumbly, their utter lack of skill in that respect brutally exposed.

There were dozens of unloaders here, and it was difficult to know where to start. It wouldn't do to wander around, asking politely if anyone knew where he might find one Rudolph Gerste. The man had contacts here, who, very reasonably, would want to know who was interested and why (or perhaps they'd forego the questions and use a knife instead). Subtlety wasn't a required skill of East Berlin's *VolksPolizei*, but Hoeschler was in enemy territory, and his warrant card (even if it wasn't presently sitting in his desk drawer at Keibelstrasse) wouldn't impress anyone. He decided to apply himself carefully, and to the female constituency.

An old lady who looked as if she couldn't lift her own spirits was dragging a fifty-kilo sack of coal across the concrete towards a line of US Army trucks. Hoeschler waited until it had been taken by a GI and intercepted her on the way back. She glanced at him suspiciously and swerved, but he held out a hand, palm up, and offered her the chocolate bar that was to have been his lunch.

'There you are, mother.'

Her scowl deepened. No one offered food *gratis* in Berlin anymore. 'Why?'

'I want to ask a question. About someone who works here.'

'I don't know anyone. I come here for the work and food. Then I go home.'

'Ah.' He pulled a face, one that he hoped conveyed sympathy (it wasn't an impression he attempted often). 'It must be hard.'

'It's *very* hard. I had sons who should have provided for me. But they're gone, dead.'

'They were heroes.'

She spat, only just missing his foot. 'They were idiots. They volunteered to fight, both of them, and died on the same day, the Crimea.'

'I'm sorry. May I please show a photograph to you?'

Karlshorst, the central nervous system of the Soviet occupation of eastern Germany, possessed a single xerographic copier - looted, no doubt, from one of the few office buildings in Berlin that managed to survive the final assault. The identity papers of every non-military visitor to SVAG HQ (excepting those whose visits were entirely involuntary) were scanned on it by a female corporal - who, according to Kurt Beckendorp, could have wrestled for Western Asia and opened bottles with her …

'I don't know them.' The old lady said it firmly, though she hadn't bothered to glance down at the image.

'Please look again.'

He held it up, in front of her eyes where she would have to make an obvious attempt to avoid looking. She squinted for a moment, sniffed, and relaxed. 'I haven't seen him.'

With a shrug she moved around him, pointing herself at the C-47 from which she had extracted the sack of coal, and paused. The chocolate was gripped tightly her hand, and something of the obligation must have seeped through the calloused skin. She turned and nodded to the rear of a queue of three aircraft.

'Find Mila Henze. Speak to her, she knows a lot of the men who work here.' She leaned forward a little, confidentially. 'A *whore*.'

Hoeschler asked an old man, who pointed out Frau Henze. Her sexual predilections well disguised, she was directing the unloading of another C-47. This one had brought medical supplies, which required a slightly lighter touch than the coal shipment. Mila Henze had a clipboard, and attached to it a sheet of paper which she was ticking as the 'plane's pilot read out a list from his own manifest. Three unloaders, all women, were transferring boxes to a truck that had edged as close to the aircraft as possible.

He had no intention of trying to question her in front of an American (particularly one who might speak the language), and if he stood around for long enough someone would ask his business. He joined a short queue of Germans waiting at the concrete's edge for aircraft to taxi in off the field. Once more, his mind fell backwards, back to that smaller, hotter airfield near Athens, where he and his comrades had stood in line to board a transport, many for the last time. One of them (they wouldn't meet for some hours yet, if *meeting* was the correct term for a mutual scramble into a shallow depression) had been Otto Fischer, in those days the owner of a reasonably intact face. Later that afternoon they had shared a nod, a cigarette, a swig from a nearly-empty canteen and the attention of some of New Zealand's finest marksmen, who persisted peevishly in trying to account for every single German who had dropped in that day. The night that followed had been as miserably cold as the day was hot, and the next morning neither he, Fischer nor any other survivor of the attacking force could believe the enemy had pulled out, somehow self-deceived that they had been beaten. It had been one of the few times in his life that Hoeschler had come face to face with blind, undeserving good luck.

He got a shove from behind. A 'plane's side cargo door was open, and the queue had become a crocodile, passing boxes along its length. He took one, turned, passed it on and took the second in the chest.

Its donor gave him another shove. 'Christ, man, *move!*'

'Sorry.' If they thought he was a hapless virgin at this business, fine. He accelerated, managed to receive and dispose at the same speed as everyone else, and the remainder of the cargo was unloaded within minutes. As the last of the boxes reached the truck behind them Hoeschler's fellow unloaders charged away to their next job, leaving him alone on the concrete. The American navigator gave him a brief nod as he closed the cargo door, and the C-47 (its nose bore a garish image of what appeared to be a show girl, her name *Lucy Mae*) slowly abandoned him too. He glanced around, but couldn't see Frau Henze.

He was beginning to wonder if he was fit for this work. On the low ledge formed by several concrete blocks, a few of the unloaders were resting between shifts. He found a spot too far from the nearest of them to risk a conversation and sat down, slouching forward as if exhausted to keep his face from becoming memorable. From there he could watch everyone entering or leaving the building (if they were considerate enough to use the main entrance), and quietly torment himself that he had achieved nothing in almost an hour in which he had been effectively overseas, exposed and powerless.

He was thinking of retreat when she sat down next to him, barely two metres away, and lit a cigarette. Close to, she was prettier than a German woman in her late 40s in the late 1940s had any right to be – a nice complexion, a kind face that had lost (or never had) the pallor of desperate under-nourishment and a way of moving that hinted at time spent on a dance floor. It was a symptom of the sexual drought that had plagued his adult life that he liked her even before he heard her speak.

'Excuse me?'

She turned, frowned slightly and offered him the pack. Generous, too. He smiled, shook his head and searched his pocket for the xerograph. 'Are you Frau Henze?'

'Who's asking?'

'No one. I mean, I was told me that you may be able to help me find someone. Rudolph Gerste.'

'I …' She took the copy and handed it back immediately. 'I don't know the name. But he works here sometimes. Why do you want him?'

Beckendorp and he had given themselves headaches with that question. Once over the demarcation line, the truth became poison – no one would want to help *VolksPolizei* do a favour for MGB, and Hoelscher had no desire to test whether western prison cells were culturally distinct from their eastern counterparts. The long-lost brother tale was too flimsy, heard too often and bound to raise suspicions from the moment in left his lips. The old comrade wondering if Gerste survived the war might work, but only if the person who heard it had no knowledge of Gerste's past from which embarrassingly unanswerable questions might be framed. Beckendorp had suggested the standard response – that is was none of the enquiree's business and that he or she should tell all of what they knew. At this, Hoeschler suggested that that he'd been police too long.

Threats wouldn't work, and Hoeschler had nothing to offer beyond a chocolate bar or two, but in a world fraught with uncertainty something fortunate was a balm, and they had decided to go with that. He held Frau Henze's eyes with what he hoped was an open, guileless expression.

'I've been asked to find him, by his sister. She's very anxious that he hasn't heard her good news.'

She laughed. 'There's good news somewhere? My God!'

'She's won the class lottery – not the big prize, but enough to keep the wolves from the door. Since they were children, they've always sworn that they'd share any windfall, and now that her husband's dead she wants Herr Gerste to have half of it.'

'That's so sweet! But why hasn't she come?'

'She's old, and lives in Westphalia.'

Hoeschler didn't know if Westphalia was one of the states to have reintroduced the lottery earlier that year. He hoped that other Berliners were similarly ignorant.

'Lucky man. I assume you're taking a commission for this?'

He put on a hurt face. 'Only for my travel expenses. Her husband was a friend.'

She put her hand on his and squeezed it slightly. 'I'm sorry, that was rude.'

Tactile, too - probably because she was used to working among men. It was little wonder the old woman had mistaken it for something else.

'I'm keen to find Rudolph. I bribed a pilot to bring me into Berlin, but's getting out's going to be hard and he might know someone who could help.'

Her face darkened slightly. 'That's very likely.'

Suddenly, Hoeschler was police again. 'I'm sorry?'

'He works where he's put, like the rest of us here. But I've seen him with people I don't want to know.'

'Not criminals, surely?'

She glanced around and shuffled herself a little closer. 'Everything that enters western Berlin comes through here, or Gatow. I've heard Americans talking among themselves, and they're angry about what goes missing. Not the petty pilfering – there isn't anyone who hasn't put a tin of processed meat into their pocket, me included. But I've heard that things go missing to order, which means organization. I've been questioned twice now by the Military Police, but I don't know anything and I'm not going to point a finger at other Germans. Your friend keeps company where my finger doesn't point.'

'Oh dear.' Hoeschler chewed his lip theatrically. 'When did you see him last?'

She shrugged, and stubbed out her cigarette on the concrete shelf. 'I don't know, I haven't been looking for him. But several days ago, at least.'

For the first time, the look on his face matched his mood precisely. She caught the frown and touched his hand again, a light tap. 'Do you want his address?'

'What …?'

'The Americans don't lose sleep over the smaller thefts, but they don't like them either. If you work here regularly you have to register, show them your papers. They record the details and keep them on file. I can ask, if you like.' She smiled. 'I get on with a couple of the *guys* in the office.'

'Would you? I'm not supposed to be in Berlin, so I couldn't
…'

'It's no trouble. But there's a price.'

'I don't have much …'

She was smiling again. 'If you're around for long enough, you can take me to the cinema. It'll be nice, being seen with a good looking man.'

He waited for almost an hour, his arse slowly numbing on the concrete, and didn't feel anything. For the first time in thirty years he had been the target of a blatant flirt, and he couldn't say that he felt any less absurdly pleased about it than back then.

23

Kurt Beckendorp had inherited his house from blameless
people who hadn't wanted to flee Berlin but who had fully
believed Goebbels' claims for the brutality of the Red Army
(one of the few matters about which he was, however
unwittingly, entirely honest) and sought refuge among
relatives in the Saar, from where they hadn't since returned.
Their revenge for this dispossession was the walnut stump.

For two years now he had set aside several hours each Leave
Sunday to get to the bottom of its root system. At first,
thinking it the sort of activity that bound fathers and sons, he
had conscripted the twins to remove the parts he managed to
exposed and separate from the rest; but as he gradually
uncovered ever-deeper, more venerable byways, he realised
that teaching the boys the sort of vocabulary that was all very
well at a Front would not do for good relations with his wife.
These days, he took only his spade and pickaxe to the bottom
of the garden, where the fence made no objection to the very
many words the German language allocated to male and
female genitalia and what they did to each other. It was as
close to a hobby as he admitted to.

Usually he set himself to the task after lunch, the Beckendorps
being a traditional family who ate their heaviest meal at
midday. Since waking that morning, however, he had been
pestered by a buzzing in his head, and needed to think. He was
aware that he twitched slightly when his head dwelt upon
unpleasant or intractable matters, and his wife invariably
noticed this. Two obvious solutions presented themselves - not
to think, or to go outside and surprise the walnut stump.

What if Otto was dead, he asked it, silently. Logic told him that K-5 had transferred his friend to the Russians for a reason, but that might have been only to ensure that a kill order was carried out. He might be chasing a book that was already closed. Beyer might have died for nothing, nothing at all, in which case the largest manhunt in the short history of the *VolksPolizei* had been set in motion to avenge a man who had asked a question that need never have been asked.

And what if Otto were alive still? What could be done? Even Major Zarubin of MGB had the power only to confirm the fact of his survival or otherwise, and for that morsel Beckendorp had been obliged to commit himself (well, Rolf Hoeschler) to scouring western Berlin for someone else who might be alive or not. What was it with people these days, that they couldn't be one thing or the other?

And what if Hoeschler got it in the back of the head from someone who didn't like questions? He turned and glanced back down the garden. At the kitchen door the twins were busy upon phase sixty-five (at least) of their construction of a ship crane, watched adoringly by little Engi, Hoeschler's boy. He had a semi-official bunk at Gartenweg 16 (mainly because the lady of the house couldn't bear that any child should be without at least a part-time mother), and one of Beckendorp's worst, most enduring nightmares was that it might of necessity become a permanent one, the latest refuge of his short, battered life.

So he had as many as three potential deaths to keep him company at the bottom of the garden that morning, and the walnut stump paid a price for it. Twice, he swung the spade too hard, lost his balance and fell, his amputation rubbing cruelly in its metal socket. Briefly, pain anaesthetized everything else but it passed too quickly, leaving *what can I do next* front and centre once more. For the moment the false

Beckendorp identity seemed secure, but too many things were happening over which he had little or no control. Zarubin hadn't pushed him about Fischer's abduction or Beyer's death, but K-5 were a constant, dark cloud hovering on his horizon. They had been asked something that shouldn't have been asked, and the enquirer – their friend in Criminal Investigations – had died very quickly thereafter. It worried him that they hadn't come asking yet, hadn't even made their curiosity obvious. He pulled on yet another newly-exposed root, and wondered why.

Lying half-awake in bed that morning, his thoughts had returned to his conversation with Zarubin, and something stirred. The present crisis, the blockade, the siege – whatever it was to be called – had created a new reality. In 1943, Freddie Holleman and family had said farewell to who they were and fled to the Spreewald, sustained by friends and a false identity until the surrender. Since then, Kurt Beckendorp had risen on the back of his imagined reputation as a good communist and some half-decent police work, getting along comfortably in an uncomfortable world but always half-expecting things to crash. Had they done so, there would have been little he might have done to save his family.

Things were different now. Zarubin had confirmed what he half-knew already - that Stalin's bluff had been called by the Americans and British. They weren't going to leave Berlin, and they weren't going to be kicked out. So there was no single Berlin anymore. It had become two cities, with a distinct border between them - only a line, perhaps, but it separated one from the other no less than the invisible border of nations. Since the end of the war, safety – if he and his family needed to flee – had been a distant dream, requiring a fraught flight across half of Germany that never could have succeeded. Now, it was a matter of four or five kilometres due west, to a place where Joint Control no longer pertained. He was one of the most senior officers in Berlin's *VolksPolizei*; the Americans or British would want to protect him, drain him, as much as K-5 or the Russians would want him extinct.

He hated the idea, but it was a door where none had been before. If the Beckendorps were discovered, finally, to be someone else, they could run. If Beyer's ghost were to come back to haunt them, they could run. If K-5 made the connection between him and Otto Fischer …

He severed the root, took a good hold in both hands and started again. *If Otto's dead and one or more pieces of shit happen, we'll run …*

A mug of ersatz coffee materialised under his nose. 'You'll never get to the bottom of it, Freddie. Cover it over, forget about it.'

'Don't call me Freddie.'

She looked around, and then over the fence. Their neighbours, the Hartmanns, were an old couple with a married son in Pankow who worked for the City Council and drew upon supplementary rations. They were hardly ever at home on Sundays.

'No one heard. When's Otto coming to stay?'

'I don't know, sweetheart. It's difficult, getting into Berlin from the West these days.'

'The poor dear. She was such a good wife …'

'You never met her.'

She pouted. 'If Otto loved her she must have been. It stands to reason.'

He sighed and took the mug. 'Which is another way of saying you have no evidence to support your opinion.'

'Stop it. She fell in love with a half-faced man, and married him, and built up a respectable business.'

'You mean she was a sinner come to good ways?'

She flushed. 'Well, it's true.'

'Yes. It's a great pity.'

'A terrible shame is what it is.'

He had long since realised that his wife would make a wonderful professional mourner. She took no enjoyment from the misery of others but had a strong empathy with melancholy - a sense that grief should be shared, bled out a little, rather than be borne alone. It was one of the reasons he'd thought to bring Otto to Berlin, to be half-drowned by tenderness (and loaded with a few kilos of her excellent, starchy cooking). He didn't know how to begin to tell her what had gone wrong with that plan.

He stared down into the large, complex pit he had created. It looked like what happened immediately before, or just after, a massed tank battle. She was right - if he followed this thing to its furthest roots he might reach Courland. It wasn't as if a walnut stump was an unattractive feature, particularly in the garden of a man who had always considered domestic horticulture to be a hobby, like golf, for dead people. Its upper surface was almost flat, and not too low to be a comfortable seat whenever he needed to flee the kitchen for a few quiet moments. He stuck his spade into the soil, silently declared an official armistice, and sipped his *muckefuck*.

She stroked his hair. 'How long are we having Engi to stay?'

The twins had given up on the ship crane for the moment, and one of them (even after sixteen years' practise, Beckendorp had to get close to recognize one from the other) was showing Engi his FDJ scrapbook. As usual, the younger boy was concentrating fiercely, as if trying to imbibe the essence of a normal boyhood, removed from want and violence.

'Probably two or three days. Rolf's doing some work for me outside Berlin. You don't mind having him?'

'He's no trouble, except for when the boys are away and he follows me around like a puppy.'

'You probably smell of his own mother.'

The moment the words were out he wondered why he'd said it. Her eyes welled up and she turned around to count the chicks in her nest. 'Poor Engelbrecht.'

She saw only the waif and not the consequences. She didn't know – he hadn't told her – that the boy was also an adept thief, a scavenger, someone who could lift a watch without bothering its owner, because that would have required a conversation about the street-life that had made such skills necessary, and he wasn't sure how much Dickens she could take.

'We'll be eating in half an hour. Is that alright?'

He shrugged. His stomach should have been growling by now, but his head appeared to have commandeered the microphone. 'You're the boss. I might have to go into Keibelstrasse later. For an hour, no more.'

She tutted automatically, but the demands of his rank had long since settled comfortably upon Gartenweg 16. He was providing for his family when so many other men couldn't; had taken them from the life of refugees and built a respected position in their fragile, strange society. He was a policeman, an unequivocally good man, a shepherd in the new wilderness. The marital flank, at least, was secure.

He watched her as she waved in the boys and returned to the kitchen, trying and failing as usual not to linger on her arse, and the prospect almost managed to make the worms in his head stop writhing. He sat down heavily on his former enemy and tried to put them in order. He didn't know whether Otto Fischer was in the world still or not. He didn't know whether K-5 were about to come looking for the person who sent had poor Beyer to pry into their business. He had no idea whether Major Zarubin was biding his time, hoping for help with his little problem while only pretending to find Fischer, a man he had good reason to wish far elsewhere. Until something emerged from the fog of all this, he had no way of knowing whether he should be planning to redecorate the sitting room or trying get his family to western Berlin before they were offered the option of Tashkent.

24

The second floor of the Criminal Investigations department at
Keibelstrasse resembled a Cecil B. DeMille crowd scene, and
it gave *UnterKommissar* Müller a strong feeling of *déjà vu*.
Eleven years earlier, he had been wasting time in a police
station in Wedding, attempting to see a client who, it
transpired, had no need of a lawyer (his confession, coaxed
out during the night hours, had been very comprehensive),
when what seemed like half the city's underworld had been
dragged in for a fleeting dawn visit. He recalled the precise
date still, naturally: 9 March 1937 had been the first day of
Himmler's 'preventive custody' policy, which neatly excised a
generation of habitual criminals from German society and
relocated them to the Reich's new holiday camps. None of
them had needed a lawyer that morning, either; in fact, their
appearance at the Wedding station had been an error on the
part of the duty officer, who had assumed the round-up to be
normal police business and tried to book them in. Once the
misunderstanding had been explained and forgiven, the
offending objects had been removed and the majesty of
National Socialist justice allowed to proceed unhindered.
Müller recollected that he had taken the trouble to attend court
a few days later to comment upon his voluble client's good
character, but then begged to be excused the obligation of
attending the subsequent execution. He saw a beheading once;
it had given him no taste for more.

He looked around the main interview room. Today's visitors –
suspected gang members and black marketeers to be
questioned on the matter of Beyer's murder - wore the same,
dully surprised expression, a mild disbelief that a regime's
attention had finally swivelled their way. They were men who
had long enjoyed the immunity that an overworked,

understaffed *VolksPolizei* unwittingly offered to Berlin's professional underbelly; men who had been too clever to attract the attention that over-ambition or excessive violence encourages. No doubt many of them were wondering why their bribes had ceased to buy invisibility, or which disappointed customer had passed the wrong word to the very wrong ear. None – or, perhaps, one – would guess that their arrest was upon a capital matter.

Much as Müller wanted Beyer's killer caught it was not why he was here, waiting for the other bulls to finish their questioning. He was in the market for gossip, rumour, a grudge waiting to be repaid. On his own initiative he had brought a packet of cigarettes, a flask of cheap almost-brandy and a small store of obscene jokes, tools to loosen reluctant memories in lieu of the air of menace he had never possessed. When he mentioned the intention to Kalbfleisch (whose own experience of interrogations was as thin as his own), the older man had approved but urged to Muller overcome his teetotaller's qualms and share a drink with them. A hint of insubordination, even incompetence, couldn't help but ease the atmosphere.

He was nervous, wondering if he had a real investigator's heart, the calm manner and quick mind that spotted the inconsistency, the half-admission, the outright deception. His *krimi* novels were stuffed with such characters, men who could pin a suspect with the steely glint in their eye, or strip away false bravado with a timely revelation. He certainly couldn't find symptoms of any of that in himself. It had taken an effort of will to push himself forward, to go to his busy colleagues and tell them what he wanted. No one had objected, or asked questions; the most distinct reaction he had drawn so far was a shrug, yet still he felt that he was interloping upon other, real policemen's business.

The first of the suspects was ready to be re-interviewed by mid-morning. Müller had booked a small room away from the main office, as much to preserve his dignity as keep the matter discrete. It held a small table and two chairs, with a small window to the outside and enough exposed pipework to remove any suspicion that this had ever been a police room. He waved his first guest inside, closed the door and sat down without offering the other chair.

He read the man's file slowly, hoping that the pause might loosen nerves. Herr Bernhardt Vohl – a slight, rodent-like creature – had been arrested several times on suspicion of black market dealing, and served a three-month sentence served during 1947 for hooliganism (a marvellous, catch-all offence, in this case probably imposed because *VolksPolizei*'s quarterly conviction statistics had needed a little boost). There was a brief note appended, speculating that the fellow was an associate – or at least supplier or customer - of several organized gangs in the Friedrichshain area. As far as Müller could see, nothing resembling evidence was provided to support the theory.

He dropped all thoughts of deploying booze, cigarettes or false bonhomie and asked the question. Vohl denied knowing anything, and Müller believed him. His eyes didn't flit around, and he didn't pause before answering - in fact, he seemed slightly relieved, as though he'd been expecting worse. When he was told to go he just nodded and left.

The second suspect was brought in by a *wachtmeister* who dropped a file on the table and closed the door behind him. This one looked terrified – of police, the room, being at Keibelstrasse at all. It took Müller all of thirty seconds to see why. The file had a single charge entry – an arrest for theft, two years earlier, a matter of a few potatoes taken from an allotment to feed a desperate family. The perpetrator was here today because the examining magistrate had shown singular compassion and dismissed the case with a caution, a decision that the arresting officer (clearly a man of long memory) hadn't considered acceptable. This was just unfinished business, a petty stab that wasted everyone's time. Müller tossed his head, and when the door had closed once more tore up the file's single piece of paper and replaced it with a blank sheet.

Over the course of the next hour he interviewed four more men. Each of them was a career criminal with at least two previous convictions (though luck or bribes had kept them out of the Erzgebirge radium mines); all claimed to know nothing regarding the matter Müller raised.

He began to wonder if his timing was unwise. These men had just been questioned with regard to a hanging offence, and probably suspected that the second interview was a typical *VolksPolizei* trick to keep hold of them until something could be found that would stick. Clearly, *nothing* was the safest thing to know about anything, so ignorance or prudence were all he should have expected. He told himself that persistence was one of the more necessary qualities of a good investigator, and every bit as valuable as a steely-glinting eye, though none of his novels ever seemed to dwell on the mundane passages of police work.

Kalbfleisch joined him before the seventh man was released to them. He dragged in a chair and two mugs of something imitating something else, and for a few moments they glanced at the fellow's file. Afterwards, Muller was almost certain that he'd spotted the detail himself, but just as the door opened Kalbfleisch tapped the page, his dirty fingernail leaving a smear that highlighted the thing.

Herr Peter Nitsch, a very large man, did not wait to be invited to sit down. He folded his thick forearms across his chest and planted himself where his defiant stare could best be appreciated by his interrogators. Müller feared that if things turned ugly the room's official presence might be maimed before help could arrive. It didn't raise his confidence by much. He smiled, trying to be affable.

'So, you're Silesian?'

'No.'

'But the surname …?'

'My great-grandfather. Why, are you pulling in Silesians this week?'

'Don't be cheeky, son.' Kalbfleisch tried his best glare, which almost visibly bounced off its intended victim.

Müller cleared his throat and asked the question. Nitsch was scowling already, so his face was braced for it; nevertheless, something less than a twitch yet more than blankness caught both policemen's eye. The detail beneath the clumsy smear on the charge-sheet begged to be introduced.

'You were arrested four months ago, for handling stolen goods.'

'*Allegedly* handling stolen goods.'

'An offence for which you have a previous conviction.'

'Which is why I was arrested again. It saves you lazy sods the bother of investigating crimes.'

This was so palpably the way of things that Müller ignored the slur. 'The arresting officer was *UnterKommissar* Kurt Beyer.'

'He didn't introduce himself.'

'But you know who he is. Being innocent of that particular crime, you must have resented his assumption. Did it bring you much inconvenience? Embarrassment, perhaps? I wonder if it caused you to commit his face to memory – you have a very careful stare, after all.'

Nitsch's face paled and he sat up, the hard man routine forgotten. 'I never saw him again after that day. Why would I care? I was out in three days. It was nothing, a rest-cure.'

Müller and Kalbfleisch exchanged a meaningful glance, the sort that bad policemen finding a tidy solution to a taxing problem might share. For once, their force's reputation for amateurism and chronic corner-cutting was doing the work for them. Nitsch's wide eyes passed from one to the other and back again as he tried frantically to work out how a small fish in a broad net had suddenly become its principal morsel.

While this torment proceeded, Müller pursed his lips and re-read the file in front of him, pretending to find more than a single item interesting. Eventually he looked up.

'We'll come back to that. You're still living at Bergedorferstrasse 54?'

'Yes.'

'This is what puzzles me. You're a known associate of several gangs who deal in contraband goods. An incident occurred near Kaulsdorf church, which is no more than a half-kilometre from your home. Clearly, it was related to gang activities, yet you claim to have no knowledge whatsoever of the event.'

'I don't.'

Müller smiled. 'Herr Nitsch, within twenty-four hours of the discovery of the three bodies the police distributed an eye-witness request throughout the area which gave basic details of what had occurred. If nothing else, you would have seen this – or, if you can't read, overheard one or more of your neighbours discussing it. It's simply not credible to deny all knowledge of the incident. It's a pity too, because all we're looking for is a little help, perhaps a finger pointing vaguely in the direction we should be looking …'

Muller had applied the gentlest stress to *all*, but Nitsch twitched visibly as it registered. 'Well, I heard about it, obviously. But only as news, not …'

'Let's speculate, then. Three men, shot in the head and not quite buried. In fact, not-quite-buried so badly that one might assume the perpetrators had wanted the bodies to be discovered as soon as it got light the following morning - unless they were disturbed in their business, of course, which they weren't. I wonder what kind of offence would bring the sort of punishment that required advertising?'

Nitsch stared straight at Müller for a few moments, weighing every word he was going to have to let loose. 'A warning?'

'It looks like it, yes. A warning to whom, I wonder?'

'I don't know. Competition?'

'That was exactly my thought. We don't know the identities of the murdered men, so we're at a disadvantage; but if this were an emotional crime, one would expect its concealment to have been more successful. I think this was all part of doing business in Kaulsdorf, or perhaps eastern Berlin as a whole. So, what sort of business?'

Nitsch's forehead was visibly moist now. 'I couldn't say.'

'I was teasing - obviously, it's criminal business. If it weren't, one would assume that disputes would be settled through a lawyer's office – or the courts, if agreement couldn't be reached. Making three men kneel down and then executing them strikes me as a little too peevish for this to have been on a point of late deliveries, or unpaid invoices. What do you think?'

'That sounds right.'

Much to his surprise, Müller realised that he was enjoying himself. He frowned, to kill the smile. 'So, this was about illegal business in Kaulsdorf. And *you* live in Kaulsdorf.'

'But I don't know these people.'

'Know? How do you know that you don't know them?'

'I meant …. I don't mix with criminals.'

Müller sat back and sighed, the way a man who'd heard it all before might. 'Really, Herr Nitsch. You were convicted of trafficking cigarettes, weren't you? Twice? This, of course, in addition to the handling conviction. But please don't worry – we're speculating, remember?'

The other man nodded.

'So, let's think in broad terms who might be responsible. I wonder if it could be one of the aüslander gangs – Poles or Balts, perhaps?'

'I thought you'd closed them all down by now.'

'That's right, we have - or at least dispersed them to places where other police have to deal with them. Germans, then; in your opinion, could it be a German gang making a point?'

Nitsch could see where this was going, and he said nothing. To 'speculate' further would put him in a place he wanted to avoid like a skin infection. Encouraged, Müller pressed a little.

'But of course, we broke most of the German cigarette gangs earlier this year. And the ones who specialized in surprise house clearances, they ran out of product almost two years ago. That leaves prostitution – which never took off in an organized way because the competition from one-woman businesses flooded the market before it ever became one. And medical supplies …'

Müller broke off, a surprised looked painted almost convincingly on his face. 'But that's right, only the Soviets have ever dealt in drugs. And they still have mountains of pillaged personal effects that their *soldats* can't take home with them.'

There was no reply, but a half-blind anwärter could have spotted the twitch. Müller turned to Kalbfleisch. 'Still, what the Ivans do is no business of ours, is it?'

'No, Comrade. Not much we can do about what *they* get up to.'

'Apart from talk about it, obviously. Karlshorst doesn't like it when some of their naughtier boys embarrass them. Do you remember the three Uzbekis they strung up last year for … what was it?'

Kalbfleisch watched Nitsch's face as he spoke, rolling out each word with relish. 'Aggravated rape, and theft.'

'That's right. Funny how they can get so upset about what they were encouraging, three years ago. And it was us that put them on to it, I think?'

'Yes sir. We caught them at it. Had to release them, of course. But we sent a report to SVAG.'

'And forty-eight hours later they were swinging in the wind. Now that this Kaulsdorf business looks to have involved Soviet personnel, I think it's only proper to send them another report, just to see what they do about it. And I'll be pleased to mention the assistance Herr Nitsch's given us.'

Their guest was hunched over, staring at his knees. He didn't seem surprised by what he's heard. After a few moments he mumbled something.

'I'm sorry?'

'You won't get them. *They* won't get them. You can say what you want. Some people can't be touched.'

This was undoubtedly true, and Müller's sense of self-satisfaction faded a little. But he reminded himself that to pass on a report to Karlshorst was standard procedure, endorsed, expected and safe. He tapped the desk.

'Just tell us what you know. Then you can go. We've dragged in dozens of people today, so no one can ever guess who said what to us.'

'I don't know any names. There's a rumour that the three corpses were part of an alcohol racket. They brought it in from across the Czech border, night runs from farms that have illegal stills. For a while it was small scale and no one cared. But then they expanded, and someone objected to the market being undermined.'

'Market?'

'For Purveyance Board Vodka. It's poured out free to the Ivans, but for their use only - the rank and file are strictly forbidden to sell or trade it to Germans. Someone further up the ladder saw an opportunity. You probably know this.'

The illicit trade in vodka had begun almost before the surrender, and was no more news to Müller than the contents of his desk drawer. 'So this is an argument about booze?'

Nitsch shook his head. 'It's about everything.'

'How very existential. Could you be more specific?'

'Everything that Germans don't have, or don't have enough of. Alcohol, decent tobacco, food, accommodation, medicines, security and small pretty things – what we used to take for granted. Everything that matters.'

'An argument about market share, then?'

'About who owns the market.'

A small distant voice was trying to attract Müller's attention, but he pretended not to hear. 'A very well-placed group, I should imagine. I don't suppose you have names for them, either?'

No group, just a man. You can tell that I don't have a name because I'm alive still. And if, somehow, I had it and gave it to you, you'd be joining me in a hole.' The finger moved slightly to the left. 'Him too, and anyone else in this building who might have overheard it.'

The voice was louder now, and Müller couldn't ignore it. 'He's that dangerous? Surely, SVAG …'

'Are happily turning a blind eye. Don't ask me why, I don't know.'

'Do you know *anything*, Herr Nitsch?'

'I know what they call him.'

Dazed, Müller closed the file in front of him. 'Might I ask you to tell us?'

'The Butcher.'

'And is he?'

'That's what I hear.'

25

Zarubin poured a large measure of Georgian brandy into a tumbler and placed it in the shaking hand of his commanding officer.

Colonel Shpak's present complexion was one that would have been very familiar to a pathologist, though the mouth moved still, ready to convey anything that might eventually come to mind. He had spoken twice in the past five minutes and said the same thing both times. The taste of it in his mouth must have been agreeable, because he repeated himself once more now.

'Marshal Sokolovsky knows?'

Zarubin wanted to slap some colour back into the face, but this was interesting – bowel-scouring, certainly, yet his mind had been bouncing around since his conversation with the Commander of Soviet Forces, Germany some hours earlier. His first instinct had been to inform Shpak immediately, but he had needed to think it through. It wasn't something that deserved less than a great deal of thought.

'He does, yes. Now listen to what he said, Maxim Petrovich, and tell me what you think.'

Shpak's eyes held his subordinate's pleadingly. 'Really? It's necessary that I know?'

'It is, really. The first part was the expected shit, obviously. He mentioned 'criminality, vigilance', 'unyielding', 'intolerable', 'vigour', 'rigour' and 'the full weight of Soviet justice', and assembling them any ten ways would have done the same business. But then I asked questions, and something very strange happened.'

'*What* happened?'

'He answered them. Not fully, obviously, but enough to get him into as much trouble as any normal man, if ...'

'If?'

'If he hadn't been authorized to speak as freely as anyone in that uniform is ever likely to. And he was speaking to nobody, a major.'

Zarubin didn't need to read Shpak's mind to know what was marching past its horrified eye. Marshals of the Soviet Union took orders – sought authority – from one place only. It was large, quaint, had very high walls, and it impeded the traffic in Red Square terribly.

'What did he ... say?'

'He told me that if we (the pronoun was out before he could stop it, and Shpak winced) manage to do this, it will have been upon his full authority.'

'And if we don't?'

'Let's not think about that. He told me that it's been a problem for a while now, and people are beginning to wonder why.'

'A while? How many times have the Americans been robbed? Are they dolts?'

Zarubin shook his head. 'I don't think his mind was on just the currency theft. Obviously, if *that* had happened before the shipment would have been guarded by a regiment of GIs. It's something … larger. The problem, I mean. What he hinted at amounts almost to an alternative economy.'

'God in Heaven.'

'And it must be a *real* problem, if Sokolovsky believes he has to cover his arse - Germany's his kingdom, almost. So that means …'

Shpak knew exactly what it meant, but saying so was beyond his head and larynx both.

'… that the source of the *problem* is being protected, and no one knows by whom.'

'And *we* are supposed to deal with this?'

'It's a great opportunity. And an honour, of course.' As Zarubin said it he wondered if he'd gone too far. Shpak was easily teased, but even he could recognize …

'What shit! It's a coffin, and Sokolovsky's slid off the lid so we can climb in.'

'But aren't you curious? Assuming that the Boss himself isn't part of the *problem* – and he isn't, otherwise Sokolovsky wouldn't even have squeaked – then it has to be someone very, very highly placed. Where? In the Army? Again, doubtful, otherwise our Marshal wouldn't be shitting himself, even if it were Zhukov. Which leaves …'

Shpak's colour shifted even further into the grey-scale. 'The Central Committee.'

Zarubin shrugged. 'I can't see any other realistic option. One or more of the nodding statues has decided to wander off the plinth.'

'Then we should find a decent restaurant, drink ourselves into a pleasant mood and put pistols to our heads, because it can't end in any better way'

Zarubin plotted his next words carefully. He had very little regard for Shpak's professional qualities, but he needed a man who could sign paper that a mere major couldn't. He was the head of the department, and, therefore, the liaison between it and others that might be able to cast some light into the very dark places they were stumbling towards.

'I wonder if we might achieve something without advertising ourselves too widely? Setting aside other activities about which we know nothing, the equivalent of a million US dollars was stolen and at least one GI killed in the process. If we or anyone else catch the guilty party, it won't come to a trial. If it did, Moscow would be admitting, however obliquely, that large-scale criminal activity can be planned and organized in the SBZ, and they won't do that. It would also mean they'd be obliged to return the money, and they definitely won't want to do that. This is the sort of case they'll want closed neatly, with perhaps two executions – one in a cellar in this building and another in Moscow. We don't have to be known as the responsible parties.'

Shpak rubbed his eyes. 'And how many avenues of enquiry do we have at present?'

'One.'

'Yes. This is the one that leads us to Herr Gerste, who betrayed your clever scheme to persons who promptly adopted it and stole the money, and who is therefore almost certainly dead or fled?'

'You put it pessimistically, but yes.'

'So, I assume our next step is to distribute leaflets, asking for information on known heisters?'

'On what?'

'Americans refer to 'heists', do they not?'

'I believe so.'

'Then the perpetrator of a heist must be a heister, I assume.'

'English isn't a logical language.'

'Do you have *any* ideas on how we might proceed, Sergei Aleksandrovich?'

'I do. You recall the report commissioned on troop morale in the SBZ?'

'That was three years ago.'

'It was. The Colonel who prepared it looked at his own unit and several others. It dealt with several matters, but particularly with criminality. It's time for a new survey.'

'Is it?'

'The principal concentrations of Soviet soldiers in Germany are within fifty kilometres of Berlin, mainly in and around the Wünsdorf complex. We've been offered MVD resources; I'm still unsure whether using them would be a good idea, but we might deploy them to examine low-level black-marketeering, fraternization, petty offences against the Military Code, and there's a good chance we'll get at least hints of the more organized stuff. Men in foreign postings are bored most of the time, and bored men like to gossip. Also, we can look at this from the German side.'

'You think Germans are involved?'

'I don't know. But some of their criminals will almost certainly know some of ours, and they might be less reluctant to betray what they know. We'll ask our *VolksPolizei* friends to assist – discreetly, of course.'

Shpak stared at his subordinate's office calendar. September's was a pleasant, monochrome image of the aftermath of the Stalingrad envelopment, a long line of ragged, half-starved, half-frozen Wehrmacht personnel being marched off to where fine tailoring, food and warmth were in even shorter supply. Though not a mind-reader, Zarubin suspected that his commander was parsing his chances of visiting the same *where* in the near future. He slapped his table and stood up.

'I'll start immediately.'

'Must you?'

'Field Marshal Sokolovsky has insisted upon it.'

'Fuck your mother! And mine, too!'

26

Fischer took it as a bad sign that this time he was handcuffed to a chair. His first visit to the administration block had been a curiously civil episode, but this one looked likely to be something else.

The guards who had brought – dragged - him here either couldn't or wouldn't engage in polite conversation, and he hadn't persevered. Once in the general office he was shoved down into the chair and restrained immediately, as if he had just been caught in an escape tunnel and dragged out of it feet first. The wait that followed was entirely expected.

Eventually, Colonel Vaisman emerged from his office and nodded at one of the guards. The cuffs came off and Fischer was propelled forward. He was relieved when his escort stopped at the door and put it between them and their commanding officer.

'Sit.' There was nothing easy about his manner this time. He was already in his own seat, frowning down at a sheet of paper. He removed a pack of cigarettes from his pocket, extracted one and lit it while reading what, Fischer suspected, had been examined and thoroughly absorbed already. Obligingly, his nerve-ends tightened in the pause.

'It seems you've been less than honest with me.'

Fischer cleared his throat. 'In what way, sir?'

'You claimed to be ex-Fallschirmjäger.

'That's right.'

'I have different information. Your name – your real name – is Richard Thomalla.' The Colonel looked up. 'You were largely responsible for constructing euthanasia facilities at Bełżec, Sobibor and Treblinka camps. It was reported that my NKVD colleagues caught and executed you at Jičín in the final days of the war, but clearly that wasn't the case. Presumably the wounds you sustained in the meantime served to disguise you, and some unfortunate fellow was taken and hanged in your place.'

Fischer said nothing but thought a great deal, quickly. He'd feared more impromptu beatings between huts, and realized now that he'd underestimated his enemy.

'How do you answer this?'

'I can't, sir.'

'It's true, then?'

'No, sir. But *no* is my entire defence.'

'This information was provided anonymously, by an inmate of this camp. What reason do I have to disbelieve it?'

'I don't know. I don't know what his motivation is for making the accusation. All I can say is that it's not true. I had nothing to do with any of … that.'

The Colonel stared at him for what seemed like minutes, and he felt every one of his pits dampen under the assault. How likely was it that the man had known a hundred similar claims for a respectable military career be overthrown by a timely denunciation?

'So, you insist you were one of Germany's airborne troops?'

'I do.'

'Yet your story isn't credible. Perhaps you should have researched it more thoroughly.'

'Everything I told you is true.'

The Colonel picked up his pen.

'Your unit?

1st Regiment, 7th Flieger Division.

Surely 1st Regiment belonged to the 1st Parachute Division?'

'7th Flieger was redesignated 1st Parachute, but only in 1943. I was already an invalid by then.'

'Your wounds – precisely where and when did you sustain them?'

'Okhvat, 14 January 1942.'

'Surely, there were no Fallschirmjäger units present among German formations involved in the Toropets operation?'

'No sir, there weren't. At Crete our division took heavy casualties, and it was stood down for reconstruction. During this time it was decided to provide more light artillery for our units, and volunteers were requested for temporary secondment to other Wehrmacht formations for training purposes. I stepped forward and was posted to the east. It wasn't the best decision of my life, but then they say that wisdom comes in order for one to regret that it didn't come earlier.'

'To which unit?'

'During the fighting for Smolensk I was attached to 1st Battalion, 29th Motorized Artillery Regiment, 29th Infantry Division, 47th Panzer Corps. In autumn I transferred north, to 2nd Battalion, 181st Artillery Regiment, 81st Infantry Division. During your New Year offensive we were held in reserve initially but then committed to relieve 123rd Infantry Division, which had taken a hammering the day before. We detrained at Andreapol, advanced to Okhvat, and I was injured almost immediately.'

It took a while for this to be committed to paper, and Fischer thought a little more about Richard Thomalla. The man probably existed, an old crony of one or more of the men he had rattled but now dead or fled to somewhere warmer than Berlin. The alleged execution by NKVD was a nice touch; there had been a great number of mistaken identities in the confusion of the war's end, a lot of unlucky fellows whose names or faces too closely resembled those of the worst sort of swine. It was very plausible, and, like any truly innocent party, Fischer didn't have convenient documentation to say who he wasn't.

The Colonel put down his pen and sat back. 'What was the Fallschirmjäger motto?'

'Faithful to Faithfulness. I'm sure most Germans who served in uniform could tell you that.'

'Your standard assault rifle during the Crete operation – what was it?'

'There wasn't one. We were issued with ordinary *Heer* armament throughout 1941. The FG-42 became our standard, but it was developed as a direct result of lessons learned at Maleme and elsewhere.'

'Who was your commanding officer in Crete?'

'Campaign, divisional or battle-group?'

'All.'

'Student, Sturm, Meindl.'

Again, Fischer was obliged to endure the stare. It was difficult to know how this was going. The Colonel seemed to be a reasonable man, but frustration could goad the best temperament; it was a question of whether he *wanted* the prisoner to be guilty.

The pen was lifted once more, but only for the job of tapping the desk. 'You served in Belgium?'

'Yes, sir.'

'And Norway, and Greece. And in all of these desperate encounters you suffered no injuries?'

'A broken fingernail, at Fort Eben-Emael.'

'So, at Okhvat you paid the price for too much good fortune.' The Colonel sighed and closed his file. 'We must have been only a few hundred metres apart at Smolensk. I escaped the encirclement, emerged unwounded from the battle for Moscow and suffered *this* at Stalingrad (he showed his wrist to Fischer; it bore a faint half-centimetre scar, hardly more than a silvered patch), where I also lost a good pair of boots and all but one of my NKVD colleagues. My own Okhvat is yet to come, I fear. There may be a great deal of interest due.'

He remove his pack of cigarettes once more and offered it. 'It may be that you've been wrongly accused. I wonder why.'

'Perhaps someone doesn't like the look of my face.'

The Colonel laughed and pressed a button on his desk. The two guards entered the office.

'*Верните его в свою хижину. Без насилия.*'

'I can go?'

'Why not? I know where you live, after all.'

Fischer had no idea what had been said to the guards, but his return journey was considerably gentler than the outward passage, and ended with a mild shove that sent him into his hut. He went to his bunk, climbed into it and studied the slats above him.

He might have saved time by inviting the Colonel to contact one Major Sergei Zarubin of MGB, Karlshorst, who possessed a detailed file on Otto Henry Fischer's wartime activities; but he couldn't be sure that Zarubin hadn't put him in here. The price of his escape from Stettin had been a promise never to return to the SBZ. He had broken that promise, been caught and forgiven for it. Now, perhaps, his lives and the Russian's patience had run out; perhaps Zarubin had circulated a photograph of a hideously notable face, with orders that if it were ever again to show up at any terminus in Berlin it was to be despatched immediately to another, one where the traffic passed in a single direction only. It was a neat explanation for what had happened. He began to think about how he might possibly chase the theory, but then another thought intruded that quite surprised him. He realised that that he really didn't care.

27

Rolf Hoeschler peered into the dark fissure between the door and its frame. A nose lurked there, its beer-glass complexion giving nothing away of what brought up the rear. He took off his cap, to give a clear view of his own face.

'I'm looking for Herr Rudolph Gerste and family.' He said it brightly, as if bringing nothing but sunlight and good tidings, and for his trouble got a long, slow hawk in a throat he couldn't see.

'Gone.' The fissure began to narrow.

'When? All of them?'

'Four days ago.'

The door closed firmly. For a moment Hoeschler considered using his boot, but recalled that he was standing in Schöneberg, at least four kilometres west of where he might impress anyone. Beckendorp had told him that the Gerste family lived in a cellar, so he applied his deductive skills, stepped off the stoop and opened a gate that led down four steps to a basement door.

No one answered his knock. He peered through the cracked, filthy window. A small room contained basic furniture – a sofa, sink and a tiny table with two chairs, immediately under the window. There were no other tokens of occupation, no photographs or gewgaws on a low mantelpiece, no coats on the door hook, no utensils or crockery on the draining board. The place had been thoroughly emptied, and Hoeschler began to get hopeful about his assignment.

An execution would have left a bereaved family, the wreckage of a life interrupted suddenly. Killers didn't do their business and then send in the cleaners, the house removals men. Herr Gerste had found the sense to flee before the consequences of his little betrayal came back to erase him. He was alive, or at least he had been four days ago.

Hoeschler didn't intend to waste further breath trying to coax a forwarding address from the landlord. It was more likely that Schöneberg Town Hall had a record of Gerste's previous circumstances that could give at least a hint of where the family might go *in extremis*. Of course, he couldn't ask questions there (they would want to see his ID first, and the genuine article was sitting in his desk drawer at Keibelstrasse), but if Fraulein Henze wasn't just being charitable about his allure, she might be coaxed into collusion with the promise of cinema tickets and a walk through Tiergarten.

He was in a good mood for the next hour, and it was hardly dented when he was stopped by an American patrol near the Nathanaelkirche on Grazer Platz and given a hard time when he couldn't produce his papers. He was told to go home and fetch them, so he was obliged to make a substantial detour, south and east to bring him back to Tempelhof. At the terminal's entrance he no choice but to show identification, and this time he handed over his papers immediately. They were genuine, but belonged to a deceased furniture polisher from Treptow, and he had no intention of testing them any more than was necessary.

A temporary workers' café-stand had been established in a corner of the main concourse, a bare, utilitarian area that provided ersatz coffee, execrable tea, and, very occasionally, rye bread for the volunteer loaders. During the past thirty-six hours he'd used it as often as wouldn't draw attention from the wrong people (there were a few regular citizens who dawdled here, pretending to work at Tempelhof only to get the extra rations, and the Americans were beginning to look at them very closely). He moved in and around it, leaving and returning, keeping a permanently harassed expression on his face as if his problem was too much work.

In fact, his real problem was curiosity. He wanted to find Herr Gerste but also take a look at the man's associates at Tempelhof, the men that Maria Henze took particular care not to point her finger at. The Russians wanted Gerste for reasons they hadn't shared, but he was obviously one of their men here. Why hadn't they sent one of their own to retrieve him? It smelled of something very much off the books, which to Hoeschler's mind meant two things - that his and Beckendorp's arses were potentially threatened from more than one side, and that saving them required he know as much as possible about *here*.

He waited almost an hour by or near the refreshments stand, until he began to get looks. Going outside, he re-affixed his disguise by assisting with the unloading of five airplanes in rapid succession, but still he couldn't find her among the dozens of Germans who crowded around the machines, termite-busy, moving to an almost instinctive rhythm of lift and pass, lift and pass. He felt like a novice at a dance academy, all elbows and feet, slowing the process considerably.

She was there, suddenly, climbing out of a jeep, laughing, waving goodbye to its GI driver, and he wondered if the sour old lady had been right about her after all. It was still early, a little after eight am; she might have come straight from her bed with the Occupier who had occupied its other side. It was what many German girls did these days, a perfectly sensible strategy to get the most from a thin, hard world.

For a few moments she looked around the crowded concrete park, and when she saw him came straight over. To his astonishment he got a kiss, slight but warm, on his cheek. She smiled.

'I thought you might not come back. Have you found your lucky man?'

'Lucky?'

'The class lottery.'

'No, not yet. The address was good, but he and the family left a few days ago.'

Mila frowned. 'Where could they go? If you walk in any direction for long enough you reach a Soviet border.'

'He might have found a better job in another part of western Berlin, too far to commute. Or …'

He looked down, as if thinking something through. Her face ducked too, to catch his eye. To a man who had accrued several decades of accidental celibacy it was very endearing. 'Or what?'

'You told me that some of his acquaintances here were wrong types. He might have crossed them and had to get out quickly.'

She shook her head. 'It wouldn't surprise me. Other people have gone, too. They had a choice of stealing from the Americans or saying no and running. One of them did neither, apparently. He's said to have died, very badly.'

'It sounds organized.'

She looked around quickly. 'It is, and it's subtle. I wonder how they manage it, with all the guards here.'

'Perhaps they bribe some of them.'

'With what? Germans have nothing to offer Americans.'

That was true, and it made Hoeschler think about the Russians once more. One of their men at Tempelhof had gone missing; but how many more did they have, and what was their job, other than to spy?

He returned her smile. 'Never mind. Rudolph Gerste is my business, nothing else. Listen, it's a bit of a trek, but the Marmorhaus is showing *Black Narcissus* all this week. Would you like to go? It's my treat, for your help.'

'What's it about?'

'Nuns. And mountains.'

She laughed. 'Who could say no to that?'

'Tomorrow evening? We could have a drink first, at Dicky's.'

'I don't know it.'

'It's a few doors down from what used to be the Mozartsalle. On Nollendorfplatz.' He had spent almost an hour the previous day flicking through a tattered copy of the *Morgenpost*, researching which venues had survived the bombing in western Berlin.

She frowned slightly, mock-concerned. 'Where the homos used to meet? Is there something you want to tell me?'

'That I've always wanted a sister?'

She laughed again, and squeezed his arm the way women do when they want to make a point. He took this as *yes*, and a problem occurred suddenly. He had intended to sleep rough once more that night and clean up at a bathhouse, but it wouldn't do. An attractive young lady deserved more from an escort than refugee *chic*, and her disgust might quell that further casual conversation he intended to have regarding Tempelhof's criminal tendency. It was going to require a bed, bath and at least partly laundered clothes, which meant either that he would be spending *VolksPolizei* money, or taking an overnight trip home, or …

He kept his gaze open, guileless. 'I don't know Schöneberg. Are there any decent cheap hotels down here?'

She couldn't have looked at him more carefully if she'd been trying to place his face. 'You aren't throwing me a hint, are you?'

With his gut trying to turn over it wasn't difficult to stammer. 'Of course not! Really, I just want a place a little closer than …'

'There's nothing around here. I've got a sofa, if you can be a gentleman. It's not comfortable, but it's definitely cheap.'

28

'Almost certainly, the Ivans did it, Comrade Inspector.'

Beckendorp said nothing until he had read the brief report. It wasn't that he enjoyed making subordinates sweat (though he didn't mind), but asking questions when the answers were less than a metre away on a page was the kind of thing that cocks did, and he didn't want them to think he was too much of one.

'They prefer the head shot from behind.'

'For official executions, yes. But this was something else, a warning. Perhaps it was the killer's signature method.'

Müller spoke confidently; Kalbfleisch, as usual, stood upon the advantage of junior rank and said nothing. Both of them were hoping that he would agree with their conclusions so they could bury the thing and be put on to finding Beyer's killer. If the Soviets had killed executed three men in Kaulsdorf, who were *VolksPolizei* to raise a fuss about it?

Beckendorp read it through a second time, sniffed and looked up. 'I agree.' It wasn't much to need another breath before saying more but he took it anyway, and in that brief pause the two investigators allowed themselves to relax.

'But keep on it, for the time being.'

'On it?' Müller was so surprised he gaped at his boss like a new recruit told he couldn't have a uniform until one became free.

'If this wasn't an official, unofficial execution it was something else, and we don't like those in our jurisdiction, even if it's an Ivan who pulled the trigger. If Karlshorst gets embarrassed, perhaps they'll put the word around to their men that it's 1948, not 1945.'

'What do we do if …?'

'If?'

'We catch him. Or them?'

'Shoot him while he's trying to escape. Or them. I'll apologize for it, say that you're too keen.'

Müller hadn't shot anyone, on or off the clock, to date. He was fairly certain that Kalbfleisch hadn't either. They had both taken the basic marksmanship course (basic, because one half-hour session was all that anyone got, a maximum of ten cartridges to be expended per man), but war and its incidental skills had passed them both by. Kalbfleisch had served in the first one of course, but as a regimental cook. Müller didn't doubt that he had been responsible for fatalities, just not with a rifle.

'Can we not arrest them?'

'Of course you can. And then they'll have to be released to the custody of MVD, who might or might not do something about it. Shit, they might *be* some of their own, in which case we can expect reprisals. It's much safer to head off that sort of thing. Everyone tries to escape, don't they?'

'But …'

'But, Müller? One of my best unterkommissars *buts* me? What, you're squeamish?'

'No, Comrade Inspector. It's just that we have a single witness – who didn't actually witness anything – and a bag of rumours. All that adds up to is the *spitzname* of the man who might be responsible – the Butcher. We can't ask questions of the Russians, obviously, and no German's admitting to having seen or heard anything. I don't know what further line of enquiry is open to us.'

'Unless he or they do it again. In your opinion, what does this most look like?'

'A warning, probably about black market competition.'

'It does. And as this is the only healthy sector of the eastern German economy right now, how likely is it that further gestures will be made?'

'Quite likely, Comrade.'

'Keep at it, Müller. Doggedness and diligence, that's the thing. Things, I mean.'

When the door had closed Beckendorp re-read the short report. The man was entirely correct, of course - this was a dead end, a waste of police time, even if only two men were chasing it. But as long as their heads were in Kaulsdorf they couldn't be thinking too closely about Beyer and who put him in the Spree. There were already enough men wasting their time on *that* one.

He quelled a familiar feeling of self-disgust. They were wasting their time because he'd put them on to it - a senior policemen, squandering resources at a time when real crime was being given a free run by the city's political crisis, and all to cover his culpable rear end. A man with more integrity might have resigned; he wondered what it would take for the impulse to even register with him.

There was a risk in continuing to push for a resolution to the Kaulsdorf murders. Major Zarubin wasn't going to be pleased if it began to point too obviously at the involvement of Soviet personnel - he'd want to know why Beckendorp hadn't quickly and quietly handed it to MVD, whose job it was to deal with criminality in the Red Army, not that of their Germans lickspittles. But then, Müller was probably right: there were very few places their investigation could go from here. As with the Beyer business, Beckendorp was hoping strenuously for failure.

Realising this didn't improve his mood. Almost since the moment Otto disappeared he had been groping several ways in darkness and hoping for the best. He almost wished for one of the many things he feared to happen - at least he could then look at a problem in hard daylight and make a start on dealing with it. Waiting for a near-inevitable blow was a wearying pastime.

The telephone rang, almost launching him into free air. That was the other thing – his nerves. He couldn't recall having felt this fragile, not even on 1 September 1939, when he'd first climbed into his cockpit and taken off to strafe the Polish nation. He picked up the receiver, listened without speaking for almost a minute and then agreed to what was being proposed. By the time he replaced it his anxieties had faded, pushed into the distance by a shockingly immediate sense of crops being reaped. He picked up his cap, straightened his tunic and limped to the door.

'Horst!'

An *anwärter* jumped up from the desk he shared with three other men in the general office. 'Comrade Inspector!'

'If anyone wants me I'll be upstairs.'

He limped to the tiny elevators, waited three minutes and then decided to punish his leg on the stairs. It took longer than strictly necessary because he wanted to think. It was futile, naturally - had he three days to prepare himself he couldn't have anticipated exactly which way his testicles were about to be squeezed. But at least he might have practised a surprised expression, a plausible denial or a few supplicant words to a Deity.

On the fifth floor he was stopped in the corridor by a raised hand and asked his business. He wore a full Inspector's insignia and still this arrogant little shit, dressed in a manner that hinted at pimpery or worse, felt he had the juice to know. In a less disordered state, his attention more upon the world's immutable usages, Beckendorp might not have put his own hand on the face that asked and shoved, hard. But a bad day had become a much worse one, and his temper didn't take crises well. The crash brought two of the shit's colleagues out into the corridor. They kept their distance, decided not to repeat his error.

The door of Direktor Jamin's occasional Keibelstrasse office was wide open. The head of K-5 was sat at his desk; he looked up as Beckendorp came into view and waved him further in.

'Close it, please.'

The *please* was unexpected. Beckendorp could recall about a half dozen occasions upon which they'd spoke, none of which had dented first impressions of a cold, detached creature, something that hid its monstrous past under a hard, bureaucratic carapace. Today, the shell seemed less well fixed in place.

A hand directed Beckendorp to a chair. For once, he didn't get the finishing-the-paperwork-first treatment. Jamin had cleared his desk already, giving his elbows room to breathe. He looked his guest straight in the eye.

'Otto Fischer.'

As an opening line it did its work admirably. Beckendorp felt his sphincter clench violently, and it took an effort of will not to break the gaze.

'Yes, Comrade Direktor.'

'You sent a man to enquire about him, why he was picked up.'

'I did, *UnterKommissar* Beyer.'

'Yes, Beyer. He was subsequently murdered – within an hour of having asked the question.'

The sphincter moved again. 'He was. We're …'

'It wasn't us.'

Three - technically, four - words, and Beckendorp wanted to be somewhere else with at least a spare morning to parse them.

'I'm sorry?'

'I'm saying to you, officially, that K-5 had no involvement in, nor any connection with, the death of Kurt Beyer. We are of course willing to lend you any assistance in finding the perpetrator, if you request it.'

Why would he think that I might think it? Beckendorp stared at the desk, as if considering the offer. *And why would he care if I did?* The head of K-5 had the power, the means and the holes to disappear even an *Inspecteur der VolksPolizei*, and no need to fear consequences after the act – a murmured 'reasons of security' would be enough to get the paperwork done and signed off before Beckendorp's orphaned men even knew about their bereavement. Yet as he thought this through, Jamin continued to stare at him like a man looking for a misplaced lip to chew.

'I've put about thirty men on the case, Comrade. I doubt we'll need help to find the swine.'

'Yes, of course.' Jamin nodded. Beckendorp waited to be dismissed, hoping to get back to his office and lock himself in, but the word didn't come. The Direktor had found his lip and made a start on working it; the side of one of his hands rubbed back and forth slightly on the desk as if burnishing it, and he appeared to be finding the view from the window (a blank wall less than five metres away) quite absorbing. Moments stretched themselves impressively.

'So, Otto Fischer.'

The second time wasn't quite as bad, but still Beckendorp couldn't recall his friend's name falling so jarringly on his ear. 'Yes, Direktor?'

'Have you discovered anything?'

With difficulty, Beckendorp kept his composure. 'Your people haven't told me anything. Who else would I ask?'

'I don't know.'

Revelation came late for Beckendorp, but it compensated with cymbals.

'You didn't order the job.'

'No.'

'But it *was* K-5 personnel.'

'Apparently. No one has admitted to it.'

'And they handed him straight to the Ivans.'

'Yes.'

'Well, to which section? They'll be able to …'

'I don't know that, either. It wasn't MVD, or, as far as I can see, MGB. In any case, why would MGB do this, if Fischer is *their* agent?'

He hasn't spoken to Zarubin, because he daren't. For a few moments Beckendorp was tempted to breathe more easily. At least two potential threats had receded slightly. K-5 weren't coming after him because they were as puzzled as he about Fischer's disappearance, and none of the usual Soviet suspects seemed to be involved either. But then common sense applied the icy douche. Someone was working two systems with impunity, and mortals couldn't do that. They were drawing upon men in K-5 who didn't care what or if Jamin, their boss, thought about it. Worse, there was an element of the Red Army or Ministry of State Security that worked with them, or for them, or turned an unseeing eye when asked to.

Who the hell are they?

Jamin seemed to be asking himself the same thing. Beckendorp had seen him this nervous only once before, and that had been in the presence of Major Zarubin, then one of his immediate superiors, at a time when, as a new fellow, he had been unsure how far his own authority extended. It was worse seeing it now. The unchallenged head of eastern Germany's internal security service (a department that Moscow had just allowed to enlarge itself massively) was impersonating a little boy dawdling at the end of his street, wondering if the local Truancy Officer was speaking to his mother. Beckendorp couldn't begin to think how *he* should feel about it, other than very badly indeed.

'Well, I'll keep you informed, Comrade Direktor.'

What else could he say? Jamin nodded, half-somewhere else already. Beckendorp stood and limped out of the office. The corridor was clear, its self-appointed sentries prudently on other duties, and he took the opportunity to glance into several rooms as he passed by. Men were at desks, reading or writing, or standing talking in small groups about matters of concern – suspects, football, the price of cheese, he couldn't say which. It was all surprisingly normal, much more like a legitimate police department than a plurality of that Word his wife wouldn't let him say, Ever.

He was still several metres from the stairwell when he began to brace himself for what came next. It was obvious that he needed to have another conversation, today. He didn't mind that in principle - he'd had plenty before now, and quite a few with the man in question. It was what he'd have to say that was giving his bowels a little more exercise.

29

He wasn't sure that he should have kept the papers, but no-one had asked for them to be returned, and he'd come to feel for them much what he imagined a parent would for an adopted child.

They were copies, of course, the originals discovered soon after the surrender and swiftly duplicated and distributed thereafter. The particular irony was that they were the fruits of Herr Speer's efforts to understand what resources he could call upon to increase armaments production, yet they had become the principal means by which the Red Army had robbed Germany of the same. To an untrained eye their exhaustive lists would seem mundane, but he regarded them as great literature, stanzas that had provided a brief but vital advantage in the art of making peace pay for war.

He had parsed their hidden meanings immediately, and, given a very specific task, applied himself with lunatic energy, ignoring the temptation of a hundred commodities that, in their variety and abundance, had transfixed his colleagues like children seduced by an abandoned sweet shop. In less than ten days he and his men had examined, catalogued and removed almost every detachable piece of machinery from western Berlin's chemical and machine-tool factories, every Hollerith from their accounting and warehousing departments, every processing schedule, blueprint and schematic from their technical offices. When the Allies arrived in strength to assert their rights over the agreed Zones, they had discovered a largely post-industrial landscape, a prize-chest robbed of its treasures.

It was a just principle, that those who suffered most from war should extract the greatest compensation. The Soviet Union had been laid waste to an extent the British could hardly imagine and the Americans not remotely conceive: scoured by an enemy whose conscious strategy had been to reconvert a populous, modern nation to a mere agricultural resource. The penalty for failure needed to be enduring, visible, and proportionate – on that, he agreed entirely with his political bosses. He just didn't believe that the compensation should be undivided.

And yet he could say truthfully that he wasn't a greedy man. Some, rising from nothing as he had, never lose the compulsion to have more - to seek satisfaction, even safety, in excess. He wasn't like that. For most of his childhood, *home* had been two rooms, a stinking hut in Pervomayskoye, the most rearward of *beyonds* imaginable. His escape, courtesy of forced recruitment into the local Bolshevik militia, had led him to previously unimagined indulgences (footwear, eating almost every day) which even now hadn't quite faded to insignificance. If he was comfortably warm he noticed it; if the simplest meal quietened his belly he savoured the feeling as would an epicure. He had little enthusiasm for the luxuries that immoderate wealth allowed - sable furs were as warm as cat, champagne was a whore's affectation, caviar he found both inexplicable and indigestible in his peasant's gut. His *enough* was much less than that of many men, not all of whom were capitalists.

He wondered, often, if he was what one might term *rich*. The word was a slippery one, meaning many things or very little. As a boy he would have regarded anyone whose belly never hurt for want of something to fill it as being rich. No doubt a Rockefeller would think a man with only one palace a pauper. Between these extremes, a host of aspirations pinned opinion upon what constituted wealth. Should he measure his place by the space required to hold his gold? The span of power upon which he could call to preserve it? The weight of blinis he could buy without blinking? He couldn't say - he doubted that anyone could, with authority. Perhaps, one day, he would endow a Chair of Philosophy at some university to study the matter – one day, when he wasn't too busy defending what he had, and intended yet to have.

One measure of wealth, partial but indisputable, was how much intelligence it could buy. It was one of the few assets upon which he spent freely, without reservation. He knew more about supply, demand and pitfalls in his market because he was willing to buy understanding, whereas too many of his competitors went after the profit with both eyes pointing straight ahead (which is why many of those same eyes were now glazed over or jellied in their shallow graves). As in war – in that other form of war - a man had to know when and how to react to what was coming.

He thought of *reaction* as he read the very brief note from an acquaintance at SVAG headquarters, Karlshorst. It was a response to a question he had asked some days earlier – a simple question but one that, having been asked, could have earned him an appointment with the firing post, had he not been certain of his correspondent. He had requested only that he be informed if a certain matter was under scrutiny, and by whom. The answer consisted of a single word, a surname, the one he had expected. It told him that he had a problem.

He always had problems, so this one wasn't something to rob him of sleep. It had several possible solutions (all problems did), though he couldn't know which was best until he saw its edges. Subtlety, forbearance and swift, violent gestures all had their place, were all capable of stopping a wound; but a diagnosis was necessary beforehand if the thing wasn't to spurt and stain everything for want of proper treatment.

The simplest response was a bullet, of course. This was Berlin, and even in more placid times a man might find the bottom of a river or ditch, gone before anyone knew to look for him. Now, with the Occupation Powers bumping chests like gorillas in a small glade, any amount of damage could be hidden under the noise. The more he thought about it, the prettier the most straightforward solution seemed. So he thought some more, and very carefully. Time, after all, was something else that money could buy.

30

Otto Henry Fischer; 21 September 1948: no offence stated.

There had been no difficulty at all, because the flow of
suspected Nazis, dissident politicians and other assorted
undesirables into the special camps had slowed from a torrent
to a trickle over the past eighteen months. Zarubin had sent a
request to the commandants of all nine, and eight had
responded within the week. One provided a list of thirty-two
men, the winner by a long nose. Three others had admitted to
double figures (just), and three to less than ten. Northern
Berlin's very own entrance to Hell, MVD Special Camp No. 1
- formerly Sachsenhausen – had shame-facedly held up its
hands to a single name.

Now that he had it, Zarubin considered what he might do with
the information. Beckendorp wanted to hear that his friend
was alive, but it was hardly MGB's business to bring light and
happiness to the German *volk*, useful though this particular
specimen was. That being so, had it been no matter one way or
the other he would have been content to put in a call to
Keibelstrasse and give the good news. But *no offence stated*
made him pause. It took a certain amount of authority to put
someone into the camps, and a paper trail was mandatory.
Fischer seemed to have gone from the world without a ripple
forming, and that was cause for concern. He wasn't going to
pick up the telephone until he had a good idea who might be
listening in.

He was thinking about the device still when it rang, and
suddenly he was speaking to the man himself. He was pleased;
obviously, this was about the elusive Rudolph Gerste,
someone he very much needed to find (or whose death he

needed confirmed). Beckendorp was a good policemen, a ferret, yet even Zarubin was surprised at the speed with which he had moved. Of course, he said he'd be delighted to have him come to Karlshorst that very morning. Use your siren if necessary, he joked.

He was in such good humour that he asked his adjutant, Yelena, to have some tea sent in when Beckendorp arrived. She said nothing to this, but the cast on her hard, lovely face suggested that she considered a German's face the proper destination for a hot beverage, rather than his stomach.

An hour later, she waved Beckendorp into the office, and immediately the morning's sunny aspect clouded over. He was agitated, tensed as if awaiting an assault. Zarubin caught Yelena's eye and shook his head slightly.

He sat down. 'Have you found Herr Gerste?'

For a moment Beckendorp seemed surprised. 'No, not yet. It isn't why I'm here.'

'Do we have any other business?'

'Perhaps. It's something you might need to hear.'

'How very oblique. Go on.'

For almost a minute, the other man said nothing as he struggled to find the right words. Zarubin sat back, trying to be patient as he recalled his day's current list of urgencies.

Eventually, Beckendorp cleared his throat. 'What doesn't MGB get to know?'

'I'm sorry?'

Again, there was a pause. The German scratched his nose, shifted his arse in the small chair it was pressing and blinked rapidly. Had he been in an interrogation room Zarubin would have been tempted to write any confession that came to mind and pass it across the table, confident that it would be signed.

'What I mean is, we – *VolksPolizei*, MGB - all have areas of responsibility. And we all know other stuff that doesn't necessarily concern us but comes to us from one or more directions as a matter of course. Then there are things we aren't supposed to know about, but hints get dropped, thrown or let slip, or we trip over information that wipes the dirty glass and gives us a glimpse. *Then* there's the stuff that we absolutely don't need or want to know, and we know not to ask. By definition, it's best to be ignorant of *that* sort of stuff. But then again, not knowing, how can we tell one way or the other? I'm trying to say, what could be kept from MGB that might or might not be important.'

Zarubin stared up at his ceiling. 'I think you're asking *who* could keep it from MGB.'

Beckendorp winced slightly. 'I am.'

'This is not a hypothetical question.'

'It isn't.'

'Are you referring to the entirety of the Soviet world, or our part of Germany?'

'The latter. I hope.'

'Mm. Good question.' No German had the right to ask it, yet it spoke so directly to Zarubin's own recent thoughts that he found it irresistible.

'MVD and MGB are separate organizations, each reporting directly to Moscow. Technically, it would be possible for MVD to mount something major and keep us ignorant of it. In practise, however, we work together in so many areas, and generate such crosstalk between us, that I doubt it could be done successfully – at least, not for long, or to any significant degree. The Army, of course, could keep nothing from us even if it wanted to; MVD have political officers at almost every rank and would report to us MGB-relevant issues - men talking to the enemy, attempts at defection - as a matter of courtesy, even if they decided to deal with the offenders themselves. There is, of course, no civilian Soviet administration in Germany, so we may assume the Central Committee aren't trying to hide anything from me. Why, what have you heard?'

'Otto Fischer was abducted.'

'I've heard that, too. Your point?'

'He was taken by a K-5 abduction squad a bare few metres into eastern Berlin, which means that they had to have had at least a little notice. Within the hour – minutes, even – he was handed over to unknown Soviet personnel, who then …. what? I don't know. But then, neither does anyone else. Unless, of course, you've known all along.'

'I haven't, I don't. Where are you going with this?'

Beckendorp sighed. 'I told you that I tried to test the water with K-5, to get a hint of the truth.'

'I recall.'

'It failed, obviously. But this morning I was summoned to speak to Erich Jamin.'

'Dear me. Do you need a character reference?'

'Direktor Jamin wasn't displeased - at least, I don't think he was, it's very hard to tell. Actually, he seemed nervous, because he has no idea how or why some of his own men disappeared Fischer. He's asked, but he's got no answers.'

Zarubin almost let his surprise show. If there was one German organization that ran with the traditional feel for rigid discipline it was Jamin's. The thought of a rogue element working with an equally undomesticated Soviet gang stirred recent, uncomfortable thoughts. It couldn't be a coincidence, he told himself, and hoped very much that he was wrong.

'You're certain that Fischer was taken by members of K-5?'

'I am. More importantly, the Direktor is, too.'

Then it was a given, and Zarubin had a swift, urgent decision to make. Whatever resources he was being offered by Marshal Sokolovsky, he couldn't gauge their loyalty, their inclination to stay on the tracks. Someone was using K-5 personnel without their Direktor's blessing, and he could just as easily be doing it with Soviet personnel (he knew what MVD and MGB personnel were paid, and it wasn't nearly enough to stave off temptation). On the other hand, he had to trust *someone*, and he doubted that Beckendorp could be bribed with the Keys to the Kingdom.

He cleared his throat. 'The task I gave you, to find Rudolph Gerste?'

'Comrade Major, we're working on it, I promise …'

'Listen. I believed that Gerste was working for me, but it seems that he had another employer.'

'It isn't an unusual circumstance, I expect.'

'No. But it's put MGB in a difficult position. Do you have a few minutes?'

Obviously, the question was rhetorical. Beckendorp sat back while Zarubin gave him the details. As he listened he couldn't stifle a slight feeling of admiration. Having lived for so long with the sordid commercial intercourses of black market cigarettes, painkillers, alcohol and the prostitution and killings that paid for and facilitated most of it, he was being offered a privileged glimpse of real crime. There was a certain respectability to more than three million Deutsche Marks, no matter how it was acquired.

He interrupted only once. 'You're sure this isn't a western gang? Why?'

'Where would they go? They can't escape unless it's through the SBZ – how could they risk that? Whoever did it must be in collusion with someone who can ensure the money doesn't disappear into the pockets of the first patrol they encounter.'

'That sounds right.'

Zarubin's bare-faced honesty was also impressive. He was admitting to a senior Berlin policeman that he'd intended to take the money himself (though for what reason he wasn't saying). This, presumably, made the business a matter of personal honour – and, probably, arse-covering. By the time the story ended, Beckendorp was entirely convinced - this had been organized by men from their side of the line.

He was fairly convinced of something else, and this was closer to home. 'This all sounds very familiar.'

'It does. Like Fischer's abduction, it was carried out by people who appear to be able to use the system without being *of* it. They must be very brave, or extremely well covered.'

'Poor Otto. I hope he's …'

Beckendorp stared at nothing, turning the possibilities over. Zarubin realised that the logic of discretion had faded the moment he mentioned the robbery.

'Fischer is alive.'

The big German nearly leapt out of his seat. 'Where?'

'For the moment, never mind. I believe he's safe enough where he is.'

'How did you find him?'

'If I tell you that you'll know everything, and it might not make him any safer. If there *is* a connection between our little problems, the last thing we need is to flag our cleverness before we know who we're up against. Besides, it's useful that you have a strong incentive to find Herr Gerste, alive or dead.'

'And if he's dead?'

'We'll improvise. How many men have you put onto finding him?'

'One.'

'That's disappointing.'

'It's Rolf Hoeschler. You'll recall that you insisted I hire him last year. You must have some faith in his abilities.'

'As an efficient thug, yes. I'm not sure he's a bloodhound.'

Beckendorp managed not to react visibly to *thug*. 'He'll keep at it. He doesn't like to fail.'

'He's in the west?'

'For four days now. His plan was to get work at Tempelhof.'

'Tempelhof. It seems to be where things happen.'

Beckendorp didn't want to be glib, but the words were out before he could bolt the door.

'Perhaps our problems are American ones.'

Zarubin laughed humourlessly. 'Comrade Stalin would agree, I think.'

31

Siegfried was shuffling his way across the hut to Poets'
Corner, where a former SDP area organizer was clearing
phlegm prior to an advertised recitation of Goethe's *Winter
Journey*. At Fischer's table he stopped, surprised.

'I thought we no longer had a gramophone?'

Fischer didn't look up. 'It belongs to the officers' mess, if
pillage counts as ownership.'

'We seemed to believe that it did, once. What's wrong with
it?'

'It's running slowly. I'm taking the opportunity to give it a full
service.'

Siegfried shook his head. 'That's fraternization.'

'It's something interesting, is what it is.'

The item, no doubt acquired from its previous owner at a fair
price, was a beautifully preserved (if not maintained), 1932
HMV model 104, a passable twin to Earl Kuhn's personal
instrument, formerly of West Side Records but more recently
gracing the Kuhn family's Bremen home. He had never
allowed Fischer to touch, much less disembowel it, so in a
way this was unfinished business, as interesting as an odd
corpse would be to an anatomist. Siegfried was correct of
course – the work counted as fraternization, if not
collaboration. But Fischer had come to find the devices
fascinating, even if he often loathed the noises they were put
to.

Siegfried peered into its entrails. 'Are you being paid for your filthy treason?'

'We negotiated a skiing holiday, at Davos.'

'Glühwein and ski-bunnies, how perfect! Can you fix it?'

Fischer shrugged. 'They've loaned me some watchmaker's tools. It's fairly simple, just lubrication really. I hinted that the work would be harder than it is.'

'MVD don't do gratitude.'

'I know. I just wanted to drag it out. And if I make a good job they might let me have a go at a clock.'

'You could do that?'

'I'll know when I've tried.'

The hut was almost full of men doing things other than biding time. Dein's approach to Colonel Vaisman had caught the man on a good day. He had agreed that theoretical classes on mathematics and engineering could be organized, and anything to do with literature and art that didn't require books. He insisted that any and all of these tutorials could be inspected without warning by MVD personnel (a pointless demand, given that all human activities at Sachsenhausen were closely monitored already), and that any tools, implements and measuring devices provided be counted, accounted for and returned after each session. It was more than Dein or Fischer had hoped for.

Winter Journey had commenced by now, but Siegfried had been distracted. He picked up a pair of watchmaker's pliers and frowned. 'Too small to be useful.'

'Useful for what?'

'For building an aeroplane, to get me out of here.'

'Yes, they're certainly too small for that. How is your device coming on?'

'I've imagined it precisely for some years now. Joachim Dein's working on a fifteen metre yacht, with the same success.'

'He's a wise man. So much more civilized than flying out of here.'

'An ex-paratrooper says that?'

'He says it because he is one. Where would Joachim sail to, if he could?'

Siegfried shrugged, 'To where we'd all go – somewhere warm and forgiving.'

It had struck Fischer before now how he had never imagined himself in far foreign parts. His war record hadn't made it necessary of course, but there was something about slates wiped totally clean that should have drawn him more than they did. Perhaps his rural Baltic upbringing made him too parochial to want to be where folk spoke something else.

The hut door opened, and the slight burble of a dozen low conversations halted. Three inmates had paused there and were glancing around carefully. Fischer recognized one of them; Dien had pointed him out previously as a former middle-ranker in the Reich Protectorate of Bohemia and Moravia, one of Karl Hermann Frank's men who'd managed somehow not to share a rope for the reprisals at Lidice and Ležáky. A bad - and, apparently, a lucky - sort.

He made a show of noticing Fischer momentarily, then gave the rest of the room the benefit of his attention. Not many of the inmates present held his gaze, though Siegfried – perhaps armoured by the tiny pair of pliers he was holding – managed a schoolboy-insolent stare that wasn't noticed by its victim.

The politician's two friends had an air of what once might have been menace, but like themselves it was a poor, shop-worn effort, deployed too often against those who, enervated by hopelessness, bad diet and disease, could have been cowed by rain. When he moved they followed, towards Poets' Corner.

They stood and listened respectfully while the Sage (who had gamely refused to pause in his oration) emerged finally from the Harz Mountains and, without pause, made a start on Charlotte von Stein. The other members of his audience kept their eyes firmly upon him, and the rest of the room resumed its several preoccupations.

Fischer returned to the bowels of the Model 104. 'They probably want to become poets.'

Siegfried snorted. 'What, to breed a culturally superior *volks-sonnet* to piss on all others?'

'I thought that this is what we wanted, to get their sort back into our warm, loving community?'

'It'll take more than a few beatings. Don't think about turning your back on them, Fischer.'

'I won't, unless it's to run away.'

Half an hour later the guards arrived to collect their graciously-loaned implements and expel the inmates from the hut. Fischer put the gramophone's fragmented parts into their case and braced himself to move quickly, to get into the safety of a group before he could be invited to a private kicking. But the politician and his friends had departed at the head of the stream, and once outdoors they kept going, towards the huts in the north-eastern quadrant of the camp where they and their comrades held vigil against the World's unpleasant Now.

He wondered if it had been a warning, that they could find him at a time of their choosing. But he knew that already: they all inhabited a compact world whose boundaries were very definitely drawn, and he couldn't always be in the company of others. If they had the will to do it, he could be dead as soon as he forgot to look in every direction.

Perhaps he was being egotistical. They may have had a genuine love for Goethe's poetry, or needed a brief holiday from planning the National Socialist resurgence. He was considering these and other possibilities when Siegfried, shuffling beside him as they returned to their hut, unerringly pinned the likely reason.

'They were showing their faces, to show that they still could. Which means they're worried about the way things are going. So like I said, be careful.'

Should I make a will? Largely by default he had come to own a fifty percent share in a successful laundry business and a ten percent holding in West Side Records, purveyors of the finest cacophony to the unfortunate city of Bremen. His only other substantial asset was a precious weight of regrets, thoughtlessly acquired but carefully hoarded. The latter he would willingly surrender at the moment of his demise; the rest his good friend Earl Kuhn would come into by right. No, it wouldn't require a legal document to put Otto Henry Fischer to rest.

They found Joachim Dein in their hut. He seemed agitated but said nothing until all three men were outside once more.

'The Commandant sent for me. Someone's been asking about recent arrivals, and he's given your name, Fischer.'

'He didn't say who asked?'

'No. But he said something else, and I don't know what to make of it.'

Siegfried had become infected by Dein's mood, and twitched visibly. 'What, Joachim?'

'That consideration of a second phase of releases may have begun.'

'We weren't considered the first time around, were we?'

'No. Perhaps Sachsenhausen houses the very worst of our kind, or perhaps it was a typical bureaucratic flip of the coin, Camps A to M only. I don't know.'

Fischer considered it for a few moments. 'It was probably the latter. There are some bad people here and a lot of others who would have served very little - if any - prison time in the western Zones. The Soviets erred on the safe side three years ago, but we're an expense they can't want to keep meeting.'

Dein pulled a face. 'In any case, he told me that while he didn't expect me to stab any fellow inmate in the back, I should draw up a list of those who might least be expected to cause problems, if released. There's a Soviet committee, apparently, that will look at it and other camps' recommendations. What happens then is up to them. But how the hell do I decide which men are more worthy than others?'

'Form a committee. Share the blame.'

Fischer put a hand on Siegfried's shoulder. 'He shouldn't do that. He shouldn't tell anyone else, and nor should we. Can you imagine how the other inmates would react? He wouldn't dare leave his hut, or fall asleep.'

'What can I do?' Dein looked helplessly at both men.

'How many can you recommend?'

'He didn't say. If it were up to him, no doubt he'd want precisely the number of men remaining in the camp – it's no secret he hates this posting. But what's credible?'

Siegfried was staring at the perimeter wall, frowning. 'If they decide to close the camp, what happens to the ones they don't release?'

'Siberia. There's no alternative, unless they re-open the pits and shoot them.'

Dein kicked a stone hard enough to carry it almost to the death strip. 'Fuck! I'm not Christ; I shouldn't have to do this.'

'Could you refuse the honour?'

'I don't know. How wise is it to get on the wrong side of the man who decides whether or not we all keep breathing? He's fairly decent. I'd like him to remain that way.'

'You might make a short list. Of the men he definitely shouldn't release.'

'Siegfried, their ghosts would haunt me, as bad as they are.'

Fischer had been watching a guard in the nearest tower. When the stone skipped within his range of vision he had casually swung around his Degtyarev. It wasn't yet pointing directly at Dein, but a slight twitch and squeeze could have lessened the Commandant's present problem by three souls at least. He turned away, slowly.

'Joachim, why don't you make a blanket proposal? Name no-one, but suggest that all inmates incarcerated solely for their membership of the NSDAP be released on the basis that they had little choice in the matter, with the remainder to be considered case-by-case? That should get half the camp cleared at least, if he agrees.'

'And I won't have had to *not* recommend anyone.'

'Exactly.'

'Good! I'll wait until tomorrow, to give him the impression I've thought deeply about it. Thanks, Fischer.'

Siegfried watched Dein walk back to his hut, waving occasionally to acknowledge a greeting. He turned to Fischer and scratched his head. 'You know that none of us – me, you or Dein – benefit by that proposal.'

'They say nobility brings its own rewards.'

'They *say*!'

Fischer laughed. 'It's a cliché, it must be true.'

'Still, someone outside's been asking about you. That's something, isn't it?'

'I'm not sure. It depends on who *someone* is.'

Fischer turned back to the watchtower. The Degtyarev had been swung away, to a point in the death strip where it and the next tower's ordnance could seriously spoil an optimist's day. It might have focussed his curiosity about the source of the bullet that dropped him at that moment, but he wasn't thinking about anything even before his head met the ground.

32

Mila Henze had lied to Hoeschler. As the final credits rolled
up the screen it was obvious to him that she had seen *Black
Narcissus* before, and probably several times. Either she was
thinking of joining the cloistered life or didn't mind repeating
the experience if it was in his company. He hoped for the
latter.

Afterwards they ate at a *volksküche* off Motzstrasse, where,
despite the blockade, the food was good enough to leave them
wanting more. He was tired by then, having slept badly the
previous night – his first - on her sofa, but the evening seemed
to need rounding off. They found a small bar on the way back,
and he squandered half of his remaining field expenses on two
weak American beers. She held his arm as they walked,
laughed at his bad jokes, maintained eye contact whenever
they spoke, and by the time they arrived back at her tiny
ground-floor apartment he was as close to trying his luck as
confessing everything.

It was a relief that his promise to be a gentleman hung
between them still, keeping him sensible. As far as she knew
he was in Berlin for a few days only, someone seeking
someone else on a simple matter and then gone, history. A
gentleman wouldn't have pressed the advantage and he didn't,
though it cost him half a night's sleep as he lay so close to her
that he imagined he could hear her breathing.

In the morning she went to the housing office at Schöneberg
Town Hall, and returned with all that western Berlin knew
about Rudolph Gerste. It was a former address he'd given
them, across the line in Pankow. Relieved, he thanked her and
said he'd go that afternoon.

She made him a lunch of soup and bread, and when it was time to leave she kissed him on the lips. It was quick, chaste enough to save her embarrassment if unwelcome, but it removed his courage and made him promise that he'd see her again before leaving Berlin. Within two hours he was back at Keibelstrasse, his thoughts dislocated still, halfway between places.

Beckendorp was at Karlshorst with the Russians, so Hoeschler left a message on his desk, changed into uniform and signed out an Opel from the motor-pool. Forty minutes later he was in Christburgerstrasse. He couldn't recall ever having visited the street. There was plenty of damage along its length but many intact, substantial apartment buildings also, giving it the air of a place only briefly between good times. To his astonishment he passed by a small group of chatting Jews, presumably on their way to or from the newly re-opened synagogue. The prospect was as shockingly out of time as that of woolly mammoths, strolling down Ku'damm.

Christburgerstrasse 19 was a dirty but elegant block with many ornamental flourishes to its façade, only slightly pockmarked by the small-arms fire with which drunken Soviet soldiers had decorated Berlin in the days after the surrender. Looking at it, Hoeschler's hopes faded. From here to a squalid Schöneberg cellar hinted at a long drop in fortunes for the Gerste family and a cold trail for any interest party who followed. He entered and went up to the second floor, already rehearsing the failure he'd be reporting to Beckendorp.

The door to apartment 26 needed some attention. The otherwise unmarked painted surface bore a small but deep gouge, as if someone had decided to ignore the bell button and use an axe instead. He decided to be more conventional.

The door departed its jamb barely enough to give a chance to the eye that appeared between them, so he stood back and smiled. For once the uniform didn't seem to deter its audience; in fact, the elderly woman who then opened the door fully seemed relieved at this visit from *VolksPolizei*. Gratified, he kept the smile in place and tried a little old world courtesy.

'I wonder if you could help me, Madam? I'm trying to find Herr Rudolph Gerste, who I believe lived here at one time. Would you happen to …?'

She coughed. 'My son. What has he done?'

'He's not in trouble, but we'd like to speak to him on an urgent matter. Really, it's just to talk.'

Her eyes moved rapidly, blinking; she checked the corridor both ways and then returned the gaze to the uniform. He could almost smell anxiety.

'He isn't here.'

'No, I didn't expect so. But if you could give me an address it would be very helpful.'

Again, the corridor was scanned. She seemed more upset than evasive – he had expected her to deny any knowledge of Gerste, but there had been no hesitation. That wasn't usual when people had things they didn't want known; there was no way to bring a conversation back from 'my son'.

She peered up at him myopically. 'Are you with the others?'

He tried to absorb this and think around it at the same time while keeping the damn stupid smile on his face. The only thing that occurred, and sharply, was that he had run out of time.

'No, not with them. Did you tell them where he was?'

'No … yes.'

'That's alright, it doesn't matter. But I do need to speak to him. As I say, it's urgent.'

Infuriatingly, she turned and went slowly back into her apartment. He forced himself to wait rather than follow, grab her by the shoulders and shake her until something useful spilled out. She returned in less than two minutes (it felt like twenty), holding a small business card.

'Here. It's my husband's old office address. The building's half-ruined, and not re-occupied. I gave them blankets for the floor … oh!'

'What's wrong, Frau Gerste?'

She'd put her hand to her mouth. 'It's my fault.'

'What is?'

'I just told them the street address, Wilhelmstrasse. I didn't think.'

'Of what?'

'Of course, they'd assume I meant Mitte. But it's Wilhelmstrasse in Spandau, at the corner with Pfälzischestrasse.'

'When? When did you tell them this?'

'Last evening, about seven.'

There was a chance, then, depending on how stupid or clever they were – on whether they'd return to beat the correct address out of her or realise what she'd meant to say. To his shame, he very much hoped the former.

'Listen, Frau Gerste. Do you get many visitors?'

'I don't get *any* visitors. Last week Rudy came to get the keys to the office; then those two men yesterday, and now you. That's three this year.'

'Then if someone knocks on your door later today or tomorrow, don't answer it. Pretend that you're not home, yes?'

The hand went back to her mouth. 'Why? Am I in trouble?'

'No, not at all. It's that we've had a few reports from this area of burglars who gain entry by pretence of something else.'

'Should I go to my sister's?'

'By all means, if you can leave immediately.'

It took every gram of his willpower to remain at the door while she packed a small bag and put on her coat. He watched her lock-unlock-lock-unlock-lock the door (stifling a near-scream as she did so), took her arm with what he hoped seemed like gentlemanly consideration and walked her out of the building and down the street to the bus-stop at her frail pace rather than drag her at his. He left her in a small, safe queue there and almost sprinted two hundred metres back to the Opel. Obviously, he couldn't go west again in his uniform - he would need to return to Keibelstrasse, sign the car back in, get changed and take the only east-west transport that still functioned – his legs and feet. Once over the line he could catch a bus or the s-bahn to Spandau, but every wasted minute was going to put Rudolph Gerste and his family closer to the afterlife.

At Keibelstrasse he didn't even think to check whether Beckendorp had returned from Karlshorst. He was back in the west less than eighty minutes after leaving Frau Gerste, and in Spandau within a further sixty. He didn't know the area and had to ask directions to Wilhelmstrasse; fortunately, Pfälzischestrasse met it in its northern stretch, only a few hundred metres south of the prison. He found the address and forced himself to pause and reconnoitre the terrain before blundering in.

Other than lacking glass, the frontage of the building seemed almost intact, but the rear was a mess, with several storeys of exposed rooms clinging desperately to their habitual altitude. A wire fence surrounded the rear plot, but it had been well-holed by foragers. The place was about as defensible as a station kiosk.

The card gave an address – *Franz Gerste, Notary* - on the ground floor. Briefly, Hoeschler glanced around for over-lookers, slipped through the fence and entered through what had once been a small office (probably that of the building's *portier*) but was now entirely outdoors. The inner door to the hallway was half-ajar and held up only by a single screw in its upper hinge. He didn't dare try to move it, relying instead upon God's gift of his narrow build to squeeze himself through.

He paused and listened for a creak, breathing, anything. The road outside was busy, bringing home its workers from their daily grind, and much could have been lost beneath its hum.

The weight of the pistol in his pocket was reassuring, but he wished fervently now that he had brought his suppressor. A gunshot east of the line could be explained economically with a brief wave of his warrant card, but he was fairly certain the Americans and their new local police force wouldn't be impressed by a *commie* shootout in their back garden. He resisted the temptation to draw the weapon and eased himself across the hallway slowly, toward the metal door-plate bearing Gerste Senior's name

His ear was pressed against the door before it occurred to him that someone else with a gun might be at its other side, ready to relieve his shoulders of much of their present burden. And now that it did, the question of *what next* pressed. Should he burst in like a policeman or knock politely? Shout a warning or try the door as quietly as possible? Müller could have advised him – his collection of American *krimi* novels must have explored every possibility, some perhaps even realistically. But Hoeschler himself was as new to this as to most other forms of police work, and his excellent paratrooper training offered no obvious lessons.

Time shoved his shoulder, urging him to *do something*, and he made a decision. The room at the other side of the door was quiet - too quiet for him to be other than too early or too late. He stepped to one side, out of the line of possible fire, and spoke quietly.

'Herr Rudolph Gerste?'

He heard it, just – a slight thing, perhaps a foot moving to compensate for how a body had reacted to the unexpected address. It was timid, needing to be coaxed, and no-one had time for that.

'Listen, Herr Gerste. I'm *VolksPolizei*, here without authority. You must come with me, now. The men looking for you know where you are – your mother told them. We have minutes at most.'

For a few seconds there was nothing, a frozen pause, then the sound of a floor moving, approaching the door. It stayed closed.

'Is she dead?'

'No, I told her to go to her sister's. She thought they were officials, it wasn't her fault. But please, Herr Gerste, your family …'

'You might be with them.'

'If I was, the door would be down by now, wouldn't it?'

He heard a murmur, at least two voices. It was an argument about life and death, probably, and how to recognise which path went where. He wanted to roar *For Christ's Sake* or kick in the wood between them, but that would have taken even more time to put right. So he waited, making fists at the hourglass that was running out in his head.

He couldn't recall that puberty had taken longer to run its course, but eventually the door opened. Gerste came first, protect his family with his body, but two small faces, peering from either side of his midriff, ruined the strategy. With a great effort, Hoeschler deployed the smile once more.

'Quickly, now.'

A small, pretty woman brought up the rear, her hands pushing the girls forward into the hall. Gerste himself, staring at their

unwanted visitor, looked ready to detonate. It wasn't difficult
to guess who had been arguing the trust no-one corner.

'Wait.'

One of the little girls had reached the *portier*'s door.
Hoeschler picked her up and stood to one side, pushing his
face into the gap as little as might give him some view of the
building's back plot. He saw a car, a well-punished pre-war
Ford, parked on the other side of the wire fence, empty.

Frantically, he glanced around the hall. The stairs rising to the
next floor were no longer rising; they lay as rubble, blocking
access to the building's northern wing and making as neat a
killing ground of the small area they occupied as an assassin
might have prayed for. For a moment the front window in the
Gerste office sang its own praises, but its sill was at least a
man's height from the ground outside. By the time the girls
could be lowered safely from it they would be starting a new
life as orphans.

'Get back into the room.'

The Gerstes obeyed, far more swiftly than they had departed
their sanctuary. Hoeschler felt for his pistol, thought again and
drew his old *Fallschirmjäger-messer* instead. It was still
pristine - he had never used it to cut snagged lines, never used
it upon another man, had no idea how useful it was for either.
He held it downwards, flipped the fulcrum, let gravity slide
out the blade and went back to the *portier*'s door.

Pressed against it he pushed gently with his body, closing it
slightly without putting too much pressure on its only hinge.
Then it was just a matter of waiting. Professionals would
check the junction and rear alley first, but two men wouldn't
be detained for long. He prayed it was only two men still, and

that one of them would be standing guard while the business proceeded. The four-inch blade he was gripping tightly wasn't up to meeting a major offensive.

He thought afterwards of bicycles and swimming, how muscles recall things. When the door shuddered and came off its hinge he pushed back, hard, had the knife up to its hilt in the man's neck before he could wriggle himself from beneath it, had the fallen Tokarev in his hand before the one by the car could think to draw his own and put two bullets, both gratifyingly suppressed, into the second man's chest. It couldn't have taken more than ten seconds, and the hands didn't start shaking for a further ten.

The problem of getting the family into eastern Berlin had been solved. He bundled them into the Ford, trying to keep his body between the girls and the fellow from somewhere east of the Urals, whose almond eyes now stared uncaringly into the Berlin sky. He told Gerste to drive and directed him from the front passenger seat while making fists of his bloodied hands all the way through Neukölln and into Friedrichshain, via the minor roads he knew were never patrolled. His head told him that the silent, horrified stares of the womenfolk couldn't possibly cause the sensation he was feeling on the back of his neck. It didn't help.

He had Gerste drive directly into the courtyard at Keibelstrasse, where the high-sided quadrangle gave a happy illusion of safety. Even so, with all the uniforms that milled around, the girls couldn't be coaxed out of the car until he cravenly resorted to a promise he couldn't keep, of cake and milk.

He was painfully aware that he had brought them to a place from which word of their survival, if it had been noticed, would almost certainly reach Karlshorst (from where, this time, he was praying that Beckendorp had returned). He ushered them swiftly up two flights, along the least-travelled corridor (it held maintenance cupboards at one end and didn't spill into the reception area at the other), then up a third and into senior officers' territory. He forgot to knock before trying his Inspector's door.

Beckendorp was in his vest, mid-way between a change of shirts, when he was confronted by a small family and his best (and, probably, worst) *unterkommissar*. His face rehearsed blankness, anger, puzzlement, revelation and relief in the time it took for Hoeschler to think of what he was going to say, and then he wasn't given the chance.

'Thank Christ.'

33

Müller was staring into the Kaulsdorf file once more when Kalbfleisch lumbered into the room with two mugs. He placed them carefully on the table and sucked a spill from his thumb.

'I've just seen Rolf Hoeschler.'

Müller didn't look up. 'Have you? Splendid.'

'He's arrested a family.'

'On what charge?'

'We didn't speak, I just saw him. He looked as anxious as a trench-pigeon.'

For a few moments Müller said nothing. He looked up, his eyes on Kalbfleisch but looking for something else, much further away.

'What sort of men can do these things?'

'Arrest families? Cold bastards, usually. But perhaps Rolf had a good ...'

'Shut up about Hoeschler! I mean, what sort of men can run criminal enterprises in the middle of Berlin?'

'Hell, just about anyone.'

'No, not these days. Two or three years ago it was rife – there was a market for just about everything and the rule of law spread about three metres around the occasional street patrol. So many people were being found dead in the street that an execution wouldn't even have been recorded, much less investigated. Now, it's different. The Ivans have cracked down, we're a bit more effective as police and most things necessary for life can be got on a ration card. Medical supplies and decent alcohol still sell well underground, but it's riskier now to be bold. This Kaulsdorf thing was *bold*. It pissed on Authority's boots in the middle of the greatest concentration of armed men in this part of Europe. Who can do that?'

Kalbfleisch burped. 'Stalin.'

'Bound to have an alibi. Alright, let's ask a different question. Who can do this?'

'That's the same question, just about.'

'I mean, who can deal in stuff anymore?'

'People *with* stuff.'

Müller sighed. Inviting Kalbfleisch to speculate was much like throwing a ball for a dog that had no mind to retrieve it.

'Who has the capacity, the opportunity, to deal?'

'The Americans. They own everything and everything's reserve stock.'

'But they don't have the means to cross the line and execute their competition in an East Berlin churchyard. It's always been a lot easier to move west than east.'

'Bless Comrade Eisenhower's naivety.'

'Quite. No, this is a matter of easterners doing bad things to other easterners. So, again, who?'

'Someone who doesn't care about the consequences.'

Müller glanced down at the file again. He had read it so many times that he could swear the print had faded slightly. 'I thought that too. But who doesn't *care*, unless they want to be out of the world? Are we searching for a potential suicide, or a dolt who doesn't think he needs to worry? Neither possibility seems likely. And then I thought something else, something awful.'

'Which is?'

'What if it's someone for whom there *are* no consequences?'

'That would be God.'

'It would be someone who had power itself or the means to coax power. If the former, then you're right, it's Stalin. If the latter, then we're back to the question of means.'

Kalbfleisch frowned into his mug. 'There aren't any rich Ivans, are there?'

'So we're led to believe. I doubt that members of the Politburo queue for black bread with their ration books, but nor do they winter in Capri.'

'And there *definitely* aren't any rich Germans anymore.'

'Not outside Paraguay, for sure. But would someone need wealth to be wealthy?'

'Eh?'

'I should have said *well-provided*. As in having access to what's regarded as wealth - or at least, resources.'

'Does it matter? Whoever did this is beyond our reach. If they knew that an *unterkommissar* and an *oberwachtmeister* were hot on the case, they'd piss themselves laughing. And with reason.'

'I know. But the Inspector put us on it, and he's a closer threat.' Wearily, Müller shoved away the file. 'Anything new on Beyer's killer?'

'Nothing. They've dragged every scum-fuck in this part of Berlin into Keibelstrasse and no-one knows, saw or heard anything. You'd think that Golem had stretched out a hand from the Spree and dragged the poor bugger down.'

'Golem doesn't have a seven-point-six-two millimetre calibre pistol.'

Kalbfleisch shrugged. 'You can't say that, war surplus being what it is.'

'They aren't going to find the culprit, are they?'

'Not unless a suicide-by-confession walks in the front door. Or we get lucky, which we never have.'

Müller raised the now-cold mug to his lips, shuddered and set it down once more. 'Hoeschler said he was being sent into the Western Zones, didn't he?'

'Yeah. Those must be *wessies* he kidnapped. The family, I mean.'

'I wonder what they did?'

Kalbfleisch nodded to a point behind Müller's head. 'Ask him.'

Hoeschler was at his desk, rummaging in one of its drawers. He was wearing rough, plain clothes that made him look like one of the thousands of manual workers who crossed and re-crossed the city's demarcation line every day, a horde oblivious to the siege that had brought the Occupiers toe-to-toe. Kalbfleisch hadn't exaggerated - he seemed anxious, or perhaps *primed*.

He looked up, distracted, when Müller approached. He had shoved his service pistol into the opened drawer, but something that looked like a large pen-knife sat on the desk still. It was generously bloodied.

'Did you have success, Rolf?' To his knowledge, Müller had never used Hoeschler's given name before, but being embarrassed by his own inquisitiveness he made the effort to be friendly.

'What? Yes.'

This was hardly more illuminating than Kalbfleisch's sparse observation, but Müller didn't know how to go on without making it seem like an interrogation. He was further discomfited when Hoeschler removed his coat and began to unbutton his rough workman's smock. A few of the other police in the room noticed and looked away, but Müller had an unmissable, front-row view of the cabaret.

Hoeschler, preoccupied, didn't seem bothered by his audience, even when the work trousers came off and were replaced by the regulation item. His lips moved slightly, a conversation proceeding without another party, and when he put a hand on to his desk to steady himself Müller noticed that it was shaking badly. That, at least, offered a chance to say more.

'A bad one, was it?'

'Bad enough.' As he said it, both men's eyes returned to the folded knife. The blood made it more menacing of course, but Müller was certain that its design wasn't meant for any domestic purpose, despite its modest size. He was equally certain that it wasn't going to find its way into an evidence bag.

A short whistle seized everyone's attention. Beckendorp was stood in the doorway, making its battered frame even less pretty. He flipped a hand at Hoeschler, who nodded and scrambled to gather his warrant card and other effects.

'Is it a breakthrough?' Müller tried a final time, desperately hoping he didn't seem as needy for news as he felt.

'I don't know what it is. But we're going to Karlshorst with it, so I imagine we'll find out soon enough.'

The word was enough to kill all of Müller's curiosity. He didn't even envy Hoeschler his exciting case anymore - there were worse things in police work than futile dead-ends. His own Russians were as yet imaginary, born of an unpleasant assumption that, if accurate, would take the case safely from him. Poor Hoeschler's were not only real but close by, prodding, ready to flush a hopeful career if it didn't exceed all sane expectations. He suddenly saw the sense, the shrewdness, of Kalbfleisch's lumbering half-enthusiasm for police work. It took a fine appreciation of how things were to risk neither failure nor success.

34

Remarkably, Fischer was allowed a visitor, as if he lay in a civilian lazarett and not what the inmates considered to be the ante-chamber to the camp mortuary.

Joachim Dein wore the familiar, despicable air of false cheerfulness that most patients would happily relapse to avoid. Thankfully, Sachsenhausen's gift shop hadn't rise to the challenge of flowers, or soft fruits. He had brought his little volume of poetry instead, with an ardent plea to have it kept hidden other than when the guards were plainly elsewhere. Then, with relish, he offered the diagnosis.

'A broken shoulder, the blade. To be rested.'

Fischer knew precisely where the damage was located. He reminded himself of it every time he forgot not to shift in his bed.

'It was a shockingly bad attempt. Was the man blind?'

Dein shrugged. 'The home-made suppressor probably fucked the trajectory.'

Carefully, Fischer turned his head and regarded his suspended hand. It was attached, via handcuffs, to a rusty iron bedstead that had lost all but tiny slivers of its original green paint 'Why am I shackled?

'You're forgetting where you are. Being shot is not permitted.'

'Then please apologize to the Commandant for me.'

Dein grinned. 'Vaisman's furious. The idiots shouldn't have used a gun, not here. He's having squads strip almost every hut in the camp, and if the weapon's found we can expect some dawn trench-digging. Our problem with the Fourth Reich may have solved itself.'

He glanced around. The ward (a room indistinguishable from most latrines except that it hosted four beds and no hole in the floor) was empty other than for its sole patient and his guest. Technically, medical staff at MVD Special Camp No 1 were available to treat inmates as well as staff, but unless the problem was infectious they almost always relied upon nature to run its rigorous course. Fischer had been surprised, therefore, to wake from his near-assassination washed, bandaged and occupying a pair of striped pyjamas (which he hoped sincerely weren't the previous administration's left-over stock).

'You're getting five-star treatment.'

'I know. Why is that?'

'I have no idea. I went to Vaisman to beg a little consideration for you, but it wasn't necessary. He'd already told his medical staff that he wants you alive.'

Fischer considered this for a few moments only. To an orderly Teutonic mind the answer came quickly - he was surprised Dein hadn't worked it out already.

'You said that he gave my name to the commissioners considering the Special Camp releases. Once he did that he became responsible for me.'

'Ah. Well, you're now the cleanest, most comfortable German in the vicinity. Enjoy yourself while it lasts.'

'I wouldn't admit to being comfortable.'

'Does it hurt?'

'Abominably.'

'Then you'll probably be looking forward to the perpetrator's execution.'

'I don't know. It was good to be doing something useful. The camp has just the one gramophone, and I was never a competent gardener.' He lifted Dein's book with his free hand. 'I don't write poetry, either.'

'It isn't a place for muses, for sure. Perhaps the Commandant will allow you to retrain his men. A gun shouldn't have been allowed to find its way here.'

'He'll kick their arses, I expect. Which means we'll all suffer.'

'It's what we're here for, to pay for the sins of our compatriots.'

Fischer glanced towards the room's only window. It was filthy, and he was lying too low to see any of what penetrated it. Unusually, the Ivans hadn't thought either to cover the room's bare walls with exhorting posters or provide a selection of board games for the use of patients, so watching the paint peel was going to be his principal occupation. He hoped sincerely for an early discharge.

'Tell me about the Ghost.'

Dein frowned. 'What?'

'Siegfried mentioned the murders here, the three mutilations. Entertain me, Joachim.'

'Siegfried should have his gossiping gland removed. We managed to keep that business quiet, and it should remain that way.'

'What did MVD do about it?'

'Nothing, because we didn't tell them.'

'What about roll-call?'

'It's almost always been a joke here at Sachsenhausen. They tried to keep a strict tally while the escapes were happening, but once everyone tired of the hundred percent failure and fatality rate they stopped bothering. You've heard it - when names are shouted out and there's no answer someone shouts back 'dead in the night'. They mark it down because it's all too feasible. Naturally, we have to produce bodies.'

'But there were mutilations in this case. Didn't they …?'

'Conduct a post-mortem? No. Inmates re-dressed the corpses, the Ivans provided wheelbarrows, we pushed them to the pits and quick-lime did the rest.'

'One of the victims was a former gauleiter.'

'Yes, Ernst Schlange.'

'The other two?'

'Nobodies.'

'No-one is nobody, Joachim.'

'They weren't *anybody*, then. I think they'd served as minor officials in the Regime. Neither were former military, or had a hand in the Jewish solution.'

'Names?'

'I'm sure they had. I just don't know them.'

'And the murders stopped at three?'

'Yes. I mean, probably. The mutilations stopped, certainly; but there have been so many untimely deaths here that a T4 Aktion might have proceeded and one would hardly notice. Perhaps the murderer just tired of embellishing his work.'

Fischer shook his head. 'Typically, a man like that wouldn't be capable of adaptation. It's more likely that he died himself before he could increase the tally.'

'So, there may be a God after all. I must pass the word around, the fellows will be pleased.' Dein stood up. 'They're all talking about you – the first man to be shot illegally at Sachsenhausen. You're quite the desperado.'

'The what?'

'It's an Americanism. A *Schinderhannes*, I should have said.'

'But Schindehannes was a criminal.'

'And a hero, too. You've managed to irritate the worst of the inmates *and* the Ivans. You're a role model for our would-be suicides.'

'Perhaps we'll all be released before they can follow my example.'

Dein shook his head. 'Some of us will never leave, other than to the East. I stole their money, remember?'

'You have no hopes?'

'Why should I? I have nothing to return to anyway - no family, a village that would ostracise me, no means of making a way in the new world. Here, I'm almost respectable. If I'm retired to Siberia I'll at least have my camp skills to ease the novelty. Hell, in a couple of years I'll be chairing their snow and lice committees.'

When Dein had gone Fischer examined the ceiling carefully, letting the bleakness of what he'd heard rouse his own unquiet heart. With Marie-Therese gone he was water in an emptying bath, reducing to a single point of oblivion, unneeded waste material. She had taken him from a state of merely being, made him see things as more than the grey infill to a life endured rather than experienced. Her absence unwound all of that, letting the emptiness flood back.

He had been telling himself the same thing since he arrived: that this wouldn't be a bad place to die. It held the comfort of company, of men who had seen their futures similarly laid to rest. Like soldiers lined up for a first-day offensive, their fears of what was to come were eased by the certain knowledge that death here was never lonely, never singular. If the prospect of a stone in a graveyard could sooth the passing soul with its thin promise of meaning, why not that of a trench in which a thousand comrades will rot gently, never to be parted?

And yet something stabbed at him, denying that small comfort. It had to be other than a symptom of detachment, or apathy, or cowardice that he could no more wish for death than a life without her. That well-beaten metaphor, of life as the waiting-room for eternity, didn't convince him as it should; the departure board held no particular entry that fascinated him more or less than where he was, or had been. He disbelieved Paradise yet had no longing for oblivion either - she had stirred him, tricked him into living life for its own sake. Even gone, her toll was upon him, her gentle mockery of his fatalism teasing him still, keeping the Fischer crust from reforming entirely.

A pan clattered, and Yuri stumbled into the ward, cursing. Yuri was an amiable idiot, his competence considered adequate to administer to an inmate's needs. He spoke German but badly, and regarded his only patient as the means by which this fault might be cured. He gabbled, asked importune questions (and hardly ever waited for the answers), gave more detail of his own life than torture should have extracted and blatantly admitted his readiness to be bribed in almost any form of commodity. Someone planning an escape would have regarded the boy as pure gold.

Briefly, Yuri manoeuvred the patient into a more convenient position and launched another assault with his soaped cloth. Fischer waited until its more embarrassing phase had passed and then put the question without first circling the matter.

'Yuri, can you get details of any of the inmates here? From their files?'

'Me, General? Only shitty-arse-wiper, don't know nothing.'

'Do you know of anyone who does? I mean, who you might ask?'

'Why? You want to check boyfriend?'

'Ha. No, it's just that I was having a conversation with one of the others here, and we spoke of a man we used to know. He died last year. Two other men died that day also, and I want to know their names.'

Yuri paused in his work. 'For what good?'

'I don't have anything better to do. It wouldn't be against the rules, would it?'

'*All* is against rules, unless *is* a rule.'

'I could pay with cigarettes.'

'Don't need cigarettes. Have plenty.'

'I could give you proper German lessons, make you speak like one of us.'

'How many?'

'As many as you want. Until you're sick of them. And I'll teach you to read German. That would get you a better job than this.'

Yuri shrugged '*Sehr gut*, General. What day they die?'

'I don't know. But the first man's name was Ernst Schlange.'

'What he here for?'

'He was a Nazi.'

'You *all* Nazis.'

'He was an official, a big man in the Party.'

'Like Adolph?'

'Like a little Adolph.'

Yuri considered this briefly. 'I do it. Tell you names tomorrow, if not in punishment detail.'

'Thank you, Yuri. What time is it?'

'Nearly meridian.'

Fischer gave his stark, grubby suite another inspection. He shouldn't – couldn't - complain. In a camp in which untold numbers of decent people had died and a lot more not-quite-so decent people had then followed them, he was being treated with what counted as shameful indulgence. Still, it was the nature of man to contemplate his good fortune and wish for more.

'Lunch time, then. Is there a menu?'

'No need. It would say all the same thing. Is what Americans call you.'

'Kraut?'

'Cabbage soup! Mmm.'

35

Beckendorp was told that Zarubin was in a meeting, and after leaving a message he expected to hear nothing for hours. Before the receiver had cooled in its cradle, however, the man himself was on the line. He said as little as could convey meaning.

'Not Karlshorst. The schoolroom.'

In the previous year, Beckendorp and Otto Fischer had stood half to attention in a bombed-out classroom at the Friedrich Orphanage in Rummelsberg, waiting to be sent to hell or worse at the whim of Major Zarubin - who, presumably for his own amusement or to remove his guests' last scrap of composure, had interrogated them while seated at a child's desk, his legs thrust out ludicrously from beneath it. From Beckendorp's stock of bad-dream material, the details of that encounter stood out prominently still.

He told an *anwärter* to take Frau Gerste and her daughters down to the other ranks' canteen and keep them there. Without once releasing his grip, he marched Rudolph Gerste down to the motor-pool, where he dismissed his usual driver and had Hoeschler take the wheel of the Olympia. The pool manager came forward with the chit for his signature but reversed course after gauging the look on his face.

It was twenty minutes at most from Keibelstrasse to the orphanage, but the silence in the car stretched it. Gerste, staring at the back of Hoeschler's head, seemed far elsewhere; he was deadly calm, anaesthetized by a glimpse of his life's end. Beckendorp wanted to know more before Zarubin shot and buried him, but had no idea what to ask beyond *what the fuck did you do* and *will it bite me?*

The orphanage still functioned as such, its bomb damage confined largely to the buildings closest to the river. The schoolroom of blessed memory was almost on the water, well away from the keenest ears of children. Between them and it, a squad of Soviet soldiers had deployed in groups of four, every pair of eyes following the Olympia as it crept respectfully through them.

Absurdly, Beckendorp felt some relief when he entered the schoolroom and found it emptied of its strange, tiny furniture. Zarubin was there already, standing by the wall whose almost complete removal by British ordnance had allowed a broad, pleasant view of the river. He turned, lifted a hand and beckoned the Germans closer with his forefinger.

He was smiling, which worried at least two of his guests (they had seen something like it before - a wry, treacherous thing). Hoeschler pushed Gerste forward.

'Herr Gerste, thank you for coming. Please, sit down if you wish.'

Gerste looked around the bare room and slowly perched himself on the low course of the half-demolished wall.

'We had a conversation recently. You recall it?'

Gerste nodded. 'Yes, sir.'

'About money.'

'Deutsche Marks.'

'That's right. I was interested in acquiring some, and asked you to gather information for me. Four days later, a quantity of the same commodity was stolen – *hijacked*, I believe the Americans say – from one of their trucks. Foolishly, they had thought to make it safer by hiding it among non-secure cargo, and its sole protection was a guard. He was killed during the operation, and the driver wounded.'

Gerste licked his lips, said nothing.

'This could all be a tremendous coincidence, but I don't believe so. It's more likely that you shared information with someone else – no, please don't speak yet – who then decided to help himself while placing suspicion upon me. It's my good fortune that I hadn't yet asked permission for the scheme, so no one knew what my busy little head had been doing – other than my immediate superior, who almost had an infarction, poor man. Really, Herr Gerste, I should be upset at your lack of discretion …'

Beckendorp had seen the routine before, though not since his *OrPo* days. A few bulls at Alexanderplatz had enjoyed deploying civilized banter and fake bonhomie during their interrogations. It relaxed the victim, made the savage beatings that followed much more effective.

'… but I'm not, because you're going to make it up to me. You'll tell me all about this other fellow, or fellows, and when you've finished we'll be tremendous friends once more. I might even allow you that two-bedroomed apartment I promised.'

Gerste's eyes passed rapidly over each of the three men and then back to Zarubin. He was anxious again, the anaesthetic worn off.

'Comrade, he'll cut me to pieces. My children …'

'Of course, yes.' Zarubin frowned solicitously, patted the sitting man's shoulder. 'And you should know that I won't do anything if you refuse me. No, really.' He glanced up at the disbelieving expressions on the policemen's faces. 'I'll simply ask *UnterKommissar* Hoeschler here to drive you and your family to one of the Western Zone checkpoints and release you. And then you can all go about your business.'

'No …'

That's your choice: freedom to find the nearest hole, or an apartment in eastern Berlin with a guard on the door at all times until this business is done. If we succeed you'll be safe. If not, then at least you'll have a little time to make new arrangements, if it's only to flee to Mexico.'

A coal barge, moving up river, caught Zarubin's eye and he turned to watch it. To Beckendorp (not, self-admittedly, an expert on marine architecture) the sight was mundane to a degree, but Gerste stewed nicely in the pause. He licked his lips, looked everywhere and back again, twitched and made to half-rise several times, during all of which the Russian gave no indication that he was aware still of the man's presence. Eventually, tiring of the barge's slow progress towards central Berlin, he turned back. His eyebrows rose slightly, as if he were surprised to see Gerste.

'Well?'

'I don't know his name.'

'Then a *spitzname*, perhaps? *The Butcher*?'

Gerste swallowed, then nodded slowly.

'Tell us what you know of his business.'

'He has about twenty men working for him at Tempelhof – not all at once, but constantly. I know there are other things he does in Allied Berlin but I'm not involved in that – only the airfield.'

'You steal for him?'

'No. I identify cargoes.'

'What use is that? Surely, by the time he knows what's come in on a 'plane it's already been unloaded and distributed?'

'I identify what aircraft are carrying. There's one in particular, that brings military dispatches: its flights are notified to Tempelhof in advance, so they can be taxied to a secure area. I bribe a flight clerk to tell me when.'

Suddenly, Zarubin looked worried. 'Military dispatches? Then this is an MGB matter. Is the man …?'

'No, comrade. It's not the dispatches themselves. One of the pilots entrusted with them regularly brings in other things, and these are what interests … the man you're looking for.'

'So you – or others – steal these *things* on his behalf?'

'There's no theft involved. It's an arrangement.'

For a moment Zarubin didn't get the point. 'An arrangement? You mean American and Soviet personnel are … collaborating?'

'In some sort of trade, yes, Comrade.'

'The commodity?'

Gerste shook his head firmly. 'I don't know. I've seen small packages, but only when I've tried to.'

'Who would know?'

'The only German who might is the one who directs us, the Russian's *kapo* at Tempelhof.'

'This Butcher's definitely a Russian? Not from another race within the Union?'

'It's how he's referred to. I don't know for sure.'

'Very well. This *kapo*, then.'

'His name is Thomas. He hires and organizes the others.'

'Where can we find him? When he isn't at Tempelhof, that is.'

He hardly ever comes East, except for instructions. He has a home somewhere in Neukölln. He's …'

'What?'

'A bad man. He went across the lines during the war, to the Soviets. When they'd finished kicking out his teeth they used him as a liaison with the partisans. Then, someone decided he was a fascist after all and sent him to the camps. The story is that the Russian got him out somehow and brought him back to Berlin. Whatever the truth of it, he's loyal.'

'Unlike yourself, Herr Gerste?'

Gerste flushed. 'I have a family, and no country to speak of.'

Zarubin nodded. 'And only Capitalism or Communism to which to pledge your soul. Don't worry, I don't wish to entrap you. Speaking for myself, giving a turd for either is too much effort. Naturally, I'd prefer that you didn't quote me.'

He paused and looked at Beckendorp, who took the prompt. 'This Russian. Has he been known to disappear people?'

'Of course. They usually turn up again, though, in several places. It wouldn't be much of a lesson if his other employees didn't know what had happened to them.'

Beckendorp offered a cigarette. 'What about disappearing people short of killing them?'

Gerste looked blankly at the policeman. 'Why would anyone do that?'

'Never mind. It doesn't matter. You mentioned one aircraft in particular - of those bringing dispatches?'

'Donna.'

'Donna?'

'Americans paint their girlfriends' names on them. It's juvenile, but it make it easier to know when he's coming into Berlin.'

'It's always the same pilot?'

'I don't know. I assume so.'

Zarubin took Beckendorp's arm and led him to the opposite side of the schoolroom, keeping his back to Gerste and Hoeschler. 'What do you care about the pilot?'

'I don't, but you might. How else are you going to flush out this Russian, if you have no idea where to look or who's protecting him?'

'Ah, that's clever. Probably impossible to arrange, but …'

'I wasn't thinking of abducting him, just interrupting the supply line. And at the only point we can see.'

36

UnterKommissar Müller was queuing at a fish stall just three streets from his home when overtime intruded unexpectedly. Half-listening to the plaintive arguments ahead of him, he had almost resigned himself to the probability that the last of whatever had found its way from the sea's shore to Berlin that day had sold out when *Anwärter* Kalbfleisch tapped his shoulder and made the matter moot.

They were at least four kilometres from Keibelstrasse, so either Kalbfleisch had followed him from the station or managed to raid personnel records for his immediate superior's *heimat* and shopping habits. Usually, he was as imperturbable as a barnacle, but this evening he looked worried.

'Can we speak?'

'I'm late for supper. What is it?'

'Over here.'

Across the street from the fish stall a bombed-out ladies' wear shop retained its doorway, the glassless side-display hosting still a poster advertising the dreary *dirndl* mode that the Führer had foisted upon a generation of German housewives. The two men stepped into it and also a pungent aroma of stale piss, hinting at a recent change of use.

Kalbfleisch gave the street his habitual one-two. 'We haven't gone far with the Kaulsdorf killings.'

'We haven't gone *anywhere*. We've speculated, worn out the file and come up with *it's probably the Russians,* which we knew already. Couldn't we have discussed this at the station?'

'No. Yes, but …'

'Come on, Kalbfleisch, I'm hungry. What is it?'

'I've been thinking about what we could do next.'

'Next? We haven't done anything against which to set *next*.'

The older man took a deep breath. 'I mean, what we might do in lieu of fuck all. Sorry, Comrade.'

'No, that's a fair way to put it. What did you decide?'

'To speak to someone in K-5.'

'Eh?'

'Do you remember Schantzi Weber?'

'The greasy little informer?'

'Yeah. We joined *VolksPolizei* on the same day, so we used to talk a lot. After he switched into K-5 that stopped, but I know he's not popular over there - even the professionals don't like fellows who betray their own, do they? So, I thought a word with Schantzi might not go too far.'

'And?'

'Actually, he must be lonely, because he gabbled. He told me that K-5 know all about Kaulsdorf, which is strange if it was just a straightforward black marketeers' execution. Someone took the trouble to mention it and then warn them off it, and they don't know who someone is.'

'What does that mean?'

'That it didn't come from Direktor Jamin's office, which is the usual conduit when the Ivans don't want Germans looking at their dirty business.'

'They must have *some* idea who first mentioned it.'

'No, they don't. And if you think about it, that's what's significant.'

Müller opened his mouth, said nothing. He had come to respect Kalbfleisch's little intuitions. They were infrequent but came with sharp edges, and he caught one of them now.

'Someone *in* K-5 started it.'

'That's what I think. How difficult is to say 'I've heard', or 'the word is …'? No-one's going to remember who first said it except the one who did. Or the two. Or three.'

'Shit.'

'Are you surprised? No Germans are closer to the Ivans than K-5, not even Stalin's *kozi* lapdogs in the Senate. You can't work with cholera and not cough.'

'So this may be about more than just competition in the black market. At least Beckendorp can't refuse to take it from us when we tell him.'

Kalbfleisch nodded. 'He'll want to drop it like a warm turd. But …'

'I hate that word.'

'If Schantzi's frightened about what it all means, shouldn't we be?'

'Because we've been investigating it?'

'That, and the fact that, if half of K-5 are bent, the same might be true of us.'

Müller shook his head firmly. 'My own arse is worry enough for me. I'm not going to give a proverbial for the rest of the service. We can't alter what we can't alter – the only thing we can try to do is to signal to certain parties that we've discovered nothing about the Kaulsdorf business.'

'Which parties?'

Müller waved a hand helplessly. 'I don't know.'

The fish stall queue had dispersed, and any chance of a decent supper that evening had vanished. Frau Anna Müller was a good cook but even she needed ingredients to work a magic other than sausage-less potato soup (their near-standard diet). Fortunately, her husband's appetite had been entirely crushed by his sincere fear for the future's pitfalls. He sighed.

'We should get rid of it now, tonight.'

'Tomorrow. The Inspector's gone out. Or home.'

'Tomorrow, then. We'll tell him about K-5, and at every opportunity we'll repeat it until he tells us never mind, forget it. Then, we keep quiet. If anyone asks, we had a brief look at the files, decided it was official Soviet business and dropped it. Who could say differently?'

Kalbfleisch nodded. 'We were only tidying an open case by passing it back. No one's going to care about that.'

Both men relaxed slightly, for once comforted by their insignificance part in whatever mechanism moved time, tides and all other things. Müller was sufficiently distracted to be impulsive, and invited his junior to supper, an honour that the childless widower promptly accepted. Anna would give him a sideways look for it, but she was far too polite to make a fuss about the lack of notice – which, coincidentally, was what both men had of their swift, efficient and violent transfer into the back of a Red Army Studebaker less than two minutes later.

37

If Fischer's back had been unusually sensitive – it wasn't, except around the wound itself – he might have felt the tiny pricks of glances that followed him whenever he shifted from his bunk to the latrine, or allotments, or wherever else the rich and varied attractions of MVD Special Camp no 1 enticed him. Having survived the only non-Soviet gunshot wound to be inflicted here since the good old days (as many of the inmates would regard them) he was, in a sense, a celebrity. Siegfried had welcomed him home from the medical block with the gratifying news that betting had already begun on the next attempt - on whether poison, staves or a skilfully thrust shift might be the means of seeing him off the premises.

When he asked the odds on a howitzer shell, Siegfried pulled a face. 'Too long to be paid out, if it happens. But then, you'd hardly be in the mood to collect, would you?'

It was more gratifying that Joachim Dein had already put out the very public word that if someone knew who had pulled the trigger they could speak and be protected. Fischer didn't think *someone* would ever be so stupid as to step forward, but with Colonel Vaisman also spitting blood about the business the would-be assassins would need bowels of iron to try anything soon.

His new audience regarded him in different ways. Some – the gamblers – enjoyed the distraction he provided from cockroach-racing. A few considered him an unwitting hero, a man who had given the finger (if while face down in the dirt) to the torch-bearers of National Socialism. His hut-mates – Siegfried excepted – deeply resented the fact that he had survived and put them in the line of any future fire. So, it was hard to know whether to feel relieved, flattered or contrite that he was breathing still.

Yuri had kept his word and provided a piece of paper. The Russian's attempt at Latin script was ugly but the two names were legible - Fischer didn't recognize either, as he had expected, but showed them to Siegfried, who frowned, squinted, shrugged and said he would do what he could (though he didn't know why or of what use it could possibly be). He asked how urgent it was, and all Fischer could think to say was 'that depends on how soon I'm killed', which the other man took badly. It was what made Siegfried both endearing and useful - he was sentimental, inoffensive and therefore popular among the inmates, who saw no reason not to share what they knew with him.

The shoulder wound, occupying as it did previously mutilated flesh which couldn't adequately support the new damage, murdered sleep and made his waking hours a struggle to find distraction. He prepared a number of elementary German language lessons for Yuri, but that took up only half a day. When he returned the poetry book to Dein he asked about work on any one of the numerous inmates' committees and was depressed to hear how long the current waiting-list stood. He considered spoiling a life-long ignorance of physics by attending one of the domestic engineering classes that he had suggested to Dein, but fear of the truly unknown deterred him. Finally, he decided to plan for his likeliest future by learning Russian from Yuri even as he taught the boy German, a transaction most suited to the modern world. This excellent plan was spoiled, however, when Yuri failed to send word that he was ready to finesse his crude skills. Feeling that nothing could be lost (nor rule broken) by admitting to his promise he sought out one of the more approachable guards and asked if he might send a message to the boy. The guard laughed and told him that the postal service in Kirghizia was not entirely reliable. He wouldn't flesh out this information with more, but offered the oblique observation that all medical supplies were carefully stock-taken, and that it took a proper fool not to realise it.

So, deprived of any diversion, Fischer placed his mind in that state of suspension he had perfected in a Potsdam burns ward and awaited information. In the meantime, Siegfried reported frequently on his lack of progress but promised to keep trying. He had been told to be circumspect, raising the matter of the murders in only the most casual, roundabout manner, and this puzzled him, because gossip was the only freely-traded commodity in Sachsenhausen.

'Why don't you just put the word around that you're interested?'

'Because I don't want one man to know about it.'

'The Ghost himself?'

'You'd make good police, Siegfried.'

'Don't be sarcastic. Just speak to Joachim, then. He knows everything.'

'He took the trouble to keep the business from the Ivans. I think he wants it to lie where it is.'

'I don't know why. He's as close to Law as we have in this camp.'

'The murders stopped - I think that's all he really cared about. When a man knows that he's never going to leave a place he becomes pragmatic about things.'

'It isn't as though he wants to. Leave, I mean'

'No. He told me he has no family.'

'Well, he has, technically, but …'

'He does?'

'A wife, as mad as a poked bear. He looked after her for as long as any asylum would have been a death sentence, but when the Reich fell he had her committed. He told me that he's no loss to her as she doesn't recognize him. There was a son, too, but he was a different sort of lunatic. Joachim hardly speaks about him, said he was a fool who went off to war before he had to. He died, a long time ago.'

'That must be hard.'

'Joachim carries a lot, poor man.'

The mundane routine of camp life was disturbed later that week when the Ministry of Internal Affairs decided to surprise the Commandant with an inspection of the facilities. An extravagantly pointless exercise, it consumed almost a full day and proceeded with all the unpredictability of a Latin Mass. The inmates were paraded and made to stand for almost two hours in uncomfortable heat while the perimeters, huts, shower blocks, latrines and medical facilities were inspected by a brigade of Ministry officials. Finally, a number of them circulated among the inmates' ranks, asking individuals whether they had any complaints. This was so blatantly an invitation to commit suicide that none of those approached thought to avail themselves of the offer. The inspectors went away with uniformly polite expressions of satisfaction recorded in their notebooks, as if hotel guests had been canvassed on the quality of their sea-views.

Sweltering in his overcoat that day, Fischer didn't notice Siegfried's attempts to catch his eye from further down the line. When finally the whistle blew almost fifty thousand men dispersed gratefully, sank to the ground to enjoy a cigarette or anxiously sought out someone who might know whether the meal that should have been distributed hours earlier that day was still a possibility. Fischer was on his way to the latrines to discharge an urgent matter of his own brewing when his hut-mate caught up with him.

'Police.'

'What?'

Josef Kerner and Eberhard Spitz, the Ghost's first two victims. They were both police.'

'Gestapo?'

'No, just *SchutzPolizei*. Kerner was a *haupwachtmeister*, Spitz a *rottmeister*. But …' waiting for the prompt, Siegfried grinned like a well-fed pike.

'What?'

'Kerner was Spitz's immediate superior. They both worked in Wismar.'

'They weren't seconded to the East?' Many conscripted police units had tainted their records in the Soviet Union after *Barbarossa*, and it wouldn't have taken much experience in an *einzatskommando* to have earned a berth at Sachsenhausen.

'Apparently not. They seemed to have served at home for the duration of the war.'

'And yet they were sent here. What did they do in pretty little Wismar to deserve it?'

'Is it? Pretty? I never went there.'

'I had an uncle there, so it was a second home, another place by the sea. It's an old Hanse town, very lovely. At least, it was.'

'Well, something happened there, for these two gentlemen to end up here.'

'I think I have the start of an idea about that.'

'You do? How?'

'It's a matter of the way things are put. How *you* put them, in fact.'

38

Potesky waited until the last of the cargo had been stripped out and the maintenance truck had sidled up. From this point, none of Tempelhof's Krauts would be allowed near *Donna* until he returned, and then only if he was to carry cargo – usually of the human variety - out of the city. This was very necessary, because one of the said Krauts, among the dozen others that had swarmed into her hold to extract the two-and-a-half tons of flour he had flown in from Frankfurt, had already made a deposit in the small, secret fuselage compartment just forward of the medical kit rack. The Bank of Donna welcomed visitors, but not out of business hours.

Today, he had brought dispatches for Camp Andrews, which meant he was going to be in Berlin for at least three hours. His record was twelve, and that visit had given him sweat patches that a laundromat couldn't remove. He was fond of Berlin the way a guy could be about a pet porcupine – it was great to play checkers with, but cuddling was definitely a bad idea.

Invariably, he flew with just a co-pilot as crew, who also acted as navigator and radio operator. Some pilots felt safer with the standard complement, but Potesky insisted upon the fewest potential witnesses he'd be allowed to take-off with (naturally, he didn't put it that way). He also tried to ensure that his co-pilots were strangers, or at best occasional acquaintances. This wasn't difficult; most of them had been brought back to Europe hurriedly once the siege started, and there wasn't one of them who wasn't longing to get home as soon as possible. Today's company was Chester – who, apparently, was from Duluth, Minnesota, had a wife (Mary) and two boys (Chester junior and Billy), and planned to go into commercial aviation just as soon as his feet touched down on US soil once more.

Potesky had discovered all of this without once expressing an interest or offering anything in return other than *nice, sweet* and *really?* However, once in Berlin, Chester laid claim to being a just-about perfect co-pilot by heading into the terminal building for some john-time and a coffee even before Donna's props had stilled.

Chester had seemed pleased when Potesky told him about the dispatches. It meant that he would have time to grab a pastry and put his head down for a couple of hours, and no-one on the Berlin run these days passed up the chance of extra sleep. For these little pleasures he passed up the chance of meeting Private Mullaney, who, unlike *Donna*'s string of co-pilots, was very well known to Potesky. Mullaney was his jeep driver, dispatches bodyguard and generally the guy to go to for things and information. More importantly, Mullaney was bought: made blind and mute by a regular stipend that allowed him to plan for a better future than Uncle Sam had in mind.

In the terminal building Potesky reported to the first of two Provost Marshals he'd see that day, though this one was a temporary appointee, head of security at what was, temporarily, Europe's busiest airfield. Once he had his pass he walked out on to the Platz der Luftbrücke, where the jeep was waiting. Mullaney offered his usual nod, said nothing and started the engine the moment his passenger's rear touched the seat next to him. He didn't glance at either of the two attaché cases.

The route was always the same, roadworks and rubble clearances allowing. It was the quickest route to Camp Andrews, save for one insignificant diversion that added no suspicious amount of time to their schedule. This was a momentary halt at a residential address in Bogenstrasse, Lichterfelde, where a retired accountant named Egon Hoffer (Potesky knew this only because the name was on the mailbox) could be relied upon to take possession of an attaché case without a word, nod or any other indication that the other party to the transaction occupied space on the same firmament as himself. For his part, Mullaney always used these moments to scan the skies for birds, the more distant the better.

Nothing about the Bogenstrasse stop was unusual today; Herr Hoffer opened his door, took the item and went back inside without even meeting Potesky's eye, and the most that either man could have said of the encounter was that the American hadn't bothered to polish his boots and the German was wearing threadbare slippers that didn't match. Four minutes later, the jeep was at the main gate of Camp Andrews, where a guard, recognizing Potesky, waved it through.

They departed the camp only minutes later. General Keyes was in a meeting, so Potesky had put the dispatches in the hands of his adjutant, made some weak joke about golf courses and pointed himself at the exit. Mullaney was sat in his jeep still, but some sleight of hand or coin had put two coffees there with him. They drank them on the way back to Tempelhof, taking their time, enjoying the late summer sun on their heads without once commenting upon it.

Donna was cleared for take-off at 4.32pm. Even before she reached the end of the strip, co-pilot Chester had offered his opinion on Berlin, Krauts in general and what the fuck Stalin thought he was doing right now, and Potesky had heard precisely nothing. He was thinking of his retirement fund, presently growing like a corn-fed Minnesotan calf in the vaults of Wegelin & Co. a small, discreet bank in the Swiss town of Sankt Gallen. There weren't many men who could say that they'd made themselves dollar millionaires from the fighting end of a war, but he was one of them. Compared to that achievement, he valued his collection of medals pretty much as he did what departed the calf's ass.

The air corridor out of Berlin from Tempelhof took *Donna* briefly over Neukölln as she climbed. Had either Potesky or his voluble co-pilot looked down at that moment they might have noticed an impeccably maintained 'Autobahn' Adler moving rapidly north-east along Wildenbruchstrasse into Treptow and the Soviet sector. The vehicle was the adopted child of the senior motor mechanic at Keibelstrasse Police Praesidium, a museum piece that he had lovingly kept from bruising service until that very morning, when Inspector Kurt Beckendorp (a fearsome man, much avoided by motor pool staff) had asked which of his vehicles was the fastest. Foolishly imagining this to be a car-lover's curiosity, he had proudly dragged the tarpaulin from his one true love and suffered bereavement without even the consolation of a *thank you*.

The Adler had caused a sensation at its launch at the 1937 Berlin Show, and any lover of pre-war German automobiles would have recognized it immediately. Americans, however, have always esteemed their own vehicles over those of other nations, and earlier that afternoon Private Mullaney hadn't spared more than a single, unknowing glance for the strange, aerodynamic shape that, at a discreet distance, had followed his jeep from Tempelhof to Bogenstrasse, Lichterfelde.

39

Müller couldn't recall ever having been punched in the face. As a child he had come off his bicycle a number of times, but the worst of that had been shock and humiliation. This was both of those things, and shockingly painful too. If it had ever happened before, he was certain the memory wouldn't have faded.

Kalbfleisch was somewhere else. When the hood came off Müller was already alone in this room, this cell, strapped to a chair without his tunic and with only the most casual grip upon his bowels. He lost that too when the first punch landed.

Being a novice it was hard for him to judge, but he was beginning to suspect that his assailant was a professional. He had been punched three times now, with a lengthy pause after each blow – perhaps two or three minutes – to allow the pain to work through, fade and give a man a little time to think about the next one. What hadn't been inflicted so far was a question. He was beginning to look forward to the question, if it meant fewer punches or more time between them.

A fourth landed, as economically delivered as the others. Müller was certain by now that his nose was broken, because his mouth was doing all the work on the oxygen supply front. The pain was greater this time, much greater, and he cried out.

He wanted to look his tormentor in the eyes, to let him know that he was not going to cause the least trouble, but the rag tied over his own made that difficult. He didn't want to beg, but he knew that he could take very little more of this sort of damage. He was sucking in air, trying to think of the least craven way to put it, when the question came.

'Who did it, in Kaulsdorf?'

'The Russians did it.' His voice was a stranger's in its own head - flat, nasal, keening.

'Which Russians?'

'MVD, MGB, Regular Red Army, SMERSH, we don't know. It's not our business to know.'

'But a Russian execution comes from behind.'

Müller coughed and spat what tasted like blood. 'Does it? It happened in Kaulsdorf, in the middle of the night, in rain. I doubt that anyone from the Ministry of Headshots was there to see it done properly. We just wrote *Russians* and passed it to our Boss.'

'When?'

'Two days ago.'

'What's he doing about it?'

'Nothing. Who would want him to? Not Markgraf, not K-5, and definitely not Karlshorst. Like I said, it's not our business. There's a large cupboard in his office with a notice, Do Not Disturb, taped to it. The file went in there.'

'Who else has been interested in this?'

'No-one. The rest of Keibelstrasse's dealing with the demonstrations or trying to catch a police killer. It was just me and Kalbfleisch.'

'Why you?'

As much as it aided his case, Müller hated to give him the truth. 'Because our chief didn't want it solved, probably.'

It went quiet for a while. The prisoner hoped desperately that the man with the iron fists was thinking things through – the necessities, the consequences, the inconvenience of having to hide bodies so well they couldn't ever be found.

He heard a throat clearing. 'I wonder how talkative you are.'

'I'm not. I have a wife and two children, and no way to stop you doing again what you did today.'

'You look messed up. What happened to your face?'

'I fell over my little girl's doggy-on-wheels, right down the stairs. It was fucking clumsy.'

The second silence was even more unbearable. That was it - he'd as good as begged for his life and the jury was now considering its verdict. How many times during the war had he sat and watched the process in court, his defence advocate's carefully neutral expression masking what he knew was coming next? He had despised himself for the part he'd played in a sick pantomime, but now he would gladly donate his remaining teeth to be back there, squeezing the shoulder of one of any number of soon-to-be-condemned clients, safely insulated from the world as it had been.

A door opened and closed again. He strained his ears and heard nothing more. His nose felt as if it had expanded to fill his face, and he wondered just how *messed up* he'd become. For a moment he feared his wife's reaction to the sight, then realised how wildly optimistic he was being even to think it. She was far more likely to be worried about the compact dimensions of her police widow's pension.

The door re-opened, and what sounded like a sack of dismembered pork fell into the room. He held his breath until the throbbing became unbearable and then exhaled, groaning. He was answered from the floor by similar.

'Kalbfleisch?'

There was a grunt, then gasping, more volume than depth to it. The sack of pork moved, shifted itself from the floor to about the height of the reconstructed animal.

'Jesus!'

Müller assumed this to signify shock at the view, which meant that Kalbfleisch had him at a disadvantage.

'Are you restrained?'

'Only by what they did to my guts. Here ...'

Müller felt hands on the side of his head, and a moment later weak light made him squint. The view was entirely of his subordinate's over-generous midriff, for which he was not at all ungrateful. This passed out of view, and the same hands began to work on the cord that had numbed his own. He was looking at a door now, a mundane, domestic item, slightly ajar. The wall that surrounded it had once held a *fleur de lys* motif, but this had mostly disappeared. It was – had been - a sitting room, not the dungeon he'd feared. The bare concrete floor, the harsh acoustic it created, had worked perfectly on his mind. Even wearing the blindfold he'd been able to see the hole to which all other points fell perfectly clearly.

Kalbfleisch's face was unmarked but pasty, and his breathing was laboured. He held his gut as if someone had opened it with a fish-knife, and nodded at Müller.

'It looks like the train won the fight.'

'Is it bad?'

'Your nose is pointing the wrong way.'

'That's what I thought.' Müller took a deep breath and tried to stand. His legs shook, but he managed not to fall back into the chair. 'Did you see who did it?'

'No. He freed my wrists and walked out. I kept the thing over my eyes until I was sure he was gone. Even if I'd seen him I wouldn't have, if you get my meaning.'

'Gruff voice, a slight lisp?'

'That was him.'

'Definitely German. I assume you told him we knew nothing?'

'Less than that, even. I just said it was obviously the Reds, and not our business.'

'So did I. I think he believed it.'

Kalbfleisch had opened his tunic and was inspecting his belly. Parts of it were already the colour of the liver it hosted. 'Personally, I don't intend to think any more about it one way or the other. Do we have to tell Beckendorp?'

'No. There isn't anything he can do anything about it.'

'Here.' Kalbfleisch held out a surprisingly clean handkerchief. 'There's blood around your mouth, too.'

'Find a window. Try to make out where we are.'

Müller dabbed tenderly at his face, not wanting to know just how damaged the nose was. There had been at least four men and probably more involved in their abduction – a swift, efficient business, putting them both face down in the back of a truck before the brain could begin to process information. He couldn't recall seeing a face clearly, hearing a voice other than his own, noticing anything beyond his feet disappearing as they were dragged neatly from beneath him. It had all been very professional, and the gruff, lisping German voice was telling him one thing, a thing he wanted very much not to hear.

'I reckon they were K-5.'

'Don't. Reckon, I mean.'

'Sorry. I can see the German Dome to the west and north. I think we're somewhere in Friedrichshain.'

'Good. We can walk back to Keibelstrasse. I need a shower.'

'You need a doctor, too. I wonder why we're alive?'

'We're police - killing us might have stirred things a little too much to be convenient. How do you feel, by the way?'

The older man grimaced. 'I'll tell you when I've had a shit and seen what colour comes out. But tell the doctor to wait around, just in case.'

40

'Why are we doing this here?'

Colonel Shpak spoke to Zarubin in his native tongue, though several Germans stood around them. It was impolite, and Shpak was a courteous man usually, but being somewhat out of his natural habitat - an area encompassing Karlshorst, Wünsdorf and the road between these two oases of Soviet territory - his carapace had hardened defensively.

Zarubin, whose own courtesy was deployed only when it worked for him, answered in kind.

'Because, Comrade Colonel, we don't know which eyes and ears at Karlshorst can be trusted with this business, do we?'

Beckendorp watched the exchange. He understood hardly any Russian, but he could smell anxiety, even from the usually-frigid Major Zarubin. He fully shared it. They had all grabbed a tail and pulled it hard before knowing what species squatted in the bush.

As if shrugging off this uncomfortable truth they turned as one to the object of their meeting. A slightly-built, elderly gentleman sat on the room's only stand-chair. He was wearing house-clothes – sleeveless sweater over a collarless shirt, comfortable moleskin trousers, an odd pair of slippers – and an air of calm puzzlement. From the thickness of the lenses in his wire-framed spectacles one might have deduced that he was almost clinically blind, though his emaciated body hinted that the condition might not be endured for too much longer. He coughed occasionally, a quiet but hollow sound, as if the frame supported fewer organs than the norm.

Zarubin turned to Beckendorp. 'This is fine work, Inspector. Did you use your own men?'

'Hoeschler, yes. I also asked Direktor Jamin to lend me two discreet men with experience of this sort of thing.'

'You went to K-5? Was that prudent?'

'I don't know. They do this sort of thing all the time, we don't. But the way Jamin's shitting himself at the moment about who does and doesn't work for him, I expect he tried hard to find the right fellows. Who's going to do this?'

They glanced at the object again. Zarubin shrugged. 'Keibelstrasse's your ground. Please.'

'Right. It's Herr Hoffer, isn't it?'

The elderly man nodded, then cleared his throat. 'Yes, sir.'

'You live in ...' Beckendorp glanced down at his notes; '... Lichterfelde?'

'Bogenstrasse 43. Since April 1922.'

'And you receive packages from American airmen.'

'From one, yes.'

'His name?'

'I don't know. I never asked.'

'And you pass on these packages to ... who?'

'I don't know. I receive instructions where to take them. It's always somewhere different.'

'But you must meet someone.'

Hoffer shook his head. 'I place them in lockers, wherever I'm told. I get about an hour's warning, by means of an envelope. It comes with a key, and that day's locker number and station.'

'S-bahn station?'

'Yes. Haven't I done it correctly?'

'What do you mean?'

Hoffer looked from Beckendorp to Zarubin, Hoeschler and Shpak in turn. 'My work. Hasn't it been satisfactory?'

Before Beckendorp could speak again, Zarubin touched his arm and addressed the prisoner directly. 'It's been … correct. Who hired you, originally?'

'*Hired?* I'm not paid. I do this for the cause.'

'Which cause?'

Hoffer looked at Zarubin as though he were a dolt. 'International Socialism. I fought for it on the streets, in 1919. Then I endured the Hitlerites, and now the Americans. But I stayed loyal, all these years.'

'Of course you did. No-one doubts that.'

Zarubin glanced at Beckendorp, who read it precisely: *A principled man. Shit.*

Shpak coughed apologetically. 'Who was your original contact, when the liberation came?'

Hoffer turned to him. 'I wasn't given a name. But he was NKGB, for sure.'

'And you were asked to take these packages?'

'Not at the time, no. When the Allies occupied western Berlin I wanted to move east, but was told to stay and await instructions. For months I heard nothing, then early in 1946 another man came to my house to explain what was required.'

'Describe him.'

'He was German - in his 40s, I would say. Nothing about him was extraordinary.'

'Did you meet him subsequently?'

'Never. From that time to this, I've met no-one except the American.'

'Does he ever collect items – anything at all - from you?'

'No, that isn't my job. It's done elsewhere.'

Zarubin gestured Beckendorp to the room's further corner, where Shpak and Hoeschler joined them. He waited until the big German's body was between himself and the prisoner, then whispered.

'This is no good. Clearly, he knows exactly as much as he's meant to.'

Hoeschler grunted. 'Do you want me to frighten him a little? It might …'

'I heard that,' said Hoffer. 'I'm cooperating, aren't I?'

Beckendorp rubbed his face. 'Fuck. We aren't going to get anywhere this way.' He went back to where Hoffer was sitting patiently.

'You have no idea who you work for?'

'I assume MGB.'

You're paid nothing? Nothing at all?'

The old man shrugged. 'The American brings me something occasionally – chocolate, or cigarettes, though I don't ask for anything. I think he feels there should be a transaction of some sort - it's how Americans are, isn't it? Anyway, I don't speak English and he doesn't attempt German, so we aren't close.'

The four men regarded their prize. He was the only accessible connection to a problem – possibly all their problems – and of precisely no use whatsoever. He was obviously, distressingly, telling them the truth as he understood it.

'Rolf?' Beckendorp was too depressed to remember to act his rank.

Hoeschler returned from some far point he was contemplating. 'Yes, Comrade Inspector?'

'Would you drive this gentleman to the demarcation line, please? And give him some money for a bus back to Lichterfelde?'

'Right.'

'Wait.' Zarubin stepped forward to offer Hoffer a cigarette.

'No, thank you. I gave up in the trenches.'

'Do you know why we brought you here, Herr Hoffer?'

'I assume it's to make sure that things are still in order.'

'Yes, that's right. Of course, we'd rather you didn't mention it to anyone.'

'I don't *know* anyone, Comrade.'

'And if anything about the present arrangement changes, you'll be sure to come back and let us know? Or at least send a message, to Karlshorst?'

'Of course. I try to do what's correct, always.'

When Hoeschler had ushered him out of the room Shpak scratched his Roman nose lugubriously (Zarubin told himself that a scratch was just that, but his boss could inject a measure of gloom into the merest action). He sighed and nodded slightly to Beckendorp.

'Well, it was an admirable effort. I doubt that anyone could have extracted a man more cleanly.'

Beckendorp returned the sigh. 'For all the good it did. How the hell else are we going to find this Butcher fellow? Put an advertisement in *Red Star*?'

Zarubin stared at his boots. 'Hoeschler took photographs of the contents of today's package, yes?'

'Once Hoffer was in the car, yes. He says it was nothing but papers. He doesn't speak English, but he thinks that they're technical documents of some sort. Which means …'

'That our Butcher may at least be partly doing the State's work, in which case our problem has become a *problem*. Get the film developed quickly, will you? I daren't take it back to Karlshorst.'

Shpak groaned. 'What can we do now?'

Zarubin shrugged. 'Take up Marshal Sokolovsky's offer of MVD support and then stomp around Wünsdorf camp, interrogating any number of Red Army personnel until something shakes itself out of the tree. Of course, there isn't a better way of warning the Butcher of who and what's coming.'

'Otherwise?'

'Manufacture evidence to suggest that we were wrong - that it was an American or *wessie* gang that stole the Deutsche Marks?'

Shpak half-raised his arms and let them drop. 'So we have a fist up our fundaments.'

Zarubin nodded, and returned his attention to his boots. There was a further option, one that he had discarded initially but had since been quietly shining its buttons as others fell into the mud. He fully agreed with Beckendorp's assessment - that the mechanics and execution of the currency robbery, and the efficiency of Otto Fischer's abduction, suggested that the same party was involved in both; a party who, for whatever reason, didn't need to consider consequences.

There was no obvious path to finding – even knowing – this party, this *Butcher*. He was too clever, or too connected, or both. Anything less than a major manhunt with the full authority of the Central Committee wasn't likely to bring him to book; in fact, anything less would be in the nature of attempting to find a mine by stamping on the ground, and Zarubin was very sensitive to the fact that it would be his foot doing the stamping. The only alternative he could see was to encourage the mine to pop up and reveal itself. There might be a few or many ways to do this, but lacking any knowledge of the man there was just a single obvious point at which pressure might be applied. It was a matter of persuasion: of convincing a mysterious, shy and very powerful person that he had made a mistake, one that needed to be rectified immediately.

Clearly, a goat was required – one that couldn't be warned about being tied to the post. Nor did Zarubin, for all his exalted authority, consider sharing his thoughts with Beckendorp (he had no intention of testing whether his MGB rank and nationality would prevent his being thrashed severely). Shpak – well, leaving him in the dark would be a pleasure, for the entertainment that his ongoing aneurism afforded. All the plan required was the understanding and integrity of just one man – a man with whom Zarubin wasn't presently acquainted. Really, it could hardly fail.

41

Fischer had been trusted with a piece of chalk, which he was using as economically as possible. His audience – eleven inmates, including Siegfried – were frowning diligently at the once-black but now much-faded board, picking out the detail amid the many scratches and gouges. He was attempting to reveal to them the innermost secrets of the gramophone player. Absent a physical example of the species, this required a degree of imagination on both sides to convey adequately. His pupils had been told to ask questions if he said anything they couldn't understand, an offer that was being taken up prodigally. No one seemed to mind; it wasn't as if time pressed upon their day's other businesses.

A number of tutorials were underway in the Humboldt, as Hut 19 had come to be known. In its now-traditional corner, the Poetry Society was turning its critical attention to Dante Alighieri, courtesy of a former schoolteacher (and, latterly, Gestapo *kriminalassistent*) who had committed *The Divine Comedy* to memory some decades earlier. An embryonic woodworking group, trusted finally with tools, had made a start on the principles and practicalities of the mortice and tenon beneath one window's excellent light. Most provocatively, the camp's choral group (some referred to it as an assault battalion) was laying into the opening verses of the *Refugee Cantata*, making all other enlightenment in the enclosed space an intermittent process. The only tranquil part of the hut was that occupied by Sachsenhausen's three disciples of Jainism (one of whom had been infected during a pre-war consular posting to Delhi), whose proscriptions against violence and promotion of a vegetarian diet - the latter prevalent within the camp but much resented - was attracting no more interest now than it had during the previous Regime.

Fischer was explaining how a musical signal was extracted by the needle when the hut's door opened and three soldiers stepped in. They surveyed the room briefly and then closed upon and surrounded the choral group's only bass-baritone. He struggled briefly in their grasp but relaxed when a pistol butt found his head, allowing him to be lifted clear of the floor. Meanwhile, his fellow singers waited quietly, directing their attention to a number of points in the room not occupied either by him or the Russians. Within moments it was over – an efficient extraction, inconveniencing only a single inmate and those followers of Protestant church music who favoured the lowest sonorities.

Gramophones and their bowels had departed Fischer's attention by now. His audience, more used to this sort of intervention, waited politely, a few with knowing expressions on their faces. Siegfried tried to mouth a reminder of what was being discussed prior to the interruption but their tutor was staring at the door still, so he got out of his seat and tapped a shoulder.

'Probably a suspect', he said quietly.

Fischer turned. 'Suspected of what?'

'Gun ownership.'

'Oh.' It was ridiculous, but the possibility that the would-be assassin was culturally accomplished flattered Fischer's ego slightly. 'Who is he?'

'He *was* police. Apparently he served too enthusiastically in an *einzatsgruppe* unit in Ukraine and hasn't regretted it since. His name is Udo something.'

Baroque cantatas and execution trenches - another dislocation better not considered too closely. Fischer glanced at the reduced complement of singers. 'Are they all like that?'

'I don't think so. Two or three of them hang around together, sometimes close to the Nazis, sometimes not. It's like they don't know what they want to be recalled for, just following orders or enjoying themselves tremendously.'

One of the group noticed Siegfried's gaze and gave him a nod.

'A friend?'

'Herbert? He's alright. Back when I first arrived he told some of his mates to leave me alone because I was SS.'

'You?'

Siegfried laughed. 'It took them a while to get it. SS - Siegfried Stolz. By the time they did, no one cared to bother me anymore. He's the one who identified the Ghost's first two victims.'

'Would he talk to me?'

'Why? You know what he knows.'

'I'd like to know what he doesn't think he knows.'

'Is that what former *kriminalkommissars* do?'

By now, all but two of Fischer's tutorial group had given up and wandered away. He shrugged at the residue, who took it philosophically and went to watch the woodworkers.

'I can't recall, it was too long ago. Is Herbert from Wismar also?'

'I have no idea. You can ask him. It may *break the ice*, as the British say.'

'Do they? How very glacial. Is he one of our Nazis?'

'It's hard to tell. I don't recall him ever saying good things about Adolph or bad about Jews, gypsies or *florenzers*. He was sent here for 'anti-Soviet agitation', which covers just about everything, including parting one's hair on the wrong side.'

'So he'll hold no grudge? About the beatings?'

Siegfried shrugged. 'You can ask him that, too.'

Twenty minutes later, when the guards came to break up that day's tutorials, Fischer dawdled for a while outside the hut. Siegfried had departed just behind Herbert, and the pair soon returned. The other man seemed slightly puzzled but not wary; he nodded at Fischer and accepted a cigarette butt. His upper lip was a mess, probably the result of a bullet passing through, and the glimpse of chest in the *v* of his opened shirt hinted at burns. It was no surprise that he wasn't disturbed by the face he regarded closely.

'SS says you want a word.'

Fischer nodded. 'He told me that you gave him the story on the two former Wismar policemen murdered here last year.'

'Josef and Eberhard? I knew them, yeah.'

'Just from here, at Sachsenhausen? Or before?'

'Before, but for a few days only. We were held together by the Ivans, at Anklam, then brought here.'

'Anklam? That's my part of the world.'

'I come from there, but Josef and Eberhard were passing through, fleeing east from the British advance. If they'd stayed in Wismar they would have been handed over eventually to the Red Army anyway, along with the town. As it was, they ran right into the problem.'

'Why were they worried about the British?'

'They were twitchy about everyone.'

'What had they done?'

Herbert pulled a face. 'They were good police, if you see what I mean. By the *book*.'

'By the NSDAP book?'

'Yeah. Never looked the other way, didn't forget loose talk, always discharged their duties with proper rigour and ended up not understanding why they weren't Wismar's most popular citizens. It wasn't the Brits that made them run. It was what their own folk would say or do about them.'

'If they ran, why did they end up in here?'

'Before the fighting ended they got snatched up by 3rd Panzer, given guns and a push towards the Front. Ivans don't like irregulars, even those who surrender quicker than Italians.'

'I don't suppose they do. Did they ever talk about things they'd done? Specifically, I mean.'

Herbert shrugged. 'Not really. They told me they'd helped to round up their town's Jews back in '40, but that was hardly a big job. They were far busier with *kozis* in fact, Wismar being a port and full of that sort. But there was nothing that would have put them in front of an Allied tribunal – at least, nothing they admitted to.'

'And they didn't make any enemies at Sachsenhausen?'

'They made one, for sure. But I don't know how, or why.'

Fischer thanked him and remained by the door of the Humboldt as he walked away. Josef Kerner and Eberhard Spitz had been nondescripts, men so *ordinary* in the Third Reich that their willingness to carry out orders was regarded as no more morally questionable than what slaughterhouse workers did to put meat upon tables. The nation had accepted the logic and justice of National Socialism's *weltanschauung* and discharged its collective conscience as a grounded metal rod did an electrical charge - the murdered men were guilty of nothing that the rest were not; as guilty as most but hardly more so, other than for their bad judgement in pointing guns at Red Army troops but not wearing the uniforms that made the manoeuvre acceptable. Killing them *had* to be personal.

'Was Herbert useful, Otto?' Siegfried had waited patiently, respectful of the silence that a master criminal investigator's mind needed to catch the faint echo of a long-neglected crime.

'I don't know, SS.'

Siegfried grinned. 'That's such a clever *sprankle*, isn't it? I never thought of it myself, not in all the thirteen years it was right in front on me.'

'It makes you seem more dangerous than you are. You should be wary of that in here.'

'You think the Ghost may come for me, too?'

'No, he's finished, though I don't know why. If he's dead, I need something else to distract me. If not, his soul's satisfied with what it's done. Either way, I doubt he's going to confess himself.'

'Then how would you find him out?'

'Logic, deduction, blundering in the dark until a knee bangs against something – as police do.'

'It must require patience.'

'Which we all have, at Sachsenhausen. Those of us, at least, who haven't chosen to commute our sentences.'

42

Müller took the coward's way and told his wife that he had
crashed a police vehicle. The damage to his face had horrified
her, and he doubted she could take the additional anguish of
knowing that it had been slowly, deliberately applied by a
craftsman. Besides, the truth might be fatal.

Being a practical woman, she was almost as upset by the story
as his face. 'But won't they make you pay for it, Albi?'

He explained that he had swerved to avoid a Soviet armoured
column whose drivers apparently did not know or care about
rights of way, and that to Keibelstrasse's motor-pool this was
not an unusual occurrence. She accepted this as a citizen of an
occupied nation would, with a frown, a pout and a compress
for his bludgeoned nose, tenderly applied.

To his superiors he offered a different story, one that he and
Kalbfleisch had rehearsed carefully. It involved a chance
encounter with a surprised group of anti-social elements,
whose swift and brutal reaction to the sight of *VolksPolizei*
was amply evidenced by the state of the victims and their
uniforms. Having met the ground at much the same time,
neither could recall enough of the detail to offer a useful
description of their assailants. It was all too credible, and no-
one at Keibelstrasse questioned it too closely.

Prudence was Müller's watchword, his life-plan, but
something with a sting had lodged itself beneath a layer and
he couldn't shake it out. He was certain that it wasn't shame -
no former counsel for the defence at the People's Court could
have admitted to that quality - or even humiliation
(helplessness was a state that most Germans had come to live

with comfortably), and as a sane man he had no urge to chase down creatures that probably killed with little more thought than he devoted to his daily shave. It was rather a nudge, a half-feeling that something was out of alignment, as if he had emerged from a play without having quite understood its denouement. He told himself that a broken nose and slight dizziness (now fading) were small burdens in light of how it might have gone. Even so, being alive should have felt better than it did.

He hadn't spoken to Kalbfleisch since they had delivered their rehearsed lie, and he suspected that they were avoiding each other. Neither man wanted to be the one to say that the Kaulsdorf murders investigation could bugger itself heartily, nor initiate the conversation on how best to ensure this. They were both familiar with the techniques that allowed the impression of industry without delivering its benefits, but even appearing to be hard at it might earn them a bullet. It was something to walk briskly away from, to deny like St Peter had Christ, only with more conviction.

Yet Beckendorp had told them to *keep at it*, knowing that it was almost certainly Soviet business and therefore untouchable. Müller couldn't guess why he'd done that. He was an enigma still - some considered him a lout, a political arse-kisser promoted far above his talents, while others (Müller among them) were convinced that he was the only functioning policeman in the upper echelons of Berlin's *VolksPolizei*. No one had ever accused him of wasting time in the job, of putting resources on things that couldn't be resolved, and yet that was where they were: a third of his men were chasing poor Beyer's killer (though Müller had noticed a slackening of that effort during the past few days as a number of *oberrats* had quietly reminded Beckendorp of their other, almost equally urgent workload) while a hapless two-man shock-army was getting nowhere and being beaten up for it. A man might look at Beckendorp and wonder what the hell he was, exactly.

It was easy to feel the weight of obligation. Müller had been raised in the job by the man, trusted with more than a uniform, and gratitude tended to smooth doubts. Yet anyone with a head knew that the three corpses of Kaulsdorf were not going to find justice, so why continue?

He was being paid, he reminded himself. If it was effectively for nothing, why should he care? He could re-read the Kaulsdorf files and do nothing until even Beckendorp tired of it, and then get moved to something useful. It was what anyone with a gram of common sense would do.

Müller rehearsed this logic for the next two days, until it nested in his head. He began to relax, and, when he next saw Kalbfleisch, he could tell that the man had come to a similar place in his own thinking. During their shifts together they spoke of anything but their ordeal and the case (even though its files lay open on the desk between them, mutely begging to be considered), and on the day that the search for Beyer's killer was stood down for want of a single clue to chase they looked at each other hopefully, knowing that they were about to disappear into the undergrowth of a hundred active cases once more. But it was on that day too that an awful revelation came to Müller, in a moment when he forgot himself and allowed that feeling of something not-quite-in-alignment to re-surface.

The shock of it (as shocks often do) overcame any sense of caution, and he opened his mouth. Kalbfleisch, who had been staring industriously at an unadorned section of wall just behind Müller's head, noticed the movement and shifted his gaze. The look on his colleague's face gave him momentary notice of something bad, but before he could get out of his chair and be somewhere else it had become a matter of record.

'I've heard it before.'

Kalbfleisch, caught in the headlamps' glare, surrendered to his role. 'What?'

'That voice.'

43

Hoeschler had been told to drop Hoffer at the demarcation line, but as the dusk thickened his thoughts strayed from business. He was in plain clothes at the wheel of an unmarked Opel, and his earlier foray into western Berlin had unlocked the day's routine passages, made it and him feel out of step. He had promised to see her one more time, and he couldn't think how or when it might be redeemed more conveniently than now.

So he drove Hoffer all the way back to Lichterfelde and then pointed the car towards Schöneberg, parking it two streets north of her apartment, well away from her route to and from Tempelhof. He expected to have to wait, but when he knocked on her door it opened immediately. She seemed surprised, pleased, and her arms were around his neck before he was across the threshold.

Afterwards, he couldn't recall any small talk or the moment at which an urge had become something more. Mila made him stay where he was while she went to make coffee, not caring to hide her nakedness any more than she had thought to draw the curtains beforehand. He obeyed, drowsing comfortably in disarrayed sheets and faint astonishment (which strengthened considerably when she returned with two mugs of the indisputably genuine product), trying to think of a way out of his story that wouldn't kill any hope of a future for them.

She teased him about nothing, play-fought, made him feel eighteen once more and then asked when he was going back to the West. He could have told her the truth at that moment, but his courage needed a longer run at it. He told her that he'd managed to find Gerste and give him the good news about the lottery, but that he was in no hurry to leave, that he hadn't managed yet to find a pilot willing to take him out of Berlin (it might have been true; he didn't know how easily such a thing could be arranged). She accepted this with a shrug and told him he could stay as long as he wanted, an offer which required another plausible lie, one that didn't come easily to mind and was only deflected by their having sex once more.

When they were done a second time she lay with her head on his chest, and an embellishment came to him. He told her that he'd had family in eastern Berlin before the war, and wanting to know how they'd fared was part of what was keeping him here (but only *part*, he added quickly). He was thinking of trying to finding them, or at worst what had happened to them, so he hoped she wouldn't mind if he was here and there over the next few days and weeks. As he said it he wondered at his own stupidity, his refusal to accept the reality of their impossible situation; but when she looked up and smiled he felt a great, juvenile relief, and when he was invited to stay that night he thought only briefly of Engi in his now near-permanent bed at the Beckendorps. Nor did it occur to him to worry about being late to Keibelstrasse the following morning, or that he was going to be sleeping in enemy territory.

Later that afternoon she washed, dressed and went to Tempelhof to tell them that she couldn't work the evening shift. He waited patiently but couldn't resist opening drawers and cupboards, trying to get a closer feel for who she was. Nothing he found was out of place or unusual. The evidence was supremely sparse, but who in Berlin had survived the surrender with much more than the clothes they wore? He replaced her pitifully few possessions carefully, anxious that she shouldn't know that he had betrayed her trust.

She returned with bread and beer coaxed from her American friends at the airfield, and they had their supper in bed after a third, equally wonderful interlude. Given that there was little propriety that might be observed still, he asked about her life *before* as they ate. She told him about her stoker father and *hausfrau* mother, an older brother, a fiancé, a dog and a macaw, all except the last Schöneberg born and bred, all now dead. She seemed less interested in his past, which didn't surprise him; a lot of people regarded *now* as the earliest moment worth excavating, and that only until it could be decently discarded for something more hopeful.

When he asked if she wanted him to sleep on the sofa once more he got a thump, a tickle and then they wrestled for a while. He was surprised by her strength until he recalled how she paid her rent, and …

And then he thought again. Germans working at Tempelhof were paid in calories, with a token 1.25 Deutsche Marks added *per diem* to give flesh to the pretence that they weren't being used as human oxen. She couldn't meet the rent with that, much less the other incidental costs of living, and yet she didn't seem to have any other employment. His suddenly-jealous mind went back to the very first character reference he had been given – *a whore*. She was pretty, full of fun and garrulous - above all, she had that easy way with men that caressed their sense of self. He recognized its effect upon him now – how, in the past few hours, he had carefully set aside almost all of his prudence and sense of perspective for the delights of her bed. If she could deploy that power at will, rent wouldn't ever be a problem.

He had never slept with a woman who earned a living that way, and knew that his shrewd analysis might be worth all of a dried turd. Still, it managed to sour the fine American beer he was drinking and closed down conversation to the point that she noticed and tried to coax him out of whatever had killed the mood. The tactic almost worked; he told himself that she was aware he had little money and no favours to offer, but even so it was difficult to shake the weight of logic. Many respectable German women had learned that a full stomach often depended upon open legs.

Later, with her body pressed against him, warm and comforting, he found it hard to sleep. He imagined his borrowed car stolen in the night; he anticipated the eyes of his colleagues upon him the following day, his guilt somehow transmitting on short-wave across the space between; he dreaded the almost inevitable question from Beckendorp, the one man who would know, beyond any doubt, that he had passed the night somewhere other than in the tiny Marzahn apartment that he shared with his not-quite-adopted son. For all of these torments he might have done what men do, and blamed a siren's hold upon his senses; but his shame was a well-developed, honed instrument, and it stabbed him now.

The burden on his conscience might have eased slightly an hour later, but he was asleep by then and didn't hear the key turning in the lock. His sluggish, wakening mind entirely misunderstood the meaning of her hands and knees upon him, pinning him, and his bloodstream had only just made a start on the erection that he thought was required when he was seized by more, larger hands, his mouth stuffed with something that tasted of fuel, sweat and cigarettes, and a cosh, brought down with carefully-judged force on the side of his head, removed any need to consider further these singular events.

44

MVD Colonel Vaisman sat back and regarded his visitor with such astonishment that he forgot himself and invoked a proscribed opiate.

'Christ on the Cross! How many people have a grudge against the man?'

MGB Major Zarubin raised an eyebrow. 'He's found trouble in *here*?'

The Colonel flushed slightly. 'The sort that gets settles with a bullet.'

'I'm not surprised. Otto Fischer can make enemies like most men make piss. The attempt wasn't successful, I assume?'

'A shoulder wound. Obviously, it's the means rather than the end that's had me turn the camp upside down.'

'You found nothing?'

'The weapon's almost certainly at the bottom of a latrine. Strangely, no-one's yet come forward to confess. Who's the man you're after? Another admirer?'

'Probably the one responsible for putting Fischer in here. He's managed to elude MGB and Berlin's *VolksPolizei* with a suspicious degree of ease.' Briefly, Zarubin gave Vaisman details of the currency theft, the illicit trading at Tempelhof and the probable involvement of Soviet personnel in both.

'This is someone with connections.'

'Almost certainly.'

'A man could earn himself some trouble, going after that sort.'

Zarubin nodded. 'He could. Which is why we must be clever.'

'We?'

This was the delicate part. At Karlshorst, Zarubin had given the frown, a nod and some considerable bullshit to his fearsome adjutant Corporal Yelena, who had then managed to palm Colonel Vaisman's file from the personnel registry. There was nothing in it to suggest that the man was other than an exemplary officer, someone who had seen more action than Zarubin had ever watched in newsreels (but then, if he was a friend of the wrong people there was hardly likely to be). More reassuring was the fact that he was *here*, suspended in professional amber despite his record, supervising the slow half-life and death of thousands of miscreants. Someone with *connections* surely would have arranged something more promising, or at least lucrative. Even so, Zarubin feared that he was about to place his balls on the table and offer a hammer with the other hand.

He held the other man's gaze while he explained what he wanted. He didn't plead, bluster, imply what service the Colonel would be doing his country by agreeing to it (that would have been both implausible and insulting) or hint at what damage to a career a refusal might encourage. He put the case as he saw it and then asked the single, simple question.

Vaisman didn't reply immediately. He looked out of the window, across the vast assembly square to the pleasing panorama of his kingdom. He held as many fates in his hands as did a corps commander, though with none of the practical power that implied. He could order executions without due process, or reduce already-inadequate rations to the point at which executions wouldn't be necessary. He was permitted – expected - to exact a slow, methodical revenge upon Germans that any Soviet citizen with a pulse would delight in sharing. And yet, for a fighting soldier the posting was poison – a slow, self-inflicted regime of moral exsanguination. Zarubin had noticed the campaign medals on Vaisman's tunic. They weren't required to be worn for everyday duties, but a man with a far nobler past than present no doubt needed to remind himself who he was.

The Colonel turned from the view. 'Very well. I'll draw up the order and we'll both sign it.'

Zarubin breathed out and relaxed for the first time since entering the office. 'Thank you. Do you know what's happening with the camps? My immediate boss is on the committee that considers men for release, but lately ...'

'No-one knows, because no-one wants to make a decision. If I had a say, *all* the inmates would be released, or shot. We're wasting huge resources upon a carefully-maintained suspension of the will to resolve a problem. I never said this, obviously.'

'I never say many things, Colonel. If we get a war, perhaps the problem will resolve itself.'

Vaisman sniffed. 'I can't see it happening. Clearly, we would want the Americans to start it, but they're too clever for that. Why take the risk, when they can beat us simply by not letting western Berlin die?'

'You didn't say that also, I assume?'

'No. And you'd be surprised how many others aren't saying it, either.'

45

Beckendorp's morning was becoming the sort that inclined a man to consider taking up strong drink, or painting. Almost an hour had been wasted on the 'phone to Comrade Pieck, Chairman of the SED, who yet again had to be convinced that *VolksPolizei* couldn't be seen to be involved in *night and fog* disappearances of troublesome political opponents (even if they were). Then, the suspension of the Beyer investigation had to be explained to his immediate boss, Markgraf, whose interest in, and concern for, a murdered policeman extended precisely to what it meant for the Force's (that is, his) reputation. At 10.15, a fight broke out on the third floor – an actual, fist-throwing affair with teeth dispersed - between a K-5 *kommissar* and a mere *anwärter* whose wife he was allegedly banging. Given the fragile relationship between political and criminal wings of the Keibelstrasse family, this had required a senior officer from both sides to attend the aftermath and forbid future reprisals, and Beckendorp's was one of the two short straws drawn.

So, though he had asked the whereabouts of Rolf Hoeschler at least twice that morning, he hadn't heard (or noticed) the answers. It was only when motor-pool führer Billy Voss came upstairs just after midday to ask about his missing Opel that an idle, distracted question became something more. This time, he spoke to every man on duty in the Bull's Pen, none of whom had seen Hoeschler since the previous day.

A small knot compacted in Beckendorp's gut. He had told Hoeschler to release Hoffer somewhere near the demarcation line, so, even driving in first gear all the way he should have been back at Keibelstrasse within the hour. He might have had some business of his own to attend in the meantime, but that would have been yesterday still, and no doctor's note diagnosing bubonic plague or an unexpected amputation had been sent in since. This was not likely to be nothing.

Beckendorp hung the *in conference* sign on his office door and interred himself, his mind racing chicane-fashion as he tried to avoid the likely truth. Hoeschler probably hadn't had an accident, hadn't been assaulted by a street gang (like poor Müller and Kalbfleisch, the silly bastards), wasn't fleeing west in a stolen police vehicle with a satchel full of banknotes. This was to do with one thing - or rather, one person.

He had to tell Zarubin. Whatever game the Major was playing to snare this *Butcher* had suddenly acquired new rules, and he needed to know. But who else? Müller? Kalbfleisch? The truth of Beyer's death had been kept from them but they knew of Fischer's abduction - would they not put this with that, and wonder what the hell their Chief-with-the-false-identity was doing? What about the wider audience? To have to admit to yet another missing *unterkommissar* on the day after they'd officially written off the first would make the department a standing joke, much and long to be relished. At the very least, a large, ugly and often ill-tempered head would have to roll, and probably with a bounce or two first.

His gut churned further as he counted the many mistakes returning to their nest. Unasked, he had acquired a problem, one that had needed a deft, subtle touch; so, he had put on his best boots and marched straight into it, eyes closed, brass blaring, assuming that the Beckendorp magic would work as it did habitually upon the twin evils of criminality and city politics. At every stage he had taken the worst path, inviting disaster if what might go wrong did so. He'd put a matter that needed the highest discretion into the hands of men who had no loyalty to him greater than that which they owed to themselves, and blithely issued what had turned out to be a fatal instruction to Rolf Hoeschler. What was worse, he couldn't say that he wouldn't have shot Beyer himself, given that the little shit was about to tell all to his friends at K-5. It was far more the fault of bloody Otto Fischer, accepting his invitation to Berlin to be comforted for the death of his wife and then getting abducted like a country dolt …

That wouldn't do, either. The fault was his (for believing that the epaulettes he wore conferred a degree of competence), and that of a system that had allowed a lumpen former street-pounder to rise beyond his talents. He wished sincerely that he could be Freddie Holleman once more – a sensibly circumspect creature, its natural habitat the safe, dense undergrowth of non-achievement. Holleman would never have juggled with grenades. He would have attracted no attention, stirred no pots, given not a ripe turd for anything but himself and his own. He would have …

His office door opened, despite the proscription hanging on its other side, and Jens Fiermann ambled in. Jens was at least seventy years old, and, like the building itself, had been inherited from an earlier age. Technically not a member of the *VolksPolizei*, he was responsible for the processing of photographic evidence, largely because he had no other discernible skills and no-one had thought themselves responsible for insisting that he retire. Beckendorp could have valued his utter lack of ambition no more than he did at this moment.

'I have your photographs, Herr Inspector'.

'Which ones, Jens?'

'Of the documents. The thing you said was most urgent.'

'Ah. What are they?'

'I'm not sure, I have only a little English.' The old man squinted. 'What is a bipolar junction transistor?'

'I'll be damned if I know. Is that what they're about?'

'Mostly. There's one page that relates to point contact transistors. I assume that's different.'

'So, something about which we know nothing, and something slightly differently mysterious.'

Jens grinned. 'Another case closed, then?'

'Leave them on the desk and bugger off.'

At least he had a reason to see Zarubin immediately. He picked up the 'phone, made an appointment and in the hour that followed swerved endlessly between two futures – one in which Rolf Hoeschler walked through the door with a perfectly elegant reason for his temporary disappearance, the other involving a humiliating confession to the man he least wanted to annoy, disappoint or encourage to think of Berlin's *VolksPolizei* as a crowd of perfect arses. It passed too quickly, and his nerves were further teased by a helpful warning from downstairs that an MGB vehicle had arrived in the Praesidium's courtyard.

Zarubin and his boss Shpak were in his office three minutes later, the scene of their recent failure to extract anything slightly useful from Herr Hoffer. Perhaps it was the memory of this that gave a long, thoughtful cast to their faces, one that failed to clear when Beckendorp laid out the photographs and spoke of various types of things called transistors.

Colonel Shpak rubbed his bony forehead and spoke to his subordinate, though in German. 'You were correct, unfortunately. This is at least partly to do with State business.'

Despite his other problems, Beckendorp was interested. 'You know what this is about?'

'Transistors are amplification devices. They receive and increase electrical power.'

'Like vacuum tubes?'

'Yes. Except that they run cool, are a fraction of the size, much more robust and will almost certainly cost far less to produce, once they're perfected. I attended a lecture on the theory last year. Clearly, the Americans have advanced the science since then. Our Butcher may be regarded as a hero, to have got hold of this so quickly.'

The two Russians thought about it, and in the pause Beckendorp decided to get the bad news out in a tied bundle.

'*UnterKommissar* Hoeschler didn't return yesterday. He's still missing, with one of my cars.'

For a moment, Zarubin's mouth hung open, but then, to Beckendorp's astonishment, he smiled.

'And you believe the Butcher has him?'

'All I can think is that his asking questions about your Gerste fellow warned the wrong people at Tempelhof. What's to be pleased about?'

'It's *something*. We still know nothing about our enemy, so any reaction offers at least a chance of learning more. If we can recover Hoeschler's corpse it may be of some forensic value.'

'I don't want to find his corpse. I want him alive.'

'Where do you think he was taken?'

'I don't know. It's possible that he went over the line and set down Hoffer somewhere in western Berlin.'

'In which case any small reservations our Butcher may entertain against hurting one of our men will have disappeared. Hoeschler shouldn't have been over there, *isn't* anybody over there. He can't be helped.'

Beckendorp had said all of this to himself already, but the pain was no blunter for hearing it. How was he going to break the news to a little boy who bore deep wounds already? To tell him that he had been orphaned once more? How was it to be *done*, even?

Shpak's sour expression hadn't changed. He turned to Zarubin. 'If he's dead in Western Berlin, we're hardly likely to find the body, are we?'

'I doubt that the Butcher would go to the trouble – or pleasure – of assassinating one of ours and pass up the chance of profiting from it. I expect Hoeschler will turn up face down somewhere convenient, as a cautionary tale. Let's hope there hasn't been too much deterioration by then.'

There were times when Beckendorp earnestly wanted to alter Zarubin's face with a fist, but the urge had never before made him forget himself. He was – would be, eventually – grateful for Shpak's presence. He breathed deeply, not trusting himself to say more, while the two Russians gathered their photographs. He even managed to open the door for them.

When he was alone once more he thought more about what might be done and tried to find better reasons than he had for doing nothing, nothing at all. After he had examined and interred the last, faint possibility he decided to find Müller and Kalbfleisch, but when he opened his office door he discovered that they had found him instead.

46

'Don't kill him.'

Like most men, he was softened by prettiness and didn't immediately dismiss the suggestion as being impossibly romantic.

'Why wouldn't I?'

'It's not necessary. He can't know anything.' Her voice was even, though the eyes couldn't disguise the fact that this was not a rational conversation. He was surprised but not jealous. Their intimacy had always been an understood thing, part of the arrangement that served them both.

'We don't know what he knows. And by the time that we do he may prefer to be dead.'

'I can speak to him. Let me do it. Please.'

The absurdity wearied him. This was an important matter, not to be risked on a point of sentiment. But she was the best man he had, and as the years had passed he valued his assets more as the pile of dead liabilities grew. It had been her who saw the danger before anyone else (himself included), and had dealt with it with more subtlety than he had thought possible. He paid her a pittance, and she earned it a thousand times over. To refuse the only thing she had ever asked would be crass.

'You can try. But …'

'I know.'

Rolf Hoeschler woke slowly, partially, and he knew immediately that something chemical was dulling his head. It was the only part of him he could move, but it wanted to be left alone, to go back to the nice warm darkness. He tried to sit upright, straining against the ropes, and managed only to reawaken the pain at the top of his spine.

The room was … a room. It was as small as a large cupboard and bare, offering no hint as to what it did for a living. The door he faced directly didn't look to be reinforced and there was no lock upon it; most reassuringly, the cement floor had no hole at its centre to remove fluids conveniently. This wasn't Karlshorst, and it probably wasn't Spandau either.

The door opened, and the woman he had only recently invaded walked in. The sense of humiliation that had been competing with his headache intensified, but something about her manner took the edge off it. She had pulled off a considerable coup but seemed less than euphoric about it, as if concerned about the pall that his beating and abduction might cast upon their future couplings. She smiled slightly, adding to the dislocation.

'Hello, Mila.' Hoeschler managed to speak calmly, and he was glad that he got it out before the view was disturbed by the third party, the one who was obviously going to be the fists during the coming conversation. He was short, thick-set, hairless and mutilated, though not nearly so as Otto Fischer, whose wounds were an everyman's lament against the horrors of war. This was more in the nature of a celebration of the worst that men did to each other. The lesions that covered his face were like campaign medals, battle tattoos that decorated without quite removing the features beneath. Only a deep furrow that ran from his forehead to the cheek via an eye socket might have proved to be lethal (though the eye, small and deep-set, worked still); the rest were brutal ornamentations, the sort that in a previous age might have earned him a permanent place at a nobleman's drinking table. He closed the door, stood behind and slightly to one side of Mila Henze, pinning Hoeschler with a fish-cold stare.

'Rolf, what did Rudolph Gerste tell you?'

'That he was very happy to be sharing his sister's good fortune.'

War Wounds shifted slightly but Mila moved too, putting herself between the two men.

'That's not true. There isn't a sister, or a lottery win. You know who Gerste is and what he does. You're police, aren't you?'

Hoeschler was dazed still, but not so much that the choices weren't obvious. He could talk, or, probably, die. He could talk, and, very possibly, die anyway. He could refuse to say anything, in which case there was no possibility that he could survive the next few hours – the stare was telling him that, quite loudly. He had no idea how ruthless Mila could or wanted to be (his ability to read her had already proved to be lacking), but he doubted that she had much of a say about it. That was something else the stare told him.

He reminded himself that courage was virtuous, and then wondered why. It was held to be an end in itself, whatever consequences followed; it wasn't required to prove itself in utility, only displayed, so that those who might recall whatever corpse was thus created could embroider their memories and say that *he had been courageous*. He wasn't sure that he didn't want a more substantial headstone.

What to do, then? He was *VolksPolizei*, and had as much sense of loyalty to the institution as to his football team (disbanded early in 1942, after eight of the first team had gone down in the penalty box somewhere west of Moscow). If he felt more it was with regard to individuals – Beckendorp, Fischer, even that smug little shit Zarubin, a half-decent man despite all the evidence to the contrary – and his fear of what they would think of him. Against that, there was Engi, who had already lost a mother and might be broken by another hammer blow. The boy wasn't blood kin – wasn't kin of any sort – but the responsibility was the heaviest thing in a life that had so far skirted the usual commitments.

He told himself that she wanted him to talk, that it must mean something. He cleared his throat. 'I'm police. It was a favour, for MGB. They wanted to talk to him.'

'Why?'

'They didn't say. It isn't their way to explain things – not to me, at least.'

War Wounds leaned forward and whispered something. Mila nodded.

'Who, in MGB?'

'A Major Zarubin, of the First Directorate, Karlshorst.

'And you did it, you found Gerste?'

'Yes.'

'And killed two Russian soldiers.'

'Is that what they were? It happened in Spandau, and nobody was wearing a uniform. I was defending myself.'

'You did that very well, for a policeman.'

He shrugged. 'The war.'

'So, what did Gerste give you?'

'He told Zarubin about what goes on at Tempelhof, how some Americans and Russians are trading on the sly. About one Russian they call the Butcher, how he runs the thing and more stuff too.'

'Describe the *more*.'

'He didn't say, because he wasn't asked. Zarubin seems to be more interested in who the Butcher is than what he's doing. I think he's being pushed by someone senior.'

Mila conferred once more, too quietly to overhear. It seemed to Hoeschler that she and the other man were more than occasional acquaintances; he was fearsome, yet she wasn't at all cowed or nervous in his presence. Even now, he didn't want to think about how close they might be.

She turned back to him. 'It was risky, coming to western Berlin. Why did you agree to it?'

'MGB don't like to be refused. In any case, my boss got something in return.'

'What?'

'A promise to find a man who's disappeared, a friend. My friend, too.'

'A man with more than one friend? He's a lucky one.'

Hoeschler smiled. 'If you saw him, you wouldn't think so.'

She opened her mouth to ask another question but paused and thought for a few moments. 'Tell me about him.'

'The description is easy. His name is Otto Fischer. He's a little older than me and about two inches taller. Distinguishing features include half a face and a badly burned right shoulder and arm. As to what sort of person he is, I'd say innocent.'

'Of what?'

'Everything, but particularly the foul luck that's dogged him. If he's ever done bad in his life, the debt's been repaid with interest.'

'Where did he go missing?'

'He came into Tempelhof on an American 'plane, got snatched by plain-clothed thugs just inside the SBZ and then handed to the Soviets. Since then, nothing.'

'Why was he here?'

'To be comforted.'

'What?'

'His wife died a couple of months ago. My boss invited to him to come and stay with the family. It's a noisy house, a place where he wouldn't have time to think about things.'

'What's your friend's occupation?'

'It's hard to say. Since the war ended he's not managed to stick to anything. His wife brought in most of the earnings, from her laundry. His latest thing was selling jazz records in Bremen, with yet another friend. I don't think he regards it as an occupation.'

The hard fellow put his hand on Mila's shoulder and tossed his head slightly. They withdrew without saying more, closing the door behind them. Alone, Hoeschler tried to think. He had spoken freely, honestly, and he wondered if one of the chemicals that dulled his head was the American drug that suppressed the ability to lie. But it was said to flatten the wits also, and he was sure that his mouth had said nothing to drag him further into the shit.

Briefly, he tested the ropes to reassure himself that he'd been tied by an expert. He could hear no outside noises, no sounds of life passing by, so a shout wasn't likely to bring anything other than punishment. He relaxed slightly, tried to breathe steadily, as if he was back in the war and about to put himself on the windy side of a fuselage. He couldn't recall that it had ever helped back then, but his instructor had seemed to think it good advice.

They returned after about fifteen minutes. Mila was holding a cup, which she put to his lips and steadied as he drank. War Wounds had brought a stool; he placed it in the corner to the right of the door and sat down, redeploying the stare even before he was settled. Hoeschler guessed that this was going to take a little more time yet. He didn't mind; it was preferable to the likely *next*.

Mila stroked his hair as he drank the water. 'You're a good looking man.'

Christ, don't say that.

Fortunately, War Wounds didn't take this as the prompt to do something about it, and when Mila dropped her face to Hoeschler's level that anything but good-looking prospect was obscured.

'Why did you come back, Rolf?'

'To see you.'

'Really, why?'

'That's it, the reason. My boss doesn't know I'm here. I took a motor-pool car and came without permission. If they knew where to look they'd be searching for me now.'

She seemed amused. 'What, you were going to propose?'

'No. I just didn't want never to see you again. It may not be possible to cross the line for much longer, so … It was a stupid thing to do, even before this.'

She held his gaze for a moment and then straightened up. War Wound's head moved to the side, to give him the clear view. He snorted phlegm and spoke for the first time.

'What do you have, besides Gerste?'

He was a Russian, obviously. Hoeschler, knowing that they had reached the dangerous moment, looked him in the eye. 'Nothing that I know of. Zarubin doesn't confide, but if he had more he wouldn't be involving us. He would have done something already.'

'Something?'

'Something more than nothing. He doesn't know if this Butcher has friends at Karlshorst or in Moscow, and he wouldn't risk moving until he does, even if he knew which way to move. Which he doesn't.'

'You don't sound as if you care, either way. Yet you're a policeman.'

'I'm a German, which means it isn't my business. If Russians want to go after each other, good luck to them. The more the better.'

That almost raised a smile. 'So not you're not moved by the fraternal spirit of socialism?'

'I'm moved by what does the most good and least bad for Rolf Hoeschler.'

War Wounds squinted. 'I think you're telling me that you can mind your business. But you must know that we can't let you go.'

'I suppose not.' Hoeschler glanced up at Mila. Her face was expressionless, her eyes on a point somewhere above his head. He hoped very much that she wasn't trying to be philosophical about the prospect of his erasure.

War Wounds turned and shouted something in Russian. Two burly fellows who entered the small room a moment later must have been waiting just outside the door; they went straight to Hoeschler, untied the single rope holding him in the chair and lifted him upright with no more effort than if he had been Mila's little sister. He didn't struggle. Twice before in his life he had faced likely death with what he had imagined to be composure but had probably been dull acceptance, a reflexive easing of those tense urges that made a man want to remain in the world. He only regretted that he wasn't going to be able to explain things to his boy; that he wouldn't have the opportunity to convince him that the Beckendorps would make a far better family than one man ever could. As for the rest, a bullet wouldn't rob him of much more than a recently re-discovered delight in laying with a woman.

And look, he thought, as he was dragged out of her presence, *how that turned out*.

47

Beckendorp was told that Direktor Jamin was meeting the new head of the DVdI, Kurt Fischer, that afternoon. He wasn't disappointed by this as the pause gave him time to settle his temper to something approaching volcanic. Repeatedly, he recited his old ME 109 cockpit checklist in his head (a technique first suggested by his wife, several years earlier), drank several mugs of tea (a beverage he despised but endured for its alleged calming qualities), and smiled at everyone who crossed his path on the third floor, whatever their rank. When he felt that he might be capable of not doing violence he returned to his office, signed the leave sheets that he had ordered both Müller and Kalbfleisch to complete and allocated the cash he had given them (with further orders to disappear for a few days) to the *sundry operations* register, a catch-all that usually hid expenses incurred during off-the-book actions. These and other administrative matters being discharged, he leaned back in his chair and stared at a small ceiling stain until the Hermle on his desk chimed five.

A glance into the courtyard confirmed that the Direktor's definitely not of-the-people Maybach had returned from its little outing to Wilhelmstrasse. Beckendorp fastened the top buttons of his trousers and tunic, and, ignoring the pain that the day's over-exertions had gifted his stump, limped back up to the fourth floor. Jamin was stood outside his office, checking appointments with a male secretary, but looked up when he heard the clump of an artificial leg on wood. He seemed quite at ease, ready to close off his day's shift at the coal-face of State Security.

Beckendorp kept the blank expression firmly in place until the Direktor's door was closed. He allowed himself to be waved to a chair and refused the offer of even more tea with a slight shake of the head. For some hours he had been rehearsing his comments, but now that Jamin's face was in front of him their order slipped and his hard-won calm evaporated.

'Two of my men were beaten up.'

Jamin's left eyebrow rose slightly. 'Shocking. You suspect hooliganism, naturally.'

'I do. In particular, *your* fucking hooligans.'

'That's ridiculous.'

'No it isn't. I can tell you precisely who carried out the beating. It was that thug you usually deploy to catch *florenzers* up each other's arses in public urinals. Jens Kohl, isn't it?'

Jamin's slab face confessed everything by allowing a little colour to show. 'What makes you think that?'

'My men were blindfolded, not ear-plugged. You shouldn't have used someone who demands that a man confetheth hith offentheth during interrogations. Actually, you shouldn't have used anyone, because it's got me interested.'

'In what?'

'In the pit you've been digging, Comrade. The one that MGB are going to be peering into.'

'Explain yourself.'

'Kohl asked my men about the Kaulsdorf killings. Why would he do that? And why would he be content to have them assume that it was Soviet business – so much so that he let them off with a pasting? And then I remembered our last conversation, the one in which you more or less admitted that some of your men are drawing two salaries. I don't need Fritz Haber's head to work out this one. Those three poor bastards in the shallow grave - you were sending a message to your competitor.'

Jamin smiled – that is, one edge of the cod-mouth went north slightly. 'How very imaginative. And why would MGB take exception to this?'

'Why wouldn't they? They don't like you anyway. You shouldn't have gone behind their backs to Stalin, asking for more men and resources when it was their place to say yes or no. You've given them the chance to point the finger and say 'look what happens when you let the fucking Germans order their own affairs. They can't control their own men, and when they do something about it they blame a Russian for the mess. *And* they're doing all of this shit in the middle of our great stand-off with the Americans.' And then, probably, they'll suggest breaking it all up and starting again.' Beckendorp shrugged theatrically. 'Of course, I'm only guessing - I'll have a much better idea once I've had a long conversation with Major Zarubin.'

The Direktor lifted the lid of a silver box, half-extracted a cigarette then changed his mind and returned it. 'Clearly, you want something. Otherwise you'd have spoken with him already.'

'I want my men left alone. All of them, forever. The fact that we occupy the same premises doesn't make them convenient punch-bags for your thugs. If you want to know what and why we're investigating, pick up the 'phone and ask. If this happens again there'll be noise. In fact, I might come upstairs with a dozen of my biggest lads and *then* go squealing to Karlshorst.' He stood up and kicked back the chair with his good leg. 'You're welcome to look at any of our cases, Comrade Direktor. Just not with feet or fists.'

He paused and turned at the door. 'Major Zarubin's has a very personal interest in this Butcher fellow and what he's been doing. He might wonder why you didn't come to him with what you know.'

When he was back in his own office Beckendorp let his head catch up with the mouth. He had threatened the Head of K-5, the man who practically ran internal security in the SBZ. In a previous era it would have been akin to telling Reichsführer Himmler to fuck his mother backwards (and then offering to do it for him). He had bluffed, blustered, added a false half-metre to his height and reach and then drawn a line in sand which K-5's heavy boot could erase in a moment. He wondered why he had felt it had been the sensible course to take; why, as his problems seeded and multiplied, he had taken off his jacket, picked up the spade and thrown manure liberally onto the crop. Otto Fischer had been disappeared somewhere, Beyer was dead, Hoeschler was almost certainly dead or about to be, and now, to garnish an excellent month's turd-gathering, Kurt Beckendorp was straining sinews to orphan his two (probably now three) boys.

At every stage in this rolling disaster his talents had been exposed for what they were. He was a water-treader who had strayed off the continental shelf, an idiot pushing an implausible impersonation of sagacity, an over-fancy uniform disguised as authority. When the Ivans decided not to kill him in '45, to squeeze him instead into *VolksPolizei* uniform, tasked with reducing the catastrophic crime rate following the Surrender, he should have kissed their collective hand and remained there, unnoticed, massaging statistics and drawing a modest but regular salary. But he had imagined his blind good fortune to be the consequence of some innate faculty. It was painful to turn upon himself the same cold eye that had mocked the new German Order in the SBZ and discover just another time-serving dolt, promoted far beyond his talents.

He sat down heavily in his chair and unstrapped his metal leg. The sense of constriction that had been growing for days was now a band of iron, pressing brutally, and he couldn't begin to see a way of prising it off. He wasn't clever enough to look beyond what was or wasn't in front of him; wasn't adept at looking sideways at a problem. If something couldn't be punched, kicked or landed upon it was beyond his wit to beat. He needed more of a head than he had. He needed …

He needed the problem itself. He needed Otto Fischer to be here, to look into that ruined face and have the old, comforting feeling that the mechanism behind it was turning smoothly, sorting strangely-wound strands into a form that made sense. Otto would know where he had been hiding, even if he didn't (Beckendorp reconsidered that and was comfortable with it); then, asked about the mystery of this Butcher fellow, he would stare at a wall for about a minute and deduce an identity, an address and reasons for whatever ailed the man, and after everything was done and settled, Beckendorp still wouldn't have the first idea how it had come about. He had never minded that; he was happier being pointed at something and told what to do. The world made far more sense that way.

He felt the walls of his large office pressing more closely than they should have done; he felt the storeys above and below him as closing masses, teeming with men who believed him to be something far other than he was – an unsubtle, former *OrPo* street-pounder far happier using his head to support a hat. At that moment he would gladly have taken an eight-rank demotion, a *schlagstock* and directions to his appointed beat, with no more responsibility than to stop hooliganism and reassure old ladies that their lost or stolen

Handelsorganization coupon books could be replaced at no expense and hardly any inconvenience. There was something about being obliged to think only of what might be for supper that could make a man long for a golden age.

'Where are you, Otto?'

48

'Where am I?'

Obviously, the tiny room was a holding cell. It had an iron bedframe that was attached to the bare stone wall and hinged so that it could be stored out of the way. The only door was a green-painted steel object, the tiny window amply barred so as to prevent all but an undernourished bird from passing through it. The question wasn't intended in a too-immediate sense.

Zarubin pouted slightly. 'It hurts to say hello?'

'Hello, then.' From his lower position on the mattress-less bunk, Fischer gave the Russian a brief up-and-down. 'You've lost weight.'

'Too many cigarettes and responsibilities. This is Karlshorst.'

'It smells familiar. Does the Red Army use a standard disinfectant?'

'I've never considered the matter. Probably.'

'I assume you want something?'

'Yes. I want you to think of yourself as a worm.'

Fischer nodded. He was a man already disappeared, of value to no-one for what he knew. What other use could he be put to? 'It wasn't you, then?'

'Of course not. Why would I?'

'I have no idea. But I can't see why anyone else would have done it, either.'

'It's a mystery, certainly. You haven't been making yourself irritating?'

'To my knowledge, no. For the past year I've helped to sell jazz records in Bremen. It should be a crime, but it isn't.'

Zarubin nodded. 'Herr Beckendorp told me about your wife. My condolences.'

'Thank you. So, whoever put me in Sachsenhausen is of interest to you?'

'Of deep interest. It appears that he – or they, I can't be sure – operates somewhat outside of SVAG's authority. You needn't know the precise details, but I have personal reasons for wanting him … discouraged.'

'Discouraged from what?'

'Anything that impinges upon MGB business.'

'Which means that he's dealing with … who? Germans? The Allies?'

'Definitely both. There's significant cross-the-line economic activity in Berlin, and perhaps elsewhere.'

'Even now? During the siege?'

Zarubin winced. 'The administrative measures, yes.'

Fischer stared down at the cell floor. A few traces of graffiti commemorated Pioneer students who had broken the former kaserne's rules and earned themselves a night's luxurious accommodation. He wondered if he would have time to add something to the literature. 'If you're baiting a trap for this man, what is it that you think I have on him?'

'I have no idea.'

'Then what threat can you make?'

'Only the fact of your presence. Clearly, he needed you to be vanished. Your reappearance will be advertised. That it's occurred at SVAG Headquarters will suggest that you're talking, which will make him eager to remove the danger.'

'You assume.'

'Yes.'

'But I don't know what I'm supposed to know.'

'It's not necessary. I doubt that you'll be speaking to the gentleman.'

'And when it's finished? Do I go back to Sachsenhausen?'

For almost a minute Zarubin didn't speak. He pretended to be fascinated by the tiny patch of visible sky through the bars, and then by the ravishing prospect of the mutilated face before him. Eventually, he shrugged. 'It depends on whether either of us survive *it*.'

'Who *is* this fellow?'

'All we have is an opinion, disguised as a name. The Butcher.'

Fischer laughed. 'How very unnerving.'

'Isn't it?'

'And he deals with the Allies. In what?'

'Goods, currency, papers, everything. It's hard to know what protection he has.'

'Connections?'

'In very short order he arranged to remove you from the streets, via a K-5 snatch squad and Red Army personnel, and put you in a Special Camp with minimal paperwork. The connections much be considerable.'

'So, unless this is a vast Old Boys' club, he's using money.'

'That seems logical, yes.'

'And he trades commodities with western parties. That also requires money, or at least access to the said commodities.'

'Again, yes.'

Fischer considered his host. The last time they'd met he noticed that Zarubin had grown into the uniform, trading the slightly nervous demeanour of an under-staffed officer in one of Europe's lesser colonic regions for the self-assurance of a man at the heart of where the next war was fomenting. It seemed now that his cockiness was leavened by something – a slight, brittle edginess, the unconscious twitch developed by someone obliged to check too many directions with just the one pair of eyes. He didn't know what *personal* business Zarubin had with this Butcher, but he knew Zarubin himself well enough to wager his best (his only) pair of camp trousers on the man having played some game too cleverly and was now looking to leave the table with his own trousers intact. It was mildly satisfying to see his excessive self-regard punctured – and curious, too, that it seemed to have blunted his thinking.

'I've been engaged elsewhere for the past few weeks, but I assume that the Soviet Union hasn't yet been seduced by the capitalist model?'

Zarubin didn't like anyone but himself being playful. He frowned. 'What's your point?'

'That it must be difficult to be a magnate in a collectivized system. Where's the bankroll?'

The Russian's eyes went to the ceiling and his mouth opened slightly. He knew as much about the free market as his briefing papers told him. He could probably explain capitalism as well as any American businessman, but in his case it would be theory undiluted by any casual understanding of its everyday symptoms and practises. He hadn't thought it through because this was astronomy, or the physics of vapour, to a Soviet officer.

Fischer waited until the eyes came back down. 'You're looking for a man with access to product. He's almost certainly Red Army, so I'd suggest either a notoriously thieving member of your General Staff or someone in a senior quartermaster role.'

The eyes closed. 'An *intendani*.'

'You have access to Occupation Forces records?'

'Yes. I mean, I can get them from MVD.'

'Have I earned some water?'

Less than five minutes after Zarubin departed the cell a private soldier brought in a jug and a bowl filled to the brim with chicken broth. Fischer drank the water quickly but took his time with the food, which, after several weeks of the Sachsenhausen regime, tasted finer than anything he could recall in his adult life. His belly distended but he persisted with the determination of any half-starved soul, and afterwards stretched out on the bare straps of the bedframe to relieve the pain of indigestion. It felt wonderful, as if life had returned from a long holiday.

He suspected that he was going to be here for some time. A man who could do what this Butcher was alleged to have done wouldn't leave a path strewn with clues - finding him would be an exercise in thicket-sifting, with trip-wires to the fore and shrapnel coming in overhead. In the meantime, it wouldn't be too difficult to bribe some nobody at Karlshorst to introduce ground glass into a prisoner's diet, or arrange a cell transfer via the stairwell. For what reason he would do this Fischer couldn't begin to conceive. Had he absent-mindedly raped the man's mother? Had his artillery team at Okhvat launched a shell that found its way into the family sitting-room? As with so much else that had occurred since 1933, events seemed to have coagulated unnoticed around him and chosen their own implications.

He was auditing his past behaviour, trying to imagine his offence, when Zarubin re-entered the cell. No more than three hours could have passed since their conversation. As he sat up the Russian took the place of his feet, dropping heavily onto the bunk, the screws that held it to the wall protesting bitterly.

For a while Zarubin said nothing. He stared at the opposite wall, a matter of two metres distant, finding something interesting in the pattern of its bare bricks. When he spoke, his voice was uncharacteristically shaky.

'Fucking *the*.'

'What?'

'The - definite article. The Russian language has no need for it, unlike German. But it was Germans we questioned about him, every time. Fucking Germans.'

'I don't understand.'

Zarubin sighed. 'Sixteenth Air Army, presently deployed throughout the SBZ and those parts of Poland that were formerly eastern Germany, is headquartered in Wünsdorf. Its directing *intendani* is one Major-General Mikhail Myasnik.'

'And?'

'Myasnik is a common name. It's also the Russian word for *butcher*.'

'Ah. So, you have him.'

'I've identified him. What I can do about it, I don't know. He's a war hero, several times over. He served in Leningrad throughout the siege, so he must be very nostalgic about how things have turned out for Berlin. Apart from the medals, he has friends.'

'You're certain of that?'

'The men who directed the defence of Leningrad came out of the war as the heroes of heroes. They stick together, as people who've been through several hells tend to. The Boss hates that, but even he's wary of moving against them. I fear that our Butcher can do the things he does because he has blood-brothers in the Politburo.'

Fischer had stopped listening. Two words had jarred his memory, dragging him back to a past conversation. They shouldn't have roused anything in him but they did, stirring the layer of indifference that had been congealing since a particular, terrible day in Bremen. He turned to Zarubin, who had returned to his opposite wall vigil and was chewing his bottom lip, a most uncharacteristic betrayal of the inner man.

'I've given you your Butcher, so you no longer need worm-bait. If you – we – survive this, I want something.'

'What?'

'To go back to Sachsenhausen.'

Astonished, Zarubin momentarily forgot his concerns for his own, beloved skin. 'Why the hell do you want that?'

'Because I'm guilty.'

'Guilty? Of what?'

'Of precisely the same offence as you.'

49

The telephone call, like all using the Soviet Occupation Forces exchange line between Karlshorst and Wünsdorf, was secured (the lesson had been hard-learned during the early Eastern Front campaign, when Wehrmacht was given egregious assistance by their enemy choosing to convey military orders on open lines). The caller, a Commissar First Class of MVD, spoke briefly and with a degree of deference to a man of almost equal rank. In a stark departure from Russian conversational etiquette, personal names were not used.

'Someone has asked a question.'

'Really? How interesting might I find it?'

'Considerably, I should think. A Major Zarubin of MGB here at Karlshorst has requested details of all senior officers of the Quartermaster Service presently in the SBZ.'

'Did he? That won't be a long list, I imagine.'

'It can be squeezed comfortably onto a single page. I understand that it was produced with impressive speed.'

'And this Zarubin's a diligent fellow, is he?'

'He's said to be *clever*.'

'Well, that can be good or bad, but I'll assume the worst. Thank you for your call.'

When he had replaced the receiver, the recipient of this information summoned his adjutant on the intercom and ordered a car, asking for a particular model. This meaning more than the form of words suggested, the adjutant spent some minutes arranging a paper trail for the benefit of anyone ask the whereabouts of his commanding officer before he returned to his desk. He then called the General's personal driver, who needed no further information than the single word *Emka* conveyed.

The vehicle was a late model but battered, and for this reason the motor-pool had decided not to honour it with Red Army markings or a pennant. Usually it was used by junior officers, men who couldn't be trusted not to take a drink or two between the garrison and one of the girl-rich villages surrounding them, and its habit of finding ditches during these outings had given the pool regular employment. In a nation in which any pristine vehicle of more than three years' vintage was a rare sight, its campaign wounds made it unremarkable, even anonymous. This, for at least one of its regular users, was a quality much to be valued.

The Emka departed the camp before dawn the following morning, its going (despite the presence of a senior officer in its rear seat) hardly noticed by the sleepy, desperately home-sick soldiers who manned the Waldstadt gate. Less than an hour later it was parked beside a barn less than a kilometre from the village of Spitzmühle, east of Berlin. In the farmhouse, the General and his driver breakfasted upon real coffee and very real cakes while the farmer and his wife stood over them, beaming, delighted to have a visit from their principal source of income. Less happy, though only recently warmed by his own breakfast, a man sat on the floor, his back to the heavy radiator to which he was handcuffed.

Rolf Hoeschler watched the men at the table carefully. In his general's uniform War Wounds looked less objectionable, the disfigurements explaining his rank elegantly. He ate delicately, savouring each mouthful as if nourishment wasn't something to be expected, and when he was done he drew a handkerchief from his pocket to wipe his fingers. His companion (a sergeant) ate as pigs do, though mercifully without the noise. While his mouth was still dealing with most of the last cake, he picked up his mug and went outside.

General War Wounds turned to Hoeschler. Breakfast seemed to have relaxed him, and the frown was elsewhere.

'Tell me about Major Zarubin.'

'I hardly know him. I worked for him briefly last year, just street work. I fucked it up, but I must have done it on a good day, because instead of donating a bullet he got me a job with Berlin Police. Since then, I've seen him only recently, on this Gerste business.'

'Who are his friends?'

'If he has any, he doesn't mention them'

'An intelligent man?'

'Not as much as he imagines he is, but that would hardly be possible.'

War Wounds smiled slightly and examined the pattern on the tablecloth, brushing away cake crumbs with a finger. For the first time, Hoeschler noticed that his left ear was almost entirely gone, the hole's entrance flush with the side of the head. It must have been a very near miss. He recalled that senior Red Army officers had tended to get a lot closer to the action than their German equivalents (probably to ensure that the lower ranks weren't having too much fun), and suffered accordingly.

'He's found me.'

For a moment the sense of the words didn't register, and then Hoeschler's gut contracted savagely. The farmer had stepped forward slightly and was looking expectantly at the General, who shook his head slightly and turned back to the prisoner.

'Herr Franke keeps pigs. In normal times they're not fussy about what they eat. In *these* times they don't waste a morsel, ever.'

He stood up, and lifted his General's cap from the table. 'But don't worry about it. You've just become useful.'

50

Beckendorp loved his wife dearly, and yet she was the only human being who could unman him entirely. She had never slapped him, or threatened to leave, or tried to crush his spirit with silent reproofs of his very many failings, and if anything else were needed to loosen his bowels it was her habit of gazing at him with such quiet, perfect contentment that only an iron-clad dolt could imagine that this was how things went usually.

Life was a journey, he'd heard (or read, he couldn't recall). Like any passage between two points it had the capacity to be fair and prosperous or a sewage outfall by any other name, and she'd done her best to make the latter - *his* latter - as much of the former as any mid-twentieth century German life could be. He was grateful beyond words, which was why he was terrified of ruining it all.

He watched her, painting an old table, its legs pointing to the kitchen ceiling like a dead horse's. She was frowning, the tip of her tongue protruding slightly as she gave the ugly piece of furniture a Mennonite transformation. He hadn't believed that light blue could turn out well, but there it was: doing much the same for the table as she had done for his heart. And now he was going to repay the favour with misery.

'Kristin?' He used her old, real name, the forbidden item. Surprised, she looked up and smiled.

'What, Freddie?'

'When did we last have a holiday?'

She laughed. 'You know when. At the lake-house, for two weeks in June, 1939. After that it didn't count.'

No, it didn't. They had returned to the lake-house in 1943 as refugees from the Reich, cowering behind drawn curtains for almost eighteen months, practising their new names until they no longer sounded wrong. It hadn't seemed at all like a holiday.

'Nine years. A long time.'

Carefully, she propped the wet end of her paintbrush against one of the sections she had yet to attack and wiped her hands. 'What are you thinking, then? Egypt?'

He laughed, despite the weight of his mood. For as long as he had known her, the Bible had provided all the itinerary she would ever desire. 'I want to see where the Chosen People went' she used to tell him, until National Socialism altered the destination and quite removed the longing. His father's lake-house apart, the only secular abroad to which he'd ever managed to drag her had been Lake Constance, for a short, romantic and rain-drenched honeymoon. To this day, he couldn't understand how their hotel-locked stay hadn't resulted in an immediate pregnancy.

'Not quite Egypt. We haven't seen Gerd and Greta for more than a year now, have we?'

He hadn't mentioned his brief meeting with Gerd Branssler six weeks earlier. She would have tried to insist that he stay with them for a few days, or just turned up at the Artists' Café on Dircksenstrasse to give him a kiss and a hug, and either would have made both men too polite, too circumspect, to talk about things that needed to be said.

'How could we go west now, Freddie? With all the roads and railways closed down?'

'We couldn't, probably. But it can't last much longer, and then the Allies and Soviets are going to have to talk. When it's over, we could visit Frankfurt for a while. That's it, for a proper while - more of a break than a holiday.'

'But ...' She paused, and looked at him as though his thoughts were wrapped only loosely, and in cellophane. 'What's wrong?'

This was it, the moment he had dragged himself towards with as much enthusiasm as if it were a stake. How many of his former lies and omissions could he put right without her despising him? He would never, ever admit to the Beyer business, because even if Rolf Hoeschler were now dead his memory shouldn't be soiled by the decision into which he had been thrust by his boss and imagined friend. If he told her that Otto had been in the east for weeks, only at a location or locations unknown, she would probably go for the skies no less impressively than those fancy rockets he had watched at Peenemünde, back in '43. If he mentioned that he had been doing favours for his Soviet puppet-master in MGB that were likely to bring upon him the wrath of a man so powerful he could bend elements of K-5 and the Red Army to his whim she would pack bags and take the twins and Engi to her sister's in Leipzig, saying nothing hurtful but letting her eyes speak volumes of betrayal. So what the fuck else could he tell her?

'I'm ... not doing well. With the Party.'

'What do you mean?'

'There's a rumour that Chairman Pieck thinks I'm not enthusiastic about what's been happening in Berlin. To his mind, anything that isn't one thing is its opposite, so I'm a secret democrat, apparently. They've stopped inviting me to meetings, and I don't think it's because of my police workload.'

Somehow, she managed to look both worried and relieved. It had never been a secret that she detested his political work (like any sensible German, she regarded all politicians of whatever conviction as scoundrels). Her practical nature, however, accepted the lifestyle it had brought, and it was hardly likely that their occupation of the pretty house on Gartenweg could survive her husband's fall from grace. There was also the question – never satisfactorily answered – as to whether the police job relied upon the political work. They could find more modest accommodation; they couldn't survive without the salary.

'What will you do?'

He shrugged. 'If we had a triumph at work it might make me untouchable for a while, but there's nothing that looks promising, except …'

'Except what?'

'I've been working with the Soviets. They have a rogue, someone who's friendly with the Amis, they think. If we find him, Karlshorst would put in a good word for me. With Pieck, I mean.'

'Is it dangerous?'

Thank God. 'It might be, sweetheart. That's why I thought of Gerd and Greta. If the worst happens it's likely we'd have to leave quickly.'

'How, with the blockade?'

He squirmed slightly, knowing that she knew the answer to that already. 'With my rank and what I know, there'd be a place for me in the West. We'd just have to get across the line into western Berlin. I could arrange that.'

'They'd call you a traitor, Freddie.'

'I know, but so what? All Germans are traitors these day, to one side or the other. The worst thing would be that we could never return.'

'If it comes to that, I don't care. Home is where family is.'

She was giving him everything he'd hoped for, and it made him feel even more wretched (if that were possible). The only remaining cliff-face to scale was the moment at which he'd need to tell her that Rolf was dead - that she had a new son to mend. He didn't doubt that she would do the job perfectly, but that wasn't the point. He was using her as a sieve, to filter all the shit he had poured into their lives, and a good man wouldn't do that.

Noticing his subdued manner, she took his hand. 'At least we'll be able to see Otto in the West. The poor man needs his friends.'

A kitchen knife plunged into his stomach wouldn't have hurt as much as the words. For a moment his resolve vanished and he almost told her the truth, all of it, the full, stumbling catalogue of missteps he'd embarked upon to save a man he still couldn't help or even locate. Only cowardice and a good idea of what she would think of him afterwards kept his lips together.

She had picked up her brush and was applying more paint to the upended table as if they had been discussing no more than the housekeeping budget, or a visit to their local park. He had never been able to decide whether she was indomitable or just impervious to life's knocks; but having absorbed his revelation she would be thinking about supper, probably, or whether there'd be enough paint remaining to have a go at the kitchen chairs also. It was admirable and frustrating, that she could so easily depart a place in which he remained to torment himself. Still, he told himself, he'd prepared the ground. If his problems were all still in formation, at least the home front had been secured.

He was taking the little comfort this afforded him when she looked up from the table and guilelessly dropped a piece of half-tonne ordnance into his calming waters.

'The boys were playing war in the garden yesterday, so most of Engi's clothes are in the laundry. When you see Rolf, ask him to bring around a couple of changes.'

51

'What is it?'

Zarubin was holding a piece of paper. This was not an unusual occurrence, he being an Intelligence officer and paperwork one of the principal arteries through which information flowed; but in recent days Colonel Shpak's nerves had tightened to the point at which a high C might have been extracted, had one of them been plucked. He stared at the object as if it was about to slither out of his subordinate's hand, flow rapidly across the floor and disappear up a trouser leg.

Zarubin's face told him nothing. 'It's an invitation. To a meeting.'

'Oh.' Shpak relaxed slightly. Meetings, like paper, consumed their waking hours, and as the invitation had been directed Zarubin's way it wasn't likely to be anything with teeth.

'To discuss what?'

'I'm not sure.'

'I hate it when that happens. You'd better look at the distribution list and give it your best guess, try to read up on …'

Zarubin cleared his throat. 'I'm to meet with our secretive friend.'

For a moment *friend* threw Shpak, and then the colour left his face once more.

'And I'm to bring Otto Fischer.'

'Oh, God. It's a snare, it must be.'

'Quite possibly. But he wants it to happen where neither of us have any authority, which makes an assassination that much more problematic.'

'Where?'

Perhaps it's better if you don't know, Comrade Colonel (the look of relief on Shpak's face needed no translation). I think I'm happy about it - at least he wants to talk. It would be as easy, and probably far more convenient, to have someone ventilate my skull. And ...' he passed the paper to Shpak, '... I may get something in return.'

Shpak read the note and handed it back. 'We must tell MVD. They can arrange a squad ...'

'And how do we know it will be comprised entirely of honest men, who aren't already taking his money? If even one of them talks I won't make it to our rendezvous.'

'You'll go alone?'

'As I say, killing me wouldn't be difficult, so protection is pointless. In any case, I want him to speak as freely as possible.'

'You find this *interesting*?'

'Don't you? A man like the General isn't supposed to exist in our system. He shouldn't have been able to divert resources, manipulate men or build an alternative economy, all of it somehow shielded from oversight and correction. If my arse wasn't in his crosshairs I could admire him - whilst deploring his reactionary motives, obviously.'

Helplessly, Shpak shook his head. 'And what about Fischer? Are you going to sacrifice him?'

'A good question. Logically, the fact that we'll be on neutral ground should work for him also. But I suppose the General could always shoot him and then offer the cast-iron alibi that the victim is German and therefore either a spy, saboteur or someone we missed when mopping up in '45.'

'This is hardly amusing.'

'You're right, of course. General Myasnik must know that if Fischer had anything damning to offer he would have done so by now, so what reason would there be to kill him?'

'You might be dealing with a vengeful person.'

Zarubin folded the paper and placed it in his tunic. 'In which case ignore everything I've said. If I disappear, protect yourself, Maxim. Get away from here.'

'Get away? To where?'

'I mean defect, of course. Cross the line. Pay a visit to Camp Andrews.'

'Are you mad? Why would they have me? Not ...' he added hastily, '... that I would ever consider it.' Even in an otherwise empty room, Shpak feared the rogue ear turned in his direction.

'You have invaluable information. They'd probably make you a general and give you a ranch in Arizona.'

'What could I tell them?'

'That the pilot of the 'plane named *Donna* is passing industrial secrets to the Soviet Union. I presume you can recall enough of what transistors are to make a case convincingly? Then you can mention General Myasnik, how he's the one who took three-and-a-half million Deutsche Marks and killed at least one of their men doing it. I suspect they'd either try to turn him or get one of their spies to put a bullet in him, in which case you'll have avenged my death. I'm not joking - believe me, in the past few hours I've thought of doing it myself.'

Wistfully, Shpak stared out of the window. 'I couldn't, really. How would I adapt to life in the US?'

'Quite a few foreigners have, I understand.'

'I don't speak English.'

'Neither do they – the Americans, I mean. If you become too homesick you could move to Alaska. We owned it once, and the climate is very familiar. Or settle in Pennsylvania; there are so many Germans there that it would be like Berlin, only with less rubble and more food.'

Zarubin's dark humour always worked well on Shpak, but the gathered clouds were darker still, and parted only briefly. 'This is a mad business, Sergei Aleksandrovich.'

'I know. If only I hadn't tried to be clever, we could both be doing something tedious right now.'

'Ah, an endless dryness of staff meetings, the mounds of paperwork generated only to begat more of the same - it would be heaven. When are you going to do this?'

'As soon as possible. Tomorrow. If the Berlin debacle blows up the matter may fester by default, and I don't trust Myasnik to be patient. When it's over, I shall be applying for a post on the committee for the reconstruction of the Dneiper hydro-electric system.'

Shpak patted Zarubin's shoulder. 'Don't worry. I'll be there already, putting in a word for you.'

52

Rolf Hoeschler realised that he was very close to killing again, or being killed. The Russian had told him that he was useful, but the farmer didn't seem to share the opinion. Every time he unlocked the handcuffs and took his prisoner outside to relieve himself he kept the shotgun aimed precisely at Hoeschler's favourite, only head (which, strangely, made bowel movements more, not less, difficult). In the evenings, his habit being to take most of his nourishment from a bottle's neck, he became playful. The wife, familiar with the routine, kept herself elsewhere, so the man who happened to be attached to the sitting room radiator had no choice but to be the principal diversion. The slaps weren't so heavy as to be onerous, but the mock executions with an ex-service P3 were becoming tiresome.

An arable farmer would have had less time on his hands, but pigs seemed to be damnably self-sufficient. The property was isolated, without any visible neighbours, its distractions too scarce even for folk who relished the bucolic life. Already, Hoeschler had noticed the blood-group tattoo on his gaoler's arm; it wasn't likely that the man's idea of what constituted entertainment could be satisfied by walks in the woods or conversations on a matter of drainage.

The trips to the makeshift latrine behind the barn offered the only obvious opportunity. Once he was squatting there he had no advantage - it would require a momentary distraction on the way to or from the squat, and a good deal of luck to manage something before his head and neck parted company. He wasn't likely to be successful, but the radiator was beginning to feel like a scaffold.

It was on the fourth morning of his rural interlude that Hoeschler decided to make the attempt. The farmer usually ate a heavy breakfast and was likely to be slower for it; also, the pigs tended to be noisier before their day's first consignment of swill, which might further divert attention. It had rained during the previous night, so both men's footing was likely to be impaired (for better or worse), and if it came to a brawl, a mud-and-shit wrestle, Hoeschler was confident he could break the bastard's neck - or, if a decent grip couldn't be had, drown him in by-product.

It was a plan of sorts, and raised his spirits as the household stumbled to life. He took his own breakfast from the farmer's wife, thanking her without getting the slightest sign that he'd been heard, and watched her husband assault his own, much larger portion of bread and bacon fat. The man's eyes were red-ringed from the previous evening's indulgence, his face pasty and bloated, and his farts were like a dawn mustard-gas assault. Had Hoeschler been surer of his recent luck he might have hoped for an aneurism; instead, he ate slowly, carefully, as men do when their minds are far elsewhere.

The farmer was poring over something interesting in his week-old copy of the *Morgenpost* and needed a third coffee to help digest it. His wife had eaten her portion quickly as always and was already clearing pots into cupboards when he barked at her, a noise without meaning to any but them. As she returned to the table to clear the empty plate and mug he hoisted his shotgun from the wall against which it had been propped, belching deeply his thanks for the meal. From his shirt pocket he drew the handcuffs key and tossed it to Hoeschler, who tried to maintain an air of beaten dullness as every nerve-ending in his body charged itself.

It was raining still, and cold, and the prisoner felt his own years every bit as much as those he was wishing upon the farmer. As usual, the shotgun's butt helped him into the yard even though he was moving, and he staggered slightly, pretending that he found the surface beneath him precarious.

'Move, dog-fucker.'

Dog-fucker obeyed. The farmyard itself was kept fairly well-swept, and he didn't trust the farmer not to keep his feet if jostled suddenly. Theatrically, he clutched the front of his pants as if a dam were about to burst, and his slightly crouching gait both reinforced the impression and made his head marginally harder to remove with a first shot.

He hadn't thought about timing, but as they both stepped into the thicker ooze in front of the barn's doors his reflexes overtook his head. He 'slipped' again, half-turning, his left arm coming up to deflect the shotgun as his foot went sharply for the farmer's knee. To his great surprise it went as well as if they had been rehearsing a theatrical fight scene, or a violent ballet. With a loud but abruptly stifled cry his gaoler went down heavily into the ordure while he remained upright still, half-dazed by the happy prospect of the muzzle gripped tightly in his hand. He swung the gun around, pushed the stock into his shoulder and aimed carefully.

'Stay.'

He hadn't planned on them both surviving the manoeuvre, but there was a convenient radiator close by, a single telephone line (easily sabotaged), and only a middle-aged woman to argue matters with. After that … what? He had no idea where they were. The journey to the farm had been a short one, but he had arrived unconscious at his previous location, so it was possible that he was now many miles from Berlin. Under a rain-drenched sky he wasn't certain where the sun stood, so a wrong decision and a good start might put him in Poland.

Ask the wife, politely. Or the farmer, very impolitely.

He was debating this, keeping his shit-covered prize carefully under the barrel, when his common sense returned. He stood back a pace and gestured with the gun. The farmer, using all four limbs, scrambled to his feet. He look frightened, and about much more than the prospect of his own weapon turned against him. Hoeschler didn't think it likely that the General operated a staged disciplinary regime for underperforming employees

Back in the house, he made the farmer shackle himself to the radiator and then went into the hall way. Next to the front door, a small table held a few scraps of correspondence. One of them was in its envelope still: it was addressed to Herr Michael Franke, *postlagernde*, Spitzmühle post office.

Spitzmühle. It sounded a faint peal in his head, one than repeated more clearly as his thoughts drifted back to a previous age. After the Crete campaign he'd had leave, a few days only, and hadn't wanted to waste it being unconscious on a succession of Berlin bar floors. He and a friend had hitched their way to the Straussburgerwald instead and spent a pleasant weekend boating on the Straussee. He recalled that there had been local signposts to a Spitzmühle – not a common name - that hadn't rated the place sufficiently important to include distances also. So, he was close to Berlin, perhaps only thirty kilometres from Keibelstrasse.

He heard movement above his head, in one of the bedrooms. It was tempting to just leave quietly, but she probably had access to a hacksaw, and he needed a head start. He went back to the sitting room and applied to his former host.

'I can hurt her, or you can tell me where there's rope.'

Briefly, Herr Franke seemed to consider the offer, as if weighing the convenience of an inexpensive divorce against the burden of having to cook his own meals; but then the scared face returned abruptly, and Hoeschler heard a distinct click to his left rear.

SVT-40, he concluded, having an excellent (and very necessary) ear for Soviet weaponry. Slowly, he bent at the waist and placed the shotgun on the ground. When he straightened and turned he realised his slight but understandable error. It was the previous model, an SV-38, though no less deadly for that. The other fellow held an American M1911, presumably one of the millions donated to the USSR in the days before Uncle Sam learned better. It wasn't nearly as impressive as the SV-38, but Hoeschler didn't doubt that it could do its job.

Between the two men, and considerable prettier than either, Mila Henze stood, hands on her hips. She had done her best to keep him alive and he'd just betrayed her trust, perhaps put her in a difficult position. She had the right to be angry, yet seemed … sad. A hopeful suitor might have called it almost regretful.

'We parked the car down the track. It's time to go.'

53

This time it was Jamin who made an appointment with Beckendorp. Anyone below the rank of Paul Markgraf himself shouldn't have expected anything more polite than a summons to the Fifth Directorate, so this was unusual. Even more curiously, the request was conveyed via a note in the Direktor's own handwriting, a novelty that might have massaged Beckendorp's sense of self-importance had it not fled already.

He had no fight left in him. A day earlier he had almost punched the face of the man who now begged an appointment, and he realised now that it had been no more than a flightless bird's flapping, all noise and hopelessness. His bombast was flatulence, his fearsome reputation a straw ... something, he couldn't recall what, but it counted for less than one of the Führer's treaties. Two months ago, he had been as sure of his place in a crazed firmament as anyone might be; now, he was lost, adrift, waiting for others to sense the blood in the water and finish him off. Why not Jamin? A knife thrust from him would do as well as any.

His stock of self-pitying analogies exhausted, he sent a note upstairs, saying that he would be delighted to meet at the Direktor's convenience. Within ten minutes Jamin's arse was in the seat directly facing Beckendorp's own, and the bastard had so little sense of his advantage as to seem slightly ill at ease.

'I've been thinking about what you said, Comrade Inspector.'

'Which part?'

'The part where you mention our present situation to Major Zarubin of MGB.'

Beckendorp had known precisely w*hich part*, of course, but he needed every moment he could steal to rouse his dull mind.

'It wasn't a threat. I was …'

'No, it doesn't matter. In a way, I'm glad it's come to this.'

'You are?''

Jamin stared at the desk between them, his mouth half-making a start on something and then losing the signal. He coughed, adjusted a shirt-sleeve cuff that was already perfectly aligned and then, finally, met Beckendorp's gaze.

'What do you think of the … situation?'

There was no need to ask what he meant. There were many matters that might have concerned either man, probably an infinity of issues and as many problems as one might shake a stick at, but the *situation* had owned the field since the previous 19 June.

'It's difficult to read.'

'It is, because no-one has a strategy for what comes next. It's what the Americans call a stand-off. We and the Allies have stood toe-to-toe and dared each other to do … well, something. The problem is that the enemy doesn't really have to *do* more than continue to supply their parts of the city with food and fuel. If they succeed in getting through the winter without large-scale civic unrest then we'll have lost by default - unless the Soviets decide to heat up the conflict in the meantime.'

'Which they won't.'

'No. There are too many unknowable quantities, not least whether the squadron of B29s that's currently stationed at RAF Lakenheath is equipped with atomic bombs.'

'Shit.'

'Indeed. A land campaign wouldn't present too many difficulties, but losing a dozen cities in the western Soviet Union to acquire Germany isn't something the General Secretary's willing to contemplate. Which leaves the present impasse.'

'You know more about it than me. Why do you ask my opinion?'

Jamin sighed. 'I don't know. Perhaps to hear something I hadn't considered. There isn't going to be a war, not over Berlin. Which means that there *is* going to be a separate, western German state.'

'Probably, yes.'

'And that means there'll be an eastern one also.'

Strangely, Beckendorp hadn't taken the argument that far in his own head, but Jamin's logic was sound. The Soviets occupied their zone and doubtless would continue to do so, but they couldn't govern it without German help. And if the capitalists made a success of their new almost-nation, the *kozis* would have to show that they could do the same, or better.

'I suppose you're right.'

'Which bring us to why I'm here. We can't continue to rely upon the Soviets for more than their military assets. We have to stand up, be Germans once more.'

'In what way?'

'In a way that Stalin's seen already. You know that Ulbricht and I went directly to Moscow, to ask for more resources?'

'In April, wasn't it?'

'So, gossip gets around. You can imagine that MGB weren't pleased about it. The Fifth Directorate was established directly under their command and direction as the means by which domestic political subversion could be monitored and suppressed. They never intended the dog to wander off the leash.'

'It must have put you in a difficult position.'

Jamin smiled. 'It did, momentarily. But then the *situation* came about, and things changed.'

'Did they?' Almost everything in and about Berlin had changed, but Beckendorp couldn't see how K-5 was affected by that.

'Very much so. Since June, Stalin's lost almost all faith in MGB's efforts in Germany. They haven't managed to penetrate USFET or the Gehlen Organization more than a few centimetres, so they have at best a fogged idea of what the Americans can or intend to do. This, of course, is what's paralyzing Moscow's intentions. To use a very tired metaphor, if they can't see the black pieces on the board, how is white going to move?'

'So you're happy to have MGB fall into the shit?'

'Not at all. We just want to see the relationship loosened a little, have them think of themselves more as brethren, not *mutti*.'

'They won't like that, losing influence.'

'It can't be helped. As Stalin's beginning to see, only Germans can conduct effective intelligence operations on German soil.'

Beckendorp thought briefly about the previous year's tortuous manoeuvres, when he, Fischer and Branssler had tried to keep K-5, MGB, Gehlen and the Black Forest's elf population happy while deceiving all simultaneously. *They* had been Germans, playing at intelligence on German soil, but he couldn't see how they'd been remotely effective other than in managing, just, to stay alive.

'I still don't understand why you're here.'

Again, Jamin paused as he searched for the best way to put it. It was strange to watch this display of delicacy from a former member of possibly the most deranged SS unit ever to be set loose on a battlefield - a creature who should have found a shallow grave next to his boss, Dirlewanger. Beckendorp couldn't decide whether it had been God (mocking the concept of divine justice) or blind luck that had put him in a Soviet POW camp instead and then gifted him a miraculous talent for persuasion.

'Having your men beaten was … a mistake.'

'I'm glad you think so.'

'It was clumsy, and counterproductive.'

'It was, as we've now got warring gangs on adjacent floors.'

'It's obvious to me that we can't continue to act as two entirely separate arms of law enforcement. We sit in the same buildings, separated only by doors, yet we share next to no information on a daily basis. 'I know …' hastily, Jamin held up a hand to quell the anticipated explosion, '… that the fault's mainly ours. We don't value *VolksPolizei*'s other directorates sufficiently, for sure.'

'You only ever speak to us when you need extra fists to break up SDP meetings. Or when you're trying to get one of my men to confess to revisionist thinking.'

Jamin nodded. 'Yet a successful socialist state needs a vigilant police force. Until now, your men have been used solely to chase crimes against the person or property, while we're deployed to counter reactionary political activity. This is, at best, fire-fighting. We must have an effective, motivated *VolksPolizei* that can preserve and strengthen the Party's position at street level.'

Another 'Stapo, you mean. Beckendorp kept a neutral expression on his face while yearning to do to Jamin's what he had failed to do the day before. There was nothing surprising here: it was a process, a despicably transparent journey back towards what they had once been. They had commenced with the bread-and-butter work of discouraging their political opponents in the council chamber (or rather, in the alley-ways to the chamber's rear) without recourse to debate or rhetoric. He didn't have too much of a problem with that – German politics had always been an uneasy marriage of high oratory and low punches, and if he was on the side doing most of the punching, well, he had a decent salary and a nice house to ease the moral pain. But the next stage of the SED's plan for this part of Germany went somewhere else, to the place the Führer and his gang had annexed and defiled already. The hearths and hearts of the people were be searched once more, impugned or scoured, marked as enemy territory and treated accordingly. The informer, already a resurrected national institution, would become everyman, creating a perfect equilibrium of mistrust. Mere sideways glances, drivel spouted from a bottle and formerly good neighbours managing to get ahead in life a fraction more quickly than the rest would bring the loyal populace flocking to their local police stations, ready to put things right with a timely accusation. Beckendorp told himself that he should be pleased, because his already-secure career would be set in a geological strata as he helped to organize and coordinate this fine work from the very top. It made the sick feeling in his stomach seem almost like ingratitude.

'Forgive me for asking, Comrade Direktor, but why am I hearing this? Surely it needs to be decided by President Markgraf?'

'It does, of course. But it seemed right that I should lay out my thoughts openly to the officer with whom I've had the most troubled relationship to date. As a gesture of sincerity, as it were.'

The cock thinks he's being magnanimous. Jamin had come bearing a gift – an ornate chocolate box crammed with fragrant offal. Moscow wanted this, so the Party wanted it also, which meant that Markgraf craved it like a fourteen year old boy offered a first sniff of *muschi*. It had all been put into motion already, and Beckendorp's part was either to object and give them a reason to bury him or to loosen his belt, bend over and await guests from the floor above.

He smiled broadly at Jamin. 'I'm sure our misunderstanding is done with. I look forward to working constructively with the Fifth in future.'

Jamin bounded out of his chair. 'I'll organize a committee to look at where we should start. Obviously, I'd like you to be on it.'

Beckendorp stood up also (though his tin leg made this a slower trajectory than the Direktor's) and offered a hand. 'Comrade, it would be a great honour.'

54

The prisoner was sewing, mending a rent in his tunic, when Zarubin entered the cell. Earlier that morning Fischer had asked a guard for needle and thread, to which the proper response would have been a rifle butt. Yet Zarubin had permitted it; he must have reasoned that a man who had asked to be returned to an MVD Special Camp wasn't likely to be planning a more immediate departure.

Still, it was irritating. The coming hours were likely to have profound implications for both their futures, and a little visible appreciation of it would have made Zarubin feel better about his own loose guts. But Fischer looked to be preparing for Church Parade, or a night out with a supremely undiscriminating elbow-warmer.

'I doubt that you need be too presentable.'

The tailor looked up, his eyes refocussing with the help of a squint. 'I'm sorry, Major. I didn't hear you.'

'Really? I imagine the lock on this door must have been fitted by one of Frederick the Great's ironmongers.'

'I was wandering, somewhere else.'

'Biarritz? Capri?'

'Stettin, before the war.'

'Your imagination needs a holiday. From you.'

'I was wondering how many criminals I caught, as a *kripo*.'

'You didn't keep a tally?'

'I recall roughly how many convictions I secured. I just wonder what proportion related to actual crimes.'

'So, the German criminal code had catch-all offences too?'

'Himmler himself gave us 'preventive custody', its logic being that any man or woman who had offended more than once was likely to do it again. We lost a whole generation of petty criminals with that one. No, I was thinking more of *arranged* offences.'

'Denunciations.'

'Also a Soviet speciality, I understand.'

Zarubin shrugged. 'It's been known to happen.'

'Specifically, I was wondering how much witness testimony wasn't spiteful, or rehearsed, or just shit.'

'How good were your conviction rates compared to, say, the period prior to National Socialism?'

'Oh, they went through the roof. By the time I joined the force in '35 the need for new detention facilities had become critical. Indirectly, our fine work gave the Final Solution a leg up. Without the *arbeitserziehungslager* the Polish camps would have needed some serious design work, rather than the mere tweaking of an off-the-shelf model.'

'So, either criminality surged spontaneously after 1932, or …'

'Yes. *Or.*' Fischer sighed, and carefully drew thread through the tear's edges.

'A curious matter to dwell upon, given the minor distractions that have occurred since.'

'Actually, it's been very much on my mind, recently. As a venue in which to contemplate the subject, Sachsenhausen couldn't be more wonderfully apt.'

Zarubin smiled. 'At this point, I might ask if you now regret your egregious contribution to a criminal enterprise.'

'You'd do better to ask what I don't regret. But it isn't my guilt that I've been thinking about - more the mechanics of it.'

'Well, we've had longer to perfect the methodology than you Germans. A man need only enter the Soviet justice system to know that his crime will be punished, once it's been decided upon. Denunciations are as sound as fingerprints – more so, because society itself has determined both the offence and the guilt attached to it.'

Fischer laughed. 'I don't suppose your defence lawyers are paid well?'

'They do it for love, not wealth. Is this going to take much longer?'

'It's finished, just about.'

'Good. We have an appointment.'

'Where?'

'On neutral ground.'

'There is no neutral ground, not in Berlin.'

'No. It was a matter of finding ground upon which neither party will have a definite advantage.'

Fischer handed back the needle and thread, stood up and put on his tunic. 'Then it isn't anywhere in the SBZ, because you couldn't say that if it were. I assume that none of the Allies have offered temporary office-space, and the Czech border is too distant to make a comfortable day-trip. Western Poland then, and somewhere near an intact bridge across the Oder, because you aren't going to trust Sixteenth Air-Army not to assist you in departing an aircraft prematurely. It won't be Stettin if you've had any say in the matter, and the Poles are touchy about Swinemünde still, so you'd be noticed there. What do they call the eastern part of little Frankfurt these days?'

Zarubin shook his head. 'With the right attitude you really would have made an excellent employee. It's Słubice.'

'Ah. Almost what it was. It's nice that tradition's respected.'

'But you're wrong about the bridge. It was destroyed, along with everything else. We have a nice ferry ride to look forward to.'

55

'This is Little Frankfurt.'

Hoeschler was sitting in the back of a Red Army truck, but the rear flap was open and no-one had told him to keep his eyes closed. He had recognized only the battered spires of the *Marienkirche*; the rest of the town was far too much of a mess still to take any reliable bearings. A small twinge in his stomach reminded him that this was almost home. He had been brought up only a few kilometres away, in the Oderbruch, and had regarded the small city as the only fragment of civilization in a world of swampland. It hurt to see what it had become.

Mila gazed out at the smashed panorama. 'I've never been here. Was it nice?'

'It was old, and sweet, and until the last days of the war mostly untouched. Wehrmacht did this as we retreated, as if Germany wasn't fucked enough already.'

'There's hardly anything left.'

'A lot of the older buildings were wood and plaster. War isn't kind to wood.'

She held back the canvas flap as the wreckage of a town passed by, and he kept his eyes on her. In profile she was even prettier, the slight snub of her nose softening high, severe cheekbones. Her hair was a mess as always, but he imagined it after a decent hairdresser had repaired the neglect, the auburn allowed to push through the grease that a shampoo-less world deemed to be *a la mode*. He wondered how she saw him – as yet another gullible mark, a near-miss, a casualty or something else. It was hardly important now, but a man with his record of near-chastity could be curious about that sort of thing.

The truck came to a halt at a small wooden jetty on the Oder's western shore, close to where the remaining piers of the old bridge thrust forlornly out of the water. His two minders – Godomar and Thomas – came around from the cab, released his handcuffs from the truck's frame and took a good hold on either side. He relaxed, not wanting to give them any reason to get annoyed. They seemed healthy lads, the sort who might enjoy a game of head football.

He was half-carried to a small motor launch, a battered version of the class that graced Italian lakes during the summer months, and pushed to its floor. The semi-automatic rifle was in the truck still, but Thomas had the M1911 tucked into his waistband, and he made sure Hoeschler had a good view of it when he sat down on the transom bench. Mila took the space next to him, her coat wrapped tightly to keep out the unseasonable wind. Godomar, having untied the boat's prow, fired the engine and pointed them due east, towards the Oder's right bank.

They were about to leave New Germany, an absent-minded entity that somehow had misplaced eight hundred years' eastern expansion. Hoeschler wondered about how he would feel about it. Directly in front of them was the former settlement of Zliwitz, a place he recalled as the least interesting part of the old Frankfurt - as full of farmers as any village, and with an odour to match. Would it seem like part of another country now, or Germany still? Did rubble have distinct ethnic characteristics, a particular odour, a sense of its past?

A foot kicked his leg, though not hard. Mila nodded to the north, and he turned to see what local colour she'd found. A Red Army pontoon bridge had been thrown across the river where the southern tip of am Winterhafen re-connected to the western bank. A column of tanks and motorized artillery was crossing it slowly, east to west - another reminder (like the dozen or so checkpoints they had passed through since Spitzmühle) that things weren't normal, even for abnormal times.

The 'jetty' at the eastern bank was a long concrete pile from some destroyed building that had been pushed into the water, providing a gently-inclining ramp to dry land. Godomar brought the launch alongside it with great precision and threw the rope to a man in a uniform that Hoeschler didn't recognize, though the red and white tab on the tunic left no doubt as to his nationality. When all four of them were on the jetty, Mila handed a piece of paper to him; he glanced briefly at it and returned it, nodding them on to Polish soil.

Close to the water there was a great deal of damage, but further inland Hoeschler was surprised to see that far more of the district's older buildings had survived than in Frankfurt itself (due, no doubt, to an over-hasty evacuation of the right-bank in the war's final days). He wondered if the pretty four-story houses that lined what had been Friedrichstrasse were still standing, but didn't think it worthwhile asking if they might do the official tour.

He was half-dragged, half marched southwards until they passed the limits of the built-up area, and suddenly he was certain of their destination. Unless they had taken great pains to find a corner of a now-Polish field in which to execute him, they were on their way to the old Otto Morgenschweis stadium.

He had last been here in April 1932, with some of his friends, to listen to the crazy man who'd just tried and failed to become President of the Republic. Adolph Hitler, surrounded by his SA thugs, had harangued the large crowd for almost two hours, but by then Hoeschler and his mates were no longer part of it. Bored, they had traded a vision of what Germany might be for a few rounds of drinks at a local bar, followed by a ten-kilometre trot back to their village. He only recalled the occasion because Herr Hitler had done some things since that had tended to stick in memory.

They entered the complex through a gate in the fence that was missing some wood and ascended the spectator stands to the arched brick promenade at the Stadium's rim. The overgrown sports field aside, it was intact still - a faithful (if much smaller) copy of the design for Berlin's *Deutsches Stadion*, and as empty this particular afternoon as the ruined site of the latter tended to be these days. Hoeschler looked down on the field and tried to recall where he'd stood a whole world ago, when Germany had imagined she'd been going through some bad times - times that seemed now to have been a very slightly distressed state of grace.

Thomas grabbed his handcuffed wrists and dragged him to one of several benches that were clustered beneath the arches.

'Sit.'

He obeyed, and to his surprise both men turned and began to walk back down the stands. He hadn't been shackled to anything, or told to wait, or given any idea of what came next. Mila was looking at him, and he half-turned to meet her eye.

She smiled. '*Ciao*, Rolf. If you ever happen to be in Schöneberg, don't forget about me.'

'You're joking?'

She leaned down, her hand on his shoulder, lips barely touching his ear, and with the greatest effort of will he couldn't stop the shiver that ran the entire length of his spine.

'Think about it.'

He watched her follow the two men down the stands and on to the field, admiring what she did for a pair of otherwise shabby workman's trousers. He felt a curious urge to run after them, to ask what was going on - even if they might keep company with him for a little longer. It was ridiculous, but here, only a spit from his old *heimat*, he felt almost lonely. It was partly to do with helplessness, of course - not knowing what part (if any) he had yet to play in something he didn't understand anyway. He rubbed his head, breathed deeply, felt the chill in his arse slowly disappearing as it managed to warm the bench beneath it.

Here under the arches, the early evening's stilled air was filled with the scents of autumn advancing. It couldn't have been more pleasant if he'd been allowed bread, cheese, a few beers and a half-decent book to pass the time. He tried to imagine the tastes in his mouth, the wonderful sense of having nowhere to be, but none of it felt as good as if she'd been here with him, trying to do the same. Somehow (it definitely had something to do with abstinence), a single, interrupted night in her bed had managed to resurrect all of the inner teenager.

He needed to get up, to go … somewhere. He had no papers so the handcuffs would need to come off, because the only way he was going to get back to Germany was via a quiet stretch of the Oder, wearing few enough clothes not to get pulled under. He was contemplating this, and how he would explain his near-nakedness to the first patrol that found him on the other side, when the space under the arches suddenly seemed full of people.

'Hello, Rolf.' Fischer sat down on Hoeschler's bench. He looked thin, almost ill – a considerable achievement for a man whose good days were the stuff of most people's nightmares. They hadn't met since the previous year, when he'd had more flesh on his bones and life in his cheeks (well, cheek). He had been married then, of course, and that was what wives were said to do to a man.

'Hello, Otto. That's Major Zarubin, isn't it?'

'Yes. I assume that the other one is General Myasnik.'

'He didn't introduce himself, but he's the Butcher.'

Fischer looked down at Hoeschler's cuffed hands. 'What have you been up to?'

'Murder, mostly. You?'

'Avoiding it, mostly.'

'I'm sorry about Marie-Therese.'

'Thank you.'

'How will this turn out, do you suppose?'

Fischer looked at the two Russians. They had taken a bench about ten metres away and their backs were to the Germans, so body language wasn't likely to give away anything (unless it involved a gun being pulled from a pocket).

'It depends upon what they want from each other, I expect. I don't think Zarubin really knows how deep or wide his problem is.'

'The General asked me about you. I told him that you know nothing, nothing at all.'

'He didn't say why he thought I should be in a camp?'

'He doesn't say much about anything. I don't imagine you have a devilishly clever plan to get us out of this?'

'Only the one that involves pleading, pitifully.'

Hoeschler nodded. He hadn't expected much, even from Fischer's well-mulched mind. 'Why are you here, by the way?'

'The General wanted me here. You?'

'The same. I can only think that he considers me worth trading.'

Fischer frowned. 'Why on earth would he ...'

'What?

'Nothing.'

'I wonder what it's about?'

'Exposure. The Soviet system's like National Socialism – there are rules, institutions and chains of command, but the real power lies in who knows who. Zarubin's worried that the uniform on his back is his only friend. As to what the General thinks might hurt him, God knows.'

'Being found out, surely?'

'I don't doubt he takes care to camouflage his business. And if he bribes enough of the right people, discovery isn't necessarily fatal. The men in the Politburo are said to have estates in the country - what level of corruption would be regarded as too much?'

The conversation on the other bench had become animated. Zarubin's hands were moving, punctuating whatever point he was making. The General let this go on for a while and then put his hand on the other man's shoulder, leaned towards him and said something in his ear. It took some time to deliver, but at the end of it Zarubin had deflated considerably. Fischer wondered what spell could bring down such a self-assured ego.

The Russians stood, and came to join their captives. To Hoeschler, the General's demeanour seemed as relaxed as two days earlier when he had sat in the farmhouse, enjoying his breakfast. He was looking carefully at Fischer's face, examining the wounds, the good and bad mixing starkly. He gestured to his own, more decorative alterations.

'Someone else who had a good war. Mine was the one before last. Where did you get yours?'

'Okhvat, '42.'

'A hard fight, I hear.'

'Hard enough. I missed most of it.'

Myasnik nodded. 'I have a question for you.'

'Please.'

'How did you know about the American?'

'I'm sorry?'

'The attaché case – how did you know? Is it USFET or Gehlen who sent you?'

For a few moments Fischer said nothing. He'd heard enough to know what was being asked, but how it applied to him …

'Are you talking about the flight into Berlin?'

Myasnik nodded. 'My friend tells me that he was watching you, that your eyes were on the case for almost an hour, as if you were trying to see into it by force of will.'

'An *American* put me in Sachsenhausen?'

'We take care of each other's problems on our own sides. He passed the word at Tempelhof and you were disappeared. It was your excellent fortune that my only female employee was on shift that day to make the arrangements. She has a tender side, one not shared by her colleagues. Had it been Thomas, you would have been underground that same evening.' He laughed. 'So, you've both gained from her kind nature.'

Puzzled, Fischer looked at Hoeschler, whose face had reddened considerably. 'I'll tell you later', he said.

'So, USFET or Gehlen?'

'Neither. I wasn't looking at any attaché case. Your friend was mistaken.'

'But he was quite certain.'

'My eyes may have been on it. I wasn't looking at it.'

'What *were* you looking at?'

'My dead wife. Whatever was in front of me that day, on the ground or in the air, I was looking at her, her body, her coffin, trying to recall her face when it was moving still. To be truthful, I don't give a first or last fart for your attaché case and what was in it.'

Myasnik looked entirely unconvinced. Zarubin coughed. 'In fact, it isn't difficult to check. I can confirm that his wife died two weeks before the flight. As for USFET and Gehlen, do you have contacts in either camp?'

'Would I tell you if I did?'

'Of course not. But last year Fischer crossed Gehlen and his USFET employers quite provocatively, so they'd be as likely to use him as they would Lavrentiy Beria. Just ask, if you have someone at Pullach. Really, your American pilot was mistaken; you used your resources that day to parry a dangerous case of grief.'

'Christ.' Myasnik's eyes went up to the promenade's low ceiling. For a while they stayed there, examining the pattern of bricks, or the grouting, or something further away, and then he turned, abruptly, pinning Zarubin with the fish stare.

'You know what I want.' He put his General's cap back on his head and walked out of the covered area. At the top of the stand's stairs he looked back briefly and gestured at the two Germans. 'Keep them. Think of it as goodwill, if you want.'

They watched him until he disappeared through the perimeter gate. Zarubin was armed and might have taken advantage of the ample opportunity offered, but there was nothing in the General's gait that suggested he expected it. Even Fischer, who had lost any ability to be coerced or intimidated, felt and was impressed by a sense of power as indifference.

He turned to Zarubin. 'You offered me up? And Hoeschler too?'

'Don't ask damn stupid questions, Fischer.'

'He said that you know what he wants. What?'

Zarubin sighed and rubbed his eyes. He was visibly agitated, a man from beneath whom both the carpet and floorboards had been pulled away. 'He wants Rudolph Gerste.'

'Who?'

'A man who worked for and betrayed us, each to the other.'

'And you have him?'

'Yes.'

'And what did you ask in return?'

'Nothing, because I didn't want to be mocked or beaten. It's implied – that if he gets Gerste he leaves me alone and doesn't point any fingers.'

'Regarding the three million or so Deutsche Marks you didn't steal?'

'Yes.'

'That, in fact, *he* stole?'

'Yes.'

'And if you fail to hand over Gerste, the General will either construct convincing evidence to incriminate you or ask a paid employee to remove you from the Officers' list? Or both?'

'That would also seem to be implied.'

'And you regard this as a satisfactory bargain?'

'Oh, shut up.' Zarubin looked at Hoeschler. 'Get back to Keibelstrasse. At least Beckendorp will be happy.'

Fischer gaped at the other German. 'You work with Freddie … I mean, Kurt Beckendorp?'

Hoeschler shrugged. 'I work *for* him, since last year. The Major put me in the job.'

'The Major has a sentimental nature. He just doesn't like to advertise it.'

Zarubin snorted. 'It's because I don't have a dog. Did you mean what you said, Fischer? About going back to the camp?'

'Yes. I'd like to see an old friend first, though.'

'I assumed so. Very well. You'll sleep at Karlshorst tonight, and be freed on licence tomorrow. I'll have you re-arrested the day after. Until then, you can socialize.'

At the gate they were met by two Soviet soldiers wearing MVD insignia and escorted to a Red Army launch that had been beached in the Alte Oder inlet. During the brief crossing, no-one spoke. Zarubin stared at the broken skyline of Frankfurt, lost among the permutations of what came next. Hoeschler, a dead man somehow breathing still, found a great deal to contemplate in the boat's wooden floor. Fischer, held between two recent conversations, frowned into the brown, choppy waters of the river by whose banks he had spent most of his adult life. As the launch came against the western bank's jetty, he turned to Hoeschler.

'Something about this is all wrong.'

57

Beckendorp beamed like a half-drunk winner at the roulette table – dazed, unbelieving yet staring at the irrefutable fruits of his mysterious good fortune. Fischer had fully expected the bear-hug and managed to brace himself for it, but Hoeschler was astonished by his own share of the assault, having until that moment enjoyed a mostly professional relationship with his boss. Once released, both men endured an incoherent welcome-cum-interrogation in silence, allowing the stream to play out unhindered. Finally, Beckendorp took a couple of breaths, gave his face time to pale a little to medium puce and turned to Fischer.

'Well?'

'Well what, Freddie?'

'Don't call me that, you silly bastard! *Well*, what the fuck have you been doing, getting arrested?'

'Staring at something, apparently.'

'What?'

'Never mind. It was an error, a misunderstanding. The Soviet Union has apologised.'

'So, you're free?'

'Yes and no. I'll be returning to Sachsenhausen tomorrow.'

'*What?*'

'It's business, not pleasure. Listen, I need something from you. Who has custody of the People's Court records?'

'I … haven't any idea. Let's ask the expert.' Beckendorp opened the door of his office and shouted, a piercing, unmusical blast. A few moments later, *UnterKommissar* Müller stepped in reluctantly. He saw and recognized Fischer, half-opened his mouth and closed it again.

'Müller, you were a lawyer in the People's Court.'

Müller winced, as he always did when the accusation was made. 'Yes, Comrade Inspector.'

'Where are its records kept these days?

'In the upper atmosphere. They went there the day the Americans bombed the Wilhelms-Gymnasium and sent Judge Freisler the other way. They were stored in the basement there.'

Fischer closed his eyes. 'Shit.'

Müller shrugged. 'Does it matter? In one sense, all cases brought before *Sondergerichte* were duplicated. The arresting jurisdictions got notifications of sentences and were required to append them to their own files.'

'Of course! And the arresting officers' names would be on the same files, wouldn't they?'

'Obviously. But how would you know which case is the one you're looking for?'

'It doesn't matter.' Fischer turned to Beckendorp. 'Fr … Kurt, I need you to do something, and it's most urgent. Can you find out if police records at Wismar survived the war?'

'Yes. The town was bombed pretty badly, wasn't it?'

'I know …'

'And the Brits held it for a couple of months before they handed it to the Soviets, so they may have cleared out any paperwork. Brits are like Germans with paper – they adore it.'

'Could you ask, please?'

'Alright. Anything specifically?'

'If pre-war paper exists still, the arresting records of two officers, surnames Kerner and Spitz.'

'All records? For what period?'

'From January 1933 to the outbreak of war.'

'Jesus! That'll be a pile of stuff.'

'I need only the names of those arrested, and no females. The sentences don't matter – after all, if they went before the People's Court, death was almost mandatory, wasn't it? And Wismar isn't a big jurisdiction. Does Keibelstrasse have a facsimile machine?'

'Yes. But I don't know if Wismar's Praesidium does.'

'Let's hope, then. If this is possible, it would be good to get the information before Zarubin's men pick me up tomorrow.'

Muttering to himself, Beckendorp went out into the Bull's pen, dragging Müller in his wake. Hoeschler, who hadn't spoken a single word since Poland, turned to Fischer.

'What did you mean?'

'When?'

'When you said that something was wrong?'

'I'm not sure yet. I need more information. Where will you be this evening?'

'At the Beckendorps, seeing my boy. You remember Engi?'

'He's yours now?'

'He isn't anyone else's. There didn't seem to be a choice.'

'That's good, then. My presence will be demanded also, so we'll have time to speak more about it. I need to know what Kurt knows.'

'About …?'

'More or less everything.'

58

Dinner was an ordeal. The boys had been sent to bed early, so there was no juvenile nonsense to wait out, and the food was more than fine – perfect, even, a marvellous combination of hearty German cuisine made even finer by the scarce ingredients that *VolksPolizei* graft had secured. Fischer ate ravenously, enjoying every mouthful. His ordeal came at the hands – or rather, eyes – of Anneliese Beckendorp. Her gaze, which didn't leave his face for a moment, was a sublime concoction of tenderness and pain, emphasised occasionally by a soft sigh and a squeeze of his hand that quite spoiled the rhythm of his getting the most food inside him in the least time. She wanted to *talk* about Marie-Therese, and that was something he would gladly have swum through a latrine to avoid. He responded to her questions only when he couldn't avoid doing so, with as little detail as possible. Still, he felt as if his soul were being audited under spotlights.

Her husband was no help. In her presence he was as assertive as a reticent sheep, and in any case had worked off his own sentimental excesses earlier that day. He just sat through the interrogation, eating, beaming, saying bloody nothing to interrupt or deter the sighs, squeezes or tender stares. Meanwhile, Rolf Hoeschler, a guest who also use the Beckendorp home as a free child-care facility, prudently kept his head down and enjoyed his portion of the slaughtered calf. It all lasted an hour, during which time no useful conversation could be had.

Eventually, she gathered the plates and went into the kitchen to make coffee, and the three men's heads closed the space between them.

'What's been going on, Freddie?'

Beckendorp told Fischer about his frantic attempts to discover his fate and whereabouts (omitting, with Hoeschler's silent but palpable agreement, any reference to the unfortunate *UnterKommissar* Beyer), Zarubin's scheme to re-allocate the Americans' Deutsche Marks and his subsequent co-option of Keibelstrasse resources to help track the mysterious Butcher. As he did so, Fischer's interest was piqued only once, when the hunt for Rudolph Gerste was mentioned.

'Who is he?'

'Nobody, I think. One of the breed of Germans who've reached the bottom's bottom and put themselves deliberately in the mud to keep their families alive. He acted as MGB's part-time eyes at Tempelhof, but he was also the Butcher's man.'

'Butcher.'

'Eh?'

'His name's Myasnik. It means 'butcher' in Russian. He's also a general.'

'Oh.' Beckendorp sat back and considered this, a pleased expression on his face. Like all policemen, he liked neat explanations.

'And now Myasnik wants Gerste. It seems to be his price for not dropping Zarubin into the proverbial regarding the stolen monies.'

Beckendorp seemed doubtful. 'Could he do that? Put him in the shit?'

'Only yesterday I had a conversation with Zarubin about the art of denunciation. All Myasnik need do is to transfer some of the loot to a bank account with Zarubin's name on it and then point the Soviet Embassy in Geneva to the evidence. But I don't understand any of this.'

Hoeschler leaned further forward. 'You said that before. Which part of *any*?'

Fischer stared at the laced table cover for a few moments. 'Myasnik let you go, Rolf. Why would he do that? Even if he was certain you'd never turn on him – which, of course, you neither could nor would – why would he jibe at the cost of a bullet to erase a man who killed two of his own in a Spandau alley? This is supposed to be a ruthless bastard, yes?'

Hoeschler nodded.

'The only reasonable explanation, it seems to me, is that you have *some* value to him alive. Did he ask you anything about Keibelstrasse?'

'Not a thing.'

'So, that's the first wrong thing. The second one is me.'

Beckendorp snorted. 'That's for sure.'

'Your lips, my arse. What I mean is, I was disappeared because his American associate thought I was on to his operation. Fortunately, Rolf's girlfriend decided not to have me properly disappeared.'

Beckendorp frowned at Hoeschler. 'Rolf's who?'

'Never mind. Zarubin found me in Sachsenhausen and got me out, and Myasnik seemed genuinely surprised to discover that it had all been a stupid, petty misunderstanding, a waste of his time and a possible exposure. I doubt that he's too happy with the American for it. But again, why the hell didn't he take out his irritation on me? At most it would have been like swatting a fly that had buzzed in his ear for too long. Instead, he gift-wrapped both Rolf and me and presented us to Zarubin, who was already on his knees, all but swearing to comply with whatever Myasnik wanted and in need of no further incentive whatsoever. Is this likely to have been gratitude? A sense of fair play? Compassion?'

'No, no and no.'

'It's wrong. We should be dead.'

Hoeschler shrugged. 'Perhaps he didn't want *VolksPolizei* on his back as well as MGB.'

Beckendorp practised his snort once more. 'A Soviet General, worried that *we* might be on his case? He'd care more about dandruff. Anyway, he'd probably welcome the chance to rub K-5's nose in it …'

'What, Freddie?'

'I've just realised something. He *would* welcome the chance. Which makes Rolf not being dead even stranger.'

'What do you mean?'

'That Direktor Jamin's got his own troubles with Myasnik. The day you landed in Berlin you were picked up by a K-5 squad, remember? They weren't doing their day job.'

Briefly, Beckendorp recalled the Kaulsdorf killings, his initial assumption that it had been Soviet business, the deliberately dead-ended investigation and his discovery of Jamin's dirty fingerprints on the crime.

'Who were the dead men?'

'Apart from being both Jamin's and Myasnik's employees? Who knows? Probably informers, rats or street-eyes – the sort who men who pocket wages from both sides and who no-one really minds losing. A message doesn't have to be expensive to be effective.'

'No ...'

'What is it, Otto?'

'Wait.' Fischer got out of his chair and went to the window. It was dark outside, but Gartenweg, having been commandeered by the Party, enjoyed a measure of street lighting. He looked at the illuminated windows along its length, the glimpses of happy, well-fed families at their evening business, their evocation of a distant German past, undisturbed by more recent unpleasantness, and saw none of it. He was searching for something else, something that dodged between the lit patches.

'Jesus.'

'What?'

Fischer turned from the window. 'I think I know why we're alive.'

'Why?'

'Because this game isn't what it seems to be.'

'Otto, if you get all enigmatic, I swear I'll ...'

'Myasnik wants Gerste, yes?'

'Obviously, because he asked for him.'

'He wants to kill him, and probably slowly, because he squealed to you and Zarubin?'

'That's right.'

'No, it isn't. The General's a pitiless bastard, but where's profit in being vindictive? He *needs* Gerste, desperately.'

'He does? Why?'

'Because it's all a bluff. He doesn't have the Deutsche Marks. He never did. He didn't steal them.'

'Who did?'

'The man to whom Gerste revealed Zarubin's plan for the monies.'

'That was Myasnik, for fuck's …!'

'No, it was Direktor Jamin.'

59

Beckendorp's mouth opened and closed several times before he got it out. 'But … Gerste was Myasnik's man – he told us!'

'Yes, he was. But you've just said that that rogue elements of K-5 picked me up outside Tempelhof, which means that the young lady …'

'Her name's Mila', Hoeschler mumbled.

'… that Mila must have spoken to someone immediately, someone who could arrange it with a 'phone call. Who would that be? Obviously, it had to be someone like her, someone working for Myasnik, but who also knew exactly who to speak to at K-5.'

'That's right. So how do you get from there to …?'

'Jamin had already sent Myasnik a warning with the Kaulsdorf executions, but he must have known that his problem wasn't solved by it. He told you that he doesn't know which of his men snatched me, yes?'

'Yeah.'

'So, he's looking to find a way of identifying his own traitors, the ones who live on the fourth floor at Keibelstrasse. How would he make a start on doing that?'

'By infiltrating Myasnik's business.'

'How?'

'He'd need a spy.'

'He would. Again, how?'

'I don't know.'

'But he had at least an opportunity, didn't he? He got his hands on three poor devils and put them into a grave at Kaulsdorf.'

'Perhaps someone informed on them.'

'Perhaps, it doesn't matter. But why would he kill them all, when he needed an 'in' to Myasnik's business?'

'Shit.'

'He took four, not three, men.'

'Gerste.'

'Who was offered a choice that wasn't a choice. After that, anything that came Gerste's way went to Jamin first.'

Beckendorp shrugged. 'So Jamin heard about the bullion. Why would he organize a robbery? He doesn't care about money, not when he can have anything he wants anyway.'

Fischer looked at his friend with great affection. Even now, as a shifty Berlin politician and senior policemen, he had a core of naiveté that the world couldn't touch.

'Power, Freddie. Something he could use on two Fronts.'

'Two?'

'Myasnik *and* MGB. He's played them both, made them think the other's the problem. And why wouldn't he? They're both part of the Occupation Forces, two bears he'd much sooner have at each other's throat than his. If MGB brought down Myasnik, fine. If Myasnik made MGB look like cocks, who benefits more than Jamin?'

'How is Myasnik exposed by this, if he didn't even think of robbing the Americans?'

'Are you serious? Jamin's probably opened a Swiss bank account in Myasnik's name already. All it needs to become fatal is a deposit.'

'Right, he'd be buggered. But surely, if Myasnik's trying to grab Gerste, he's worked out that Jamin's got the money?'

'He suspects it, at least. But to get at the head of K-5 he needs 'evidence' of his own.'

'Gerste. He needs Gerste.'

'So, where *is* Gerste?'

'Zarubin put him in an apartment in Treptow, with a single guard on the door. It won't be enough.'

Fischer shook his head. 'I wonder if Jamin's already dealt with that potential exposure. You might check what's been fished out of the Spree in the past few days.'

Hoeschler's face had taken on a yellow hue. 'The two men I killed in Spandau - they weren't trying to hurt Gerste.'

'No. Or rather, not immediately.'

'Otto?'

'Yes, Freddie?'

'I get what you've said, I think. None of it tells me why Myasnik decided not to put you and Rolf in the ground.'

Fischer drew a shape on the table with his finger. 'Because this is a three-cornered fight. Jamin, Zarubin and Myasnik are all circling - though remarkably, Major Zarubin seems to be the least informed person in the ring. If you're one of them, what do you do?'

'Try to win' said Beckendorp, simply.

'Yes, but one knockout at a time. For the moment, Myasnik's got Zarubin where he wants him - on the ropes, thinking he's about to be fingered for the Deutsche Marks. Jamin's the real danger, the man with the money. So, we were a no-cost gesture to keep Zarubin looking the other way. Rolf's a policeman, I'm someone who's turned out to be no-one – what's the harm in letting us live, *if* we can be of use?'

Hoeschler scratched his head. 'But if Myasnik doesn't get Gerste, then … what? He isn't going to just cross his fingers and hope for the best. He'll go after Jamin the hard way, before he can be fitted for the robbery. And after that, why not us?'

Fischer nodded. 'We have to hope that Jamin moves quickly, then. Freddie, you work on the floor below - do you ever speak to him?'

Beckendorp laughed sourly. 'We're becoming best mates. He's putting me on a committee to work out how best to weld our departments together.'

'You have to see him, tomorrow morning.'

'And tell him what?'

'The lot, everything.'

60

Early the next morning, Fischer went to Keibelstrasse with Beckendorp and Hoeschler. He had been there once before in his entire life - and, as before, was bundled into the building via a minor back entrance. He was beginning to be intrigued by its elusive front façade.

Beckendorp left them both in his office and went to put a note on Jamin's desk. He was gone for longer than expected, perhaps ten minutes, and returned with a fistful of paper and a curious expression on his face.

'This is for you.'

Fischer took two of three sheets, while Beckendorp read the other.

'Obviously, Wismar has a facsimile machine. Their Commander tells me that your question was asked by the Soviets, three years ago. It's why the information's already been identified, extracted and copies kept in a file marked *Josef Kerner/Eberhard Spitz*. He says not to bother with whatever's biting me, as they were both off'd to the camps at the end of '45 on the strength of what's written here.'

Fischer scanned the list of cases and found it almost immediately, about halfway down the first sheet. He sighed. 'Thank you, Freddie.'

'It's Kurt again – we're out of doors. Or Comrade Inspector.'

'Sorry. Here …'

'You don't need this?'

'I've got what I need. You can burn or file it.'

Beckendorp shrugged, crumpled the paper and dropped it in a waste bin. 'That's it? And now you're going back to Sachsenhausen?'

'As soon as Zarubin's men get here.'

'Why, for Christ's sake? If you don't need to?'

'Don't worry - it's a visit, not a sentence. I'll be back in Berlin by this evening.'

'And then what?'

Fischer realised that he had been avoiding the question, because there was no *then*. He had no plan, no intentions even. If he took Earl Kuhn's offer to be bought out of the laundry business he could think things through at his comfortable leisure, insulated from the precarious circumstances that the majority of Germans toiled through each day. Yet he doubted that a chest of Rhenish gold guilders would be sufficient to carry him through to a decision, to a purpose that might, eventually, flesh out as a *future*. He was on the seas still, cast adrift by her going, caring little for whether a shore would loom eventually.

It wasn't that he didn't have choices. Freddie would pester him to remain in Berlin, perhaps take up semi-permanent residence at Gartenweg 16. Gerd Branssler would try to convince him that, now the Gehlen Organization had relocated to Pullach, he could safely search for opportunities in Frankfurt, the capital of the American occupation forces. Earl Kuhn would beg him to return to Bremen, because … well, because. He was blessed with friends, good friends, and had nothing to offer them in return. She shouldn't have died, or he shouldn't have survived the war.

'I don't know. Really, I don't.'

There was a knock on the door, and before Beckendorp could say anything an *anwärter* pushed his head around the door.

'Sorry, Comrade Inspector. There are two Ivans outside, with a chit. They've come for someone.'

'Already? It's only seven am.'

Fischer stood up. 'Zarubin probably drafted the order yesterday. It doesn't matter, we'll speak this evening.'

The *anwärter*'s head had only just disappeared when the shift *oberwachtmeister*'s replaced it.

'Comrade, Inspector, Direktor Jamin says an hour from now would be good. But in the courtyard, please.'

61

Beckendorp took a cigarette from the pack that Jamin offered
and leaned back heavily on the bonnet of a *VolksPolizei* Opel.
Shifts were switching, so the courtyard was bustling, allowing
a discreet conversation to proceed unheard.

Beckendorp had tried and failed to think of a way to broach
the matter delicately, so he waited until Jamin had taken a first
drag and let it spill.

'A few weeks ago, the Americans were robbed of more than
three million Deutsche Marks as it was being transferred from
Tempelhof to the Länder Bank.'

Jamin nodded. 'I heard that.'

'I think you did it.'

The Direktor's eyebrows went up, but he was smiling. 'I
didn't, not personally. Otherwise yes.'

There was something about an unexpected admission that
could throw a conversation, and it took several seconds for
Beckendorp's gears to re-engage.

'You robbed the *Americans*?'

'It's strange that you sound incredulous, Comrade Inspector.
You've just accused me of it, after all.'

'*Why?*'

'Political necessity.'

'Theft is a political necessity - in a socialist system?'

'Put like that, it sounds improbable. Believe me, it's true.'

Beckendorp couldn't see why Jamin was putting up his hands to it so readily. He seemed relaxed – pleased, even, to be confessing, as if it wouldn't get him an appointment with the hangman. Even the Direktor of the Fifth couldn't declare economic warfare on the enemy without …

'You were authorized.'

'I was ordered, actually.'

'May I ask, by whom?'

'Of course. By Josef Vissarionovich Stalin. Personally.'

'Oh, my mother's fucking ghost!'

'He congratulated me on the idea. Really, I feel almost bad about having stolen it from Major Zarubin.'

'But he was only going to plant the money in someone's bank account, to embarrass them!'

'Which is precisely what's happened, though it's going to embarrass another someone.'

'Who?'

'That, I won't say. I'm not sure I'm supposed to know.'

'So it isn't Myasnik?'

'Ah. You know his name. No, not him - though certainly he'll be affected by it, and probably mortally.'

'A criminal punished, then.'

'Oh, he isn't much of a criminal – more a trespasser. It was what made this a matter of great delicacy, something to be danced around rather than charged at. Myasnik's a patriot, though not of the prescribed variety. He's been responsible for gathering a great deal of classified intelligence from the Americans.'

'And his loot?'

'He keeps some, certainly; but most of it goes east, to the cause of resurrecting his city. No, it wouldn't have been possible to move against him on the basis of what he was doing, only of what he is. And the General Secretary doesn't care for what he and his friends are.'

'So this wasn't all to embarrass Zarubin, to make MGB look bad and K-5 good?'

Jamin laughed. 'No, though that's happened by default. Myasnik and Zarubin met two days ago, in Poland. I assume that the General demanded that Rudolph Gerste be delivered to him?'

'How did you guess?'

'It's logical. Gerste has the knowledge he wants, the evidence that might incriminate me.'

'So, you're going to make sure that he doesn't find Gerste?'

'I said *might* incriminate me – Myasnik doesn't know that Stalin himself has his hand on the business. No, I've already made sure that Gerste is out of reach, but for a different reason.'

'You killed him?'

'Don't be offensive. He and his family are on their way to Lübeck. I even provided a little money - Deutsche Marks, actually. I found that I had a small stock remaining.'

Beckendorp thought about that. The only other person who might have any interest in Gerste (other than three generations of female Gerstes) was …

'If Gerste can't be produced, Myasnik won't be pleased.'

'I imagine not.'

'I thought you weren't trying to embarrass Zarubin?'

'I doubt that a red face is what Myasnik has in mind for him.'

Zarubin was probably the most intelligent intelligence officer in MGB Berlin. He was also Jamin's former boss, and knew more about K-5 than any other Russian. Beckendorp recalled having sat in Jamin's office a year earlier, watching the Direktor more or less shit himself every time Zarubin opened his mouth. A man could get tired of that sort of anxiety.

'You don't want him …'

'Of course not. But I need to tell you that a little before dawn this morning, a GAZ Pobeda with MGB plates was found abandoned near the Invalidenfriedhof, a little to the east of the demarcation line. I called Major Zarubin to inform him of this, but he couldn't be found. I therefore asked to be transferred to his immediate superior, Colonel Shpak. Do you know Shpak? A most amiable man. Anyway, they couldn't find him, either. This was very unusual, because I don't believe that either man is on leave at the moment.'

'Christ.'

'No doubt the Americans bundled them on to the first 'plane to Wiesbaden, where they'll have much to talk about. I must, say, I'm rather disappointed. The Major was something of a mentor.'

Jamin stubbed out his cigarette, nodded an end to their conversation and went back into the building. He looked pleased with himself, and it was no wonder - he had played chess with pin-less grenades, and won handsomely. Myasnik's fingers had been prised from K-5, Zarubin persuaded to accept unwitting guilt for the sins of MGB and thus Beckendorp, now tainted horrible by association with the latter, could be expected to welcome a fist up his arse every time Jamin felt like playing puppets. Sugar-wrapping all of it, he had the sincere gratitude of Stalin for having the genius to think up someone else's plan. And what had been the price for all this? Three-point-five million American-minted Deutsche Marks that weren't his anyway.

At least, Beckendorp told himself, he had inadvertently tied himself to the coming man, the fellow of the hour. He could stare into the mirror and despise what he saw, but there was something to be said for self-hatred endured in considerable comfort and anticipation of a solid pension. He would collaborate enthusiastically in the great task of keeping the people right-thinking both on the street and in the council chamber; grow old in the service of a cause that required great devotion and only moderate competence; retire with enough of the right sort of gossip committed to memory to ensure that no-one would ever dare disturb his golden years. It was hardly glorious, but he wasn't burdened with too many expectations of himself. He could handle shame quite well, though sometimes he wondered what Kristin felt about his work and what his boys might think of him one day, when the last gram

of their adulation had worn off. And Otto, well, he had a
gentle, cruel way of mocking a man without actually saying
anything that …

Otto.

Fischer had hoped for a car, however modest, but Zarubin hadn't been inclined to indulge him. One of the Soviet soldiers gestured at the truck's tailgate and he climbed in. At least he wasn't cuffed this time, or obliged to travel with an indifferent pair of eyes pinning him.

They reached Sachsenhausen before 9am, and the chit smoothed Fischer through the gates with no more ceremony than if he had been the lice inspector. At the Administration block, Colonel Vaisman inspected it curiously, and then, to Fischer's relief, returned it.

'Do you want him summoned?'

'No, sir. If it's alright, I'll go to him.'

It was long after breakfast, so the camp's guests, having put themselves outside some fine cuisine, would be taking the air, or setting themselves to their chosen area of study (be it electrical engineering, poetry or observing the passing clouds), or contemplating the vastness of the human condition from their bunks. Fischer, as he had expected, found Siegfried Stolz at the latter task.

'Otto!' Painfully, Siegfried pried himself upright and grasped Fischer's hand with a surprisingly hearty grip. 'You're back! Why, for God's sake? Are you missing our Nazis?'

'I wanted to speak to you. I'm not being re-admitted.'

Siegfried seemed touched. 'To me? Is that worth setting foot back in this place? But tell me, they're all asking – who is it that you're betraying?'

'What?'

'To be released. We decided it must be that - innocence surely wouldn't be enough. If you have any other names, I'm to say that you should share the list with those who can use it.'

'It wasn't that. A Russian needed me for something, a piece of work.'

'Ah. Espionage. Or are you now a good communist?'

Fischer smiled. 'No. Listen, Siegfried, I want to talk about something you said to me.'

The older man shrugged amiably. 'You're not getting the blueprints for my aircraft, if that's what you're after.'

'The Ghost. The murders.'

Siegfried's playful manner faded abruptly. 'Why? Leave it, Otto – it's old shit. You don't have to think of such things any more. You never did, come to that.'

'It's the not-quite-dead police in me. I have a question, just one. Is that alright?'

Siegfried sighed and sat back on his bunk. He seemed resigned, ready for something expected.

'Joachim Dein was a mayor. He stole his village's agricultural payment.'

'He's paying for that, with interest.'

'He is, certainly. What was his village?'

For a moment, Siegfried's mouth worked noiselessly, as if an internal censor was checking the detail. 'Penkun.'

'I've never heard of it. Is it anywhere near Randowtal? In the Uckermark?'

'I … yes. Why?'

'It answers something. We spoke about Joachim's family.'

'Did we?'

'About his mad wife, and a son. It might be that one was responsible for the other.'

Siegfried shrugged. 'Who can say, with insanity?'

'You told me the son was an idiot, because he went off to the war before he needed to.'

'Do you know a better definition of idiot?'

'I thought you meant that he'd volunteered, rather than be conscripted. But I also thought you said 'the war', and you didn't.'

'I recall that I did.'

'No, you said *he went to war* before he needed to, not *the* war. You didn't use the definite article. I hardly noticed, except that it's a strangely archaic way to put it if you'd been referring to a specific conflict. But then you're from Breslau, and it's an old-fashioned place.'

'It *was*, in the days when it wasn't Poland.'

'I might never have thought any more about it, except that a similar point of grammar arose recently. Joachim's son was an idiot because he went to war against an enemy he could never defeat, didn't he?'

Siegfried stared at the hut floor, and said nothing.

'But that isn't my question. The Ghost's first two victims here, Kerner and Spitz? Your Nazi friend told us they worked together, in Wismar. You didn't know that?'

'Until then, no. I just knew that they'd both been police'

'He also said that they'd rounded up undesirables, as good police did back in the good old days. Queers, gypsies, Jews, communists ...'

The twitch was slight, but Fischer noticed it, and when. 'He was a kozi, then? Joachim's boy?'

'Yes.'

'Joachim would have hated that, probably. Is it why the son left home, to work so far away? Still, he found himself among his own – as your friend said, there's nothing like a port for *kozis*, is there?'

'How did you know?'

'I've seen the arrest record – a summary only, it didn't state the offence. Caspar Dein, aged twenty-two, arrested on 12 June 1935, at Wismar; tried and found guilty of subversion in the People's Court, Berlin, 3 August 1935; executed at Plötzensee Prison, two days later. And this is why you've kept Joachim's secret all this time.'

'Is it?'

'He was avenging precisely the crime that you committed, Siegfried – though against another young man, another *kozi*. You must have felt God's hand upon the business.'

'You're very clever, Otto.' The expression on Siegfried's face suggested that this wasn't a compliment.

'The third victim puzzled me. As the – by then former – Gauleiter of Brandenburg, Ernst Schlange wouldn't have had anything to do with the arrest or prosecution of Dein's son, because it was Mecklenburg Gau business. But then I spoke to a man who once worked at the People's Court, and I realised I might be looking at it from the wrong direction. He knew Schlange, vaguely, as they had shared a profession - a substantial man, he told me, born into the largest estate in the Uckermark, at Randowtal. And before he was ever a hopeful young Nazi he was a lawyer – a Doctor of Law, at that.'

As he spoke, Fischer watched Siegfried's face closely. Whatever the older man hadn't known about the careers of Herren Kerner and Spitz, *this* wasn't news to him.

'Someone who was desperate to help his only son might have turned to an old acquaintance, a friend from the same *heimat*, a man who knew the system intimately. He might have fallen to his knees and begged even, hoping that friendship might work some miracle. I imagine that a refusal would have hurt considerably. And even if it didn't, that he had mentioned the business at all would have been enough. When Kerner and Spitz were murdered here, Schlange would have known immediately what it was about: a young man having *gone to war*, prematurely.'

Siegfried's hands clutched the thin, filthy mattress beneath him. He seemed genuinely distressed. 'Otto, you can't hurt Joachim.'

'I don't intend to.'

'No I mean you *can't*! He's torn open his own back with the flail, racked himself for it. Believe me, the only hurt you can do is to make him realise that you know. Please don't!'

'Siegfried, I didn't come back to denounce Joachim. He's a good man, the best of men. His son had been killed, his wife driven mad by it – who wouldn't have done monstrous things to avenge that?'

'Then why are you here?'

'It was the sort of thing I used to do for a pay-packet. I needed … no, I *wanted* to know.'

'Vanity, then.'

'Perhaps, but more because it made me feel less like I should be dead. Don't worry about what we've said. I won't speak of it, ever.'

They shook hands solemnly, a scarecrow and a *krampus* observing the proprieties. As he walked back to the Administration Block, Fischer realised that he should at least have tried to bring some small gift – soap, perhaps, or chocolate. The Commandant was a half-decent man; he might have allowed it.

Vaisman's door was closed and Fischer was told to wait, by a sergeant who looked as if he would have preferred to use his boot instead. Fischer obeyed, standing half to attention, inmate-style, in the corner he decided would be least likely to be needed by the other men in the room.

The Colonel was on the 'phone, and his voice, though muffled by the intervening wood, was agitated. Fischer couldn't hear a word of it, but people who receive unexpectedly bad news sound much the same whatever language conveys it. He hoped the problem wasn't personal; the inmates hardly needed a change for the worse.

Eventually, the 'phone met its cradle violently, and about two minutes of silence followed. The door opened then, and Vaisman, his face still several shades darker than its usual hue, stormed into the general office. He shouted something to one of his men, who hurriedly pulled a ledger from a shelf next to his desk and offered it unopened. Vaisman turned, gestured to Fischer, and went back into his own room.

The small knot that had settled in Fischer's stomach twisted slightly. He closed the door behind him and waited as the Colonel examined the ledger, found an entry and carefully ripped it out of the book.

'Is something wrong, sir?' It was possibly the most pointless, idiotic question he had ever asked aloud, and yet it felt better than saying nothing. For a few moments, Vaisman didn't answer; he was staring at his ceiling with the expression of a man trying to recall something, his lips moving slightly, reciting possibilities. When the eyes came down and focused, Fischer realised that the man had been upon several businesses, far away.

'Mm? No, nothing at all, now. I've just had a call from someone. I don't know him, but I'm extremely glad that he took the trouble, and only sorry that the nature of his good deed makes it impossible to return the favour. That piece of paper you're carrying – may I see it again, please?'

Slowly, Fischer removed Zarubin's chit from a pocket and handed it to Vaisman, who re-read it then tore it into several pieces.

'But Major Zarubin ...'

'There *is* no Major Zarubin. I believe we'll find, eventually, that there never was. Which means that you're guilty after all.'

'Of what offence?'

'Of abominable luck, certainly. But I'll think of something more conventional for the file. Don't worry, we've had no new arrivals since you left us the other day. Your old bunk is available still.'

The guard on the gate was new to his job (as was everyone else here, it having been only four days since the Soviet Control Commission officially transferred the camp's administration to officers of the new German Democratic Republic), and wanted to do things correctly. The papers looked to be order, but they had been handed to him by a full *Inspecteur der VolksPolizei*, a fearsome fellow whose artificial leg added to a sense of dislocation. He put through a call to the administration block and then, feeling somewhat exposed, resumed his post. The visitor leaned against his car, a black, impeccably clean Olympia that some besotted owner must have preserved in a deep, dry shelter for the war's duration, while his police chauffeur sat inside, staring blankly ahead, gloved hands on the wheel. Silence, a state with which the guard was already becoming familiar, pressed unusually in that pause.

Almost five long minutes had passed when the Commandant himself emerged from the gate door with an *anwärter*. He offered his hand to the officer rather than a salute, briefly checked the paperwork and handed it to his subordinate, who retraced his path with commendable speed. For a further fifteen minutes the two officers waited, sharing a smoke and discussing football, the weather and whether the new Ministry of State Security should, indeed, be named the Ministry *of*, or *for*, State Security.

Of seemed to have achieved a preliminary consensus when the gate door opened once more and someone stepped out. The guard was standing to attention and couldn't turn, but after the Commandant had shook the senior policeman's hand, wished him a good day and re-entered the camp, the new arrival stepped forward into view. A momentary glance confirmed that this was – had been - an inmate, his shabby, faded clothes and emaciated figure complemented considerably by a quite terribly mutilated face. This was not in itself so shocking, as the guard had already noticed that Sachsenhausen hosted a number of men whose war might have been considered punishment enough, had their fates been decided by less vengeful arbitrators. What disturbed him considerably was the long, tight embrace that the inmate and senior policeman shared and the tears on the latter's cheek as they parted and climbed into the Olympia. He wasn't one to judge, but tenderness seemed to him a dangerous innovation, and boded ill for their infant Republic's future in a harsh, unsentimental world. 'Stapo would never have condoned that sort of thing.

Even before the war, the ambitions of members of Leningrad's political elite were mistrusted by Stalin. Their leadership during the siege of the city by the Germans increased their prestige enormously, and, at the war's end, several of them gained important roles on the Central Committee.

One prominent associate of these men, Nicolai Voznesensky, had chaired the State Planning Committee during the war and supervised the eastward transfer and reconstitution of industries in the path of the German advance. He continued in post following the war's end, until, in March 1949, he and several other members of what Stalin considered to be a Leningrad clique were summarily dismissed from office and arrested.

Ostensibly, their 'crime' had been to organize a trade fair in Leningrad to help fund the city's recovery, but during the trial Voznesensky was also accused of having enriched himself illegally. Monies were said to have been discovered in a foreign bank account in his name, but their source was never established and definitive evidence was not offered. On 1 October 1950, following a secret trial, he and six other accused men, all citizens of Leningrad, were found guilty of treason and executed later the same day. A purge of their associates in government and the Red Army followed.

The Berlin blockade ended officially on 12 May 1949, when all land routes into western Berlin were re-opened. The episode had been an unequivocal strategic disaster for the Soviet Union: not only had the airlift succeeded in feeding and fuelling the besieged western sectors but also seriously undermined the eastern city's economy and vastly increased the western Allies' prestige in most Germans' eyes. Eleven days later, a new West German Government was formed, and, on 24 August, became one of the fourteen founding members of the North Atlantic Treaty Organization. Stalin's tacit admission of defeat came on 5 October, when the German Democratic Republic was formed.

MVD's special camps on German soil were handed over to the authority of the GDR in January 1950. About forty percent of the original intake of prisoners had died during the previous four years from a variety of causes – bullets, disease and malnutrition being the most prevalent. In addition, there had been a number of phased releases undertaken since 1948, and an indeterminate number – of Germans and politically-unsound citizens of formerly free eastern European states – were transferred from the SBZ to camps in Siberia prior to the handover. The remainder comprised some 14000 men. The GDR, wishing to demonstrate its moral ascendancy over its West German neighbour (whose failure to adequately chase or prosecute known war criminals was already staining its reputation), organized a series of show trials involving approximately 3400 of the surviving inmates (all NSDAP members, the majority of whom were found guilty and given long sentences, or, in the case of thirty-two defendants, executed), while most of the others remained in camp custody until they died or extreme frailty occasioned their 'humanitarian' release.

Printed in Great Britain
by Amazon